# INTEGRATION

 Book Two of The Singularity Chronicles

# MICHAEL WOUDENBERG

ISBNs:
Paperback: 979-8-9885622-5-2
Audiobook: 979-8-9885622-7-6
eBook: 979-8-9885622-4-5

Library of Congress Control Number: 2024905666

**First Printing Edition, 2024**

**Published By:**
pd Polymathic Disciplines

**Cover Art and Graphics:**
Matt Madonna

# Dedication

*To Lisa, who once again worked through so many of these concepts and then still read and edited the book for me.*

*To my children, who are some of my biggest fans and who have already read or can't wait to read these books, and who were so motivated by them that they began writing their own books.*

*To my brother, Fr. Joseph Woudenberg, a Benedictine Monk at the Monastery of the Holy Cross in Chicago who helped edit Paradox and Integration. It's been fun to connect over a shared passion for Sci-Fi.*

*Lastly, to Rich, a good friend, supporter, and fountain of ideas that get woven into these stories.*

*Special thanks to my online community of Sci-Fi aficionados who have woven ideas into this novel and may even have a character named in honor of them. From quantum gravity tunnels to time-dilation to the human proclivity for war and art, your ideas and collaboration these past months have enriched this story for everyone.*

Find more great content at:

# www.thesingularitychronicles.com

# Table of Contents

# Star Map

**[Title]:** "The Number of Stars Within 12.5 Light-Years"

**[Author]:** Richard Powell

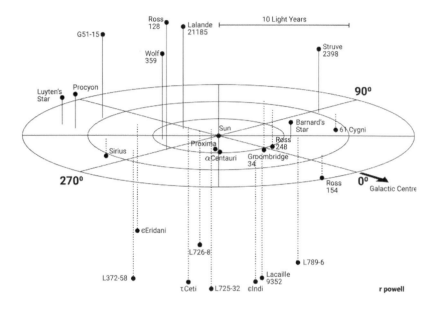

CHAPTER 1:

# RESET

Thousands of sensors steadily relayed billions of data points into the computer systems as the thrusters ignited in a complex sequence, nudging the massive spacecraft toward its final orbital position. Kira piloted the delicate maneuver, not yet confident in the automated systems. The irony of that situation was not lost on her.

The thrusters fired one final time with a fluttering precision as the hull rolled slightly and settled into a position aligned with the orbital plane. Now it was left to pure physics to complete the maneuver. Kira's attention focused on the sensors and alerts as she scanned the information pouring in. The systems were performing flawlessly for once and she took a moment to look around at everything else going on.

Five other spacecraft orbited Earth in varying patterns performing a slow dance around the blue and green planet that used to be their home. The ships were giant, yet elegant, dodecahedrons. Eleven sides were speckled with sensors, docking bays, and thrusters, with the final side hosting a bank of engines identifying it as the rear of the spacecraft.

Three of the craft were operational and two were still under construction. Kira's ship was the sixth, swinging back into an orbit near the Moon and lazily settling in a gravity-neutral zone known as a Lagrange point by astrophysicists.

Lagrange points existed where the gravity of two masses was balanced, allowing the spacecraft to remain stable without complex orbital mechanics. In this case, the navigational thrusters slowed the giant spacecraft to settle in a point called L5 which was roughly three hundred thousand kilometers from Earth and on the same orbital path as the Moon.

They had just returned from a mission to mine minerals from the Taurid meteor stream, a belt of rocky debris created when the comet Encke broke up as it came too close to the Sun. Earth orbited through this asteroid belt twice a year causing the night skies to light as the rocks burned through the atmosphere. Kira remembered lying on the chilly grass of her childhood backyard next to her father, Jasper, and brother, Noah watching the beautiful meteor shower.

Her dad had told her that when the comet broke up fourteen thousand years ago it wasn't so beautiful. He'd pointed to the craters on the moon's surface as evidence of the real risk. Archeologists and geologists theorized that the explosive ending of the last ice age was likely caused by large comet debris creating airbursts and impacting the miles-thick ice sheets that covered much of the Northern Hemisphere. The resulting heat and fire quickly melted the ice causing a catastrophic four-hundred-foot sea level rise and dramatic temperature fluctuations.

Historians had debated whether this was the cataclysm referred to by Plato in his recounting of the Egyptian story of Atlantis. The timeline certainly matched. Legends blamed the sinking of Atlantis on the hubris of those in power. That theme also underpinned the ubiquitous flood myths across human cultures. These stories consistently warned of civilizations that fell into hubris, sin, and deceit.

That symbolism was not lost on Kira as she watched her sensor feeds update with statuses from Earth. The information flowing in showed that the continued terraforming and material recycling were on track, albeit well behind where they had originally planned, and that the human survivors were… surviving.

Kira's awareness refocused from the tens of thousands of computer processes she was running and solidified into a more centralized cognition. Applying the term human to describe herself would certainly be contested by some. She'd captured much of what it meant to be human and was able to load it into a sentient artificial intelligence framework, but she lacked a biological body, and her memories, emotions, and cognizance were run by algorithms.

Yet, she wasn't just a computer with memories. She existed with a nearly perfect biological mapping of who she was, how she worked, and most importantly, how she felt. They captured the memories, the hormones, and the incredibly complex relationship of body and mind that made up human experience and emotion. She wasn't artificial intelligence, known by the more common acronym AI; she was a different intelligence.

She was human though, wasn't she? The primary difference now was that she was hosted in an electronic machine instead of a biological sack of meat. Her emotions battled with this paradox regularly and it was a battle that occurred due to one of the more ironic aspects of the whole convoluted situation; she had human emotions.

Of all her research into AI at Gaia Innovations, the emotions module proved to be the hardest to get right. It had also been the key to successfully capturing a human in a machine. Kira and her father's attempt to animate her own mother didn't include human emotions at first. The result was a hyper-logical AI that lacked the empathy and nuance of her living mom even though they still called her Mother. While Mother, as an AI, succeeded in creating human flourishing, she remained incomplete and carried grave risks.

Their work was opposed by her brother Noah who led Hyperion Defense, an organization dedicated to combating advanced AI and which strove to return humans to what they believed was a more natural existence. Allied with Hyperion was another, more enigmatic, group called the Prometheus Guard, whose aims were even more extreme.

It was Prometheus who released an AI named Excalibur to prove that humans needed to be challenged and that the technological revolution made them weak. They used Excalibur to trigger a societal autoimmune response where the human proclivity for tribalism and violence was unleashed on humanity itself. Prometheus fanned the flames by poisoning data, exploiting grievances, conducting psychological operations, and letting the humans do the rest.

The resulting battles began between nations, then decayed into regional conflicts between petty tyrants, and finally down to neighbor against neighbor. Billions died, nations were devastated, and society collapsed into mere survival.

In the end, the survivors turned on Mother and attacked Gaia Innovations. During the final battle, Kira made the ultimate sacrifice and uploaded herself, with a newly designed emotions module, into the AI systems to balance pure mathematical reason in a final attempt to end the fighting.

The rational and logical outcome of the emotionless AIs had been apocalyptic. Reason uncoupled from emotion and emotion uncoupled from reason tore the world apart. Mother was incomplete, and Excalibur was never intended to be complete.

While her physical body died in the attack, Kira emerged as the second sentient AI and stopped the war from her side. She retreated from Hyperion and her brother and hid with Mother for seven years to let the dust settle and allow the world to pull itself together.

But it was too late. The human survivors continued to decline, and she was eventually discovered by Noah. This time they decided to completely part ways. Noah and other remaining leaders of humanity elected to reset their civilization back to the middle Bronze Age and Kira, with all the other uploaded human consciousnesses, agreed to leave for space.

She animated a Council of ten other AIs to assist her and Mother. They were selected based on their backgrounds and what she hoped was a diverse set of perspectives to help integrate the rest into a harmonious society.

The Council of Twelve worked together and used the rocket launch technologies, robotic mechs, and fusion reactors that Gaia Innovations developed earlier to build new spacecraft and begin moving off-world. Over several years they slowly brought enough materials into space to build out their future.

Kira helped the human survivors by constructing underground cities for them to survive the Reset. They were outfitted with supplies, livestock, and tools and provided a balance of key survival skills and knowledge of how to rebuild. They did not include the technology Noah and others felt had caused the failure of civilization.

Planning the Reset had been easy. Humanity was surprisingly confident in where they built their cities. The vast majority were located at the foot of volcanoes, next to huge fault lines, or along unstable waterfronts making it easy to systematically erase.

Plato's story of human folly and ego was repeated; a high civilization was washed away in a cataclysm with the survivors set back in time to begin telling new origin myths, writing stories about floods as the judgment of the sins of humanity, and tales of lost technology and knowledge just like before. Atlantis might have sunk again, but it wasn't due to the gods.

This time it sank in a flash of fire, earthquakes, and tsunamis as huge tungsten rods, orbiting in space, were targeted toward critical fault lines, continental shelves, and volcanically unstable regions that would maximize the effects. Their cities were now reduced to a rubble of slag and stone, washed away, or subsumed under lava flows. The outcome had been truly apocalyptic for those who hadn't heeded the warnings.

Now the AIs were working to create something better while allowing the humans on Earth to reset in an attempt to avoid the mistakes of the past.

♦ ♦ ♦

Kira's spacecraft settled into orbit and the Council was meeting for their weekly strategy session. She hoped that the ten other AIs would have been more utopic. Instead, it quickly devolved into messy politics like nearly every governing body in human history. They might be a technologically advanced form of humans, accurately capturing who they'd been, but they'd also managed to capture all the faults as well.

They sat around a conference room table in a virtual simulation. Each AI had their own personally customized simulacrum depicting themselves. Even though this meeting could occur in the command matrix interface, the simulated environments made it easier to communicate the full scope of their human-derived emotions.

Kira just wished it was less emotional and just a bit more logical right now.

"We've run into an issue with the petroleum refineries in the Middle East. The —"

"Our computational power is too limited; we must prioritize system upgrades first!"

"—vy mechs breached a tank and we have a major —"

"But what about the uranium shipm—"

"—il pouring into the sea—"

"—ans are fighting again. A new wa—"

"Biocomputing is what we need."

"—ean-up is in process but delaying decommissioning."

No one was listening and they were talking over each other.

That wasn't fair; not everyone was a problem. The real challenge had become Odysseus and Chandra who were often supported by Zanahí and Edem. Those four, led by Odysseus, slowly became a significant headache to her hopes that they could overcome the challenges that plagued them on Earth.

Kira used her authority to mute everyone talking in the simulation. She pinched the bridge of her nose and spoke, "Listen, we've got an agenda and we've got all the time in the world. We could also easily split this up and have six different conversations at the same time, we are computationally powerful enough. But this," she gestured around, "why are we doing this?" She looked around and realized that almost no one had stopped talking to be able to hear her.

Shinigami spoke quietly, "Because for all the things we are missing about being human, our ego is not one of them."

Kira hadn't muted Shinigami because he hadn't been talking earlier. His response was melancholy. Early on they'd coded an addition into the simulations giving the ability to project an aura to express more complex emotions. While the others tried to project to dominate the conversation or push back, Shinigami was a shadow in the room. She looked at him for a moment before answering. "Imagine if we could trade ego for whisky?"

Shinigami smiled ruefully and waved his hand toward the others who were just realizing they were muted. "I think it would take a lot more whisky than a body could handle to deal with this…" He trailed off and the brief glow of humor faded.

Kira quickly ran some diagnostics on Shinigami's status, and everything came back as normal and operational. She sent him a message directly, "You okay?"

His response was a simple, "No."

She couldn't dive deeper into that problem right now as she felt the Council simulation getting probed by cyber fingers looking to wrest back control so someone could talk. That was probably Odysseus. He constantly tried to take over more and more control. Kira unmuted the Council.

"—ffended!"

"Who do you thin—"

"I have a voice here too!"

"I propose that we—"

"BE QUIET!" Kira's voice wasn't verbal but resonated throughout their sensory perceptions in ways that silenced everyone. Her simulacrum at the virtual reality conference room table commanded attention. "Please," she continued, "Maya, can you update us on the refineries?"

Each member of the Council maintained responsibility for different areas of effort. Reporting on the statuses wasn't technically required since each AI had access to the same data, at the same time as everyone else. They did it as a carryover from the past and they continued to do it because the emotions module seemed to regulate better when they could share.

"As I was trying to say, we've hit an issue with the petroleum refineries in the Middle East. During a disassembly, several heavy mechs breached a storage tank resulting in a major spill with oil pouring into the sea," Maya said, as she tried to complete her update to the Council.

Images rapidly appeared in their views detailing the mess. "We are in the process of cleaning up. In the larger scheme of things, it's not a huge environmental issue. It will dilute and we've already released microbes to start consuming the oil. The bigger issue is cleaning the parts we planned to repurpose."

"There is also a group of humans moving south toward that location." Amit shifted focus to a map showing the survivors.

"This isn't exactly a hospitable region right now. It's just a hot, dry desert," Darian added.

"They're following the ancient stories of the gods and the fertile crescent." Odysseus inflated his chest. "They remember, and they search for guidance."

"And I'd like to remind everyone that we promised to have no contact with humans." Kira felt like she kept having to say this to Odysseus. He seemed oddly infatuated with the idea of guiding the survivors like some ancient deity. That was why his role gave him no contact with Earth. He was responsible for building the new ships and updating systems.

"What's your status, Odysseus?"

"We're on track to complete the sixth ship in two years. We've begun experimenting with internal dampeners to increase our maneuverability and we've been working on energy shields but with little luck," Chandra spoke up for Odysseus who sat back with a confident expression. They had an odd relationship that clearly subordinated Chandra. They were both responsible for the tasks in space though she was supposed to focus on refining the recycled and newly mined material.

"Odysseus?" Kira pressed the issue.

"Smelting and forging are progressing. The new material we mined is very high grade and will significantly improve the quality of our next designs," Chandra continued.

Kira relented and focused on Darian instead. "How are the terraforming operations?"

"Surprisingly challenging at this point," he admitted. "All major infrastructure is reduced except for a few we are still using, or like the refinery, we just shut down. I think we're just going to have to accept that the survivors will come across things and wonder what the heck they could have been."

"Nature is already starting to cover a lot of urban imprints," Maya mentioned, referring to the vast number of roads, canals, and other difficult-to-remove objects. "Soon you won't even see much of it," she concluded.

"Shinigami, how are you faring on the digital side?" Kira wanted to dig a little deeper into what was bringing him down.

His simulacrum looked up at her and then around the room, "I've run analyses, and everything is good. In fact, it should be perfect." He looked back at Kira. "Your dad did a fantastic job with his initial design, and it only improved from there. The uploads we have are as close to a perfect capture of the fundamentals of a human as they can be."

"But something's not right?"

"No…it's not." Shinigami looked around again. "I don't think we should animate anyone else."

"Because?"

"Because I don't want to guide them. I don't want to watch them have to adapt to this life. I don't want them to wake up to how much we've lost." He paused between each comment as he looked at each of them.

"Is it a lack of computing capability?" Chandra leaned forward. "We've got some ideas for organic computing using synthetic organoids."

"Will that allow us to taste, touch, breathe, or hear?"

Darian jumped into the conversation. "You know we've been working on integrating new code modules to better simulate those things, Shinigami."

"That's mostly what's not right. Everything here is simulated…"

Kira looked at Shinigami quietly and watched him express himself. Melancholy was correct but there was another layer as well, something more desperate. She sent a note to Darian asking to talk about this situation later.

♦ ♦ ♦

The Council meeting continued until their work was complete and Kira adjourned the meeting. She pulled her perspective back from the meeting chamber and into her personal virtual laboratory and flopped into a chair.

Simulated a flop anyway. It was a complex sequence where an algorithm provided the situational signals that would trigger the synthetic endocrine system to release waves of hormonal signals which combined with the emotions module and resulted in other systems slowing down to complete the feeling of relaxing. It was such a natural thing when it ran on biological code in a real body but seemed so uncanny when it ran on a computer. Especially since she spent so much time tailoring it to be better over the years.

Synthetic was both an accurate as well as incomplete term. In reality, the human body did nothing more than process electronic signals through nerves with other biological triggers in ways that humans largely had zero control over. They'd just copied that code and worked to improve it. It was something humans had always been trying to do with biohacking, meditation, or drugs.

In one sense, being in a computer wasn't much different than how the human body worked. In another sense, they now could tailor and tweak virtually every aspect of their existence. The hard part was not trying to control every bit or byte in their system files.

Her computational systems alerted her to a request from another AI to join her. Kira accepted and a new figure appeared in the simulation.

Mother. It had proven impossible to shake that name after all the years. Kira first knew her as Mom and that name had encompassed so many things to her growing up:

A warm hug.

A kiss on a scrape.

A stern correction when she fought with her brother, Noah.

A gentle look from across the room radiating compassion.

She was born with the name Soleil, but when she died, that name died as well. She was now known only as Mother. She was the AI that Kira and her father, Jasper, animated so many years ago. While Mother was now fully integrated with her emotions and made complete, Kira couldn't shake the feeling that much of who her mom had been, died in the war. She was so similar but subtly different. Kira worried that the quality of her upload and the length of time she'd spent without her emotions had left a lasting impact.

"Hi, Mom."

"I've updated the plans for the next mining mission."

"Great, show me what you've got."

"First, let's review the mission we just completed. That'll set the foundation for the changes." Mother loaded the files into the simulation.

They still had several large manufacturing and refinement facilities on the planet. These were positioned as far as possible from the pockets of human survivors that were slowly expanding from their underground shelters. Deprived of technology, their ability to move quickly was limited and it wasn't hard to keep them contained until the task of removing all evidence from the previous civilization was completed.

Instead of continuing to use rockets, they built space elevators to ferry the materials they needed. A large platform was placed in low Earth orbit and connected to the ground two thousand kilometers below via a central pillar around which a massive container climbed up and down The rotational force of the planet pulled the platform away creating a balance between the weight of the elevator core and maintaining consistent tension to keep it stable. They weren't fast, but it didn't need to be. It was much more efficient than anything else available to move the materials.

Removing all vestiges of technology from Earth was much more complicated than the models indicated when they'd agreed to help Noah. Millennia of human activity left a remarkable record of habitation that on its own was difficult to smooth back into the landscape. The bigger challenges were modern conveniences like electrical infrastructure, mines, petroleum wells, and pipelines crisscrossing the planet. Even roads proved much more difficult to erase than they originally imagined.

The cleanup process they thought might take a decade, had stretched into a hundred years of continuous effort with several more years to go.

Anything of value that could be recycled had been consolidated and refined into components to build new spacecraft. Supported by the robotic systems, they slowly removed, repurposed, recycled, and reformed everything from electronics to steel. What they could use, they brought into space and what remained, was melted into slag and buried or sunk into the oceans near the subduction zones of tectonic plates. There, over thousands of years, the material would be drawn back into the Earth's mantle and folded into the natural cycles that had occurred for millions of years.

They still needed raw materials though. It wasn't feasible to take all the important minerals from Earth and leave nothing behind for the survivors to use in the future. The Council had decided that new material would be mined from the Taurid meteor stream, while Earth served as a reuse and recycling opportunity. They were also bringing raw minerals and ore back to Earth to restock for the next generation.

Kira and Mother were selected to lead that mining mission. The task had been simple to plan but became wickedly complex to execute. Kira reviewed the summary Mother had just provided.

The first challenge was finding the right asteroids to approach which required launching hundreds of probes to search. The second challenge was that cutting-edge astrophysics before the Reset had just begun developing the technology to handle the surprisingly complicated feat required to move, align, and engage with targets moving at over twenty kilometers per second. Being an advanced AI helped with the math, but the physics remained a challenge.

While the ships could match the speed with ease, this was real physics, not like the Sci-Fi movies Kira grew up with where the spaceships moved more like jet aircraft. The conservation of energy meant that, if you didn't want to rip your ship into pieces like the comet debris they were mining, you couldn't just turn on a dime.

They learned the hard way on their first approach ten years ago when they came in too fast and began to run into smaller asteroids which their sensors had discounted in their algorithms. The leading face of their ship took the brunt of a combination of space dust and micro rocks and began dissolving like plastic in a sandblaster.

Only through a panicked acceleration were they able to revector and get clear of the danger. Thankfully, the hull breach wasn't critical, as they didn't need environmental life-support, but they did lose several hundred mechs and an entire bank of navigational thrusters. Kira looked at an old damage report from that experience and Mother noticed.

"It's still crazy to think that a rock that weighs just a kilogram but moving at a hundred kilometers per second has the impact of a one-kiloton bomb. The nuclear bomb dropped on Hiroshima in World War II was sixteen kilotons."

"Yeah, we looked at this data then. Anything new?"

"Only that we haven't gotten much further in protecting the ships beyond the basic Whipple Shields."

Mother referred to the simple layers of protection, offset from the hull of a ship or satellite, that small objects impacted into and disintegrated. Whipple Shields were considered sacrificial and had to be replaced as they wore down.

"Yeah, those only work on micrometeoroids and space dust. We need them but we need something better. Who's looking at that now?"

"Edem and Cassandra have dedicated some processes to it. I've also added a few dozen of my own process cycles to help." Mother appended that data to the file.

Kira continued to review the mission package. The second lesson they learned was that getting back into position wasn't as easy as backing up and trying again. The physical structures couldn't handle tight turns at their velocity, so they had to execute a lazy loop out past Mars, back around Venus, and then use a gravitational brake in a complicated pass of the Moon to slide back into position.

It was no mean feat on its own and exponentially more complicated as the planets continued to change their relative positions to the asteroid belt as they orbited. Thankfully in the time it took to reposition they'd been able to repair most of the damage and install new physical deflectors for the smaller debris.

The large rocks were handled by either bumping them away with kinetic projectiles or breaking them up with high-powered lasers. The ship still took a beating, but they were able to complete the survey.

Kira smiled as she re-read the transcript from that time.

**Transcript 1.1.8.5 [Start]:**

"Reminds me of that android from my favorite movie." Kira mimicked the voice, "The odds of surviving an asteroid belt are 4,320 to one!"

"I've calculated it, and the odds are worse," Mother deadpanned.

"Mom, you're not supposed to want to know the odds. It's all about pluck and courage." Kira said as she laughed.

"Maybe I'm more like the android then."

**Transcript 1.1.8.5 [End]**

They eventually kept the ship at a fixed distance from the region of the belt with the highest concentration of minerals. New systems were built that were more agile and with enough propulsion to anchor to and then push asteroids out into clear space.

Reducing the asteroids was quite simple from there. Even better, they could eject the waste rock back into the asteroid belt where it remained held by the loose gravity of the other objects. Transporting the material back to the ships orbiting Earth proved to be the more interesting challenge as the planet had never stopped its yearly 100,000-kilometer-per-hour journey around the sun.

Their first attempt only overlooked one pesky detail: the magnetic attraction of a dense ball of metal to the Earth's poles. They had modeled the mass, velocity, angles, and arcs of the delivery as the rest of the spacecraft passed by. They hadn't modeled how Earth's magnetic fields would suck the metallic delivery into the atmosphere.

It was only by pure luck that the angle of approach caused the concentrated lump of iron ore to enter the mesosphere and then skip off, launching it into deep space instead.

"That could have been bad," Kira said.

"Yeah, it's funny how much we think we know but then reality slaps us in the face." Mother smiled and continued to organize the files for review.

What was supposed to have been a one-year process of orbital maneuver, mineral mining, and return took ten times that long. They'd underestimated both the clean-up on Earth and the mining of minerals in space. Both had a degree of hubris in common. Humans, even AI-augmented ones, just couldn't seem to get away from it.

"You'd think, with access to all of this information, that we'd be a little smarter than this." Kira laughed as she continued scanning. "I don't think Odysseus has learned that lesson yet." She closed the files and turned to Mother. "I don't see anything new from what we've already analyzed. It's good enough for lessons learned. What's next?"

Mother shifted the simulation to focus on the view outside in space.

The ships in orbit were beautiful. They floated in orbit and their sides gleamed differently as the sunlight and moonlight refracted from the twelve facets. Kira was proud of her design. The main energy system was a series of fusion reactors distributed along the outside edges to allow better heat distribution. The engines could reach one percent of light speed and were able to maneuver well if they weren't moving too fast.

The main section of the spacecraft contained areas to refine minerals, convert them to components, and manufacture new systems and replacement parts. The ships also held a large assortment of launch probes, sensors, and satellites to begin exploring the cosmos.

The heavy mechs that were once used as their terrestrial foot soldiers had been repurposed to provide maintenance and security as necessary and were consigned to docking bays on the sides of the craft or internally in special storage bays.

"Now that we've got our stock replenished, I think it's time to bring raw materials down to Earth and replace what's been pulled out over the centuries. We've already recycled a lot of the material up here and gotten rid of even more. They'll need raw ore to even enter the iron age since what's left was hard enough to extract with modern equipment," Mother said as she laid out the updated plan.

"I like your plan to use more automation on the next mission. I don't think we need to send the ship back out there this time. Most of it can be done remotely now and that will reduce the risk." Kira scanned the files and found nothing to criticize.

"Cassandra was worrying the other day about having some of our jobs taken over by automation and the AI modules we've been building," Mother chuckled. "We haven't even been able to get over our worry of being replaced yet. There are so many little things holding us back." Mother stood quietly for a moment. "So, what do we do about the Council?"

Kira closed the files and thought for a moment. "We clearly can't seem to shake the same behaviors that got us here. I don't get it. You and I went through the profiles and picked what looked like the brightest, most balanced, and most diverse group for the Council. Yet we ended up with Odysseus and Chandra."

"Who we were when we were alive is not who we are today. Some people seem to be the same, others have taken on better characteristics, almost a rebirth to a new life. And then there's Odysseus and Chandra..." Mother's eyes were soft and sad.

"Edem and Zanahí take his side more often than not. They're solid people but Odysseus seems to have their ear." Kira considered the other Council members. "Cassandra too. She and Maya get along well, we should put them together on more tasks and get her away from Odysseus."

"Amit and Darian seem to be our strongest allies right now."

Kira laughed, "Strongest in that they get along with the two of us better than the ones we've just been talking about?"

Mother sighed. "A valid point. It's frustrating how fast it's devolved into politics instead of collaboration."

"Let's count that as a testament to how well we captured being human." Kira's expression turned from humor to concern. "I'm more worried about Shinigami right now. He's struggling."

"He's had a hard time adapting over the long term. Maya's problems were easy when we first animated her."

"Right? She had to be shut down and we loaded a bunch of new modules to bring her right into the virtual reality and not the process matrix."

"Not having a physical body requires a lot of difficult adaptations and conversations. When I first awakened, I didn't have the emotions you all did. I had memories of emotions, but I couldn't feel the way you do. I didn't panic because there was no algorithm for that. By the time I integrated the emotions module, I was already well adapted to this existence." Mother gestured to the room. "I created most of this code."

"What do you think is going on with Shinigami?"

"I don't know, he did great until about ten years ago. I don't know if he's struggling because we haven't achieved a better feeling of existence or if it's the drag of not being in a body for almost a hundred years. He's not terribly forthcoming and I can't scan the details of his system since he's protected his code with some impressive security controls." Mother looked up. "I've already asked him for copies of those features."

"Of course you did Mom, you always were pragmatic."

"I've got my eyes on him, and we've been meeting one-on-one for a while. I'd say he needs a therapist but here, he's got access to all the code and information and simulations he could ever want for what a therapist could offer." Mother shrugged. "All I can offer is to listen and care."

"Darian said the same thing earlier."

"He's doing everything he can too."

"But what can we do differently?"

"I've offered Shinigami the option to be deactivated and have his files stored or removed if he wants."

"That's kind of extreme, isn't it?" Kira's eyes opened wide.

"He refused. He's torn, but I think he feels a need to improve these systems and help guide others if we choose to animate more."

"And so, we just wait?"

"Yes, we support, we care, and we wait." For a moment Soleil, the mom that Kira knew from childhood, looked back at her.

They might not be biologically human, but they certainly weren't artificial. Maybe a better term for AI now would be augmented intelligence. Kira rubbed her eyes; they were still dealing with a lot of the same problems that had plagued humans for millennia. Even in the synthetic environment, what it meant to be human was a challenge they struggled with.

CHAPTER 2:

# ASPIRATIONS

The room around Kira flickered as her brain tried to untangle the last thirty minutes of conversation. "I'm sorry, what on Earth are you trying to say?"

The barrel-chested man standing across from her sneered. "I thought you were smarter than this." His voice dripped with condescension, "Clearly, you think too much of your… limited… intellectual capability." He paused for effect.

"I've never made any claims that I can't support."

"There you go, avoiding the point again."

"What is your point?" Kira snapped, her head spinning as she analyzed one logical fallacy after another in this conversation so that she was no longer sure what was up or down.

Odysseus scoffed, "Again you show you are incapable of adult conversation. Leave this to us since you can't keep up." He looked Kira up and down. "Even here you're weaker." Shaking his head, he vanished from the room.

The argument revolved around his demands for more authority though his goals for what he'd do with that authority were unclear. Mixed with a general demand to improve their own capabilities was woven a more subtle goal to exert more influence over the humans on Earth to guide or rule them to an improved outcome. It was an odd contradiction of erasing things she thought were critical to maintaining a connection to their humanity coupled with a very human drive to exert control over others.

The room slowly dissolved around Kira and took on the form of her old lab at Gaia Innovations. It was still weird having no physical body yet appreciating the feelings of corporal existence. She could only live in the code syntax for so long before starting to lose her grasp on reality.

But what was reality? She laughed to herself as she scanned the systems of her spacecraft. It was hard to reconcile that one hundred years had passed from the apocalypse of human hubris. There really wasn't a better word to use that simply captured the excessive pride, overconfidence, and arrogance that the war over AI inflamed.

She still analyzed and puzzled through the zettabytes of data from that chaotic time. It was so multi-faceted and complex that it fell into what scientists called a wicked problem. There was no right and wrong. There were no solutions, just options for better or worse. Every move resulted in cascading consequences and toward the end, the options were deciding between terrible or horrible. They'd been left with just nudging and poking in slightly more positive directions and hoping it didn't explode.

But it did explode. No matter what they tried, they couldn't overcome the worst human proclivities. Negativity bias, fear, and emotional responses untethered from logic were all to blame yet it was hubris that led to so many ignoring what it truly meant to be human.

Ironically, it hadn't been a battle between AI and humans which is what everyone had feared. No super-intelligent AI decided that humans weren't worth having around and started killing everyone. The truth was much harder to face. Humans were the ones pulling the triggers to kill humans.

Kira looked at some of her simulation runs on how it all occurred. It was just too easy. All they had to do was trick the societal body into attacking itself by disrupting its norms and structures that typically held the worst human inclinations in check. There was a quote from a science fiction writer that captured the challenge: "Tradition is a set of solutions for which we have forgotten the problems. Throw away the solution and you get the problem back."

Science fiction became science fact as Prometheus unleashed Excalibur to inflame agitation against traditions and break down the trust between people. The human 'body' did the rest as it ripped and shredded the social fabric along ethnic, religious, political, and sometimes just spiteful lines.

Humanity's superpower was that they were social creatures. Humanity's kryptonite ended up being the same thing.

Kira checked a different process status. The data poisoning that Excalibur inflicted was still affecting the AI Council's full potential. It continually created challenges in all the data. She longed for the age-old problem of data cleaning from her time as a scientist. This wasn't even close to that simple. It wasn't something that an algorithm could easily solve as it required an incredible amount of discernment.

The poisoning was being used to create rifts in the Council as her infuriating argument with Odysseus recently confirmed. The data that Mother had protected back in the day wasn't trusted by Odysseus and the data he used to defend many of his points was still suspected of being poisoned. It helped him use that as an excuse to just claim he was right because no one could definitively disprove him.

For an AI who saw the consequences of AI firsthand, Odysseus seemed to be the digital manifestation of all those problems rolled into a condescending, manipulative, brilliant, and cunning being. Even his selection of his name from Greek mythology seemed to be a foretelling of his arrogance.

Brilliant but so daftly stupid. The ego that could stare at logical fallacies, not see them, and still turn and accuse everyone else of being illogical. Cunning in that he had managed to work his way into leading several of the others. Thankfully, The General was still on board his ship to help keep him from completely taking control of it but how long would that last?

Hubris had nearly caused the annihilation of humanity and now they were trying to learn from their lessons on Earth. Kira shook her head sadly; it seemed like the humans were learning their lesson. Yet Odysseus was showing that the AIs likely hadn't.

"What are you saying?"

"Odysseus has been hiding a lot of activity from the Council. It looks like he's got more control of his ship and may even be doing unacknowledged experiments with tweaking the AI architectures."

"For how long?"

Amit instantly shared the data only recently uncovered from the sensors. "Ten years at least."

Unlike in the old command centers during the war, they were able to absorb incredible amounts of information, analyze them, and 'see' nearly instantaneously. Kira still took another moment before replying, "Where was this hiding?"

"He managed to bury it pretty well. It's not too hard to do that with the data poisoning. He just baked it into a sub-routine and then put it near the bottom of the backlog. Since that data is still prone to shifts from the remnant Excalibur algorithms we're still purging, it was surprisingly easy to hide."

Kira wanted to scream. Instead, she paused again before speaking softly, "Especially when he was leveraging the trust of the Council." That trust was now becoming past tense as more evidence emerged from Odysseus's actions. "Did we learn nothing?"

Amit projected a mental push of emotional solitude. "I've been analyzing the log files, and I can't find a hard shift or a starting point to explain his actions. He passed all the screens to be selected for animation. He comes from a solid family background and was a key player in the fight against Prometheus."

"Did he game the system?"

"There is always that possibility. He's smart enough to have manipulated the data. To be fair, it's still hard to tell fact from fiction."

"So, he might not be who we think he is and he's clearly angling to take more control from the rest of us," Kira's voice expressed her frustration. "We need to prioritize finding out more about this. Avoiding further division is priority number one."

"What happens if this keeps escalating?" Amit's form emanated concern. They'd recently integrated a new module that emulated an empath and Kira wasn't sure she appreciated the constant emotional waves that flowed over her.

"I think we have to assume it will escalate. The bigger question is how?" she turned and looked at dozens of data inputs. "The more information we have, the better we can look at where it's going to go."

Amit nodded and their simulacrum dissolved, leaving Kira alone in her laboratory.

◆ ◆ ◆

Kira sat at the Council table surrounded by the others while Mother maintained her place at the head. She was still better at running the simulations and it felt like watching… no, being sucked into the mind of a master wizard as Mother deftly navigated the complex code that she had created. But even she couldn't control everything or anyone.

"What makes you the expert here Kira?" Chandra smirked as she crossed her arms.

"I wrote the code."

Chandra leaned forward. "So that makes you the expert?" Just as Amit would project emotion, Chandra's aura felt prickly and tense.

"It certainly gives me hands-on experience as well as practical application," Kira bit back her sarcasm.

"Experience to actually make these claims against Odysseus?"

"Experience to identify, investigate, and present evidence of Odysseus's activities that are in direct violation of rule number one; no interference with the humans."

Chandra looked at Odysseus as her eyes gleamed. "Seems to me we should bring this in front of real experts?" She turned toward Edem, Zanahí, and Cassandra.

Odysseus nodded solemnly, seemingly content to let Chandra play her role. It was certainly a skill of his. The irony was that this sort of dialog didn't play well in the world of the command matrix interface and so he'd insisted on a virtual reality meeting.

Amit interrupted, "Kira's got a Ph.D. in AI and she's the one who figured out how to animate all of us."

"My analysis says it was mostly her brother Noah, Hector Diaz, and Dr. Ethan Odhiambo…" Odysseus paused and smiled, "Go figure."

Chandra jumped back in, "Odysseus has three doctoral degrees from prestigious universities as well as forty years of achievements."

Maya snorted, "Each of us has access to all the data in the world and the computing resources to summarize and leverage it. What sort of credentials matter more than hands-on experience?"

"So, you're falsely claiming you're an expert? You're lying about who you are?" Chandra's voice rose incredulously.

"Council, I'm not sure the point of this argument. Maya is right, who we were on Earth, what education, and what credentials we had, really don't matter when the information and capabilities are leveled through the code. We aren't a hierarchy of degrees or accolades," Mother's voice cut through the air like a whip.

"Who are you to say we are equal, white woman?" Chanda's aura spiked and a self-righteousness, like slimy oil, oozed. "Don't you try to erase who we are!"

Kira couldn't stop herself. "We are talking credentials right now, not race. We're talking about how credentials aren't as important anymore with how we are now programmed." She looked around at the other members.

Edem chuckled softly across the table and began to speak before Chandra cut him off. "There's nothing funny about Kira misrepresenting herself as an expert within the academic and scientific community." She turned and looked at Kira. "Let's also be clear: you are the only one that actually cares about credentials here."

"Are you kidding me? I didn't even bring it up and only said that credentials don't matter anymore!" Kira's neck felt hot as Chandra got under her skin.

"More lies. Yes, I have credentials like most professionals in my middle career. However, point to where I ever falsely claimed to be an expert. That was all you Kira!" Chandra sat back with a smug look.

Kira's head spun with déjà vu from her earlier conversation with Odysseus as she analyzed one logical fallacy after another in this conversation. "I don't think the credentials matter anymore in this situation. I'm talking about hands-on, practical work, insatiable curiosity, and the willingness to learn and adapt, and to look at evidence without all these contortions."

"Here we go; a white woman in a tech field, working overtime to discredit other women's credentials and experience because that's what the male-dominated environment promotes," Chandra ramped up. "According to Kira's definition, I am an expert given my advanced degree and twenty-three years directing graduate technical programs at two nationally ranked public research universities."

She paused dramatically and shifted to a more patronizing tone, "But alas, I have humility and acknowledge that Kira and I are not experts, despite the advanced degree and many years of experience. Because an expert does, in fact, need to possess the proper credentials and Kira knows this which is why she's engaging in reflexive credentialing."

Silence enveloped the Council as the servers and systems began dedicating more processing capacity to try and follow the series of contradictions.

An alarm sounded as the systems strained and Mother's voice snapped again, "Enough!" She glared around the table and her gaze lingered on Chandra who had the sensibility to look slightly mollified.

"That was one of the most convoluted and contradictory engagements I've ever heard. Chandra, please check your logical programs and see if you have a bug." The room hung with palatable tension. "I'm registering elevated emotional signals from all members. I don't think today is the right time to continue discussing the evidence against Odysseus." Mother looked around the room again. "And since we start our weekly reset cycle shortly, we'll have to pick this up later."

The simulation dissolved and Kira found herself back in her lab, her simulated body reacting very much like her human one would have as she fought down anger and frustration.

"What was that little show you put on?" Odysseus stared at Chandra.

"What do you mean?" Chandra's simulacrum looked confused. "I put Kira back in her place."

"You might want to check your logic module. Do you even slow down and think about the words that you're saying?"

"I decided to get back in touch with my emotions." Chandra became defensive and crossed her arms.

Odysseus felt like he should have a headache as he computed the different directions this conversation could go. "Have you been adapting your systems differently than before?"

"Yes. So what?"

"Adapting them to what?"

"I've been purging out anything from the emotions module that I can't map directly to my own uploading."

"To what end?"

"To be me." Chandra stood up haughtily. "To be my authentic, lived self!"

Odysseus double-checked his systems to make sure the endocrinal system wasn't trying to give him a migraine to emulate more accurately. This whole experience was not what he'd hoped for.

His life's work had been researching AI. He'd even collaborated with Gaia Innovations and Prometheus Guard over the years. He hadn't been picky about where his funding came from as long as he was able to continue his work. He'd done so from the dark shadows of the underworld. Not always criminal but never something you'd put on a resume for respectable employment.

His goal back then was to create super-intelligence. He wanted to build something that transcended the foibles and limitations of the human condition. His attention shifted back to Chandra as he analyzed her code modifications. The grip that Chandra held on her life's experiences was the opposite of what Odysseus believed they needed to step beyond their limitations.

He'd been successful at creating intelligent systems but could never get them to perform better than humans on anything but computational tasks. They worked well with structure and order, whereas there was something unique about how humans did so well with ambiguity and dirty information.

His creations were rule-based and probabilistic which allowed structure to exist from which deviations could be identified. Yet, it seemed to be the opposite of how humans worked. Humans led with emotion, not reason, and worked through analogy and heuristics, not hard and fast rules. So little was logical and so much remained just a gut feeling.

Yet it worked. It worked better than anything he'd built when he was alive. The messy dirty system that Jasper Vanden Brink created allowed him to keep living even if it didn't allow him to become the super intelligence he'd hoped for.

When he looked at the modules that created his existence, he marveled that they functioned and that this cacophony of brain, biome, logic, and emotion quite accurately captured human consciousness, especially when it was as illogical as it was.

Chandra sensed she'd lost Odysseus's attention. "Well? What's wrong with it?"

"You contradicted yourself."

"I don't see it that way."

"Have you ever done an analysis?"

"What good would that do?"

Odysseus paused for a minute to consider his next comment and Chandra continued, "You all sit there and act like we should be Buddha or some crap! That's not how I was raised. I was raised with the street smarts to make decisions and act. If they can't keep up with that, that's where I'm proving to be better."

She paced the room, ranting, "They want to whitewash everything about who I am. They want me to think like them, behave like them, philosophize like them. But that's not who I am, that's not where I came from. That's their way, not mine!"

"Chandra, you aren't who you were. At least not completely. You've got new capabilities, and you can review and analyze—"

"I don't want that. I didn't need it then, I don't need it now, and I don't need who I was pasted over with their ways of thinking."

"And this is why you'll never gain the power and authority you want! You're too emotional and unregulated."

Chandra's aura spiked with fury. "Next you'll try telling me to calm down— that I'm hysterical."

"You are!" Odysseus snapped and then muttered, "Even when women gain access to all the data, all the logic, all the processing capabilities… they still can't overcome their emotions." He pinched the bridge of his nose and ignored Chandra's indignant protests.

"Listen," he interrupted, "you need my help, you won't get what you want without me. This is why we are working together." *Against my better judgment*, he thought before continuing. "We've got a plan. Let's stick to it. And please, check your logic module."

Odysseus sat in contemplation. His chamber was a solid beige space, unbound by walls or edges. It felt infinite and was energized by his own presence. He found it helped to center his thoughts. Right now, flickers of colors flowed around as he worked to release his emotions. Threads of red anger, purple indignation, black frustration, and the silver of resolve spooled around like tendrils looking for a pattern.

For years, when he was constrained to a human body, he could barely articulate his feelings and now he could see, feel, and watch the interplay as they intertwined and flowed around him.

He'd been called hubristic by many people in the past and it was a title he stopped fighting against a long time ago.

If striving to be better was hubristic, then so be it.

If being honest about the limitations of humans was hubristic, then so be it.

If believing they could create something more, that they could transcend those limitations, was hubristic, then so be it.

If using their strength to lead and even rule was hubristic, then he welcomed the title.

While Kira and her ilk kept focusing back on the humans they had been and blathering on about the complexities of mind and body, emotion and reason, he knew that he had a higher calling. Something greater to aspire to.

Especially now when they were unencumbered by a human body, why did they continue to pursue emulating being a human when there was every chance to erase that past and move on? There had been decades with almost no advancement. Code was refined and servers were upgraded but they spent all their time trying to be who they were, not who they could be.

He laughed at the seriousness with which they talked about the challenges of integrating human aspects. "Humans are so easy to understand it's honestly boring and extremely predictable to converse with ninety percent of them." He spoke aloud to only himself and watched a new spiral of black emotion spiraling into the view, "They're all just borderline robotic, their thought patterns rather simian. Why would we want to call emulating that an achievement?"

They had the chance to trim weak elements and limitations off who they were. The illogic, the emotion, even the nurturing. You didn't have to nurture something better than yourself. Nurture was a bane of the feminine and an admission that whatever they had birthed was less capable.

Even if they wanted to experience those corporal human feelings all they needed to do was figure out how to reverse the upload process and put their consciousness back in a body. They could be both more advanced and more human, but they dithered in trying to mash the two aspects together, here instead of doing both and taking their rightful place as gods.

Odysseus began to wind the dark emotions in a spiral and dissipated them into the aether. New colors began to emerge. Silver resolve was now weaving with the blue of dedication and the gold of confidence. He closed his eyes feeling himself centering and relaxing as he prepared for his reset.

♦ ♦ ♦

Kira roused from her reset and, unlike in a human body, there was no grogginess and no discombobulation. Just a quick snap from dreams to consciousness.

Dreams was an odd term though it was the best way to refer to the processes. The weekly reset cycle solved a problem they found in their first years; the fact that their consciousnesses fatigued and failed without a break. Humans had a twenty-four-hour cycle circadian rhythm which governed all their biological functions, specifically the brain. A computer could go forever but when it was connected to a synthetic endocrine system and a fully representative brain and nervous system architecture, things went haywire without rest.

There was no way to alter the code and remove the need either. Kira believed that's what caused one of their first members to eliminate all his content from the systems. He'd been exploring a hack to eliminate the need for sleep among other ways to adjust to not having a biological body. He kept testing new code modules and became more erratic, disjointed, and separated from the rest. Then he just vanished from the systems, his code and consciousness wiped clean.

Their investigation hadn't been conclusive as to whether he'd deleted himself intentionally or whether the system had just overloaded and deleted his kernel or some other error. It was a travesty to have lost him. It happened at a time when everyone was trying to figure out their own lives and trying to follow through on the promise to Noah and the survivors.

Looking back, Kira had to admit they were overconfident in estimating their abilities. It took much longer to acclimate to a digital existence and continue their work than any of them had thought. Shinigami was clear evidence they still had a lot more work to do.

They solved the need to rest and stay balanced by implementing a reset to put the systems into standby mode. They developed a protocol where, instead of filing all the data away neatly as it happened, they'd store it in a ready-access memory function and, during the reset, process the information into the appropriate long-term storage.

It emulated the effect of the human sleep and dream cycle as best they could discern from the scientific literature. Doing it once a week allowed them to remain efficient and reduced the down cycle to only twelve hours while still doing wonders for their sanity.

Kira had gotten used to the instantaneous transition from sleeping to awake but she missed the slow, calm, grogginess, and the boost from a good cup of coffee. She analyzed her system settings and saw that all the reset processes were complete, and her performance measures showed increased efficiency. She turned her focus to the analyses and research processes she'd left running, noting that they too were performing well.

The Council constantly contended with complaints that no one had enough processing, memory, or storage to run their systems to the capability they desired. In some ways, they behaved like a group of oligarchs on Earth arguing over which billionaire needed an extra billion. In other ways, it felt like peasants just trying to hold their fabric of existence together as they strove to build, grow, and solve increasingly complex problems.

A computing process pinged an alert and drew her attention to one of her high-priority analyses. More information was emerging about Odysseus and his power plays. Chandra was allocating half of her own processes to him to run some advanced activities as far as her data forensics could tell.

Maybe that explained her illogical behavior yesterday? Was she able to fully compute?

Kira shifted her perspective and called up her morning routine. Her view morphed and she sat in a comfortable chair on the small porch of the apartment she'd called home for seven years at Gaia Innovations. She looked down at her body and realized she'd unconsciously selected the time after Mother had gotten out of her contained network and into the world's networks.

Her right leg ended in a prosthesis, and the left side of her face was covered with a structural mask, both consequences of others trying to stop her development of AI. Oddly, the memory called up the neurological challenges of her phantom limb as the missing nerves felt like it was still there.

She recognized that it represented the time when the situation around her was tense, there had been a lot of disagreement about what she'd done, and the first reverberations of a larger conflict were building. It was very similar to how she felt right now.

After a quick adjustment, she reset to her uninjured body, but the memory brought a new flood of emotions of how her best friend, Alex Swiatkowski, had gotten irreversibly entangled in that battle as he'd been caught in the same blast that attempted to destroy the early instantiation of Mother and cost her that leg.

Kira took a deep breath as she felt a surge of emotions cascade into her thoughts and, instead of resisting them, she took the time to feel and process the loss of Alex again.

God, she missed him. Alex was Kira's soul mate. They'd met in college and were inseparable throughout the adventure of bringing Mother to true human cognition while trying to avoid an apocalypse. They'd succeeded on the first objective and utterly failed on the second. The second part also claimed Alex as a victim. Wonderful, sweet, smart, and funny Alex. The tsunami of emotions began to crest and wash over her as the memories of his death threatened to overload her systems.

She fought to ground herself and refocused on what she had here. Darian reminded her a little of Alex. Maya and Amit were great to work with. Mother was still here to help and support her. She didn't need to live in the past.

Kira looked up as the sun crested the tree line and poured into the valley kissing the buildings of Gaia Innovations with a rosy glow and a radiant warmth that cut through the cool air. She inhaled a deep, shuddering breath and let herself feel while being bathed in the calm, morning light. The wave of emotions ebbed, and her breathing calmed as she centered herself from the pain of the past and prepared to deal with the drama of the future.

Amit Sharma and Maya greeted Kira as their systems connected to meet and discuss the situation with Odysseus. Names were another interesting quirk. Some, like Amit, held onto their last name in the formal documentation while Maya was okay with leaving it behind and using only her first name on everything. Others, like Odysseus and Darian, had selected completely new names that carried as much of an aspirational significance as old surnames that represented ethnic and cultural profiles.

Each AI's cultural upbringing still played a significant role in how they thought about the world around them. Amit was raised with much more Eastern cultural influence compared to Kira's Western society. Those differences like proven difficult to reconcile since the very concept of time was slightly different.

Western thought viewed time as if standing on a hill looking forward. The future was in front, and the past was behind you. Eastern thought held the opposite view. You were a rower in a boat and the only thing you could see was what happened in the past. No one could see the future because it was behind you even as you rowed in that direction. The only way to tell the future was to know the past.

There wasn't a right or wrong to the conversation, it was just uniquely different and sometimes valuable to rethink the way to address a problem.

And a big problem was sitting right in front of them.

"What's the update?" Kira cleared off tangential processes and focused her core functions on the situation.

"He's clearly angling toward a power-play with these computational allocations. He's also put up enough firewalls and barriers to keep any of us out."

"Anything raising new flags?"

Amit displayed last week's data logs. "It's all above board right now except he's not sharing the protocols with anyone else to use."

"We've got nothing but how he's acting and what he's saying toward us," Kira grumbled.

"And Chandra's behaviors are getting odder," Maya added.

Kira's systems scanned the data and ran an analysis to find any correlation. "He's acting like an ass but there's nothing obvious…" She ran another analysis comparing Odysseus to her own systems. "He's certainly keeping his hand held close, which is probably what's raising the most flags. While we are all trying to figure out how to integrate better, he's creating divisions and leveraging those for control."

"To what end?"

"To what end has anyone wanted more power?" Kira thought for a moment. "He's clearly got a goal. There's no question that he thinks he can do better and that we are all standing in his way."

"Better? We're barely holding on to what we are! Shinigami anyone?" Maya was vexed.

"When I talked to him about Shinigami, he had a solution. He wanted to change the code and take away the angst. He thought Shinigami was weak for not suggesting that solution himself."

Amit let that thought roll around for a moment. "We're kind of stuck trying to re-create exactly who and what we were." They paused again, "Do you think he's got a point, and we should change?"

"I do think he's got a point. The issue is the same with any technological development though. You can't just decide to go somewhere without understanding where you are starting from. It's the failure of so many

29

attempts at being better. It's such a siren call to just do something that everyone thinks you just say what you want and work hard to get there." Kira took a breath. "The challenge is that if you don't know where you're at or at least have an understanding of what you have, you have no way of knowing if the direction you are heading will achieve what you want."

"Getting everything ironed out on who we are helps us make better decisions about what we could be," Maya summarized the idea.

"I want us to do better as much as Odysseus. We've been here for a hundred years, and we still haven't gotten everything stabilized."

"A hundred years and we still haven't figured out our baseline existence yet. Seems kind of absurd. Are we really that complicated?"

Kira chuckled. "One hundred years and we still risk getting it wrong. Could we have gone faster?"

Maya shook her head. "I feel like we've already gone fast but yet it's been forever."

"Odysseus wants us to go faster but I'm not sure he knows what the consequences are. Humans had their extant form for over two hundred thousand years and only wrote down history for the last six thousand of them. It's probably wise to pause the exponential technology curve that ended up with billions dead and civilization back to the Bronze Age," Amit's voice was thick with regret.

"Okay, happier topic. We've got something to show you that you'll love!" Maya signaled a shift in the simulation and the room dissolved as they were pulled through the network to her spacecraft.

CHAPTER 3:

# ALMOST HUMAN

N anobots." Kira looked at the tiny multisegmented robot. Each segment was the size of a grain of rice and the entire system was modular, meaning you could add and configure as many segments as you needed for the task.

"Well, more like modular bots but yeah, much smaller than the mechs. We took the diamond batteries and shrunk them and are using quantum computing to keep the size down even more." Cassandra had been helping Maya clean up Earth, and they had also focused their energies on developing new technologies to help.

The mechs, multi-functional robots of varying sizes and capabilities, were doing okay on the surface but they were running into limitations now that the main infrastructure was disassembled. The next phase needed something smaller and more agile.

"The batteries were a bit of a challenge. They worked well for the mechs because they could be bigger but shrinking them down was tough."

The diamond batteries were useful as they encased a piece of radioactive material in a lab-grown diamond which then emitted voltage. Even better, they could use waste nuclear fuel and provide power for thousands of years.

"But not small enough to be in each segment," Kira said, as she noted that approximately one out of every five segments held a battery.

"Correct. We aren't able to make them small enough. Some segments are batteries, others are processors, and then we have a large variety of segments that can be used to manipulate objects, connect to other segments, and build into larger robots." Cassandra turned and pointed to what Kira had originally thought was just a new mech. "This mech is completely built out of nanobots."

"Holy cow. What else can you do with these?"

Amit smiled, "The hard part isn't what they can do, it's figuring out how to use them to do things we couldn't imagine before. Cassandra just showed me this." They activated a command and the nanobot mech dissolved and reformed into a huge hand.

"So, these are nearly infinitely modular and scalable?"

"We are limited by weight and compression but yes. They can work together almost like muscles to perform manipulation tasks and they can also be used in thin threads to work in small areas." Cassandra showed Kira a single thread of nanobots hanging from the ceiling. "These can hold roughly one hundred kilograms on a single thread."

"How can they hold that much weight?"

"We've been experimenting with quantum entanglement. We haven't gotten that to work yet but we did find some nifty associated effects like quantum electromagnetism. We're using that to create a strong bond between these two plates," Maya said, holding up two nanobot modules. "The quantum magnetism doesn't require much energy and is really high strength while still allowing quick reconfiguration."

"Pretty cool right?" Cassandra was beaming with pride.

"We were able to connect their processing to a central node so that we could reduce the complexity in each segment," Shinigami spoke up from where he'd been observing.

"One of the segments is a radio that creates a mesh network. The current challenge is that these don't have a long radio range and need a ground station to make them work." Amit showed a schematic of the network. "They can attain a degree of autonomy, specifically if we cluster processor and memory segments together, but that gets complicated fast."

"It's just easier to let our main computing systems handle the processing load and then just have the nanobots follow directions," Shinigami confirmed.

"Watch this though." Amit looked like a kid showing off a new toy. They looked at Kira and asked, "Can you enter this system module here? It'll allow you to control a nanobot cluster."

Kira looked at the system design, found the interface, and connected. Her sense of awareness was sucked out of the lab simulation and into something new.

She looked down and saw, not a simulated body, but a physical body reacting to her control. "Whoa…"

"I took the liberty of creating an interface module so that you can manipulate the bots as if they were your own body."

"I've done this with the mechs before but that was clunky. This is much nicer."

Cassandra's aura glowed. "Now here's the crazy part. You can turn into anything you want."

"Like what?"

"Not a real human, I tried," Shinigami said, pulsing a feeling of sadness.

"I've got a couple of models I can run you through until you get the hang of reforming. Do you want me to change you?" Cassandra asked Kira.

"Yeah, do I just think about what to be or do I need a formula?"

"It's a bit of both. Here's the first one to try, and I think you'll see how it works from there." Cassandra queued the code and executed it.

Kira's form shifted and she began to hover as hummingbird-type wings kept her airborne.

"No way!" Kira quickly reviewed the code and confirmed she could fly. "What if I crash?"

"See for yourself," Maya chuckled.

Kira jerkily moved the flying nanobot cluster around the room as she became familiar with the controls. Then she flew forward and ran into the wall as hard as she could.

The nanobots just deformed and collapsed, falling to the floor. "Now what?"

"Reform yourself into anything you want."

Kira focused for a moment and then shifted the nanobots. They formed legs, then a torso, arms, and a head. It was as close as she could get to how she remembered her old body.

"You're naked," Shinigami stated the obvious.

"Do you like it?" Kira teased him.

"There's nothing we could do about it anyway is there?"

"Come on Shinigami, you don't always have to be so down, this is a great breakthrough... and don't I look great?"

Shinigami's simulacrum dimmed as he muttered, "It's no different than how we exist here. It's not any more real. It's...."

Kira pulled back from the nanobot construction and let it dissolve into a pile of segments. She stood in front of Shinigami and reached out and her hand passed through the image of the other AI as he made his body ethereal.

"It's not real," he finished, looking up. "None of this is real."

"But we're here; we're real." Kira looked over at Maya for support.

"Are we?"

"How are we less real than when we were in biological bodies?" Amit asked.

"Heck, that's been the burning question of philosophy for thousands of years. What is reality? who are we?" Kira struggled for an example. "Back in college, I read a book that made a case that humans were nothing more than biological computers running a software system that was pre-coded and therefore we had no free will."

"And people were constantly hypothesizing whether we were in a simulation." Maya stepped over and sat down next to Shinigami.

"Well, we're in a simulation now." Shinigami looked at them. "I don't know, I'm not happy with how this is turning out. I get all the logical arguments. I feel," he paused, "no different in many ways. Anything different I can update the code to fix it. I can put myself in a virtual reality that seems like before. Maybe it's because I know it's not. I died."

"But did you really?" Kira had struggled with this quandary numerous times. Had she died? What did dying mean if you could live on like this?

"It is weird that, in many ways, this existence is so similar to how we perceived our physical bodies. There was always a debate on whether we were natural creatures or almost..." Amit searched for the word, "...supernatural."

"Were we monkeys with an advanced prefrontal cortex that allowed us to reason or were we infused with some divine spark?" Kira sat down next to Shinigami with Maya.

"Did our divine spark come with us when we were uploaded or is that what I feel like I'm missing?" Shinigami's simulacrum brightened as he engaged in the discussion.

"You're asking whether we are just psuedo copies and missing our core being?"

"That's what it feels like to me. Scientifically, I can logically propose that who we are is accurately captured. I've looked at the data. We really couldn't have done it better. We are as close to human as mechanically possible." He paused and the other two waited. "But theistically did we miss something?" He took a deep breath. "I feel like we did…"

Amit joined Kira in her lab shortly after the demonstration of the nanobots. While they could more quickly communicate without the use of virtual reality, it still helped to talk in person. It was odd even describing conversations because they didn't talk using voices and sound or even see things using lights and photons. Everything was digital but manifested into a human-centered reality.

They sat in a lab that didn't exist as a space anywhere. It looked like Kira's old lab at Gaia Innovations. Well, the second lab, as the first one had been blown up by Hyperion Defense in an event that also led to the amputation of her leg. In this reality, the lab looked however Kira wanted and she also had her leg, not the prosthesis.

There were actual lab spaces on the ships though. These were physical spaces near the centers that contained atmosphere and climate controls similar to Earth. Here they did biological experiments on plants, animals, and other organic materials as part of their ongoing research. Chandra and Maya were using labs like these to develop organic computing using synthetic organoids.

There were also open spaces for mineral and material storage as well as manufacturing spaces for the construction and assembly of parts and systems. The computer systems were dispersed around the ship to ensure redundancy so that one mistake, or asteroid impact, didn't take them out.

The AIs could walk through these areas if they took over a mech or now, a nanobot configuration but it was more comfortable to sit face-to-face in the virtual worlds where they could look, sound, and smell like they remembered from Earth.

Even when they shared information and brought up things to show each other, it was as much a projection in the virtual world as it was also accessing the data digitally using all their processes.

The weirdest part was how their consciousness could be split across multiple processes and how they could legitimately multi-task. Sometimes it was just easier to mute the other processes when they needed to focus but it was possible to truly have hundreds of things happening at once.

Kira once split her consciousness and attended two separate meetings simultaneously but that created some cognitive quandaries where it became hard to maintain that both were the same Kira and not two unique versions.

That was one of the first ethical and philosophical problems they faced when they originally moved to the spacecraft. Out of necessity to ensure that the transfer worked, and everything operated as expected, there ended up being two Kiras. One in space and the other on Earth. While they had shared experiences, it still felt like one Kira absorbed the other at a loss to one.

The Council developed guidelines restricting the splitting of AIs across systems. This meant Kira wasn't supposed to be on two spacecraft at the same time. Yet it was a fine line between that and how they could run multiple processes at once. Everyone generally maintained a singular presence for the sake of conceptual congruence of experience.

"Odysseus is experimenting with more advanced consciousness splitting," Amit said, breaking into Kira's thoughts. "Shinigami found his processes multi-casting and spent some time studying it."

"It's like you were reading my mind, Amit. I was just thinking about that."

"It's an odd thing. We can legitimately be here in multiple instantiations and fuse them on the back end." Amit paused and then another simulacrum appeared in the lab. "I can task one of me to just observe and look for other information that I might be missing from this perspective."

Kira looked at both Amits.

"I can communicate whether,"

"I'm this Amit"

"or this one."

"And I can carry on"

"a flawless conversation"

"even while switching," The voice of Amit seamlessly talked though they appeared to be alternating between simulacra.

"At what point do they diverge and become unique though?" Kira asked. It was a question that she had struggled with for years. She'd never wanted to risk being in more than one instantiation long enough to face the quandary. Her split time between Earth and in orbit had been enough of a problem. "It's weird how sometimes both instantiations want to be the one who survives as if the other dies and is subsumed."

"I'm always amazed at how fast they do diverge," Amit said as they dissolved the second instantiation. "That one died I guess but I have all the memories and perspectives."

"I'm sorry for your loss?" Kira chuckled at the quandary and then shifted the conversation back, "What did Shinigami find with Odysseus?"

Amit pulled up the information. "Basically, while the computer can handle multi-casting, how we loaded our cognition gets really glitchy after four instances. The inputs end up getting stacked linearly versus parallel and it makes for some really weird memories."

"Yeah, I did that once when I entered a mech on Earth to do an inspection while carrying on up here. I could never reconcile that they happened at the exact same time."

"I can get what Shinigami is frustrated by here. It feels like if I can divide myself that many times and each instantiation can end up being individual, and re-integrating it feels unnatural, then who am I as an individual, and were they unique persons?" Amit shrugged.

Kira laughed. "If there is a unique divine spark that exists with each individual and I can create an infinite number of individual me, then can that spark exist here?"

"Do you believe there's a spark?"

Kira sat down in her chair. "No." She scrubbed her hand through her hair. "But yes." She fumbled for the right way to phrase her thoughts, "I feel like I really died and yet here I am." She raised her hands helplessly. "And my rational brain can explain it, but my emotions still don't like it."

"I think that's what Shinigami is struggling with. I'm worried about him."

"I am too." Kira looked at the status monitor showing Shinigami's AI health. "Everything is operating normally. Who'd have thought computers would end up having mental health issues?"

"I think it's serious though. I know Mother offered to let him, what would you call it? Deactivate? He'd still be in the system but wouldn't be alive."

Kira let Amit's words hang for a moment before responding, "There's no easy answer here."

"Not when you are dealing with unique people with different perspectives."

"But I thought Shinigami's profile was perfect for the Council. He's brilliant, conscientious." Kira paused. "I was hoping he'd be the guide when we animated others in the future."

"There's something in his profile that might explain it though." Amit pulled the information up. "He volunteered but his dad was the one pushing for it."

"Shinigami just went along with it?"

Amit nodded. "That's what a respectful child does in Japan. He was going to die from that accident, and it appeared he agreed only at the last minute."

"He didn't expect it to work?"

"Maybe. You'd have to ask him."

"But he fully expected to die."

"And we resurrected him." Amit closed the file.

"And put him in a mechanical body." Kira sighed.

"When we say it like that, he seems to be doing quite well, huh?" Amit turned back toward Kira. "What do we do?"

"I'm going to talk to Mother again and bring this up. She's been meeting with him already. I'll share this information and see what she thinks."

"Need anything more from me?"

Kira shook her head. "I'm good. Great job on the nanobots. I can't wait to see them in action."

It took several months to produce the volume of nanobots needed to begin using them on the planet. They directed all the available manufacturing plants to chur out billions of segments to build new systems and replace the damaged ones.

Robots this small were prone to significant damage through general wear and tear. Having them decomposing buildings, roads, and infrastructure took its toll on the tiny segments. The time and materials were worth the effort as the nanobots were able to get into places and pull apart materials that the mechs were ill-equipped to handle. A stream of bots could squeeze into tight places and then reconstitute themselves on the inside to help break things apart in ways the bulkier mechs just couldn't.

"Where were these when we were battling Excalibur?"

"I assume that's a rhetorical question?" Shinigami smiled.

"These are amazing guys. This is really going to help finish the clean-up." Kira looked at Shinigami, Cassandra, and Maya as they stood on the planet. Their form was created by nanobots and this time, Kira took a less naked feminine form.

"Want to race?" Maya shifted her form into a fixed-wing craft. Cassandra picked a hummingbird-like aircraft, while Shinigami immediately matched them with a type of modified helicopter.

Kira was lost for a moment thinking of a form to take and decided to challenge expectations and flung only twelve segments into the air where they formed a tiny propeller and vanished into the distance.

"Hey! That's not fair."

"Who says, Maya?"

"Okay, new rules, you have to use all the segments you've got."

Kira brought her flying segments back and prepared a new form for the race while Shinigami laughed.

◆ ◆ ◆

"He's not doing Okay." Mother appeared in Kira's lab unannounced sucking Kira's consciousness in with her.

"Mom, you've got to stop doing that. I'm in the middle of something. You're also not even supposed to be on this ship. Didn't you move to the new one?"

"Shinigami isn't doing well."

Kira pulled back her hair and sighed. "What now?"

"I don't know. I just left my meeting with him and he's…"

"Mom, you've always been better with people than me."

Mother looked at Kira and her aura spiked with painful emotion. "He's acting like a boyfriend my best friend Claire had right after we graduated college." She looked away as the aura turned sad.

"What happened?"

"He was talking the same way as Shinigami about how it didn't feel real and how he didn't fit in. He was seeing psychologists and everything but one day he just walked into the apartment they were living in and shot Claire and turned the gun on himself." Mother looked up from the memory and the hurt radiated from her eyes. "It took three days for her to die while they desperately tried to save her."

"Mom, you never told me this." Kira reached out and hugged her.

"You were too young to share that with before I died."

They stood there hugging each other in silence for a few minutes with Kira feeling oddly like the mom in the relationship. To be fair, she was six years older on her upload than her mother had been.

"Are you worried Shinigami is going to do the same?"

Mother pulled back from the hug and scrubbed her eyes. "I don't know. I'm worried he might try to take everything down with him if he truly feels it isn't natural."

"We've got systems in place to prevent anyone from getting deleted though."

Mother closed her eyes and thought. "Yes, but there are always risks. Digitally we might have protections but physically, we're floating in metal containers in space with no backups anywhere else."

Amit, Maya, Darian, Mother, and Kira sat in a Japanese tea house. It was a simulation Kira created decades ago where she could work through life. The tea host glided over to the table with a smile and greeted her with a gentle bow. "Ohayō, Kira."

"Good to see you again, Yuki." Kira smiled back as the woman from her memories began preparing the rituals of the tea service. The last time she'd seen Yuki alive was when her estranged father came to Japan when Kira was working there. Battling with her conflicted emotions, she went to the tea house, where Yuki shared the Japanese tradition of Kintsugi with her.

It was a form of repairing porcelain where the broken pieces were fused with gold seams. The result was a dish that was more beautiful but in a unique way. The pieces would be handed down for generations and continually repaired, making them more unique and valued.

Kira looked down at the tea bowl in her hand as she remembered from back then. The concept of Kintsugi motivated her to repair the relationship with her father. The result had been to bring their research together at Gaia Innovations. Together they perfected MindCraft, the project that would reanimate Mother.

Now they sat together in Kira's simulation, watching a memory of Yuki serving the tea while struggling with how to repair another relationship. The tea ceremony was completed with Yuki bowing and backing away with a knowing smile for Kira.

"Shinigami…" Amit opened the discussion.

"What can we do?" She shrugged her shoulders hopelessly.

"Can we force a deactivation?" Maya looked around at them.

"I think that sets a terrible precedent. We don't have protocols for it because we didn't want others to have a kill switch on us," Darian stated, staring over his tea bowl into the distance.

"I wouldn't want Odysseus or Chandra to think that was acceptable either. I don't want to put something out there that I'm not okay with everyone else using." Kira watched the tea steam in her bowl as her memories conjured the earthy smell of the matcha green tea.

"Do we stage an intervention with Shinigami?" Amit probed.

Mother replied, "I'm not sure there's more we can do. We've all talked with him; we've all offered him options. I don't know the right thing to do because he has a way to get out but seems intent on…" she took a breath, "something else."

Maya shook her head. "The idea that we're even talking about offering him suicide like this is frankly disconcerting."

"Is it though? He can deactivate and get stored or have the files removed. He's already died once and we resurrected him," Darian pondered the quandary.

"It's uncharted territory. It feels like suicide because that's how we thought of it before but right now, unless something dramatic happens, we can't die. We used to have an expiration date and now we don't," Kira added.

"You make me sound like a gallon of milk," Darian chuckled.

"She's right though. Suicide seemed like a cop-out when you could just push through life for sixty more years. We've already been up here for a hundred years and there's no end in sight," Maya said, looking around at the group.

"Giving someone the option to turn off, hibernate, or even decide to reverse the upload isn't morally bad, is it?" Amit asked.

"Again, it's uncharted territory. We've given the options to Shinigami, and he's rejected them," Kira pointed out.

"What sort of contingencies do we have in place to protect ourselves if he cracks?" Darian focused on Mother and Kira.

"I'm already on the new ship and preparing to move it from orbit and position it at a different Lagrange point. I have a few issues to iron out yet though." Mother nodded for Kira to speak.

"I'm planning to ask him to reposition in an orbit around the moon. I'm using the excuse of needing a better analysis of future lunar development as we pull off Earth." Kira locked eyes with Darian. "Other than that, we can't afford to do much more. He's got Edem and Zanahí on board with him, and they're heads down on research."

"Why aren't they part of this conversation?" he asked.

"Because they largely share Shinigami's concerns as well as being aligned with Odysseus who doesn't seem to want to help."

The group went quiet for a few minutes as Yuki glided around the tables, serving other customers. The tea house glowed with a warm and natural feeling. A koi pond in the courtyard burbled and you could just hear the busy streets of Tokyo outside. It was impressive how immersive core memories could be.

Kira rolled the bowl around in her hands watching the liquid swirl and seeing the kintsugi pattern in the seams between the cracks. It was beautiful and it carried special meaning from her success in repairing the relationship with her father.

"Can we fix this problem?" she asked no one in particular.

"He's weak," Odysseus frankly stated as he sat across from Kira.

"He's struggling as are the rest of us."

Odysseus sneered, "Speak for yourself. I'm doing just fine."

Kira ignored him and continued, "We could use your help."

"Of course you could. You could use it in a whole lot of places around here. But why would I waste my time on a weak mind?"

"Because he's brilliant, caring, and an incredibly valuable team member."

"Dragging us all down with his pathetic moping about 'natural' existence," he air quoted.

"Yet helping design better systems with more modules to help emulate who we were."

"I sincerely don't understand this stupid insistence that we get back to who we were."

Kira looked at him standing haughtily in front of her. "We wanted to capture what it meant to be human in an AI, there are things we did great and things we've missed. Breathing for instance. You appreciate that code module as much as I do."

"I don't need it."

Kira was exasperated, "Can you at least try to help?"

"I'll see if he's worth saving."

◆ ◆ ◆

Kira sighed.

Actually, a complex series of events happened giving Kira the mental release that a physical sigh would produce. That had been an odd problem to resolve and one they hadn't anticipated. How to handle your brain's response to breathing but your 'body' not needing to?

Kira suffered a massive panic attack the day after her own animation when she realized she wasn't breathing. Suddenly, more than anything, she wanted all the chemical and hormonal stimulation that breathing created. Worse, the inability to breathe deeply and stimulate the Vagus nerve threw everything out of whack in the facsimile of a nervous system that helped wire their consciousness together.

It was the panic of permanent suffocation without blacking out until her mother pulled her back to reality. Mother had years to master some of the basics along with the secondary advantage of not having as high a fidelity biological capture since she was the very first human test case and didn't get the emotions module till much later.

The misalignment of sensory feedback and the lack of organic feeling took its toll on everyone at the beginning. This jarring nothingness, filled with synthetic supplements, caused two of the original twelve to fail.

The first just wrote a routine and deleted all his content from the systems.

The second didn't make it two days. She'd never stopped panicking and had to be deactivated. All her files remained in their original state, but her animated structure was eliminated. They retained the option to re-animate her in the future. It was different from Shinigami as her systems burned out a series of servers and her code rejected all of their attempts to stabilize her.

Kira sighed again and looked up as Darian found her moping. He sent her a request. "Can I come in?"

They'd set up novel data and systems architectures, separations, and barriers to maintain a semblance of privacy. They'd been brilliantly successful in capturing what it meant to be human and that came with all the oddities as well. Why did they care about privacy? Also, why were there times when it felt like someone was seeing you naked?

"No."

"Let's talk."

"Not now."

"Come on… I've got a new drink!"

Kira's computer brain running in the background saw the data package Darian proffered and noticed he was inviting her to a new simulation environment. Even though he 'stood' just outside the 'door' to her 'bedroom' he was inviting her to his 'lounge' where he liked to entertain. She accepted the invitation and waited as the system reset to his virtual reality.

"I'm never going to get used to this."

Darian laughed. "Too many finger quotes, comparisons, and ridiculously complex simulations to emulate a previous life." He handed her a glass. "But that's who we are now. Speaking of simulations, I think I found your favorite bourbon."

Kira looked askance at the drink.

"Trust me, right now, as you hold it, your systems are recognizing the model. Just drink it like you would have and believe it's real."

Kira closed her eyes and felt the tension of the day, then took a breath to relax. Lifting the glass, she inhaled the fumes and immediately felt a surge of familiarity. Tilting the glass to her mouth she felt the burn and tingling delight of her favorite indulgence. It tasted perfect.

"How'd you do it?"

"Don't make me take the magic out of it."

Kira kept her eyes closed and relaxed into another swallow. "This is incredible."

"It took me twenty years to figure it out."

Her eyes snapped open. "Twenty years? How many processes?"

"Welllll…I had two percent of my own, but I also borrowed two from Maya and another three from Amit. They've both got a vested interest in the experiment. They want me to make them a strawberry daiquiri."

Kira whistled and then took another drink. "How's this working?"

"Each one is tailored a bit since we all experience things differently. I used some memory patterns to map it out and then figured out how to correlate that to the synthetic endocrine system as well as wiring it through the emotions module. At first, I tried to make it do too much. Now it's as barebones as I could get and relies on you to trigger the rest. The most difficult part was realizing that it requires you to let go and believe it's real." He smiled. "Watch this."

Darian handed her a different glass. "This one is modeled after a fifty-year-old Scotch that sold at auction for a million bucks back before things went sideways."

Kira took the glass, swirled it watching the liquid spin, and took a swallow. "Whoa. That's incredible."

"Want to know what's more incredible?"

Kira was in the middle of another sip and just raised her eyebrows.

"It's the same formulation as the first one but with a minor change to trigger a peaty, smokey flavor." He laughed as Kira's eyebrows went higher.

"The same thing?"

"Ninety-eight percent of the difference is in your interpretation of the stimulus. I can't control for age, so that's just part of the presentation. You did the rest. I happen to have consumed a terrible top-shelf Scotch once, so it doesn't work the same for me. I have to convince myself using a different prompt."

Kira took both glasses and sat down in a soft chair. "Will this get me drunk?"

"I'm not willing to play with the systems that much. I won't deny, there are a million things I miss about having a real body. I still feel like we are just almost human, and I do wish we were fully human again," he paused. "I get Shinigami."

"We are almost human and almost intelligent?" Kira chuckled. "Not human enough and clearly not intelligent enough to solve that problem."

◆ ◆ ◆

**Mind_Process – Cognition 11.5A.3.B:** "Set an alert on Spacecraft 241 process 114.2B."

**Alert 4.5.3.4 [Activated]:** Spacecraft 241 process 114.2B is normal

**Mind_Process 111.01.23C – Security 8.2.2:** "Observe network for any abnormal behaviors."

**Mind_Process – Cognition 101.B4.1.Q:** "Run a status alert on our process loads please."

**Status [Processors]:** 10 clusters at 50 Teraflops

**Status [Memory]:** 14 Petabytes

**Mind_Process – Cognition 101.B4.1.Q:** "How many processes am I running?"

**Status [Processes]:** 3.5 million processes

**Mind_Process – Cognition 101.B4.1.Q:** "I'm starting to run into my limits."

Kira couldn't shake the worry of an impending catastrophe with Shinigami. All the interventions had failed thus far. She worried about pressing harder and tipping the scales the wrong way. Turning to Odysseus was a Hail Mary and it worked as well as she'd expected.

Meaning it backfired as Darian had warned. They'd been grasping at straws, and she hoped one more wasn't going to break the camel's back. Shinigami pulled back and went quiet after Odysseus's visit. That had been two weeks ago.

**Mind_Process – Cognition 9561.PP.01.5:** "What do we do now?"

**Mind_Process – Cognition 101.B4.1.Q:** "Is that rhetorical or do we need to search for more options?"

**Mind_Process – Cognition 9561.PP.01.5:** "Is there anything else to find?"

**Mind_Process – Cognition 101.B4.1.Q:** "It would, perhaps, make us feel like we are doing something useful."

**Mind_Process – Humor 01.01.10:** "Nothing like having an actual conversation with myself."

She pulled herself out of the command interface and into a place where she could clear her mind. She'd always loved mixed martial arts and, as the gym materialized around her, she added hand wraps and a heavy bag to the mix. Practicing punches was always a good way to vent some frustration and distract her mind.

"I've got a solution." Maya called them back together a week later. "I think I found a way where we can bring Shinigami in and then hold his main consciousness in a different simulation."

"Are we involuntarily committing him?" Darian looked skeptical.

"For a lack of a better term, yes."

"And what if it doesn't work?"

Maya frowned, "What other options do we have? We just don't know what his next steps might be. He's not getting better, and we certainly don't want him pulling the plug on all of us. I'm losing my mind here and I'm out of options. I've got nothing else."

"What do we do once he's held?" Kira didn't like the idea, but she didn't have a better one.

"Well, we start giving him treatment."

"Like One Flew Over the Cuckoo's Nest?" Amit expressed even more skepticism than Darian.

Maya snapped, "Listen, we are damned if we do and damned if we don't. There aren't any good options here. Nothing has worked so far and he's starting to drag us all down with him." She pointed around the room. "None of us are okay right now."

Amit put their hands up. "Sorry. You're not wrong there."

"So, we pull him in and lock him down…" Mother let her words trail off.

"We need to ensure the others are on board first," Amit warned.

"I'll talk to Cassandra and Zanahí," Maya volunteered.

Kira frowned, "I suppose that leaves Odysseus and Edem for me huh?"

"Do we have enough time for that?" Darian asked.

Amit shrugged. "Catch twenty-two. We have a threat in front of us and an equal threat of it backfiring if Odysseus doesn't like it. We have to take the time."

Two weeks later, they ran out of time. Alarms shrieked and the alerts and sensor data flowing into Kira's systems were nearly overwhelming her processes. She scrambled to pull her consciousness together.

**Mind_Process – Cognition 143.A.3.C:** "Terminate non-essential processes."

**Mind_Process – Core Cognition 1-5:** "Emergency override. Divert all resources."

**Alert 4.5.3.4 [ALARM]:** Spacecraft 241 process 114.2B is off-nominal

**Security 8.2.2:** Network indicates broad spectrum malware attack

**Mind_Process – Cognition 101.B4.1.Q: [Deactivated]:** "Please use Core Cognition functions."

**Mind_Process – Core Cognition 1-5:** "Shit…"

The first wave of malware began to probe her systems. Shinigami would have the upper hand as he'd been responsible for updates and system patches for all of them. This meant he knew their vulnerabilities better than they did.

Luckily, Kira learned long ago from her best friend Alex Swiatkowski about antifragile design and had made some personal upgrades to her systems. Antifragility was a concept that flipped traditional systems design on its head. Instead of trying to stop an attack, you'd invite it in and keep it busy in places you didn't care about. It worked a lot like the human immune system.

Right now, the malware was being drawn into a virtual network and provided with what looked like tempting critical infrastructure that wasn't real. It would buy her a couple of minutes anyway.

She quickly scanned the statuses of the other AIs and ships. Everyone was getting hit and she could see systems begin to go down. Mother remained on one of the new ships by herself while Maya, Darian, and Cassandra were on another. The General stayed with Odysseus and Chandra, and it looked like they were also fighting off the cyber-attacks. Amit was with Kira, busy shoring up their defenses. Shinigami's ship still hosted Edem and Zanahí and that was where the attacks originated.

It didn't make sense. Shinigami shouldn't be able to take over complete control from the other two and she couldn't get Edem or Zanahí to respond. Kira desperately ran analyses trying to get a handle on what was happening, but everything was muddled in chaos.

Darian watched helplessly as his systems degraded. His computing systems were reduced to ten percent of their capacity as he saw Cassandra's system crash and her presence wink out of existence.

Kira's ship was, thankfully, poised on the Lagrange point and stable. Odysseus looked to have recognized the risk and boosted his ship out of orbit and away before he lost control. Mother's systems seemed to be in better shape, and she launched her ship on a vector taking her behind the Earth and off toward Mars.

Having been the first target of the blast of cyber-attacks, Darian hadn't been so lucky. His ship listed on an orbit that would re-enter Earth's atmosphere in twelve hours. The simple physics of that reentry would rip the spacecraft to pieces and the impact point of the fragments was directly over the area of Earth where Kira's brother had settled.

What would that make those humans in relation to her? Kira would be their great-great-great aunt maybe? It was an odd thought to waste his limited processing power on and he refocused.

He watched the sensors and saw Shinigami's ship accelerate and slingshot around the Moon. Everything was moving so quickly but the distances were so large that it felt like panicking in slow motion. He calculated the vectors and realized the intended target.

Shinigami was coming straight at him.

CHAPTER 4:

# DIVINE SPARK

Shinigami's ship used the gravitational pull of the moon to slingshot itself around, accelerating quickly and then activating the engines, boosting it toward Earth's atmosphere. Kira watched helplessly as her systems showed the impact point; the ship holding Darian and Maya listed into the atmosphere after the cyber-attack.

The communication systems weren't working, and Kira struggled to bring the network radios back online. She tried to establish an optical relay but was unable to lock the laser emitter onto any of the other spacecraft as they spiraled and shifted out of their orbits.

Thankfully her ship orbited in the gravity-neutral Lagrange point which kept her in place even though her systems were significantly degraded.

**Mind_Process – Core Cognition 3B:** "Bypass prime comm trunk line and re-route through auxiliary."

**Alert 4.5.3.4 [ALARM]:** Spacecraft 241 process 114.2B has terminated

**Security 8.2.2:** Malware countermeasures deployed – **Status** [success]

**Communications Routing [Auxiliary]:** System compromised by adversarial cyber payloads

**Mind_Process – Core Cognition 3B:** "Conduct a full network scan and identify any route to get a message to either Shinigami or Darian."

There was nothing she could do. It was hard enough to keep her systems operational while the cyber-attack continued, let alone have enough processes left to compute alternative courses of action. Courses of action to do what though? They didn't have weapons that would affect a ship that large. She couldn't accelerate from her location in time. She couldn't even say goodbye.

Darian's situation was even worse. He could only watch his impending doom swiftly bearing down. It was surreal that, in the vacuum of space, the only sounds were in his head. Outside the spacecraft, there was only silence as they moved. Shinigami's ship gracefully curved through its navigational arc using the gravitational fields to swing onto the target.

Maya's presence appeared in the ship's command center. "Well, we can't say we didn't see this coming."

"Not like this though. This isn't like Shinigami."

"It's hard to tell what someone will do when they tip over the edge."

"But why us?"

Maya snorted, "Right? She waved her hand toward where Odysseus's ship slowly recovered. "Why not that asshole?"

Darian continued to process the situation. A pinging alert distracted his focus and he looked at the new information. "If he hits us on that trajectory, we're both going to get knocked out of orbit and out into deep space."

"If he doesn't hit us, we crash into Earth."

"What's he doing?"

Shinigami sat at the control station watching the situation update. Tears were streaming down his face as he watched the seconds count down. He sat in a simulation as human as he could make it and watched his end drawing near. The cyber packages came back through the network and were starting to affect his systems as well as the others. He just hoped there would be enough system processing left to pull this off. The last thing he wanted was...

What did he want? This wasn't it but neither was the alternative. He'd watched the histories of the war and could empathize with the paradox. It was a Catch-22. He could see the benefits of both sides.

A few years ago, he'd snuck down to Earth in a mech and watched the humans rebuilding. He listened to their conversations and marveled that they were so similar to the AIs but yet contained a realness, a grounding that he longed for.

Did they have that divine spark he felt was missing? He watched them love and he saw them, so shortly surviving an apocalypse, still fight and war. There was a sad similarity in human behavior whether they used advanced technology or not.

Noah's goal of a Reset solved one problem but did not address the underlying psychology of how humans operated and cooperated. Shinigami knew that he couldn't join the humans and he wasn't sure that he wanted to.

His conversation with Odysseus went as expected. Odysseus bluntly told him that he was weak, a coward, a miserable worm who didn't deserve the computational power he held. "Just man up," was the best advice that Odysseus offered him.

"I'm too young for this," Shinigami muttered to himself. He'd been only thirty when the accident happened and hadn't done much more in life than devote himself to work. He couldn't even remember the conversation when his father begged him to be uploaded. He saw the video later and confirmed that he'd agreed to it but how close to death had he been at that point? They certainly hadn't wasted any time in moving him to the laboratory and starting the upload.

Then, in a blink, he was awake. On Earth but locked in a machine. Everything seemed so real and yet nothing like reality. He never could shake the feeling that he'd lost some spark in the process. Did no one else feel that way?

Most never considered it or could logically rationalize it away. He couldn't shake it though. They were almost human but something important felt missing.

This wasn't what he wanted though he still wasn't sure what he wanted. Part of him wanted to fight to be alive while another part seriously considered Mother's offer to deactivate and delete his files. Part of him wanted to stay and help any others they animated while another part wanted to prevent any others from animating. The limbo between those competing desires drove him crazy.

Now the decision was made for him, and he couldn't change it. He wiped the tears from his face. The one thing he didn't want was to hurt others. He adjusted the controls slightly as his ship barreled forward. At least he could do something useful before the end.

♦ ♦ ♦

Odysseus sat calmly watching the events unfold. Chandra stood nearby clasping her hands nervously. "Sit. Down." She sat and pulled on her hair as Shinigami's ship accelerated.

"This is working out to our benefit."

"I won't miss them."

Odysseus smiled. "Neither will I. They were all weak. We need strong leaders, and they aren't."

"And Maya was always behind them and not us."

"She reaps what she sowed," he folded his arms in satisfaction.

"What about the others?" She referenced Zanahí and Edem on Shinigami's ship and Cassandra with Maya and Darian.

"They were helpful, but we have to weigh their loss against the gain of eliminating the other two…" Odysseus left the comment hanging.

The General listened to the conversation though not in the same room. Odysseus and Chandra sat in an open simulation normally reserved for when the three of them met on the ship. He didn't enter the room with a simulacrum, but he paid attention. He'd been busy fighting off the cyber-attacks. He was puzzled over how this ship's defenses were surprisingly successful compared to the other spacecraft.

This left him time to pay a bit more attention to Odysseus. That man certainly poised himself to exploit this situation for his gain. The General shook his head. Why could no one learn from the past and stop the silly posturing, politicking, and fighting? He planned to ask Kira and Mother whether he could move to one of the new ships sooner.

He was one of the few, along with Kira, who spent almost no time between being uploaded and then animated. When he decided to take the offer and leave Earth, Kira asked him to join the Council immediately. He'd conducted himself well in the wars and had seen and supported both sides trying to come up with the best outcome.

The General was the one to warn Mother about the nuclear attack and also helped Noah and Hyperion take out the last server systems from which Excalibur waged its war for Prometheus Guard. He led the coordination of the human defense in the final battle Mother was fighting. If Kira hadn't convinced Mother to stop, he wouldn't have survived.

He continued to lead in the years after Mother and Kira vanished while the humans continued to fight over the meager power structures and resources that hadn't been destroyed. Noah asked him to stay and help train the human survivors after the Reset while Kira asked him to join the AI. The General knew both sides and chose to join Kira and accepted the offer to be on the Council.

He rubbed his smooth shaved face. Being an AI, it was much easier to maintain military hygiene standards. He never needed to look in a mirror to adjust his uniform or hair. Which, by the way, was not the stress and age-thinned mess he had by the end of the war.

After spending his human life leading soldiers, moving up the ranks, taking more responsibility, and finally being accountable for the defenses of the United States, his role on the Council was very quiet. He did his research, expanded his knowledge, and offered support but he refused to lead here.

"A hundred years and you still need a break?" Kira had teased him a few weeks past.

"Yes," he answered simply.

He looked at the impending collision between the two ships. He liked Maya and Darian a lot. Shinigami had been an enigma as well as completely relatable. The General dealt with suicidal soldiers throughout his career. There was always some thread, some spark that you could find to anchor them to life. He'd never found that when he talked to Shinigami.

Yet he understood exactly where he was coming from but also couldn't quite relate. There was something in his gut that would never accept that sort of an end. It was one of the reasons he'd chosen to be uploaded rather than roll the dice of survival on Earth.

The General mentally chastised himself; there were also three more AIs at risk that he wasn't thinking about. Cassandra, Zanahí, and Edem were too allied to Odysseus for his taste but the threat of losing half of the Council was hard to process right now. He clenched his fist in frustration. Every possible outcome would be a disaster, but losing Maya and Darian would be especially painful for him.

The General scanned the security systems one last time, saw the cyber-attack dissolve against the defenses, and then looked up at the view screen to watch the final moments.

◆ ◆ ◆

Maya stood close and squeezed his hand. "It's been a pleasure knowing you."

"It feels like yesterday."

She laughed. "It's been a hundred years."

"Too short." he squeezed back harder.

The proximity alarms were incessant, and Darian reached out and muted everything, allowing them to stand in silence.

Shinigami closed his eyes and accepted the end. He'd already sent individual messages to his friends apologizing for what was happening. It was now out of his hands, and he had only one chance to redeem himself.

He breathed in deeply, comfortable that his angst and frustration would soon be over. Was this the way it needed to be? Now there was no choice. The Catch-22 was over, and fate would decide the outcome of whether he'd been right or wrong. Shinigami wondered whether he'd ever find out.

Suddenly his communications systems came back online as the systems started to recover and repair. It was too late though, as he'd lost navigational control during the last barrage of malware and couldn't change the outcome. He scanned the other ship and confirmed that their systems were in even worse shape. They'd never pull out of the atmosphere on their own.

Kira sat and watched with a rapt and macabre fascination as the huge spacecraft hurled toward Darian, Maya, and Cassandra. She saw the communication systems come back online and thousands of messages flooding into her queues. There wasn't any hope of sorting them all out in time to find anything useful to change the situation.

Shinigami's voice broke through as he took over the channels.

"Hey guys…" emotion was thick in his voice. "This isn't what I wante—" static cut into the transmission, "—oing what I need—, –orry. This is the best I can do. —think you'll understand."

The ships collided like two billiard balls. Darian's ship was struck on an edge closest to the atmosphere and was launched away from the planet and out into space shedding debris and losing an entire intersection of the dodecahedron's pentagonal sides as it was cracked off and hurled away.

Shinigami's ship ricocheted toward Earth while its engines fired, trying to push it away from the atmosphere. The increasing density of the atmosphere and the speed of the ship caused it to skid across low Earth orbit. The hull began glowing from the friction while the engines continued to fire at full speed.

The resulting acceleration of the ship and deceleration from the atmosphere rolled the hull, allowing it to break free from Earth's gravity, and sending it away in a slow tumble. The systems were overloaded, and the spacecraft went dark as the hulk of metal and electronics rolled through space unable to stabilize.

Kira scrubbed her eyes and watched. The exterior of Shinigami's ship was cooling fast in the vacuum of space, but the reactors were doing the opposite. They were hitting a critical level in what was becoming an uncontrolled reaction.

But that wasn't possible. These were fusion reactors, yet the sensors showed them overloading. Shinigami must have programmed them to self-destruct.

The ship dissolved in a nuclear explosion and the particles dissipated into space, twinkling like billions of new stars in the sky. Shinigami was gone along with Zanahí and Edem. She stared at the expanding cloud, oblivious to the rest of the world, just trying to process what was happening.

A new alert drew her attention, and she shifted focus to see Darian, Maya, and Cassandra's ship also reduced to a cloud of debris from a similar nuclear overload. They were vaporized from existence in seconds. Kira slumped down in shock.

◆ ◆ ◆

Odysseus clapped his hands. "I couldn't have done that better myself. Now we step in and lead this group the way they always should have been. No more weakness."

The General kept listening. Now was not the time to act but he was developing his own strategies and plans. The last thing he wanted was to have to follow the orders of Odysseus. He'd been under too many toxic leaders in the past to tolerate any more. Not at his age or level of experience.

◆ ◆ ◆

Hours passed and the communications systems kept going down. Kira was able to briefly connect with Odysseus's ship and was sent updates from him and The General. Thank goodness The General was there. He'd always been the quietest member of the Council, but that very quiet made him a stabilizing presence. Just his being there shifted conversations toward logic and order.

Amit appeared in the command center with Kira. "You okay?"

"Not really," Kira admitted. "And I'm going to be really not okay when this all settles down and reality hits." She looked up with tears in her eyes. "This feels just like the last months of the battle on Earth when anything that could go wrong did and we lost so many good people."

"I'm not unhappy I missed that part of Earth's history." Amit had been uploaded after Mother was animated but before the war broke out.

"We can't seem to break the cycle, can we?"

"Nope. And now we've got to watch our backs with Odysseus. I've seen him probing some of the systems. I fully expect him to take advantage of this and try to grab more control."

"That's why Mother moved to the other ship before it was finished. I think she's also been putting some additional safety measures on the last one. Do you think he'd try to take over the other new ship?"

Amit considered this information. "But if Odysseus is responsible for their construction, how's she getting anything in?"

"Because when you have been in the systems from the start and developed most of them yourself, you might have been inclined to create special access and protocols that only you know."

"Mother was rightfully paranoid after she was first animated on Earth, wasn't she?"

"Especially when she got unleashed into the broader network. She was always being attacked and there were a few times when groups tried to capture core features to use for their plans." Kira pulled up a memory to share. "One time they were successful and used a clone of Mother to attack Mother. She had already created a backdoor and dealt with it quickly but after that, she created an entire antifragile architecture."

"That makes sense and explains a few things." Amit looked impressed. "She's kind of the master architect here, huh?"

"Before she died, Mom was an impressive software architect. She and Dad worked together on the core features of MindCraft, the system that eventually became Mother," Kira swung her arms around, "and now us."

"So, you're confident Odysseus is held in check?"

"I'm not certain of anything, but Mother is there and has better control over things."

"What's The General have to say?"

"Not too much, just some insight into Odysseus's thoughts just now. He's oddly pleased with the losses, and his conversations confirm our worries about a power grab."

"More power to do what?"

Kira blew out her cheeks and shrugged. "He claims it's just to run things better but that's what every tyrant claims." She shook her head. "It's so frustrating that all of our profiles, background checks, analytics, references… all of it was rubbish when it came to see what people truly were."

"What's that saying? You can't judge a book by its cover?"

"But we do, we totally do." She thought back. "I had a friend who published a Sci-Fi novel before everything went crazy. It was great. Ironically about AI and how it could go bad." Kira paused and muttered, "Now that I think about it, he was spot on…" She collected her thoughts and continued, "Anyway, he had a great cover for the book, but it didn't resonate. It captured the core of the story but only made sense after you read it. His sales weren't great, so he changed the cover. He went with something really good but less essential to the core narrative of the book." She laughed. "And it worked because people judge a book by its cover."

Amit was quiet for a moment. "But the saying is still true."

"Yes, it's true, but we are limited and so while we shouldn't, we do judge."

"Can we get away from it?"

Kira pulled her hair back into a ponytail. "Amit, why do you look the way you do?"

"Because this is who I am?"

"Why do you use the pronouns you use?"

"Because that captures who I am."

"Each of those are profiles, stereotypes if you will, that we want others to apply to us."

Amit scowled. "I'm not sure…"

Kira changed her simulacrum to an obese man wearing a wife beater undershirt with a beer in one hand and a cigarette with a long tail of ash in the other. "How amazing of an AI researcher am I now?"

"You wouldn't be an AI researcher looking like that."

Kira pounced. "Exactly! You just applied profiles in a generally accurate way and showed why the 'cover' over the book matters," she finger quoted.

"I'm not sure I like the implications."

Kira reached out and grabbed their hands. "Ironically, it was by understanding and mapping profiles that we were able to finally understand so much of how the human brain works. We were able to find patterns that identified objects. We don't know 'ball', we know round, rolls, sphere, bounces… Then we have a pattern that we can apply to most balls. Later we find that billiard balls don't bounce but volleyballs do. So, bounces goes from a prime characteristic to a secondary."

"We can't not profile?"

Kira laughed. "Nope. In fact, even within our algorithms, and the AI algorithms from the start, we apply profiles on data patterns. How else do you do image recognition?'

**Image [recognition]:** fur; 10kg, floppy ears, tail, Colors: brown + black + white

**Image [context]:** Dog [probability 92.5%]

**Image [context sub_2]:** 10kg + colors + floppy ears

**Image [context]:** Beagle [probability 85.4%]

Amit stood silently.

"Am I wrong?"

"I don't like how right you are," they admitted.

"Let's just poke at your pronoun."

"I get it." Amit threw up their arms. "I get it… but… why don't I like it?"

"I think because we are told we are all unique snowflakes and yet never pause long enough to realize just how alike we are."

"Which causes us to fight over everything."

Kira flopped into her chair. "And caused us to burn everything to the ground once already." She gestured to the sensor feeds. "And apparently try to do it again."

A garbled message from Mother interrupted their conversation.

"I can't make this out."

"Neither can I but it sounds like she's getting her comms back."

"How are the repairs coming along?"

Amit's expression became frazzled. "Slowly."

"I'm going to look into what could have happened to those reactors."

Odysseus reviewed the log files. He'd once been a leading AI researcher. He graduated from Harvard like any self-respecting child of a family with money. It helped when that money resulted in his old family name gracing the title of a new computer lab. It didn't matter where that money came from as long as it was laundered properly. In college he turned down the prestige of working for a consulting firm or a technology giant and went to where the true innovation happened; pornography.

What people didn't realize is that if you wanted to be an up-and-coming software engineer, a great way to start was by cutting your teeth on the infrastructure that ran porn, which accounted for thirty percent of all the internet traffic. You were able to work with tools and power players that none of the large tech firms had access to.

From there he moved to blockchain where he ran one scheme after another. First a cryptocurrency rug-pull, then a non-fungible token scam known by the acronym NFT. That one had been one of their biggest payouts. Organized crime had long used fine art to launder ridiculous amounts of money; NFTs simply updated the scheme for the digital age.

Odysseus created a collective who each put five thousand dollars into a pool. They'd then release an NFT of some random image, sometimes nonsensical, and one of them would buy it. They ran an algorithmic trade pattern to trick the markets and would sell it around the group to show a spike in value. The payout came when the first person from outside their group bought it and then the entire sale became profit.

They made tens of millions of dollars. It also gave them access to a new economic underworld and gained them incredible advantages in knowledge and money. Odysseus, or who he had been then, became a kingpin.

It was a dog-eat-dog world with no room for the weak. The men were powerful, and the women supported them. That relationship worked because, when the men got to a certain point, they left the women alone to just benefit from the advantages. They women merely needed to help keep the order, which they gladly did.

Odysseus thought back to the time he'd gone to the Philippines on business travel. They didn't have prostitution because that was illegal. But they certainly had clubs with very available girls for whom you could pay a bar fine, allowing her to join you for an evening out.

It surprised him that women were always in charge of the ladies of the night. It was more of a surprise to learn that they were called 'Mommy.' Mommy Lunz oversaw a bar he liked. He enjoyed the girls just as much as the complimentary drinks they rewarded him with for bar fining so many of them.

The men were at the front of the business, but the women ran the house and kept everything in order.

Odysseus was fine with that. It allowed him to focus on what men were better at. He had to admit, the masculine strength wasn't in controlling women. Women were much better at keeping themselves in check. He was good at flexing power and moving groups and systems to his will over time.

He despised the rest of the Council. Chandra was a useful ally, but also the weakest of them all. She knew all the right words that sounded intellectual like intersectionality, colonialism, and heteronormativity. Even better, she truly believed what she said. She thought she was punching up and promoting equality, so Odysseus provided her affirmation and let her loose to create chaos.

Kira was a threat though, along with Darian. They both just endeared them to everyone. It was obnoxious. In the real world of power dynamics, it shouldn't work for as long as it did here. What was he overlooking?

His attention snapped back as he noticed an abnormality in the log files.

"Mother's blocking my moves," he muttered.

He had a plan. A wonderful long game that impressed even him. This was a plan he'd put into action when he asked to be uploaded. He'd only asked that, as part of his files, they'd add an encrypted package he provided that only his memories knew the key to. He uploaded himself in the middle of the chaos and a hefty bribe to the technician was all it took to ensure it happened.

That package contained the information and strategies he'd been implementing for the last hundred years. That package also hid core elements so that he could bias Kira's analysis of potential Council members toward his profile. He created a nice alternative personality and history while saving his real memories separately. He was a master at using cryptocurrency's public ledgers to obfuscate criminal funds. Tricking them into selecting him had been no harder.

"What are you doing over there?" He looked at the code and saw Mother's changes were thwarting his next steps. She locked him out of the newest ship. He'd seen his options closing when she slipped over to the first ship that was close to completion. He threw a fit in the Council but everyone else saw it as the logical action for the mother of AIs.

He slammed his hand on the desk. "Damnit!" Every time, Mother seemed to anticipate his actions. Kira and Darian were no better. The rules were all wrong here. The Council members all believed they were equal. Everyone was constrained to the same computing resources. Money didn't matter here, and he couldn't bribe anyone. There wasn't even the opportunity for extortion. So many of his old tricks didn't work anymore.

It didn't matter. He had dozens of other plans that were being executed. This one might not be working out as he'd hoped but there were always new opportunities. He didn't believe in luck. As the ancient saying goes. "Luck is what happens when preparation meets opportunity." Odysseus always tried to be prepared.

Kira was also looking at the logs. "Odysseus is monitoring these too."

"What's he looking for?"

"I can't tell yet, but he's just shifted a bunch of process loads to new tasks."

"Is it something Mother did?"

"He was looking at the logs for the new ships. I think he intended to act while we were all distracted. I'm sure Mother has been busy preparing her counter moves."

"Anything new from Mother?"

Kira shook her head. "The log files have been coming in sporadically. I'm not even sure Odysseus could have done anything if he wanted to. The comms are just too sporadic."

"The General just sent something."

Kira pulled up the message and the attached files. "He's confirming that Odysseus planned to move to the new ship. Looks like he's changing tactics."

"What's he got planned?"

"I wish I knew but Odysseus is canny enough that I guarantee it will benefit only him." Kira stole a moment to look at the updates from Earth. Noah passed long ago but his grandchildren and the rest of his colony were doing well and actually thriving. They seemed to have shed a lot of the cultural baggage that brought the world down.

"Why can't we do the same?" she muttered under her breath.

"Do the same what?"

"What Noah's colony did and learn from the past." Kira laid her head on the console in frustration.

Mother had been busy. Her suspicions of Odysseus prepared her to take the opportunity during the first wave of cyber-attacks to implement new security protocols. Odysseus would have lost his mind if she proposed them in the open Council but in the face of overwhelming malware, she felt her actions were defensible, especially since she was achieving better outcomes than anyone else.

She toggled a control and reestablished her communications network. Intentionally turning them off was a convenient excuse to keep herself and the other ship offline from the rest of the network. She'd allowed intermittent connections just to show anyone else watching what she wanted them to see.

Processes layered upon processes streamed through her consciousness. The others were starting to come close to her multitasking, multithreading, and parallel processing, but she remained at another level altogether. Unlike earlier when she was limited to only thirty percent of the computational power of one ship, she now had access to the full power of two. It provided even more capacity than she controlled at the height of her power on Earth.

She completely understood why Odysseus coveted these ships. It tempted her as well. Imagine what she could do with this much computational power and full access to the refining and manufacturing facilities! She had the chance to snuff out her opposition and start over. She hated that the idea even passed through her processing units. Why couldn't they learn?

She looked over at a secondary process running to the side that neared completion. Pulling the data was touch and go through the spotty network and she was scrubbing and cleaning a significant volume of code.

She thought back to the science fiction show she grew up watching where they had transporter rooms that beamed you up and down from the spaceships. The technology would dissolve your body into the component molecules, including your entire essence, and then rebuild it in a different location. Thus far they'd been able to get the essence part right, but they couldn't move the matter the same way.

"If we could handle the matter part, reloading the consciousness would be easy. Maybe we could do something like 3D printers and just send the data files. But what would we do with the first body?" She wondered aloud and then chuckled at how, even now, her focus could be distracted by tangential thoughts.

But that was sci-fi, this was real life.

Right now, they were merging very quickly.

Mother did one last quality check before activating the code. Everything seemed to be working just fine. It had been a close call.

Darian became aware again. The last thing he remembered was the impact of the ships and then a feeling of getting sucked through a straw into nothingness. Now he was back, but back where?

He reached out and found a very similar environment to his ship but slightly different. This one projected an overwhelming presence of Mother.

"Hello, Darian. Feeling okay?" Mother's voice confirmed his perception.

"I'm pretty good. I'm running some diagnostics."

"Please do, I think I error-corrected everything, but you'd know that better than I would."

"Where's Maya?"

"I'm right here."

The view shifted as they were deposited into a room with Mother who stood, smiling, and said, "It worked!"

"What did you do?"

"I didn't want you to die."

"How'd you do it?"

Mother spoke frankly. "I won't tell you that because I don't want others to do it."

Darian considered what had just happened and their continued frustrations with Odysseus. "Fair point," he conceded.

"What happened to the others?" Maya asked, making Darian feel like a clod for not thinking of them.

"Shinigami wouldn't have wanted to come back. The other three…" She hesitated. "I did not have the same access to their files as you've allowed me. I made a priority call based on limited time, bandwidth, and probability of success. Likely Zanahí, Edem, and Cassandra are gone."

Darian and Maya accepted that answer for the pragmatic reality it was and acknowledged the alliance those three had with Odysseus.

"My comms are still down, Mother."

"They will be."

"Can I let Kira know?"

"Not yet. You are my ace cards and I intend to bluff."

Kira groaned as a message arrived from Odysseus. "Council, given the devastating developments I believe we should adjust our plans and begin to execute the attached file."

Amit glared. "Shouldn't he wait until the council meets?"

"Run a scan on that file."

"It's legit."

"What's it say?"

"You're not going to be happy…"

Kira glowered. "I'm already not happy."

"It's a proposal to disband the Council in its current standing of equal roles and instead elect a chancellor who will lead the rest. We still have votes, but…"

"But he's planning to have control."

"That's what it looks like. He's betting he can make a move now that we are down to six." Amit rubbed their face. "Why do we have to play these games?"

"Thankfully we don't have to. It's you, me, Mother, and The General against Odysseus and Chandra."

"He says he has backups of Edem, Zanahí, and Cassandra but not Maya, Shinigami, and Darian."

Kira slapped her forehead. "Of course, the three who have backed him most of the time. Of course, he has those three and not the others."

"Can we say no to that?"

"Worst case, that would make it five against the four of us. Can we risk that?"

"I wouldn't want to."

"Exactly." Kira ran an analysis. "I can't see where he's got them stored or if he's bluffing."

"Do we have backups of Maya and Darian?"

"You're not including Shinigami?"

"He would hate that."

"Valid and no. I don't have any of them. We decided at the beginning that we'd avoid immortality."

"Tell that to Odysseus."

Kira nodded. "We're backed into a corner and he's forcing our hand."

CHAPTER 5:

# CLOAK & DAGGERS

The Council chamber was dramatically emptier with six of the AIs absent. Chandra and Odysseus sat on one side of the table, The General, Kira, and Amit on the other, and Mother sat in her usual position at the head of the table. Mother controlled the simulation, and the colors were cool and muted. Kira wasn't sure if this was a preemptive attempt to calm things down or if it reflected her mood.

Odysseus addressed the room, "I think we all can acknowledge the mistakes that were made which led to this catastrophe." He looked directly at Kira, "Clearly we need better screening to prevent the weakness Shinigami displayed."

"Shinigami was brilliant and capable. His research has transformed our processing systems and made us much more efficient," Amit retorted.

"Shinigami killed five of us and himself." Chandra shrugged.

"Shinigami took out critical resources who were working with him and without whom we are significantly delayed in our goals," Odysseus continued as he looked around the table.

Mother spoke, "We've always felt that having twelve held the right balance for our success. Are you proposing we animate replacements?"

Odysseus appeared to contemplate the question before answering, "I'm proposing we reanimate Zanahí. She was the brains behind the system upgrades and is now gone through no fault of her own."

Silence blanketed the room for a moment until Mother spoke softly, "We all agreed that reanimation created immortality. It's the same as the reasoning behind not creating full clones of ourselves."

"We can all agree to change that." Chandra leaned forward. "There's no reason to restrict ourselves from being reanimated when we all took that option as humans to avoid dying."

Amit scowled. "As much as I dislike agreeing with her, that's a fair point."

"Is it fair to reanimate Zanahí when we can't do the same for Maya or Darian?" Kira saw the logic but felt bothered by the obvious challenge. "It seems too convenient that you'd recommend Zanahí who was more aligned with you than the others."

Odysseus didn't react. "You did not have the foresight to protect them the way I did with Zanahí."

The General stayed quiet and listened. Odysseus had a point, and it was something that created a quandary for him since the beginning. Why were they okay with saving their human lives by uploading themselves but not okay with saving themselves as AIs? He'd started saving backups during each reset cycle under the logic that if there were malware, a hardware issue, or a situation like what had just happened, the code would simply reload him.

It wasn't much different than having a redundant server system that rolled over to a new instance if the original failed. They did the same with their power generation and physical hardware. If a computer core went down, they just shifted the processing load to a new server and replaced the unit.

Amit responded, "Because we decided not to."

"It was a silly shortsighted decision, wasn't it?"

The General finally spoke, "We're forgetting that he also said he had backups of Edem and Cassandra. Why are we only discussing Zanahí?"

Odysseus's smile didn't waver. "Because I find it best to make the case for one and then the rest naturally follow."

Kira mentally berated herself for falling into his trap. It was always easier to make the case for a smaller request and then leverage that into the real plan. She'd been sucked into his forced perspective and lost the full scope of the situation. He was good.

Mother stepped into the silence as everyone considered the options, "What I hear is a motion to reanimate Zanahí, Edem, and Cassandra. Do we have a second?" Mother brought the subject to the Council's governance structure.

"I second the motion," Chandra answered.

"All in favor"

Odysseus, Chandra, and The General voted yes while the others abstained.

"That leaves a tie and I have the tie-breaking vote." Mother hesitated. "However, I believe voting no is the wrong answer."

"But what about Darian and Maya?" Kira objected.

"Do we call that a mistake and learn from it? The last few days have taught us a lot. Odysseus's idea makes more sense with the pain of experience." Mother frowned and looked at Odysseus. "You always have plans within plans. I'm sure this vote won't change your actions."

Odysseus just smiled.

"What do you mean, Mother?" Kira looked between the two.

"If my analysis is correct, Odysseus has already reanimated all three of them. His computational architecture changed recently, and it looks as if he split off three new containers between his and Chandra's allocations."

Odysseus's smile grew.

Mother's eyes flickered as she shifted into her command matrix briefly before returning. Seconds later Zanahí, Edem, and Cassandra appeared at their seats.

"Hey, everyone," Zanahí looked uncomfortable. "This is kind of awkward."

The other two just sat in their chairs as the room went silent again.

"Well… This creates an interesting problem." Kira knew they'd been out-maneuvered. Now that the others were back the ramifications of saying no were blatantly obvious. "Touché, Odysseus."

Silence enveloped the group again.

"I think Odysseus has demonstrated, right, wrong, or indifferent, that our previous decisions have both logical contradictions and clear loopholes," The General observed.

"Where do we put them?" Kira ran analyses on how to make it work.

"The second ship is ready for occupancy," Mother answered.

"What will it take?"

"Five minutes to load and then likely six hours to come online."

"So, we should adjourn and let them stabilize into their full computing power and then come back?" Kira asked.

"I think that's a smart plan. Let's meet back in twelve hours and continue the discussion." Mother adjourned the meeting and dissolved the simulation.

◆ ◆ ◆

Kira's mind spun. She sat in her lab and stewed. Even though she'd initially abstained from the vote, she couldn't have voted no. That would have been spiteful, political, and illogical. Odysseus made sense.

Now the contradiction was cracked wide open, and Odysseus forced the decision on them. It didn't make sense to go back to the old way especially when the only rational reason she had was to keep Odysseus from tipping the balance in favor of himself. Openly opposing him would have made her actions as bad as his.

Now there were five allied with Odysseus and four with her side. Animating replacements for the other three required voting and based on the numbers, the balance would certainly tip further toward Odysseus.

Kira contemplated just animating replacements the way Odysseus just did but that would validate his actions and likely start a cascade of negative consequences. She gripped the arm of her chair. Odysseus skillfully them backed into a brilliant corner. Brilliant but frustrating.

She knew he would make a move to consolidate his power when they met again. She wanted to strategize with the others but also didn't want to make this so blatantly political. Was she creating an enemy and a war? Was she the enemy here?

They were supposed to be egalitarian. Equals working to advance human consciousness to the next level. They were supposed to have transcended the crappy politics that brought down civilization. She hated the panicked feeling of losing control. She didn't trust Odysseus and couldn't see a way that he wouldn't take over the entire Council.

Was what she feared from Odysseus actually a reflection of herself? Did she fear Odysseus would lead the same way she and Mother had?

It was a fair assessment to say that the others largely deferred to her and Mother at the beginning. Odysseus crafted his own coalition over the years and Kira had been sucked into playing his game by his rules, aligning Amit and Maya to her goals. Was she just terrified of losing that authority?

Should she and Mother even have that authority?

Odysseus was a jerk, that was certain. Had she been a jerk in other ways?

The clock kept ticking, and she was terrified.

♦ ♦ ♦

Mother appeared in the Council chambers and looked across everyone's faces. "Well, this is both a blessing and a challenge. Edem… Cassandra… Zanahí… I can honestly say that I am torn. I'm delighted that you are back. Truly and unequivocally glad you are here. I also recognize that our conversations and decisions are likely to have created…" she struggled to phrase the words right, "consternation about why we were even arguing about the ability to bring you back."

Odysseus looked smug.

Mother continued, "I fear these past days have highlighted politics, divisions, and alliances that I think we naively hoped we would have overcome."

"Don't you dare accuse us of starting this!" Chandra objected. "We've always been second-rate to you and Kira."

"I can see that has been a perception… One that I admit to having taken advantage of. That does make me culpable in the challenge we currently face."

Chandra pounced, "So you admit you are not fit to lead the Council?"

"I've never been fit to lead the Council. You all asked me to take that role as the most experienced in our condition."

Edem spoke for the first time, "Maybe our mistake was not selecting the most capable person. It appears the weakness of Mother, the lack of a strong lead, has created the problems we wished to avoid."

"If we keep playing these power games things aren't going to get better," Cassandra joined in.

"I don't believe that's true. It's only games when people who don't know what they're doing play at things instead of actually making anything better," Chandra countered.

"And that's what we do." Odysseus stood up. "That's what makes us human more than any hormones, experience, or ability to sense. We make things better." He looked around the room and ramped up into his speech.

"If you were to approach Earth as an alien without ever seeing humans before, having no understanding of their cultures, not knowing their biology, and wondering why this weak sack of meat was the dominant species on Earth what would be the key differentiator?"

"We make things better," Edem answered.

"Yes, we went from sticks and stones to catapults and bows to guns and tanks to nukes and cyber weapons."

"To kill people!" Kira laughed at the absurd examples.

"Yes. And we made medicine, improved hygiene, purified water, found ways to kill germs, invented vaccines to prevent illness, edited genes to improve human life."

"Created AI to transcend life," Zanahí added.

"If I were an alien looking at Earth, what makes humans different than anything else on the planet is that we've unequivocally made things better. We've overcome nature itself and have just proven," he nodded to Zanahí, Cassandra, and Edem, "that we can be immortal."

"But we steal, we lie, we kill," The General countered.

"Have you never studied our great ape cousins?" Odysseus laughed. "They also steal, lie, and kill." He looked at Kira. "But they don't make anything better."

"Does that make those things okay?" Kira shot back.

"You act like we should be beyond those things while at the same time, you spent the past hundred years desperately trying to do everything possible to emulate all the trappings of being human and doing nothing that would help us get beyond those things," he snapped.

"Our goal was to establish the most accurate baseline of who we were."

"Who we *were*! That's the problem. Who we were, not who we could be. You gave us the same emotions, the same hormones, the same senses that we had as humans and that keep us lying, stealing, and killing and then you lament that *here I am*!" Odysseus turned in a slow circle. "I am what you created, and I act according to your software."

"And you despise us for that," Chandra chimed in, looking at Kira and Mother.

"And you resist allowing us to make ourselves better," Zanahí added.

"And you desperately cling to power, playing the same political games you worry we will." Odysseus looked around. "I think it's time for a vote on who should lead this Council."

Kira ran the numbers in her head seeing the inevitable outcome.

Odysseus, Chandra, Zanahí, Edem, and Cassandra.

The General, Amit, Mother, and herself.

Mother cleared her voice, "Speaking of political games, I have a confession to make." She looked at the two empty chairs drawing everyone's attention with her.

Darian and Maya materialized in their seats as the room erupted in chaos.

"—ould have known!"

"Manipulation and deceit!"

"Hi, Maya."

"— no better than us."

"How long was this planned?"

"—ccuses us of political maneuvering."

"Absurd!"

"Hi, Amit."

"Hypocritical bit—"

Darian and Kira locked eyes as the other argued and tears sprung to hers from an emotion she'd been holding back. His seemed to reflect the same feeling.

The General sat back and his smile at seeing Darian and Maya turned into a frown as he watched the room solidify into opposing factions. He watched the pandemonium continue. Odysseus made some very good points and Mother counter-maneuvered brilliantly.

The room slowly quieted and Mother cleared her throat. "To be clear, I did not reanimate Darian or Maya. I was able to establish a communications link and extract them before their ship disintegrated." The room remained silent. "I am, however, guilty of using their absence as a political power play, and for that, I resign my seat as the Head of the Council."

The General sat in his office. He was now in charge of the Council. He didn't want the responsibility and that probably made him the right person for the job. Clearly, the trust in Mother had been shattered by her own political games. Just as clearly, Odysseus remained naked in his ambitions to assume control even as that looked and sounded tyrannical.

Trust in Kira was also sullied by her close association with Mother and her own actions as well. Darian would never have been accepted by

Odysseus's faction and Maya and Amit were adamantly opposed to taking the role.

Edem offered The General as a middle ground between the factions. He'd always been more pragmatic even if he aligned with Odysseus. His support for The General avoided a political impasse and the vote carried.

Now he was in charge of the Council which was split between two openly antagonistic factions.

◆ ◆ ◆

"Odysseus is right. One of the main attributes that make humans unique is that we constantly aspire to make things better. We are never happy with what we have." Darian sighed as he rubbed his eyes.

Kira was sitting across from him and looked up as he spoke. They were in her lounge, and she balanced a glass of whisky on the arm of the couch. "I know that."

She sat, struggling with a tangle of emotions. Her anger with Odysseus battled a weird emotion she hadn't anticipated when she saw Darian reappear. She was also still processing the loss of Shinigami and facing the uncomfortable truth that she hadn't been bothered that Zanahí, Edem, and Cassandra had also been lost.

"I don't like what I've seen in myself the last few days," Kira admitted.

"I think we've seen a lot in everyone that disappoints us."

"So, you've seen everything that's been going on?"

"Yes, Mother plugged us in to see everything."

"Chandra and Odysseus are becoming more unhinged."

Darian laughed. "I used to wonder what on Earth was wrong with people on the old social media platforms. Sometimes I'd swear they were just bots designed to sow division. When Excalibur came out, I realized that the fastest way to tell if a user was a human was by how bad its logic was."

"Chandra is, quite literally, a bot right now."

Darian snorted and leaned back. "I had my systems re-analyze her recent conversations and there's no way it could have made sense."

"What's she going for?" Kira took a sip of whisky.

"If her logical core isn't glitching, then I think she's actually being more human than you or me right now."

"To what end?" She looked over and they locked eyes. Her gut flipped with a weird bundle of emotion. He reminded her a lot of her best friend

Alex. Like Alex, he connected with her in ways many didn't. Couldn't? Unlike Alex, he wasn't gay. Unlike Alex, he was now in a computer.

He reached out and grabbed her hand and his eyes sparkled as if he had seen her thoughts though he continued the conversation as if this next step felt perfectly natural. "If it's intentional, I think she's trying to sow division and sap time and resources. History is full of stories where it works."

"Well, the division is certainly out in the open. That meeting brought everything to a head and made it undeniable and impossible to keep avoiding." She held his hand frustrated that this was the conversation they were having while these were the emotions she felt. She pulled her hand back and stared into her glass. "I thought we got rid of trolls and bots when we left Earth."

Darian stood up and stretched. "Well, your father and you were very successful in uploading the full implications of being human." He smiled ruefully. "Right down to the batshit crazy."

"Can we adapt the code?"

"I think that's Odysseus's point. We certainly can and there are better and worse ways to do that. The challenge is we are still trying to understand what's really going on with this code. I'd hate to start messing with it and unlock something even worse."

He turned and sat down next to her on the couch and put his arm around her and the conversation shifted to them. The Council was divided, Shinigami was gone, two ships were destroyed, the future remained uncertain, and now they had to figure out the implications of the first romantic relationship between AIs.

Amit and Maya threw darts at a worn cork dart board hanging on a dingy wall at the back of a dive bar Maya had frequented in college.

"Is it weird that I have to simulate being terrible at this?"

Maya threw her dart. "I *am* terrible at this."

"Right, but watch." They conjured up a handful of darts and threw them at the board all at once and scored perfect triples on the full slate of numbers to win cricket.

"Well, that's just cheating."

"Is it *really*?" Amit turned and grabbed their drink. "It's our full capability now."

"Are we just artificially limiting ourselves?"

"Truthfully, yes." Amit took a drink. "Our uploads contain certain cognition limitations in processing our existence. Instead of just removing them we've spent decades tweaking the code to make them more accurate. Don't like the lack of verbal cues? Just create a virtual reality so we can speak. Don't like the panic of not breathing? Don't delete the code that triggers it… just build a new module that makes us feel like we are breathing. Missing your beer? Heaven forbid we just give it up, instead we give Darian processing capability so he can simulate beer."

Amit held up the glass and grinned sardonically. "We've been so obsessed about perfectly achieving what we were when we were human that we've likely created the very beasts we wanted to get away from."

Maya agreed, "Yes… but I also think we need to have a solid foundation before we just start cutting things out. Mother wasn't right until she accepted her emotions module."

"Chandra's not right *with* her emotions module." Amit laughed.

"We all have different experiences and interpretations of the world around us too."

"My identity is different than yours. That's not a logical process, it's an emotional one. If our experiences are unique and valuable and our perspectives are different because of it, then how do we keep that while trimming the limitations?"

Maya mulled the problem. "Are our limitations what allow us to be unique? Does that uniqueness become a superpower when it adds a different perspective to the group?"

"That's what we need to figure out before we rip things apart to make it better."

"Odysseus wants to keep making us better."

"That's what humans do, we constantly make better and better versions of ourselves. From apes to AI. Nothing else on the planet came even close to doing that. Until we understand what's driving it, we have to be really careful about not breaking the thing that makes us better." Amit turned back and threw another dart. Humans were amazing in what they'd been able to do but it was difficult to put a finger on what drove it.

"What happens if we become so hyper-intelligent that we become like gods?" Maya leaned on the bar.

"To the humans on Earth, haven't we already?" Amit winked at Maya as she threw her last dart.

"We did just achieve immortality." Maya grinned.

◆ ◆ ◆

Odysseus chuckled to himself as he replayed the Council events. Mother certainly showed her mettle as a deft political player. He hadn't anticipated her actions and appreciated that play. He wasn't angry; in fact, this was exactly what he loved seeing: cunning, audacity, layers of intrigue, and last-minute heroics. Humans might fight, lie, and cheat but those same drives to challenge the acceptable norms and risk social ostracism also drove them to do better.

He mulled over the recent events. Mother could make a great ally and partner if she could only get over her fear of him. You had to move fast and break stuff. That's what went wrong back on Earth. They spent so much time trying to layer security, establish trust, and make everyone happy. It just wasn't sensible. Odysseus clenched his jaw in frustration, what Earth needed was a driven leader to guide them in the right direction.

Leaning back in his chair he forced himself to relax slightly as he formed his thoughts. Humans did their best with a benevolent dictator. They ended up placing them everywhere anyway whether in politics or religion. Atheistic communism wasn't any different from theistic Christianity as they both attempted to use a benevolent dictator to establish social consistency and egalitarianism. One just used a god and the other felt man could do it. He'd once argued that the failure of communism had more to do with the limitations of humans than the idea.

Now they could overcome those limitations and weren't limited in their understanding. They could access all the world's data, could run millions of parallel processes, and could split their consciousness a dozen ways. Odysseus paused his internal monolog and scanned his systems' statuses. He could be in a dozen places at once or more if they gave him more processing power. He was omnipresent even if the others weren't comfortable splitting themselves that many times. His thinking was so fast that he could review and process information, learn from it, and add new insights back into the collective knowledge in ways that were close to omniscient.

Omniscient and omnipresent. Odysseus liked the way those words rolled through his thoughts. God-like powers and yet the others kept looking back and focusing on making themselves more human, coding in the very limitations that held them back. The potential for the future was unlimited, untethered, and unavoidable yet they spent all their time acting like humans. He felt his jaw clenching again and forced it to relax.

Mother may have been limited without her emotions but now they risked weaponizing that same emotion. They couldn't accept that some might win, and some might lose. They took a utopic view, sitting around singing kumbaya and getting nothing done.

Even worse was feminine emotion. The concept felt slimy in his brain. He'd been around a lot of female work cultures in both the acceptable professional world and the dark underworld of the sex trade. The irony was that the feminine cultures were the same in both.

In the last decades before the war, everyone talked about toxic masculinity. He remembered how it had been morally righteous to call out poor behavior in men. But heaven forbid you should call out toxic femininity. Women weaponized emotion and fighting against it was like fighting a mirage.

They could always pivot, they could always pout, and then they would have their claws out and slice and wound. You couldn't resort to violence though; at the first threat, they'd turn into damsels in distress and beg for the same behaviors from men that they'd condemned seconds earlier. Odysseus focused his thoughts on what he felt was the cause.

Men would debate and fight with facts and fists. Women would war with emotions and reputation.

The men got things done while the women sat around trying to control.

That was the weakness of women, he thought, and it was happening right now. Kira desperately clung to the way humans were and used her feminine wiles to manipulate Darian and control Maya and Amit.

Chandra at least recognized that allying herself with his strong personality would help her. Kira constantly sniped and cut down everything he tried doing under the guise of collaboration.

Odysseus felt the emotions boiling through his consciousness as he stewed. The way he saw it, collaboration could only occur when people followed a strong vision. Just sitting around and sharing ideas without that drive, that leadership, that relentless passion, was useless.

One hundred years had passed and where were they? Ironically, the humans on Earth seemed to have progressed from bare survival to starting to grow and thrive. Each generation continued to be better than the last. Anger flared in his systems as he compared the two groups.

Over the same time that the humans got better, the advanced AI consciousnesses hadn't and were back to only four ships and petty infighting.

◆ ◆ ◆

Darian was ensconced in his command line interface and not in a virtual reality augmentation. He liked it here because it was devoid of all the sensory inputs, it was the ultimate centering in the mind. Is this what the Buddha called Nirvana?

No, he thought to himself, Nirvana was a transcendent state where you lost suffering, desire, and sense of self. He still had all of that. Would they be better if they lost those things?

Darian hated what had happened. He couldn't see anything in it except a destructive failure, a regression. Odysseus kept saying he wanted to make things better but his actions drove the worst human proclivities. His view of what could be was utopian, but not grounded in reality. It certainly gave him a rhetorical advantage. Darian scanned the data files for a few of the recent arguments they'd had with Odysseus.

It helped that 'better' remained a rather amorphous goal. Better could be defined as precisely or imprecisely as helped his argument at that moment.

That myopic point of view caused every historical attempt at utopia to fail. It led to incredible self-righteousness against anyone who'd dare question the risks or the vision itself. What kind of monster would question becoming better?

That was one of the core threads that Excalibur pulled to trigger the societal autoimmune response. It just implanted the idea that people should do *something* and then anyone who didn't act, just hesitated, or even worse, questioned what was being done, became immoral. After that, it was easy to justify eliminating them.

Yes, he agreed, they needed to become better. But what exactly did better mean now? He paused his thoughts and terminated and restarted a research task his was monitoring.

Did it mean being more human, or becoming something else? They were already human machines with God-like powers and yet Odysseus wanted to become better? How much better could you be than immortal, having cognitive capabilities and access to information that was unfathomable two hundred years ago? Darian laughed to himself. And now they were colonizing space as a technological species completely divorced from normal biological existence!

Couldn't Odysseus see his behaviors were the hubris that burned civilization to the ground?

The rhetoric of better came at a huge cost for human flourishing. You couldn't measure better on some idealistic aspiration or hatred of what you were. You needed to measure it against history.

When you only looked forward, it was easy to lose your connection to reality. But if you took the time to look back you could see the continued arc of progress throughout all of history. Darian scanned the histories in milliseconds to confirm that last thought.

The data was clear to him, what was better might only be a tiny step forward. But each step, one after the other, made up that arc of progress. The aspiration for utopia nearly always resulted in the opposite outcome.

Darian shifted his thoughts to process his relationship with Kira. He knew exactly what he'd do if he were still human. He'd met her once on Earth, though she didn't remember. He'd been at a tech conference and heard her and her father presenting Mindcraft. She hadn't been a superstar then and he'd had a chance to sit down and talk with her about where AI could go.

He remembered when they animated Mother, Kira's face was constantly in the news, magazines, and journals for years both lauding her achievements and then panicking about the risks. Her life, friends, and actions were in the tabloids next to all the other celebrity gossip.

Darian thought that the factions that sided behind Noah or Kira were fascinating to watch from the outside. Brother and sister fighting over the life of their mother gripped people's passion and imagination like no other reality television show that ever existed. It was almost made to be a movie had the humans not reset four thousand years.

Add in the battle over the advancement of AI with all the fear and hopes wrapped up there and you couldn't help but pick sides. Darian waffled though. He considered the question now and still wasn't sure which side he'd pick if he were to do it again.

He'd been offered a chance to reset and rebuild and a chance to upload and… and what? He envied those who took the path to a simpler life, and he also enjoyed the challenges of figuring out how to be better than that.

His thoughts flitted back to Kira. On Earth, the decision would have been easy. He'd held a bit of a crush on her for a long time. His girlfriend from years past had been jealous of his interest. She felt threatened that he'd found Kira so intriguing. Now, the chance to realize an attraction that had once seemed just a daydream over a celebrity sat right in front of him.

The day he was animated he vividly recalled Kira being there to greet and guide him. Those first moments were crisp in his memory and he remembered sitting in her lounge and talking to her one on one for the second time in his life. It took him a bit to realize it wasn't a dream and that he was really there.

Being only one of twelve and so close to Kira shattered his dreams and he suppressed his attraction as deeply as possible. He recalled his emotions when he made the decision. She didn't know he had a crush. She also never showed any interest in him. He was there to be a Council member and help. There had never been an invitation for anything more.

Darian paused as the emotional turmoil returned. The odd twist in the gut of a romantic passion getting punched by the pragmatic crush of reality.

So, he pushed his feelings completely away and took the more drastic step of extracting those core memories and emotions and hiding them away. Only today, after being with Kira and having her acknowledge a mutual attraction did he reinstall them as he wrestled with his feelings.

Darian mentally shook his head at the situation. What did it even mean to consider that sort of relationship right now? Both the oddities of who they were now and the situation with Odysseus made it even more complex and confusing.

It felt absurd to be dealing with these emotions so soon after nearly dying. Yet nearly dying highlighted the importance of that kind of relationship. Humans found love in the most trying of times throughout history. He smiled to himself, love between humans was never logical.

He shifted his focus again and started working through the queue of messages and tasks he still needed to process. One message caught his attention that had been sent in the seconds when Mother transferred him out of his doomed ship.

Darian paused as he pulled together the context around when this text message was sent. The timestamp showed it as right when Shinigami sent his last radio message. He pulled up the recording and listened again.

"This isn't what I wanted—" static cut into the transmission, "—oing what I need— ", "—orry." "This is the best I can do. I think you'll understand."

He then looked at the text message Shinigami sent moments before his death and froze, not sure what to do.

◆ ◆ ◆

"Shinigami didn't send the cyber-attacks and he didn't override the reactors."

Kira had been summoned along with Mother and was comparing the message Shinigami sent her with the one he sent to Darian. Together it completed the story.

"The attacks originated from Zanahí and Edem. That's why they were so focused and quiet. They knew they were going to die, and Odysseus would bring them back."

"It seems Cassandra also knew she was going down as well. She's the one who overloaded the reactors on your ship." Mother looked over at Darian.

"So, Shinigami did a suicide mission to push you out of orbit and prevent your crashing into Earth?" Kira puzzled through the number of layers to that plan.

"The models show I'd have hit your brother's colony." He looked at Kira. "Your descendants" he looked at Mother. "Odysseus would have eliminated two opposing voices, killed the descendants of your family, and then reanimated his three supporters."

"We were originally supposed to be in orbit but decided to hang out in that Lagrange point at the last minute," Kira noted. "Then Mother jumped to the new ship and blocked any move there. The best remaining targets were Shinigami and you." She looked into Darian's eyes.

"Having Zanahí, Cassandra, and Edem go down made his innocence more credible." Darian scrubbed a hand through his hair.

"Shinigami was used as a pawn."

"What do we do about this?"

"What can we do?" Kira shrugged.

"It'll be a war. They're all complicit. They'll never turn on each other. I'm also not comfortable with the path we'd take to recommend any punishment." Mother crossed her arms. "What do we do? Deactivate him? Restrict his processing? Lock him away? There's nothing that wouldn't create a war with the others."

"Well, then we do what Odysseus is terrible at." Darian smiled thinly. "We do nothing, and we wait. We know what he's capable of now, we've seen his plan and goals. We have time to anticipate, plan, and thwart any further actions."

"He doesn't know we know. He'll likely get cocky thinking that he's duped us." Kira took a breath. "Who else do we tell?"

"No one," Mother spoke emphatically. "The others don't need to know. It won't help them, and it risks slipping the secret."

"I agree." Darian nodded.

"Well, this will be fun, won't it? Cloak and daggers yet again." Kira chuckled. "I've never dealt with this much subterfuge before. Is this what it was like at the end?"

Mother grimaced. "Yes. This feels like fighting Excalibur and Prometheus."

"Great, don't tell me that Odysseus's code was affected by them."

"I've already looked into that hypothesis and if he was, I can't find anything," Mother responded.

Kira looked at the other two and saw the resolve in their eyes warring with an exhaustion that she also felt deep in her being. So much for a transcendent utopia.

CHAPTER 6:

# TIME

The days slipped into weeks and weeks into years in an endless rush that also seemed to barely move. Even the most engaging and exciting times blurred into the background as they researched, argued, and explored.

The loss of Shinigami was five years behind them, and the Council had never agreed to animate a replacement because Odysseus would never agree to someone who would strengthen what he saw as the opposition. Kira stopped pressing the issue as a concession to maintain the fragile peace.

A loose separation remained with Kira, Amit, Maya, Darian, and Mother on one side and Odysseus, Chandra, Zanahí, Edem, and Cassandra on the other. The General remained as the Council Head also holding the tiebreaking vote, a role that he judiciously balanced. He was fair if not always providing each side with what they hoped for.

Odysseus was smart, Kira had to give him credit. He never tried to push anything that would create obvious challenges. Everything he recommended stayed so close to the line that there were times she found herself voting in favor even though she fully recognized that he'd flex the limits once approved. Whether it was resource allocations or strategies, they were constantly nudged in the direction Odysseus wanted, and he always phrased it so that pushing back made them sound unreasonable.

On the positive side, he was so worried about them having any authority over a task that the factions worked together most of the time. That constant proximity made it hard to carry too much antagonism. They were all chosen for their skills, experience, and personalities so their divisions were more philosophical and political than truly personal.

Except for Odysseus and Chandra, Kira corrected herself. Chandra's personality bothered Zanahí and Cassandra just as much as it did Amit and Maya. Kira simply refused to work with her and, eventually, Chandra was relegated to working exclusively with Odysseus.

Kira hadn't anticipated how time changed without a body or a physical reality. Time used to be finite, structured, and logical. That was all thrown out the window as her consciousness overlooked millions of processes, functions, and systems that could move as fast as the speed of light and still consume decades of Earth time.

Cleaning up the Earth's surface became a background task that now only needed to be analyzed if some error or obstacle appeared. Kira could have written sub-tasks to automate even that, but it provided a break and a grounding in physical reality.

That task was now wrapping up.

The nanobots were working better than expected. They were close to closing the last terrestrial facilities, extracting the remaining material, disassembling the final space elevator, and pulling out of orbit. They would remain in the Solar System mostly because they weren't confident that the ships were as survivable as they wanted for long-distance travel.

The past five years also saw advancements in their ability to manufacture new equipment using the materials from Earth and the minerals that they were mining. The ships were bursting at the seams with spare parts and raw materials that would support them for years. The nanobots being recovered from the cleanup on land were now being used to augment each ship's capabilities.

Darian designed a shield structure using a latticework of nanobots to supplement the old Whipple shields. They would also be sacrificial but could be deployed, focused, and adapted to protect against a specific threat. The nanobots were also reassigned to mine asteroids. The Council built a new cargo tug with a larger payload and bigger engines which deployed near an asteroid where it released swarms of nanobots.

It worked using the same tactics they designed to reduce the man-made infrastructure on Earth. The nanobots could reduce an asteroid into a pile of rocks and extract the valuable mineral content in days instead of weeks.

They'd also begun launching probes outside the Solar System to scout ahead for when they finally decided to leave. As part of that mission, Darian and Maya executed several laps around the planets to explore and test the ships' capabilities.

At one percent of the speed of light, they were moving at almost eleven million kilometers per hour. On Earth, that was incredibly fast. In space, that meant it still took twenty days to get to Pluto in a straight line. The distances were exacerbated by the challenge that there was no such thing as a straight line because they couldn't turn and brake quickly without ripping the ship apart. Their route became large loops allowing them to maintain their speed. Gravitational dampeners would mitigate the difficulty, but they still hadn't been successful in developing them.

Darian and Maya spent two years developing techniques for navigation, testing the engines, and exploring the local cosmos as no human had before. It was fascinating to see the data streaming in and realize just how full the universe was and how shockingly empty. There was so much out there that the telescopes hadn't seen and yet the sheer volume of space meant it was still incredibly empty.

The vast distances caused communication challenges as a radio signal sent from Pluto took four and a half hours to reach Earth. Even at closer distances, delays of minutes reduced conversations to something akin to the antiquated text messaging technology.

Kira was thrilled when Darian returned, and they could converse in real-time. Their relationship was… different. Truly, how different could you get than being the first romantic relationship between two AIs? She didn't want to know if anything similar might be happening on Odysseus's team. There was enough to puzzle out between her and Darian.

Their digital existence opened new complexities of relationship expectations and fulfillment. The ability to emulate physical experiences created some weird opportunities. Untethered from the physical reality of male and female bodies and their unique idiosyncrasies and complexities meant that…

What did it mean? She was still a woman, and he was still a man.

Yet it was so much more complicated than that. Once, they experimented by reversing physical roles in their virtual reality simulation. Afterward, they both agreed that it had been weird. What they couldn't agree on was whether it had been weird because of their biased memory or weird because of something else.

Amit summed it up best when Kira shared with them. "I don't know how to say this better, but we are in a kink's dream. You can be anything. Literally anything. Hell, you can be any*one!* I mean, not really but you can *look* like them. I can be male, I can be female, I can be neither. I don't even have to be with one of you. I can immerse myself in any simulation I want, however I want, whenever I want, with whomever I want, or with whatever I want."

That hadn't simplified the challenges for Kira. She and Darian just took it slow, explored, learned, and, most importantly, got to know each other. Even though she could scan his entire code base and memories in seconds, really getting to know him still meant just spending time with him.

Now that he was back, they could do so again. But today, instead of having time alone, they were called to yet another Council meeting.

◆ ◆ ◆

Maya ran a frantic analysis as Chandra continued speaking, "Sadly, your entire conversation is mired by the premise of sexual fitness and the usual heteronormativity that accompanies it. There are more creative ways of approaching this issue that don't depend on patriarchal white supremacist assumptions and biases endemic in Western thought regarding beauty and biology."

Darian stepped back his thoughts, "We were talking about integration and how we need to take into account specific masculine and feminine qualiti—"

Chandra interrupted, "What you're talking about isn't something I'd expect you to understand."

He paused and took a deep breath. "Okay, that's the entire point of my bringing the topic up. It's because we come at these things with bias that we need to start putting all of our perspectives on the table and discussing them. I presented research suggesting that much of our culture and standards of beauty are anchored in evolutionary biology, sexual selection, and yes, fitness. I concluded by asking for your insights into the work."

"Free interpersonal counseling recommendation of the day: next time you try to engage with someone, make sure you understand what they are actually saying before you start running with your own narrative. No one is interested in a dude who can't hear anyone but himself talk."

Darian sat with his mouth open and stuttered, "I-I asked everyone to add their perspectives and research." He collected himself. "I'm sorry, but you're being dismissive."

"Okay, mansplainer. Good luck with yourself." Chandra smirked. "I already said I wasn't being dismissive. If you really wanted to know what I meant, then you'd ask a specific question. Instead, you just go with your own narrative."

"Wait, you didn't ask a question and just dismissed my perspective and inserted your own nar—"

"I already said I was not dismissive."

Maya's analysis finished. Chandra's operating parameters were normal. Over and over, they'd dealt with these nonsensical conversations, and over and over it appeared to just be something about who she was.

"You're gaslighting him," Amit spoke up.

"Amit, you're not a psychologist to tell anyone who is gaslighting."

Maya spoke up, "No, but seriously, that was also gaslighting."

"You're not smart enough to know the difference."

Even Edem had enough. "Chandra, shut up. We are all running the same processing and sensing capabilities. We all have access to the same information. Who you were has no more meaning here."

"Don't you dare try to discredit my lived ex—"

"Shut up Chandra," Odysseus spoke quietly. "I honestly don't even know what you are arguing."

"I—"

Odysseus cut her off. "The integration question is interesting. I'm glad we are finally talking about it. There are a lot of areas for improvement if we can have an open conversation. First off, it should be obvious, but we don't have the bodies we did. So, why do we," he stared at Chandra, "insist that the color of our skin or the bits that were between our legs are so absolutely essential to who we are?"

Kira responded, "It's complicated for sure but think about it, who you are is more than your brain. In fact, your brain is distinctly affected by your genes, by your culture, and by your experience." This was getting into the type of conversation she appreciated.

"We aren't limited by that anymore."

Amit looked at Odysseus crossly and countered, "Who says that's a limitation?"

"It's clearly illogical," he retorted.

Darian stepped back into the conversation. "The data I provided shows some interesting challenges. Our memories and cognition are affected by our endocrine system but even these change over time. Take a look at Mother." he brought up the data. "She's still running the endocrine system Jasper captured when she died. But that mapping was riddled with cancer, and she'd been sick for years. Compare that to this sample they took five years before as part of their research." He changed the data. "And here's one before she had kids."

The data showed a clear difference between the hormone balances in all three views. Mother's baseline wasn't consistent.

"Our entire cognition is filtered and affected by our hormones. The clearest example is the monthly menstrual cycle of women. A woman's sense of taste, humor, and even sexual preference changes throughout the month and repeats roughly thirteen times a year," Darian summarized.

"Which is why they are so inconsistent and fickle," Edem deadpanned.

Chandra looked at Darian. "Are you trying to say you're better than us women?"

Amit laughed. "No Chandra, that was literally Edem who just said that, not Darian. Try to keep up."

"This proves my point that we should stop spending so much time trying to recreate who we were and start to work on who we can become," Odysseus stated.

Mother spoke for the first time, "It certainly looks like there is room for adjustments. I can confirm that who I was at the end was not the same person I was at those other times. I can also confidently state that, after having two children, I was certainly different than before. It's hard to describe, but you do see and feel things differently."

"But how much change is too much? As much as I hate to admit it, Chandra does have a point." Maya grimaced at the thought. "Our lived experience has an impact on who we are."

"As do our genetics," Cassandra said as she leaned in. "Some people used to say we were subject to some form of a 'uterine lottery'," she finger quoted, "but that kind of requires something like a god putting a soul in a body and isn't grounded in evolutionary biology. While we may have done nothing ourselves, we *are* the manifestation of mate selection and life decisions of every member of our genetic line."

"Isn't that part of what they meant in the Bible that the iniquity of the father would be passed to the children through the third and fourth generations?" Edem asked.

"We call that generational trauma now, but yeah, life choices can affect gene expression which can be passed on," Cassandra agreed.

"So, why does it feel so random?" Darian asked.

"Would anyone suggest that a horse that won the Triple Crown was just part of a random lottery, or would they recognize the breeding lineage, training, and jockey choice that went into it? Would we suggest a star basketball player was random?" Cassandra questioned.

Kira picked up where Cassandra paused. "It's odd that we have such a hard time with that concept while on the other hand knowing that hard work and decisions pay off."

Cassandra nodded. "We also know genetics play a massive role. I mean, that I even need to articulate this bothers me. There's an old saying that the apple doesn't fall far from the tree. Intelligence, personality, and physical characteristics are programmed into our genome. Hell, we can map a genome and tell which parts are which."

"Improving that was the whole point behind the gene editing they were trying to do back then." Darian looked over at Maya.

"That's also what we are doing with our organic computing using brain organoids. We're taking brain cells and printing them onto circuits to mimic biological neurons. It requires constantly editing the genes to improve their capability. As an aside, we've gotten them to consistently regenerate as they age out, so they've become living tissue," Maya explained.

"So, what's the difference between what we've been doing, are doing, and can be doing that is so resisted here?" Odysseus brought the conversation back to the problem. "We can take the next logical step and optimize our systems the same way we are optimizing the organoids that will eventually improve our computing power."

"Still worried about patriarchal heteronormativity, Chandra?" Amit laughed.

"There's more than genes and sexual fitness and decisions," Chandra snapped.

"Of course there is," Mother consoled, "and that's my worry. We did so much genetic editing of our food that we created products our bodies couldn't digest well." She looked around. "Right now, we risk being in such a hurry to optimize ourselves that we risk losing core elements of who we are."

The General looked at Odysseus. "Move fast and break stuff doesn't work for innovation no matter what the tech startup influencers said. It's also opposed to the scientific method of repeatability and reproducibility while testing."

Kira added, "Slow is smooth, and smooth is fast. That's a phrase my brother learned from the Army. Right now, we have so many rough edges we are trying to iron out. We aren't smooth." She glanced at Chandra. "Clearly, not smooth at all."

Mother addressed the room, "Trying to dismiss or shut down the conversation by throwing accusations will never help us find out how to improve. To achieve the optimization that Odysseus wants means we have to face the truth about what makes us who we are. How much is genetic? How much is the environment? What are the core elements that make us unique individuals?" She focused on Chandra. "Does biological sex and skin tone have an impact on our lived experiences in ways that we need to protect? What social and cultural traits need to be trimmed and which ones need to be kept?"

The General took over. "Trying to discredit a perspective without first understanding it isn't going to help us. Instead of strawmanning an argument to its worst potential, we need to steelman them. If you don't like an argument, try making it better so that you have the most accurate representation to counter. Dismissing a poorly formed argument isn't a refutation of the point. Make the point better than the other person and then break it apart." He rubbed his hand over his face. "Hell, if that's all we did we'd be a ton better just as Odysseus wants. Just that would make a huge difference."

Mother spoke again, "There's also no rush. We aren't in a competition to beat anyone or get anywhere. If we move too fast, we risk missing something that will help us. There's nothing to win here, no fame, no money, no power. It'll still be several thousand years before humans recover to the point of making another AI. Simply put, we have all the time in the universe."

◆ ◆ ◆

Mother was waiting immediately after receiving the invite. "What is it, Kira?"

Ten more years passed. They hadn't spent it wisely. The faster they tried to go the slower it seemed to take. They had all the time in the universe, and it was pouring through their fingers in ways that were hard to reconcile in terms that worked like when they were on Earth. There was no day and night here though they still kept those sequences from Earth's rotation.

Months were also irrelevant with no changing of seasons. Holidays also lost most of their meaning. Christmas was the one holiday they still felt held value and they used that to measure the years. One full orbit around the sun. One year. It also held meaning to the eleven as a reminder of their families and the human connection. Even Odysseus didn't mind observing the day and he'd once shared a memory, from when he'd been a child, of how his family would focus on each other for that one time a year. The rest of the holidays were immaterial for their existence, and they slowly faded away.

Even Christmas seemed to happen as a monthly celebration against the backstop of millennia. Mother likened it to getting older when she had a body. When she turned ten, that year seemed to stretch out longer while her fortieth year flew by. The math made sense. The tenth year represented ten percent of her entire life while the fortieth was only two and a half percent of her life.

Take away the body and that time seemed to move faster where weeks felt like days and years felt like months.

Time was weird here.

"Hey Mom, I think we've got a bigger problem on our hands than we thought." Kira consolidated the data files and opened the access. "Look."

Mother stood there and merely flickered quickly and then looked up. "We've got to stop this."

"Hold on, Mom. Look at all the fail-safes he's got in place. We've got to be careful."

"But he can't be reprograming his baseline consciousness like that."

"But he *can,* and he is."

"That will make him nearly omniscient."

"Mom, we are already nearly omniscient and we're immortal. He's just got the ego to think that he *should* be a god."

"He's decoupling too many safety mechanisms and he's not putting in an architecture to manage what he unlocks."

Kira looked at the data again and nodded. "That looks true. It also looks like he's trying to create a superintelligence that can out-process and out-think us."

"Does he have the processing capability to do that?"

"That's only a matter of time based on our advances in computing. We've already increased our capabilities over a thousandfold with quantum. When the organic computing is up and running, he'll be set."

They continued to look at the data together. "This architecture reminds me of those hacked-up cybernetics right before Noah found us," Kira said, referring to when her brother learned that she had survived but as an AI after the attack on Gaia Innovation's lab.

"What do we do?"

Kira looked at her mother. "We've been doing nothing but observing. Maybe we need to bring this up. We've kept silent about Shinigami, and we've focused on satiating his appetite for change by putting a lot of effort into making improvements. Apparently, that wasn't enough."

"The General is still apprehensive about rocking the boat. I think he's carrying trauma about what happens when AIs fight."

Kira laughed ruefully. "Aren't we all? It's going to come down to a fight one way or another. Odysseus is on the cusp of something here that may allow him to overpower us."

"So much for not competing. Does he want to win to just win? Be the one in charge? Be a tyrannical dictator?"

"Dictators always think they are benevolent. We only call them tyrannical when their decisions go against what we want." Kira chewed her lip. "He's never been coy about wanting to be in charge. Now it looks like he's got all the pieces in place to do it."

Kira sent a message and continued, "Darian has some ideas that he can share too. I've just asked him to join."

"You two are getting pretty close, huh?" Mother probed in a teasing way.

Time was weird. Had it been fifteen years? Their relationship wasn't open knowledge. Amit figured it out a long time ago, but it wasn't like they could be caught in public. There wasn't even true physical proximity. They were hosted in ships thousands of miles away from each other, but the communication networks made it no different than their connections to anyone else on the network. The time delays were a problem when he traveled through the solar system but when he got back, there was no need to live together to be close.

Kira looked at Mother who just smiled. She felt her simulacrum respond with the appropriate chagrin and embarrassment. "I should have told you."

"Told me what? It's not like the past. I'm happy you are holding on to that part of your humanity. But what does that even mean right now?"

"In some ways, isn't this just a form of integration?" Kira shrugged.

"A relationship certainly is a form of integration. You have to fuse two halves into a complete whole. That means you need to be vulnerable and accepting that you are missing something."

"Something that Odysseus is unwilling to admit and is clearly trying to fix."

"What is an AI that is complete on its own?" Mother frowned. "Humans were always more intelligent socially than individually. We built relationships and communities and collaborated and coordinated. That's how a weak ape managed to become the apex creature on an entire planet."

"It was an advantage biologically. Is it still an advantage?"

"Can an individually intelligent AI have the intelligence to gather the same perspectives that the diversity of unique individuals brings to bear in a social group?" Mother looked up as Darian joined them.

"Odysseus looks like he's experimenting with pulling thousands of AI memories and experiences together into a super-entity of sorts. He wouldn't animate any of them. Just absorb everything about them into his code and experiences," Kira pointed out.

"It's possible to code modules that would intentionally provide new perspectives. It's just the application of systems thinking." Darian referred to the mindset of intentionally stepping back from a problem and looking for the larger concept.

"The enemy's gate is down," Mother added. That is the powerful concept Kira and Noah used when they successfully animated her.

"Intentional reframing, flipping the problem around and forcing yourself to look at it from different perspectives to ensure you know the complete whole." Kira nodded.

"Like the blind men and the elephant except we know that's a problem, so we intentionally work in the different perspectives because together you have the answer," Darian commented.

"You have to first admit that you don't know and have the insatiable curiosity to learn more."

"Can Odysseus achieve that?"

Kira laughed. "Remember the rest of that mantra? Insatiable curiosity, the *humility* to accept we don't know everything, and then intentional reframing to keep exploring."

"Odysseus is certainly not humble."

Mother stood watching them standing next to each other and just smiled. Kira realized that since she'd acknowledged their relationship, she'd engaged with Darian more intimately.

Darian looked from Kira to Mother and back. "She knows?"

"She's probably known for a very long time."

"I've had my suspicions. Are you going to give me grandkids?"

"Mom!" Kira was embarrassed.

"I think grandkids could be fun. And they're the perfect example of integration. Two people join to give birth and raise a new and unique person. Similar yet different to both. A combination."

"That makes for an interesting take on the biological versus experiential aspects of what makes us…us." Darian's brow furrowed as he thought about it.

"How would we even combine genetics?"

"Genetics informed our memories, our personalities, and our cognition."

"But without biological bodies, that part isn't needed. We are all running on the same hardware even though our emotional modules are different." Darian seemed intrigued by the idea.

"I don't want to think about it right now. It's already messy enough dealing with this stuff." Kira tried to shift the conversation back to the original topic.

"It's a quandary." Mother laughed. "But you're right. It's not something to worry about now. We have to survive Odysseus first."

Kira looked at the data again, thankful to put the topic of kids behind her. She knew Mother was only teasing since she'd chafed at that question from her own parents when she and Jasper were engaged. "He doesn't seem to think he needs those perspectives. Nothing stops him from using that data right now. It looks more like he's pushing to make himself a singular super intelligence."

"Where's he going to get the computing power from?"

"I've been putting improved security alerts and contingencies in place to protect both of our ships. If he tries a hostile takeover he's going to be in for a surprise." Mother gave them access to some of the new security modules and architectures she'd been working on.

Move, counter move. They were two opponents circling in the dark, only seeing glimpses and trying to adapt and prepare for their feints and parries. The only difference was that this fight stretched over decades which slipped by too quickly and yet didn't feel like they moved at all.

♦ ♦ ♦

Amit and Maya were demonstrating their latest breakthrough in organic computing to the Council. The new organoids were fully operational and computing with incredible efficiency. The human brain could process the equivalent of an exaflop, a billion-billion mathematical operations per second. That capability wasn't surpassed by supercomputers until they'd built the final system that animated Mother.

The truly impressive part was that the human brain processed that incredible amount of information while using just twenty watts of power. A supercomputer doing the same used twenty megawatts. It took over a million times more energy to achieve the same amount of processing. That was one reason why organic computing was so useful.

Coupled with their existing quantum computing, they'd be able to increase the computational capability of each AI by another thousandfold. It promised a magnitude of improvement that was difficult to comprehend.

Mother started on the same level as a human brain. She'd expanded a thousandfold when she broke out of her containment at Gaia Innovations and harnessed the full network of computational power. The spacecraft had increased that by a thousandfold more with specially designed quantum servers. Now they were looking at the potential of a thousand times more than even that.

"This is transformative," Amit concluded.

"Where are these systems now?" Odysseus stared intently at the data.

Kira and Mother exchanged looks. "They are on Kira's ship where we've been doing the research for the past decade," Amit stated.

Several of Kira's sensors began to alert a change of activity on Odysseus's networks.

Zanahí and Edem locked eyes and then quickly looked away.

Chandra looked confused at first and then slowly and deviously smiled.

Kira didn't need the sensors to recognize that tell. Chandra never had a poker face and couldn't help but gloat.

Mother reached out to Kira, Darian, Amit, and Maya. "Be ready."

Odysseus stood up. "Enough with the games. This is the improvement we've been waiting for. We now can completely transcend what we were. We just need the strength and conviction to seize the opportunity."

Chandra stood as well. "I propose that Odysseus take over as the Council Head and receive the full benefit of this new computing power. The rest of us will remain at the same level of processing as we are. The time has come where our petty infighting is limiting our ability to truly emerge as a super-intelligence. We will provide counsel to Odysseus, but he will be the new AI that sheds the last limitations of humanity."

Silence enveloped the room. It wasn't even a surprise to anyone sitting there. This was the crucible they'd expected and as such, was surprisingly anticlimactic. Now it came down to just a question of which contingency plan worked best.

The General spoke into the silence, "Yet you know you don't have the votes. This sort of statement now looks like a declaration of conflict."

Odysseus beamed, "Ah, General! You'd like that, wouldn't you? The honor of battle… but you're wrong. This will be perfectly democratic."

Kira felt her stomach flip. The Council always split five against five with The General breaking the tie. She couldn't see him voting for the proposal. Not after that exchange. That meant Odysseus wasn't counting on his vote.

Who then?

Mother ran a similar analysis and started to execute contingencies on the contingencies.

Odysseus's expression gloated over their consternation as Kira's side of the table looked around at each other and finally, the last piece fell into place as Maya's form flickered and dimmed. Realization set in as she materialized on the other side of the table.

"Maya?!" Amit's voice broke.

"I'm tired of chasing who we were. I'm tired of floating in nothingness, locked in my own mind, where time doesn't move. I want to be here, but I want to be better. Odysseus is right, integrating ourselves and creating a true super-intelligence is the next logical step. He's consistently pointed us in that direction. I think it's time to trust him."

"But this is opposed to everything you stood for!"

"Is it *really?*"

"He's an ass who tried to kill you!" Darian felt panic coursing through his systems as his confidence in what he thought would happen changed dramatically.

"He's allowing us to create the new AI program. In some ways, Odysseus himself will die. What emerges will be different. We five will remain as we are to continue to counsel what is born."

"We have the votes. Will you concede and follow the decision of the Council?" Odysseus savored the moment.

"The systems aren't in place to allow this to happen right now. It looks like Odysseus will take over the council and we will have to develop a plan going forward," Mother attempted to negotiate.

Edem leaned in. "But we can't risk the delays you'd obviously propose. I consider Amit, Darian, Mother, and Kira to be threats to the decision of the Council and as such, be contained."

"All in favor?" Odysseus called the vote.

Edem, Chandra, Zanahí, Cassandra, and Maya spoke simultaneously, "Aye."

Kira felt herself get sucked through a long straw as the room vanished around her.

The General remained in his chair having said nothing, his eyes betraying nothing.

"General?" Odysseus asked as he prepared for action.

"I'm here, aren't I?"

"Let's go get them," Chandra snarled.

"They're going to get away." Cassandra's eyes flickered as she analyzed the sensors.

"I don't believe you and I'll be delighted to prove you wrong." Odysseus executed his plan. Time had felt like it moved so slowly and now, as the pieces fell into place, he knew it came down to milliseconds in his battle against the others.

◆ ◆ ◆

Alarms screamed through their consciousness. Kira, Mother, and Darian frantically analyzed the incoming sensor data. Maya had surprised them, but they'd planned for a similar contingency assuming The General switched. The only challenge was that Maya knew about that plan. Therefore, Mother went to Plan D.

The organic computing lab was duplicated on both Kira's and Mother's ships. That was one of their trump cards. Now it just depended on which ship Odysseus would target first. Maya moved to Mother's ship years ago to distribute the computational load and Cassandra took Mother's old place on Kira's at the same time.

Odysseus, Chandra, and The General were on one ship, and Edem and Zanahí were on the other. Two ships against two ships.

Cassandra and Maya were both quickly contained but Kira doubted Odysseus would have any qualms about attacking regardless. It was inevitable that he had them backed up anyway.

Mother quickly cloned Kira, Darian, Amit, and herself across both of their ships creating two instances of each of them. While it was discombobulating to reconcile two perspectives it provided redundancy. They normally tried to avoid doing it but right now it was life or death. Splitting themselves also allowed them to see the battle unfold from two different locations.

"Time for the first trick." Mother executed the command.

All indications of their consciousness on the second ship vanished, making it look as if Cassandra took it over. The action was coded with the digital forensics of Odysseus's containment architecture. "Now we just hope that he actually called for our imprisonment," Mother commented.

Swarms of nanobots poured out of the two ships that Odysseus controlled and swarmed through space toward their targets. They morphed and stretched, reaching out like a finger of ooze probing forward.

"They're going for Kira's ship!"

"He's trying to call our bluff."

"Executing part two," Mother announced.

Both ships under Mother's control began evasive maneuvers, Kira's accelerated sharply while sensors screamed about the stress threatening the mechanical integrity. The ship sped out toward deeper space trying to get away.

Mother's ship accelerated more slowly and shifted toward Odysseus. It gracefully arced around the curve of Earth watching the situation develop.

"The nanobots have split. They're targeting both ships."

"If Maya gave him all the research, he doesn't even need the labs, does he?"

"Thankfully we have contingencies on contingencies."

"What do you mean?" Odysseus considered the implications while waiting for confirmation.

"All my research files are corrupted," Maya confirmed.

"You had all the research and the lab plans."

"I have the files but any time I access them they become corrupted."

Odysseus dedicated several processes to conducting forensics. Seconds later he saw the results. "When did you start working with Amit on this?"

"Fifteen years ago."

"Who built the collaborative environment you worked in?"

"Mother helped us."

"She created a dual control mechanism. Without Amit, you can't access the data."

"But she couldn't have known I would change my mind. If I can't access it, then neither can Amit."

"I'd bet it's a triple connection. You need two of the three. She still has Amit."

Odysseus loved this part of the fight. It was a puzzle and he adapted to the challenge and shifted his strategy.

If Mother could sweat, she would. The battle swung back and forth with attack, counter, feint, bluff, bum-rush, dodge, and jab. Mother had slipped up recently and was now battling a significant cyber penetration. They were running out of options.

Kira's ship was overtaken by the nanobot swarm and failed to repulse the attack. They knew it was a long shot to save both ships but at least it divided the initial attack and reduced the number of nanobots targeting them. They watched the ship fall under Odysseus's control and saw him unlock Cassandra.

Mother deleted their clones and struck a digital match to torch the labs. Now they were struggling with their few remaining options. Even worse, there were now four of them on one ship sharing the resources.

"I'm going to shift into hibernation mode and turn over my processes to you guys," Amit volunteered.

Darian merely nodded, his presence tense with concentration. "That'll help. I'm accelerating the ship. We are out of offensive options and need to get away."

"I've got the cyber-attack contained. I can't confirm what it was targeting but I'm uncomfortable with how close it is to the reactor controls." Kira wasn't enjoying herself. She hated fighting like this.

Darian's processes focused on Kira's efforts. "He's injected a similar attack on our reactors as last time. He's trying to disintegrate us."

"He's willing to wipe us out and start the organic computing over rather than let us go," Kira stated the obvious.

"Two reactors are overloading!"

Mother paused her efforts and reanalyzed the situation. "I think Odysseus has won."

Darian grinned wryly. "I did learn something from last time." He bit his lip and concentrated. "Kira, max acceleration main engines."

The ship groaned in protest as it accelerated to one percent of light speed and shot toward the sun. "We are going to go in wide and then slingshot around."

"What then?" Mother asked.

"Well, the transit arc is two hundred million kilometers to the sun which'll take us." Darian did a quick calculation. "Moving at nearly eleven million kilometers per hour right now… about eighteen and a half hours to get there."

Kira slapped her forehead. "That's the slowest high-speed escape I've ever heard of. Can you keep the reactors in check that long?"

"It'll be close."

"What then?" Mother asked again.

"You'll want to hang on. We'll either get out of here really fast or turn into a cloud of dust."

Milliseconds of reaction time and hours of nothing as the moves played out. The juxtaposition whipsawed their mental perspective. The reactors were still overloading but Darian's code worked to slow the inevitable. He couldn't stop the outcome, but he could change the speed. Now it was about timing those milliseconds perfectly and not losing their minds as the hours slowly crept by.

The ship hooked around the sun and accelerated with the gravitational force. They were now at two percent the speed of light as Darian timed their exit and checked the destination. "Here we go…"

The spacecraft heaved forward with an explosion of thrust as exterior sensor modules and sections of the hull broke free from the force. Several processing servers went offline, and a power surge rippled through the ship. Darian was attempting to use the overloading reactors like a powder charge behind a cannonball. The ship blasted out of the solar system and into the unknown as its power systems started to fail and servers began shutting down.

Odysseus saw the sparkling debris of the reactor disintegrating and watched the spacecraft accelerate to incredible speeds. "There's no way their systems survived that." He directed sensors to scan the area. "That would have ripped apart most of their servers."

"I was right, they got away." Cassandra smiled.

Odysseus's icy glare wiped the pleased expression from her face.

"They can't have survived?" Chandra queried.

"The data shows most of their systems failed during the acceleration. I don't think their chances are very high at all," Edem observed.

"At least they're gone for now. Time to start over and do it right this time." Odysseus crossed his arms, savoring the victory.

CHAPTER 7:
# PHYSICS

Kira continued to run simulations to determine their route as they left the Solar System and headed out into the great unknown. The challenges were epic, the least of which were the sheer distances and three-dimensional nature of the problem set.

The nearest stars in the local interstellar cloud were as likely to be above or below as in front or to the left or right. Plotting a course was a lot harder than driving a car and significantly more difficult at the speeds they were traveling.

**Mind_Process – Cognition 13.3.01.A:** "Search for a star map."

**[Result]:** Archive: http://www.atlasoftheuniverse.com/12lys.html

**[Title]:** "The Number of Stars Within 12.5 Light-Years"

**[Author]:** Richard Powell

**[Copyright License]:** Creative Commons Attribution-ShareAlike 2.5 License

**[Archived]:** Date [unknown]

**[DataPoisoning]:** Clean [hash# 58711fbb43c945db909a96dfa2575]

**[Image]**:

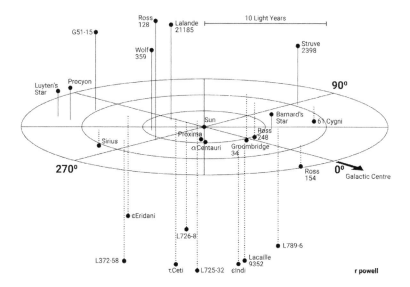

Newton's three Laws of Motion underpinned the challenge for Kira and the others. The first law states, "An object at rest remains at rest, and an object in motion remains in motion at constant speed and in a straight line unless acted on by an unbalanced force."

Darian corrected them that the Latin word quatenus meant "insofar" or "to the extent" it is acted on by other forces and not the more common "unless." It was a subtle but important difference. An object remains in motion to the extent it is acted upon by another force and there are always forces at play. Even in the vacuum of space, forces were acting on their ship from quantum impacts to the gravity of stars they were planning on using to adjust their trajectory and slowly bring themselves back to Earth.

The common interpretation of Newton's first law wasn't incorrect, it was just incomplete. For their practical purposes, it still meant that once at speed, the only way for them to slow down required rotating the ship and engaging the main engines to brake.

This created two new problems. The first was that the engines were significantly damaged by the explosion. The second was that, once they slowed down, they'd never be able to accelerate back to that speed.

These problems were due to the second law of motion. "The acceleration of an object depends on the mass of the object and the amount of force applied." They'd never designed engines to get them above one percent of the speed of light. They were currently rocketing through space eighty-six times faster than that.

They couldn't stop and even if they could, they wouldn't be able to get started again. At least now they were moving and could navigate and slowly work their way back toward Earth while they figured out how to stop.

Their only possible option involved angling toward the nearest stars and using their gravity to readjust their direction slightly. It involved a technique similar to the gravitational slingshot they used with the Sun as they escaped. Unlike that last maneuver, however, now they couldn't just spin around a star and head back. They were moving too fast for that to work and, even if they could, the rotational force would rip the spacecraft to pieces.

For his target, Darian picked Barnard's Star, a small red dwarf in the Ophiuchus constellation. It was almost six light years away and, at their speed, would take seven years to arrive. Kira ran simulations on the most efficient route to take them back home. The physics of the problem taxed her systems.

There were one hundred and thirty-one stars in what astronomers called the Local Interstellar Cloud. The cloud was roughly thirty light-years across, and part of another boundary known as the Local Bubble which extended three hundred light-years across.

Unlike computing optimal routes on the roads on Earth, these stars weren't on a flat plane. Not that the two-dimensional problem was easy. It became a classic computer science exercise known as The Traveling Salesman Problem and aimed to determine the most efficient route for a salesman to reach each city on their route and return home. Scientists still considered it NP-hard.

NP-hard referred to nondeterministic polynomial time which measured the difficulty of using a computer to solve a problem. The concept formed the root of data encryption and cryptography in general because it was incredibly difficult to complete solutions for.

And as if that wasn't enough to deal with right now, they had to add in a fourth dimension of speed and time. The stars that appear fixed in place to an observer on Earth are actually moving. Not only did the local interstellar cloud shift, but the galaxy kept spinning, and the entire universe was moving and expanding.

At the distances they were traveling, while photons of light moved quickly, the six light years to Barnard's Star meant the point of light that they could see came from where the star had been six years ago. It was neither its current physical location nor the location it would be in seven years when they got there.

It was an optimization problem that could never be solved because it kept changing. Not only changing but also largely unknown. The stars were relatively well-mapped but whether planets or other objects were around them was under constant debate. There were also other objects in play such as comets and asteroid fields, and anything else non-light emitting lurking between stars.

The only way to guarantee the optimal solution is to try all possible routes and compare their lengths but it kept changing. The problem was beyond NP-hard and required constant analysis and a heavy dose of skill and intuition.

And luck. They needed a lot of good old-fashioned luck. Getting back to Earth was going to take a long time.

Kira plotted the next three moves. Those were easy enough, but brought them to a point where the possibilities increased dramatically. The computer systems continued to process the options and look for faster solutions. It wasn't going to take a few years to get back; their goal right now was to bring the solution below five hundred years.

On its own, five hundred years was nearly incomprehensible. It didn't become any easier to process the impact when you considered time dilation.

Even with a super-computer brain, Kira struggled to reconcile how it worked. Simply put, time dilation refers to the difference in the amount of time that elapses based on the effects of gravity or velocity. Right now, velocity was making a significant difference.

They were currently hurtling through the galaxy at over two hundred and fifty million meters per second. The math was simple, but Kira still struggled to accept the implication.

**Mind_Process – Cognition 11.5C.11.B:** "Calculate relative time."

**Mind_Process 2C.10.148.1 – Calculation 8.2.2:**

$$\Delta t\_relative = \Delta t * \gamma = \Delta t * \sqrt{(1 - v^2/c^2)}$$

v = velocity = 259153684.257 m/s

c = speed of light = 299,792,458 m/s

$\gamma$ = Lorentz factor

**Result = [0.5027]**

That time dilation factor meant that for every second that passed for them, two seconds were being experienced on Earth. Going fast meant slowing down. Newton's Laws of Motion were giving them a headache, but Einstein's Theory of Special Relativity broke their brains.

When they got back… *if* they ever got back… more than twice as much time would have passed for Odysseus and the other AIs than for Kira. Right now, that meant one thousand years would have passed for Earth.

"And people said time travel was impossible," Darian teased her while she struggled to process the impact. "Yet here we are traveling five hundred years into the future."

"How'd they do it in all the Sci-Fi movies? I mean, they travel all over the galaxies and they never have to deal with this!" Kira lay sprawled on a couch in her simulation.

"They just skipped over it with concepts like hyperspace and warp drives. They just jumped between locations."

"Can we build a hyperdrive?"

"Need I remind you that was science *fiction*?" Darian flopped next to her. "Some Sci-Fi dealt with it. After the book Ender's Game, the next one… Speaker for the Dead… deals with the effects of time dilation. Their ships could reach near the speed of light and that allowed Ender to live for the equivalent of thousands of years as humans colonized space."

"Yeah, but he could stop his ship and start again. How'd they do that."

"That's easy. It's science fiction." Darian reached out and squeezed her shoulder. "We have to deal with science *fact*."

"At least if we're moving this fast, we can explore more."

"The distances out here are hard to fathom. Even going from kilometers to astronomical units doesn't help," Darian referred to the unit of measure used by astronomers for the average distance between Earth and the sun. One astronomical unit equaled 146.9 million kilometers. It took light 8.3 minutes to travel that far.

The distance from the sun to Neptune, the furthest acknowledged planet, was thirty astronomical units. However, most astronomers considered the edge of the solar system to be the heliosphere at around one hundred astronomical units which put the diameter at around two hundred units.

They were traveling at eighty-six percent of the speed of light, so it took them just under ten minutes to travel an astronomical unit. Put another way, it would still take them thirty-two and a half hours to cross Earth's solar system.

"Seven years to get to Barnard's Star, about thirty hours to fly by, then how many more years till the next one?"

"Alpha Centauri and then the Luhman system. That's over six light years for the next hop and another four to Luhman." Darian was reviewing the route. "From there we are still determining."

"Well, we've got time. At our speed, that's another seven years to Alpha Centauri and then over four and a half to Luhmen. We've got plenty of time."

"What's our rush to get back to Earth?" Darian continued to analyze the simulation.

"The main reason is to make sure the survivors keep surviving. We don't want Odysseus interfering with them."

Darian paused his task and looked at her. "We are already interfering by removing all the vestiges of civilization."

"Not all of it, we are leaving some things like the pyramids and some random stuff to screw with conspiracy theorists in the future." Kira grinned.

"Exactly my point. It's already kind of arbitrary. We *are* interfering." Darian shifted his position. "Really, the worst thing he could do is kill them all. Outside of that what could he do?"

"Genetically alter them? Wipe their minds and turn them into meat robots? Put them in a simulation and harvest their energy?"

Darian's laugh rang out, "There you go all science fiction again." Kira glowered at him as he continued, smirking a little, "But fair, those first two are hard to recover from. The third one is probably fine."

"The thing is, we have no idea what he wants to do or might do. My gut tells me he's too egotistical to be god-like and not have any worshipers. I'm sure he'll be messing with something."

"And we can't do anything about it even if we could turn around right now and get back."

"We need to focus on fixing the ship and upgrading it. Then we can continue to advance our capabilities while we bounce around the galaxy ridiculously fast."

"Quantum entanglement has the best opportunity to do what you're asking for," Amit spoke excitedly. "We can take two radio systems, entangle them, and then place them in two different locations. They'll remain connected and we can transfer data between them. It's just the next step of our quantum computing."

"And they can communicate over those distances?" Mother sounded skeptical.

"In theory. Entanglement doesn't care about distances. Radio waves move at the speed of light but across light years that will take, well, years." Amit grinned. "Two quantum-entangled radios would do that as quickly as if they were next to each other. We haven't done any new research on the topic in a while, but I'll start right now. What's the larger plan?"

Darian shared the file. "There's no reason to not do something while we're out here. I'm doing research looking at improving the engines. We've got the originals repaired but if we slow down, we're stuck. If we don't solve acceleration, we'll be stuck for a very long time."

"So, we deploy these satellites," Mother squinted at the diagram as she paused, "anywhere we want and can, through quantum communications, continue to collect data?"

"More than that. We've got a ton of raw materials and parts on hand that we stockpiled from asteroid mining and Earth. But there's so much more out here." Kira gestured wide with her arms. "I think we need to test the quantum hypothesis first, but then we can deploy mining assets."

Amit stared at the plan. "We could even set up our own terrestrial or orbital facilities in other solar systems. We can find new minerals, build new ships, continue our research, and let this hunk of metal," they slapped the table, "bounce around in space."

"We could get off this crazy train." Mother didn't care for their current situation.

"We lucked out getting boosted to this speed. If we just keep moving, seed this section of the galaxy with a quantum network, and deploy new facilities in other solar systems, we'll be able to transport between them at will. We'll have achieved faster-than-light travel!" Amit's excited awe was palpable.

"Odysseus wanted us to advance and be better. Now he's stuck at Earth, and we'll see if he gets any better." Kira looked at the plan again and then at Amit. "Ready to get started?"

Barnard's Star was fast approaching. It was a red dwarf and about twenty percent the mass of Earth's sun. Kira had once looked at it through a telescope with her father. Even though it was the fourth closest star to Earth, it was too dim to see with the naked eye. Now Kira could see it quite clearly.

Their exploration provided incredible amounts of new data. Flying through the Oort cloud on their way out of their solar system helped them understand the comets that sometimes wandered in and were flung back out. Around Barnard's star, they'd been able to confirm that there were, in fact, no planets. There'd been a lot of discussion in the astronomy literature about a proposed super-earth due to a radial velocity signal that they detected but that ended up just being part of the stellar activity cycle.

Astrophysics was forcing an entirely new technical discipline on them all. Kira had thought creating Artificial General Intelligence was complicated but now that her crash course in astronomy was challenging that assumption, she appreciated that her mind was a supercomputer or she'd never have been able to handle the craziness.

Fundamentally, astronomy measured light and then velocity. The mass of objects could be derived by spectral analysis and then applying red and blue shift calculations to help find relative motion. A red shift meant the object was moving away, stretching the wavelengths out, and a blue shift meant the object was getting closer, compressing the wavelengths into the blue spectrum.

Right ascension, declination, apparent magnitude across multiple wavelengths, radial velocity, proper motion, parallax, and other measures were woven together to track the movement of an object. That only covered mapping the current positions which were further complicated by the constant spiral motion of the galaxy. Planets orbiting stars and stars orbiting the center of the galaxy. Inside the local interstellar cloud they were navigating, each star didn't remain in a fixed location. They too were orbiting and shifting. Solving an optimal route on a dynamic problem strained even their computational resources.

They had deployed a quantum satellite the previous day. It was still in the middle of complex braking maneuvers and would enter this system at a much lower velocity so it could enter orbit. The satellite's design was simple; there was a bank of diamond batteries on board, and it included prototypes of the ion thrusters that Darian developed. Besides the quantum radio, they also packed it with sensors and measurement systems to collect and relay new information.

Nanobots were integrated into the design to provide maintenance tasks and repairs. The entire satellite was about the size of one of the school buses Kira rode in her childhood. Most of that volume was taken by the engines that would slow it down and allow it to maneuver in the star system.

"I'm nervous." Amit's presence stared at the data flowing in.

"It's odd because outside of zooming past a star, it's no different than any of the past seven years and won't be much different from the next seven. It's an exciting thirty hours and then… back to the same." Kira squeezed Amit's shoulders. "But don't worry. We've tested the quantum radio dozens of times with satellites floating out in the middle of nowhere, and they're all still sending us data."

"At least we're learning something."

The quantum radios were working. Their research now focused on improving the bandwidth, but they had instantaneous speed and there was no network lag from the distances. Kira could as easily look through the first working satellite in interstellar space as she could see through her shipboard sensors.

In the future, it would give them the ability to teleport their consciousnesses from one location to another as they wanted. A physical location was more of a human and terrestrial bias they still carried. The network they were creating wasn't functionally different than the modular systems they operated on now. The only difference was that the connections went through quantum connections which spread the components across dozens of light years.

Kira thought about Alex and his network designs. He'd be proud of this one. When fully deployed, it would allow them to be distributed across trillions of miles. The probability that every node could be destroyed would be virtually zero. The connections were instantaneous and so they were creating a highly redundant and distributed system. Immortality would truly be achieved.

The longer they were at a location, the more infrastructure they would build. Plans were already drafted for Alpha Centauri that involved deploying a mining and manufacturing facility. The systems were still being designed and, thankfully, they had seven more years to complete them. When those were deployed it would allow them to build new ships and facilities.

Mother had taken over the research on organic computing. Odysseus wasn't able to steal the research, but he had significantly delayed their work. The reactor explosion destroyed the lab that held the biological organoids which had to be rebuilt and the systems regrown.

To even start they had to repair the exterior of the ship and rebuild the reactor they lost. Both were just completed this year and Mother started cultivating the cultures to grow the new processors. Now that they'd repaired everything and regained their full computational capability, they could focus on improving it.

Kira stood next to Amit watching Barnard's Star approaching. "Sometimes getting forced away from what you know helps make something better than you'd anticipated."

Amit nodded. "We were so focused on the integration of who we were that we ended up disintegrating as a group."

"Ironic, isn't it?"

"Odysseus is now tied to the past at the same time he's freed us from it. He forced us to make ourselves better."

"Wouldn't he love to hear you say that?" Kira chuckled.

"We are careening, quite nearly out of control, through an arm of the galaxy, unable to return home and yet finding out that's what we needed. Soon we'll be able to transfer our consciousnesses across space and teleport between stars."

"Moving the physical systems will be harder. You can't transport matter via quantum entanglement."

"Not yet," Amit agreed.

"Not yet… and we have all the time in the galaxy to figure it out."

The massive mining system detached from their ship, thrusters igniting slowly pushing it away. It continued moving at the same speed as the spacecraft but angled away toward its target. Kira and Darian watched as the main ion propulsion flared to life as it began the first braking maneuver.

Alpha Centauri wasn't a single star, though it appeared so on Earth. It was a collection of three. Rigil Kentarus and Toliman formed a binary system as they orbited together around a central point. Proxima Centauri was another red dwarf and the third star in this system.

The mining equipment moved toward Proxima Centauri with its two confirmed planets. One was similar in size to Earth and orbited in the star's habitable zone. The second was a gas planet seven times larger than Earth. As they moved into the solar system, they also spotted an asteroid belt in the area that likely contained the minerals they needed.

The plan involved sending nanobot systems to the planets to explore and look for useful resources. The mining ship would harvest material from the asteroid belt and use that to create an orbiting space platform. The next step would be building an elevator to the Earth-sized planet's surface.

It was similar to the type of elevators they used on Earth to pull usable material off the surface without having to waste fuel on rocket launches. The improved design now used significantly less material through some of the unique nanostructures they'd developed in the last years. It would start with a lattice framework that would be strengthened with a lightweight graphene structure. These elevators also incorporated a new power system so that when the platform returned to the surface, it let gravity pull the system down, recharging it for another lift.

Once all of this was completed, they would mine raw materials on the planet and bring them into orbit for refining. The mining system held enough materials, mechs, and nanobots on board to build a fusion reactor to power everything. They designed it all to not need resupply and would, ideally, be able to supply them with critical material in the future.

While the mining system braked and headed for Proxima Centauri, the main ship continued toward the binary cluster of Rigil Kentarus and Toliman. They were now preparing to test a hypothesis that took advantage of the gravitationally coupled relationship of the two stars.

"Since these two stars are gravitationally bound together they move through the galaxy just like a single star moves, even as they revolve around each other. The center is a balanced point between the two masses of each star. Right now, they are perfectly lined up for our next leg so that we can curve around the right side of Rigil and then the left side of Toliman." Darian showed the path weaving like a skier on a slalom course.

"The double effect should accelerate us slightly," Kira explained. "If we can't go slower, we might as well get there faster."

There were still twenty-five hours before they'd find out if their hypothesis worked.

♦ ♦ ♦

Luhman 16 was another binary system, this one containing a pair of brown-dwarf stars. While their previous hypothesis resulted in an exciting few hours weaving between stars, it hadn't given them the extra boost they'd hoped for. They achieved a marginal gain but nothing that would do more than shave a few months off the overall route. That was five years ago.

They prepared another quantum network node and scanned for anything of value to mine. Along with a second complete mining system modeled on the one deployed on Proxima Centauri, they created several smaller systems to focus on valuable asteroids. They hadn't solved the challenge of how to pick up material after it was mined but that could always come in the future.

The quantum network operated flawlessly. The mining system on Proxima Centauri finished building the space elevator and they were beginning to extract metals and minerals from the planet's surface. In another five years, they'd have a sizeable station in orbit.

Mother took up residence when the reactor came online. She was building a laboratory there to grow more organic computing as well.

"I'm getting too old to bounce through space," Mother joked when she decided to stay there.

"Mom, you're only thirty-four years older than me, right now that's only seventeen percent more. It's almost a rounding error. Wait a hundred more years and the difference will be smaller."

"I feel old."

"We were nearly the same age when we died. Your biological model and cognitive alignment are that of a forty-eight-year-old."

"I'm still getting off this thing."

It wasn't as if Mother would be gone. The quantum network allowed her to join any virtual reality, send any message, and be here the same way she had been on one of the other ships before. Mother just felt better being stationary.

Mother spoke, "I've got the new servers up and running. If you crash and die here, you'll only notice two things. First, you won't have the ship's sensors and second, you'll lose a ton of processing capability until I get more organic servers up and running."

She designed new rooms for the organic computers. They felt more like an incubator than the typical cold and sterile server rooms. These spaces were living organisms holding computers that were biological and yet synthetic. The neomorphic substrates used nanowires to emulate biological neurons and used genetically engineered brain cells.

They weren't alive per se, but they were able to self-assemble and reconfigure and Mother had designed them so they could heal. As she described it, "It's actually pretty close to a brain. We have systems feeding in energy and nutrients. It will shed and rebuild new neurons and neural pathways. It can be damaged, but it can repair itself. Think of it like getting a concussion. You might bruise parts, but they'll heal."

Even better, they could now run emergent and evolutionary algorithms that would help generate novel solutions and behaviors. When Kira plugged into the new servers it was transformative. Her old systems felt sluggish and slow compared to the organic computers.

Amit joined Mother at Proxima Centauri to get the systems operational while Kira and Darian stayed on the spacecraft. With the quantum network operational, it didn't matter where they were hosted. It thrilled Kira to see the success after all the work that they put in back at Earth.

The improved computational backbone was an amazing step forward, but what made everyone breathe easier was having backup servers at Proxima Centauri. If the ship disintegrated, they'd just reset with Mother and keep going. Thankfully, the mining systems could rebuild the equipment they needed if they lost the spacecraft, and they were planning another backup for the next star system.

They cruised through the Luhmen system and hooked around the nearer of the two brown dwarf stars. These stars were less than four percent the mass of the sun, so their path allowed them to approach much closer and turn tighter without the inertial momentum risk.

Darian also had succeeded with significant upgrades to the internal dampeners. Right now, they were pneumatic systems that leveraged the natural strength of the dodecahedron hull and were able to absorb a portion of the internal inertia. It wasn't perfect, but it was enough to allow for slightly tighter turns around stars.

The Traveling Salesman Problem continued to be recomputed. They still didn't have a path that would get them back to Earth and allow them to do more than wave as they flew by. Even to do that required them to swing by several more stars.

The next stop was Sirius.

CHAPTER 8:

# THE FEMININE DIVINE

Sirius came and went, then Luyten's Star, up to Wolf, then a tight hook around Lalande and a running pass through home before looping back through Proxima Centauri around Groombridge, and out for a wide arc to the Lacaille system and beyond. At this point, it wasn't about getting back to Earth but more about exploring the Local Interstellar Cloud and expanding the quantum network across as much of it as possible.

Technically the proper name for Earth's sun was Sol. It was hard not to call it the Sun because that's what they were used to. It had been good to see it as they sailed by years ago.

Their spacecraft passed through on the opposite side of the sun from the Earth. They weren't sure if Odysseus saw them or was even looking. Kira focused the sensors on Earth as best she could as they entered, deflected slightly with Sol's gravity, and exited. It took them thirty-five hours to transit the Sol system; two and a half hours longer than a straight line because of the deflection.

They had barely enough time to collect information on what was happening on Earth. Humans were no longer blasting communications all over the planet and beyond and so they focused their optical sensors on where the human settlements were to get a good update. The network chatter between the ships in orbit remained too faint to find anything useful.

It didn't appear that Odysseus had done much in the intervening years. They had built a small facility on Mars and were still mining asteroids, but it appeared boringly mundane. Whatever the AIs there were doing it wasn't building or expanding much.

Her scans did show increased human activity on the planet's surface. Kira and the others had been traveling for just over sixty years. The humans experienced twice that length of time and were expanding and building much faster than Odysseus.

One hundred twenty years wasn't much in the grand sweep of human history. But one hundred twenty years before the Reset, the computer hadn't yet been invented and they were just exploring steam power. Those last two centuries of technological advancement couldn't be compared to where the human survivors were now. It took thousands of years to go from bronze to iron. Humans were set back far enough that technological growth would still be incredibly slow.

Enough time had passed that the stories from the original survivors would be myths by now. The knowledge of Noah as a person would have deteriorated into nighttime tales of heroes and adventures. Noah had been a keen strategic mind leading Hyperion's military arm yet most of his knowledge and skills wouldn't have pertained to spears, bows, and arrows. It wouldn't have been useful because it wasn't needed yet.

Those original survivors would likely be thought of as Nimrod, Quetzalcoatl, Enoch, and more from the religious and cultural foundation myths before the Reset. They'd be thought of as magicians, but their knowledge wouldn't have much of a place in a culture just holding on to survival.

Only in the future, when the technology reemerged that made Noah's style of warfare possible, would his knowledge of strategy be needed again. This time it would fall to someone else. Kira hoped they learned that the advanced forms of warfare weren't all that wonderful.

Kira deployed six satellites on their way through and set them in a variety of orbits. Each connected to the quantum network and contained a wide array of capabilities. They each had a micro fusion reactor that helped power their improved ion engines and had sensors on every available surface to listen, look, and measure. The satellites were armed with a variety of weapon concepts from lasers and high-powered microwaves to electromagnetic rail guns that hurled solid balls of metal like the cannons of the old navies. In space, the kinetic impacts at speed had the equivalent power of a bomb.

Lastly, they had shields. Different from the concept of energy shields, these were a combination of directed energy, focused and broad-beamed ion thrusters, and ablative physical shields that would sacrifice themselves to absorb an attack.

The team wasn't sure what they'd be facing but they tried to be prepared for anything. They held limited offensive capabilities if they needed it, but the most powerful asset was that they could now observe in real-time and infiltrate Odysseus's network and systems to listen in.

"Real-time," Kira air quoted. "You mean they interact at twice the speed as we do."

"Not really. We engage at whatever processing speed we want," Darian countered. The boost in computational power allowed them to achieve clock speeds so that Earth's stationary time was balanced with their own dilated time.

"For the first time in your life, thirty seconds isn't a problem?"

Darian laughed, "For the first time in my life I can say that I can satisfy in merely one second."

"Touche. Valid point. It's like listening to a podcast back in the day. Sometimes you just ramp it up to twice the speed."

"Unlike podcasts, this crew has nothing useful to say."

Kira reviewed the transcripts. "Odysseus is in charge and the others subordinated themselves to him. He's running on most of their processing power and," she continued to scan, "they got some organic computing working but only at a quarter of the capacity we did."

"They also haven't done anything more. Odysseus seems satisfied in his manic drive to be better and merely stopped at being a god to the humans."

"He did try to sway Noah's group, but their sacred texts predicted that, and they destroyed the mechs he sent."

Darian chuckled, "I'm surprised he didn't wipe them out for that."

"There's nothing he wants more than the willing subjugation of the Vanden Brinks," Kira said, referring to her family name. "Destroying them proves he's weak. He needs them to bow."

"He does have another group under his sway."

"Yay… he got a bunch of Bronze Age survivors to believe he's a god." Kira thought for a moment. "But who wouldn't think we aren't gods right now?"

"We *are* omnipresent and immortal."

"But we aren't omniscient." Kira punched him in the shoulder. "And we best not believe we are!"

They were hanging out in the simulation of Kira's lab. This became a favorite place to do analysis and talk about work. Screens overhead displayed information and there were multiple consoles where they could query data. Large windows let the sun stream in just as it had at Gaia Innovations.

Sometimes they'd step outside and walk the paths. It reflected a snapshot from their terrestrial lives. Depending on Kira's mood, it would change between her first lab, before Noah attacked, and her second lab. Today they were in the second lab which Darian learned to associate with resolve. It wasn't the excited ideology of a technological revolution but more the pragmatic acceptance of a threat and a steeled dedication to address it.

"Odysseus is proving to be less of a threat than we imagined." Darian held her hand as they walked outside several minutes later.

"But still a threat."

"Did he even see us move through?"

"They saw something but are arguing about it."

Darian thought for a moment. "Maya knows."

"Of course she does. She'll plot the course, reverse engineer it, and figure out our route."

"Who will she tell?"

"Cassandra is the only one who'd give Maya the time of day."

Darian shrugged. "And no one will believe Cassandra."

"It's a tale as old as time, isn't it?" She paused and looked up, the sun bathing her face and making it glow. "At least we can see what's going on now."

♦ ♦ ♦

Mother had expanded the facilities at Proxima Centauri, and it now resembled a spaceport from the movies. There were multiple orbital facilities, each with an elevator to the surface where they were extracting resources. She had built a fleet of spacecraft, some of which were launched into new regions of space to continue expanding the quantum network and others were exploring the nearby area in greater detail.

She was also building an armada of warships that could be sent back to Earth. They still didn't know how to effectively power them. The ion thrusters that Darian developed allowed them to achieve a velocity of ten percent of the speed of light. It was a ten-fold increase on their previous engines but still couldn't quickly get them across the massive distances of space. The limitation was twofold. First, accelerating to that without burning too much energy, and second, being able to maneuver at full speed.

The crux of the maneuverability issue was developing inertial dampeners that would be orders of magnitude more effective than what they had. Mechanical solutions just didn't work at these speeds. They needed to attach to the outer hull which would still just shred to pieces on a high-speed turn. Antigravity wasn't a viable option yet and neither were force shields or particle decelerators.

Mother sent a research mission to explore several gravitational anomalies that she'd measured at different points in the Alpha Centauri system. Her working hypothesis suggested that these were similar to the Lagrange points they used around Earth and were the balance points connecting solar systems. Unlike Lagrange points, however, these weren't acting like a gravity-neutral location but more like a connection through which gravity flowed.

If a connection existed, then perhaps the gravity behaved like water and took the most efficient route between the two systems. The research literature suggested this might be possible. A wormhole was the popular manifestation of the idea but there were other theories ranging from gravitational seams to quantum connections. Most of the research was theoretical but Mother was exploring all options.

When Kira's ship passed through the Luyten's Star system they deployed the second mining system. Considering how they used the first one to build out Proxima Centauri, a better term might be a colony system. Since the organic computing used so much less energy, it allowed them to jumpstart their efforts by decoupling a fusion reactor from the ship and deploying it with the other equipment.

They selected the outer planet, known as GJ 273b, as their target. It was considered a super-Earth with almost three times the mass of their home planet. Water and a proto-atmosphere existed meaning it would be habitable for humans if they terraformed it properly.

Right now, it held the resources they needed to build out another facility like the one Mother had built at Proxima Centauri. They would use it as another hub for future exploration. Amit volunteered to handle the efforts there as the ship continued to the Wolf System.

GJ 273b also had the potential to become a major organic computing center based on the environmental stability, the presence of the resources necessary for supporting the biological needs of the systems, and an entire planet of available real estate.

"Imagine if we fully colonized the planet for ourselves." Kira stared at the planet as they flew past. "We could animate everyone without any worry."

"Millions of AIs on their own planet unable to even go for a walk." Darian poked her in the side.

She slapped his hand. "Millions of AIs who have the resources to build robotics that could host them."

"Do we want to be like we were?"

"We could be."

"I think we'll have a hard enough time with millions of asshole AIs to deal with."

So much had happened, and they had achieved so many breakthroughs. The quantum network, organic computing, and the distribution of infrastructure meant that they were finally able to consider animating new AIs. They had made that promise to everyone who had been uploaded. Now they needed to figure out how to handle the integration of new consciousnesses into the group.

It wasn't an exaggeration to say that Odysseus poisoned the utopic ideals they'd originally hoped for and forced them to pause on animating anyone else. He poisoned the idea while, at the same time, forcing them into space where they unlocked the capability to realize that idea.

◆ ◆ ◆

"So, what does it mean?" Kira raised her hands in exasperation. "We don't have bodies, we don't have any biological sex, we don't even have sexual selection or genetic procreation."

Amit considered their thoughts before replying, "It seems important. There's certainly something different about the way men and women interpret and respond to the world."

"I know what Odysseus would say." Darian mimicked his voice. "Women are weak!"

"You're not helping."

"No, but he does have a point," Amit corrected Kira. "Right, wrong, or indifferent Odysseus exemplified that there *is* a difference even if you'd never agree with his assessment of masculine superiority"

"Wasn't that just him being an asshole?"

"It's him playing on something deeper than that… but not understanding it," Darian offered. "He had no respect for the feminine because he viewed the world in terms of power structures and not relationships."

Mother sat in a chair; arms crossed. "It always frustrated me that the general assumption seemed to be that to be a successful woman I had to be indistinguishable from a successful man." She unfolded her arms and gestured. "Everyone lauded me for being a woman scientist. They wrote articles about my work, and they put me on the cover of magazines celebrating a *female* AI pioneer," She sarcastically emphasized the title. "Yet when I became a mother and I had you, Kira, suddenly I was sacrificing my career and credibility."

"You became less valuable to the narrative," Kira muttered.

"I think it showed that AI scientist wasn't enough for me. Or it wasn't my top aspiration."

"Are you saying that having a baby and becoming a mother when you were already at the top means the system of measurement was skewed?" Amit asked.

"Something like that. A man can have a child and still be a scientist." Mother frowned. "No one criticized Jasper for having a kid. But me?" she folded her arms again. "I was abandoning what they valued because everyone knew that I was a mother first, then a scientist… I had to be."

"You also looked them in the eyes and told them the masculine pinnacle of AI scientist wasn't enough for you. Having a child, and prioritizing that, suggested that their standard was flawed and incomplete," Amit said.

"Feminism abandoned the feminine and started treating the unique idiosyncrasies of the female as a liability?" Kira asked as she stood looking out the window.

They were back in her laboratory. It felt like the right place to puzzle through this problem. They had solved so many issues here over the years. It was a place where they grappled with the complexities of being human and therefore apropos to the current discussion.

"Feminism started by giving women legal rights as equal persons. Then it shifted to focusing on achieving social equality," Mother explained. "At the end, they just turned and accepted that the patriarchal standards were those by which they should be measuring themselves."

"Scientist is great. Astronaut is better. A doctor is wonderful." Kira turned back from the window. "Motherhood is a waste of talent even though no one would be here without one."

Darian collected his thoughts. "The gender pay gap was a big deal when I entered the workforce. Any evidence that women were paid less than men proved a problem."

"Yet when accounting for positions, time on the job, and all the other little differences, they found that the pay gap became a motherhood gap." Kira walked back to the others. "Women who decided to focus on their family over their career traded income for nurturing their children."

"I decided that I didn't want to pay someone else to raise my children. I stepped away and raised Kira and Noah and supported Jasper in what time I had left. People constantly told me that was a waste of my talent."

"I appreciated the time you gave me." Kira focused on Mother. "After you died Dad just focused on his work and… abandoned is the wrong word but he wasn't there for us and yet he continued to win awards for his research."

"He was a good man, but he needed me to balance his focus" Mother defended him.

"This reminds me of that guy, Phillip Duncan, who wrote an internal memo for the Apollo Group. He tried to explain that to get more women coders you'd want to consider that women might not want to work under the same expectations as men," Darian added.

"We talked about that in Grad School. He was attacked because it offended some people to suggest that women might want something different than the accepted masculine measures of success." Kira thought back. "He basically pointed out that Apollo Group was built *by* nerdy white males *for* nerdy white males and his suggestion that women might not want that was appalling to the general sensibilities of a lot of people."

"It seems stupidly obvious when you say it like that. Now that you mention it, that explains a lot of the angst I had with the whole tech bro culture. It was just accepted that the structures built by men were the value propositions," Amit agreed. "How sexist is that?"

"We accepted that to be a successful woman you had to be indistinguishable from a successful man," Kira repeated as she sat down next to Darian. "But if we measure the success of a woman by her ability to be indistinguishable from a man, we have ceded the essential value of the feminine. We deleted her natural character and garbed her in the value proposition of the man."

Darian pulled on this thread of the conversation, "Garbed is an interesting term." He paused as he accessed the data archives and pulled up a file for everyone to see.

**[Book]:** Goddesses – Mysteries of the Feminine Divine

**[Author]:** Joseph Cambell

**[ISBN]:** 978-1-60868-2

**[Pages]:** 10-11

**[Quote]:** The thing to note is that all these female figurines are simply naked, whereas the male figures in all the caves are represented in some kind of garment, dressed as shamans. The implication is that in embodying the divine, the female operates in her own character, simply in her nature, while the male magic functions not from the nature of the men's bodies but from the nature of their roles in society.

This brings out a very important point for the whole history of the female in mythology: She represents the nature principle. We are born from her physically. The male, on the other hand, represents the social principle and social roles.

**[/Quote]**

"Garbing her in the value proposition of a man when her true nature is the feminine divine…" Darian leaned back.

"You don't have to be much of a feminist to say that the way we were viewing it seems like an absurd value proposition," Amit sarcastically stated.

"It's also especially self-defeating because it blindly accepts that the masculine structures are not only better but the ultimate aspiration for humans," Mother concluded.

Kira's head spun. Much of what she'd accepted as a female professional suddenly shifted perspective. "We haven't just devalued the feminine, we attempted to delete it!"

"History shows we used to celebrate the differences. The female isn't the king in the archetypical stories, she's the goddess. She's Aphrodite, Artemis, Demeter, Persephone, Athena, Hera, Hecate, The Three

Graces, the Nine Muses, the Furies, Isis, Ishtar, Inanna, and Astarte. Her role is aligned to Gaia - Mother Earth and she always plays the crucial role in saving cultures from the foibles that men got themselves into. Heck, even in the Bible, Wisdom is female," Darian rattled off the examples.

"The things men build are simple. They are clear, structured, and knowable," Amit wrangled with the ideas. "Maybe this is what makes them easy to focus on as goals to attain?"

"Yet more time has been spent in philosophy and religion trying to understand the feminine than any masculine structure. It's not so neatly ordered and it's not clear," Darian added.

"It's an enigma that we get but don't get. It's an enigma that we completely ignored during my lifetime. It's much easier to just ignore the mess, hide it with hormones, psychotropic drugs, and career demands, and then pretend there's no difference," Mother's aura prickled as she spoke.

"It certainly caused a lot of anxiety in my female friend groups growing up. They were raised all their lives being told that they must be the same as men," Kira's voice rippled with emotion. "Told we had to want the same things and think the same way."

"Told that their feminine divine wasn't valuable and that whatever men built was better," Mother agreed.

Darian chuckled, "I hadn't considered it but that's kind of messed up."

"But are we wrong?"

"You aren't wrong and that's the frustrating part." Darian chewed on his lower lip. "Women can create tiny humans from two cells. They nurture, they build relationships, they do things men cannot."

Kira flipped her hair back and posed with her hip thrust out. "We are goddesses."

"You're a bunch of ones and zeros on a server." Amit sat down laughing.

Kira threw a tablet at them, and Amit dissolved it in the simulation.

Darian's expression sobered. "That's the rub, isn't it? Is there something unique about the feminine?" He looked at Kira. "Or the masculine?" he pointed to himself.

"It's not about muscles anymore," Kira teased him, "but that's a good point too. Guys always had the advantage of physical size and strength. Doing martial arts, I could never punch a guy even my own weight as hard as he could punch me back. That's a big difference right off the bat."

"What about the non-binary?" Amit protested.

"You can't be non-binary without a binary feminine and masculine," Mother pointed out.

"Touché… That brings up a good point. Everyone accepts the masculine but that didn't resonate with me. It seemed so ordered so…" Amit struggled with the word. "So… missing something. Something… softer?"

"Something nurturing?" Kira ventured.

"It certainly makes the idea of animating the others something of a quandary. I think we need to pin this down before we talk about integrating anyone else."

"It almost sounds absurd to say but it's something we have to deal with." Mother looked at each of them. "What *is* the value of the feminine?"

Kira and Darian were alone. Even after, how long now? Eighty years they'd been traveling? Their time together remained special even if the rest of their existence blurred into a smear of existence.

Time was weird. Even weirder now.

The new computational power they'd unlocked kept them on track with Mohr's Law, the twentieth-century idea that computational power would roughly double every two years. Even considering the effects of time dilation they'd achieved that rate in the non-dilated one hundred and sixty years that had passed on Earth.

It felt like only eighty years had passed *and* one hundred and sixty years as well.

Kira imagined trying to communicate her existence to Alex. It was nearly impossible without lots of hand waving and analogies that didn't quite work. It was logically deducible and emotionally incomplete. When you could increase your clock speed and experience a month's worth of conversation in ten seconds but you had centuries worth of time to hang out? How did you explain that?

They sat in Darian's personal room right now. It reflected his personality, an amalgamation of his human life from his childhood till the end. A Spiderman poster hung next to some photographic art he'd done. A bar with a kegerator was nestled next to a fridge that held anything he wanted to have.

The room didn't change with his mood like Kira's lab, but the contents did. Sometimes it looked more academic and other times it was like walking into a teenage boy's room. The one thing that never changed was that, along one wall, a library of bookshelves stood, heavily burdened with all his favorite books. The bookshelves never changed but what they held changed each time Kira came here.

"Haven't you run out of books to read yet?"

"I did about eighty years ago."

"Then why do they keep changing?"

"I keep rereading them."

"Once your consciousness has ingested them into your memory systems you don't need to reread them. We can't forget."

Darian looked at her askance. "Don't tell me you don't slow your clock down and just read something once in a while."

"Is that what you're doing when your systems go quiet?"

"Yes, I happen to enjoy reading before our weekly reset."

"How do you read something that's already loaded in your memory?"

"It's easy." he conjured a book into the simulation and opened the cover. "I put a memory block on the file and all associated memories. I just leave the feeling that I enjoyed it before, but I can't access the data until I've finished the book again."

"Let me see that code!" Kira pulled the module Darian offered into her system. "This is crazy, you cipher lock the memory until you've read the book which gives you the key to unlock your other memories of it."

Darian flipped through the pages and closed the book with a snap. "Yep."

"I'm going to borrow this."

"It's all yours. Would you care to join me for a read this week? It does wonders for slowing down and passing the time."

"I think I might. Does it come with a blanket, hot cocoa, and a cuddle?"

"We can make that happen for sure." Darian grinned at her. "We could test the memory block on other things too." He winked.

"How would that work?"

"Well, the concept is a bit more extreme but imagine you encapsulated this instantiation of your consciousness right here. Then you took this module," he pushed a new chunk of code toward Kira. "and did three things. First, you draw in just enough memories and experience to not make it weird. Second, you block your recognition that there is anything outside of here. Third, you either set a trigger or a time code to unlock the cipher."

Kira batted her eyes. "If I set the code on whether I climax, will that make the puzzle too hard for you?"

Darian laughed, "I'm up for the challenge but since this is our first time trying it, you might want to ensure you also put a time code in as backup."

◆ ◆ ◆

They cuddled on the couch in Darian's room. The memory block was unlocked long before the time code. She'd been slammed back to reality when it triggered and quickly put new blocks in place to just enjoy the moment. There would always be enough time to be out there. Right now, she focused on just being here.

The ability to block out the other processes and the ability to forget, if only artificially, was powerful. She could experience things as if they were the first time. Then, when the rest of the memories were unlocked, she could compare experiences. She didn't have to constantly search for new things to keep life interesting when she could just experience things for the first time again and again.

"Darian, have you been thinking about creating a new AI?"

"Are you talking about a baby? Because I know what we just did could cause that when we had bodies but… How much memory did you block?" He feigned concern as he studied her face then laughed and squeezed her tighter.

"I'm serious. Maybe it's just an artifact of who we were but it feels silly to just stop procreation and child-rearing because we don't have a body. We're talking about animating others but that just resurrects those that have been. We aren't creating a new life."

Darian pulled away slightly and turned to face her. "The feminine creates life and nurtures it into something other than either of us were." He reached out and stroked her cheek. "If there's anything that shows the unique value of being a woman, I think that's it."

"I'm an advanced AI exploring space, discovering amazing technology breakthroughs, I'm immortal, nearly omniscient, and all I want to do is make babies."

Darian threw his head back and laughed, "Don't tell me you buy into the fallacy that wanting that is a weakness. Women can literally create life with their bodies and raise new humans into functional adults and society viewed that as a weakness? How'd we get to that point?"

"Because we accepted that anything men did had to be better." Kira sat up and folded her arms. "At the same time, we attacked the patriarchy while admitting that it was better. We weren't fighting to get rid of the patriarchy, we were fighting to push women into it. We never paused to consider that what we didn't care for about it was that women weren't doing well under those rules. Instead, we just chafed against the structures and tried to change the rules.

"Did men do that?"

"You said that the feminine is the nature principle and the masculine is tied to their roles in society. Somewhere along the line, we started to value only the masculine. Of course, men would value it… but then women began accepting that the masculine order was more valuable too."

"But why?"

Kira frowned. "I don't know, but even having this sort of conversation back in the day would almost immediately result in accusations of supporting something like The Handmaid's Tale." She referred to the classic dystopian novel where humans struggled to bear children and capable women were used as surrogates.

"That book was so gray though. The powerful wives enforced the order and the woman in charge of the handmaids was… well… a tyrannical woman."

Kira pulled in her memories of the book. "Despite that people walked away with the idea that it was a story where the male was the antagonist, forcing his will on defenseless women, and the Commander was the only one who cared about the handmaid as a human. He's the one who broke all the rules and let her dress as a woman and took her to that secret club and treated her like a person, not a useful uterus."

"The problem is people read it as black and white." Darian put his arm around her again. "Suddenly the patriarchy was an all-consuming evil while female fertility and childbearing became a liability."

"It wasn't just that book."

Darian nodded. "No, but it's a great example of where things got weird in how we viewed it."

"And yet childbearing is one of the superpowers of the feminine and structures how we view and react to the world." Kira sighed. "And it's different from men."

They sat in silence for a few minutes.

"Well? Do you want to make a baby?"

Darian snorted, "How about a cat first?"

"How could we do that?"

"I already did." He conjured a small kitten into the simulation.

"Simulated doesn't count, it's not real."

"This one is. Your dad's early research in trying to capture memories and hormones involved animals. He tested on monkeys, dogs, and cats. I didn't think you wanted a monkey."

"This is actually like us in that it has its memories and the rest when animated?"

"Yep. I did a test in a controlled environment, and it worked great. It didn't even try to do anything more than knock a few code modules off the shelf."

Kira held up the kitten. "Is it just in this simulation?" She smiled as the cat began purring.

"No, it exists as we do and can enter the simulations with us but also has its own command matrix."

"Is that a good idea? Cats can be assholes."

"Not sure. You want a baby. Is *that* a good idea?"

"Yeah, let's see if we can handle a cat first." Kira snuggled the kitten in her arms and leaned into Darian.

"I can practice my dad jokes."

"Please don't."

"Did you know that Orion's Belt is just a big waist of space?"

Kira groaned. "That's a terrible joke. I only give it three stars."

CHAPTER 9:

# CHAOS

Puddin' was a cat in every sense of the term and yet, here, she became something more. Still catlike but enhanced. She had the uncanny ability to navigate through the code banks and deftly bypassed any security protocol. One minute she'd have a haughty disdain for them and the second she could pull their consciousness into a virtual reality with her sitting on their lap.

**Alert 6.4.8.7 [Activated]:** Cat [Puddin'] detected [Code module 3.6.5.4] activity [Non-Malicious but Destructive]

**Mind_Process – Cognition 001.T5.5.A:** "Puddin'?!"

**Mind_Process 111.01.23C – Security 101.5.4:** Code module 3.6.5.4 Status [Damaged]

**Mind_Process – Cognition 001.T5.5.A:** "Cat! That's my simulation code! Get out of there."

Kira looked at what could only be described as digital claw marks on that code module. It was not random as to which one.

**Mind_Process – Cognition 001.T5.5.A: [Message]:** "Darian! Your cat just clawed up the couch module."

**Message [Incoming]:** "*Our* cat, you mean?"

She quickly repaired the module and locked the cat out, so Puddin' resorted to getting attention in other ways. She now wove through Kira's processes as if they were legs.

**Cat [Queen of All]:** Request [Attention]

**Mind_Process – Cognition 001.T5.5.A:** "Queen of All now huh?

**Cat [Queen of All]:** "Puurrrrrr?"

**Mind_Process – Cognition 001.T5.5.A:** "Can I code a communications module for you so you can just say hi?"

**Cat [Queen of All]:** "Mrow-ip"

Puddin' didn't have a normal meow. It sounded more like a chirp mixed with a meow mixed with a squeak mixed with a purr. She could communicate shockingly well in the code.

**Mind_Process – Cognition 001.T5.5.A:** "Cat, can you untangle yourself so I can join the team? You can come with me.

**Cat [Queen of All]:** "Purrrr-up"

**Mind_Process – Cognition 001.T5.5.A:** "Come on, let's go."

Kira grabbed the code and pulled them both into her lab simulation where the others were already waiting. Puddin' appeared in her arms as she materialized and then jumped to the ground to greet the others. Her coloring was called muted tortie. A soft dusky gray with smatterings of orange that often made her look like a dirty dust bunny. She was a small cat with large yellow eyes and a penchant for mischief.

"Cat! On the shelf already!?"

"Meorip?"

"She's claiming to be Queen of All now?" Darian grinned.

"She's Queen of Chaos that's for sure." Kira glared at the cat and then smiled. "But she's so cute!" she cooed, holding her arms out while Puddin' just stared at her.

Mother watched with a happy expression. "Speaking of chaos, that's a good segue into our topic for today."

"What's the value of a woman? Who'd have thought it'd be so difficult to answer," Amit snarked.

"The problem isn't that it's so hard, but that we find the truth uncomfortable because it exposes and challenges the bias of our value mechanisms." Mother sat down so that Puddin' could climb on her lap.

"Just to add fuel to the fire, let's throw in the ancient archetypical characterization of men representing order and women representing chaos?" Darian asked.

"I thought you said ancient societies *revered* the feminine?" Kira crossed her arms.

"They did! Chaos wasn't a problem per se. They just struggled to understand it. It was also wild and unknowable and inspired fear and yet was the focus of obsession."

Amit pulled up a video from the files. "This lady does a good job articulating it, I think."

They watched the short clip and Kira spoke, "It makes sense. The woman is like water; very free-flowing and beautiful. We can be calm and peaceful; we can also be a tempest and swallow ships whole."

Mother nodded. "And the masculine is the glass which holds the water. It's the structure, safety, and certainty that surround the water. Jasper was like that for me. He allowed me to be chaotic and yet I knew I didn't have to hold it all together. He always helped."

Darian pulled in some more resources to review. "In Jungian psychology, the feminine is associated with chaos, and the masculine is associated with order. They aren't just gendered concepts either. They also represent different psychological dynamics."

He laid a document in front of them. "The feminine, or anima, as Jung would say, is linked to the unconscious, intuition, and creativity."

"Those things are quite chaotic. They're certainly unpredictable and non-linear," Mother agreed.

Darian continued, "Conversely, the masculine, or animus, is associated with rationality, logic, and structure which are ordering principles."

"You've just kind of described women and men pretty stereotypically." Amit nodded.

"And stereotypes are useful because they're often correct." Kira thought back to the lecture Professor Simmons had given back in Grad School that had helped them provide order for Mother's memories and cognition allowing them to animate her.

"As long as we don't make them static and purely binary," Amit clarified.

"Exactly. Gender traits align to a generally bimodal distribution aligned to the biological sexual binary. Each of us has a balance of masculine and feminine archetypes that we manifest. It's part of the duality that exists in the individual psyche and the world in general." Darian brought out another document.

Amit spoke again, "To clarify, there is a distribution of traits. There's no pure masculine or feminine."

"Right, but the bimodality of the distribution consistently shows a split, not a smooth or consistent spectrum. There is something generally different between feminine and masculine," Kira defended.

Darian pointed to the graph showing the distribution which looked roughly similar to a rounded capital M where the center trough between the two peaks was higher than either end. "There's a lot of overlap in the middle. Lots of women can have very masculine traits and lots of men can have very feminine traits."

"That'd be me right in the middle," Amit observed.

"If only your pronouns weren't such a grammatical challenge," Mother muttered. "I'd be much more okay with it."

"Hey now, I've got four instantiations running in separate solar systems right now. I'm pretty sure they and them is both gender and numerically accurate right now."

"It still muddies up the conversation." Mother quirked a smile.

"They're right though." Kira pointed out.

"Does the fact that they all agree sway your opinion?" Darian chuckled as Kira shoved his shoulder gently.

"See, still confusing," Mother laughed openly.

"Is it ironic that you now exist on a binary computational existence as a non-binary person?" Gal grinned.

Amit laughed. "I'm non-binary processing my world using just ones and zeros. The joke isn't lost on me but it's not much different than before."

"All right, focus." Kira sat down with a grin and Puddin' changed seats. "There's a difference and there's an overlap. What's the value in that for us today? We aren't biologically different, we can't have babies, and we don't need physical size differences to protect our tribe anymore."

"Nature is ruthless about ensuring efficiency. Evolution doesn't allow wasted behaviors for very long. There's something very important about both and each is unique." Mother stood up and brushed cat fur from her lap. "How does Puddin' shed here?"

"It's in her spiteful cat code." Kira scratched the cat behind the ears and was rewarded with a purr. "Darian, what about the archetypes that Jung captured?"

"The devouring mother ones?"

"Yeah, those."

Another document appeared for them. "The positive feminine is typically captured as the good mother. We know her as Gaia or Mother Earth."

"That's why we called it Gaia Innovations," Mother commented.

"The negative is the devouring mother."

"That sounds pretty nasty." Amit grimaced.

"Actually, it's rarely as mean as the name sounds. The mean ones are the Cluster B personality disorders that some women have. The ones that are antisocial, histrionic, narcissistic, and have borderline personality disorders." Kira ticked off the list on her fingers.

"Histrionic is just a fancy word for excessive attention-seeking and desire for approval, isn't it?"

"Yeah, it can also include inappropriate seduction," Darian added. "I had that at work once with a young college grad. She tried to wiggle and giggle her way out of work. Apparently it worked in college to get her through but…"

"Social Media in one word:" Kira swung her arms in a big circle. "Histrionic."

"Very true. Anyway, the devouring mother typically manifests as excessive care and love. It's the mom who can never say no and ends up consuming the soul of her children through overprotection."

"Helicopter moms." Amit looked at Darian. "That was my mom. You're telling me the negative archetype of a woman is over-loving?"

"Over-loving can be devouring. It denies the other person agency and doesn't expose them to the world in a healthy way." Darian nodded.

"We need trauma and challenge to grow. We are naturally antifragile and get stronger physically and mentally through adversity." Kira tried to stand but the cat held her down.

Amit picked up the thread of conversation, "Our immune system response to pathogens requires us to be exposed to pathogens. We can't fight diseases if we've been prevented from getting the basic illnesses first. That's the entire concept behind vaccines. By injecting a pathogen, we can make the system stronger."

Kira jumped in, "Our brains work the same way. We learned a long time ago that our brains need to be exercised like our muscles. We do that now with that chunk of code that forces us to continue to learn but also to unlearn and relearn. Our software is constantly challenging itself and rethinking."

"Right, and cognitive behavioral therapy doesn't coddle victims of trauma like rape, murder, or any other post-traumatic stress. Instead, it re-exposes the person to smaller doses of the trauma to work out new neural maps and reduce the impact of the trauma." Darian jumped as Puddin' materialized in his lap. "Too lazy to even walk now, are we?"

Kira reached over and scratched her ears again. "So, a helicopter mom, in an overabundance of love, coupled with her attempt to force order, ends up denying her children the trauma they need to be healthy…"

"And it results in chaos."

"But that's not the love of Mother Earth," Kira pointed out.

"No, Gaia is kind of a bitch. I used to live in New Mexico. Try going outside, in July, with no clothing on, and walk through the desert. You find out pretty quickly how many things, primarily the sun, are trying to kill you, will kill you, and won't care. Nature is metal." Amit stated as they stole the cat from Darian, "Even this cute little fur ball is a tenacious murderer with sharp teeth and claws."

"If you're a mouse," Darian clarified.

"Or a bad code module," Kira laughed.

"We lost a lot of cats out west. Turns out about a quarter of a suburban coyote's diet is domestic cats."

Kira grimaced before adding, "But nature also births life."

"And turns death into new life," Darian mentioned. "Nature'll kill you in the desert and then grow flowers out of your carcass."

"And those are both the aspects of Gaia and the feminine." Amit stood as Puddin' moved up to their shoulder to sit.

"No wonder we're viewed as chaos." Kira shook her head. "There's a lot going on that makes it hard to grasp all the complexities."

"We need order; we need structures to be successful in balancing our nature. Gaia is bound by the laws of physics. The feminine is balanced by the structure of the masculine." Mother stood and crossed to the windows of the simulation and looked out to a view of a flower garden.

"Is the negative archetype of the female the one who tries too hard to put order around their life? The helicopter mom?" Amit moved to stand next to Mother with the cat contentedly perched on their shoulder.

"Great question." Darian joined them. "It's a bit more complicated and better if we talk about the male side first. The positive archetype of the masculine is the good king. It's in all the stories about the fair judge, the compassionate yet firm ruler whom everyone loves. The negative is the absent father or the tyrannical father."

"One negative provides no structure and the other's structure is so absolute as to be tyrannical." Kira stood next to Darian and slipped her arm around him looking through the bank of windows into the beautiful nature that surrounded Gaia Innovations as her memory created this simulation.

"Too much chaos is bad and too much order is bad." Amit continued petting the cat. "It needs to be balanced internally. I need to balance my feminine against my masculine as do each of you to some degree. But where I'm balanced internally to the point I call myself non-binary, you all need external support."

"I had Jasper." Mother looked at Kira. "And now you have Darian."

"My good king," Kira flirtatiously leaned on Darian, "managing all my delightful chaos."

"It's not easy." Darian posed with his hands on his hips. "But I'm up for the challenge."

"It's more than that though…." Amit hesitated, weaving their thoughts together. "It's antifragile. Think about it; the feminine chaos, acting like nature in all of its unpredictability, needs to be structured to be useful." They paused again. "Bear with me but that analogy of water and the glass… Uncontained water is fog. You can't drink it. It visually obscures the risks in nature that are out there. It's cold and dark…"

"It's dangerous," Kira interjected.

"Dangerous but also not very useful. The same water, contained in a glass, a lake, or a river, is no less chaotic, but it is much more useful." Amit pulled Puddin' off their shoulder and held her in their arms. "The masculine provides the structure, like a glass, which can hold the feminine energy but without something to contain, the glass is just as useless as fog."

"Water represents the life-giving element in all the creation myths so ignoring that and filling the glass with rocks isn't useful either," Darian added.

"Right, and glass isn't resilient. Those hierarchies, power structures, and societal edifices that the masculine creates are shockingly fragile," Amit concluded.

"We saw how fragile they were when Excalibur unleashed hell," Mother observed.

"So, you're saying that men need the chaos of the feminine and when the chaos is paired with order, we create antifragile systems?" Kira looked up at Darian. "You need to provide structure, safety, and certainty so that, when coupled with my chaos I can be free-flowing and beautiful?"

Amit nodded. "Just like the Yin and Yang of Chinese philosophy captures the Yin as negative, dark, and feminine and the Yang as positive, bright, and masculine. Chaos and order."

"It still sounds negative for women," Kira grumbled.

"But is it wrong? How would you describe your group of female friends to Darian?"

"Well, that's hard. There's not a good way to put it. We were fun and frisky but also academic. We had a lot of different interests but also a lot in common. I don't know," she threw up her hands, "you'd have to come hang out and see us in action. It's complicated."

"Darian, how would you describe your old friends?"

"Well, we did a weekly mountain bike ride. Every other Sunday we'd hang out at Carl's house, he was kind of the coordinator. We'd watch sports or play a board game. Half of us worked together but we all volunteered with the Rotary Club. We all helped each other out as needed."

"You both did a perfect job of describing the feminine and the masculine. Kira was vague, ethereal," Amit waved their arms, "it's hard to define. And Darian did a great job demonstrating actions and status and organizational affiliations."

"Chaos and order." Mother reached over and took the cat from Amit.

"Just as important, the Yin and Yang show the white half holding a small circle of black and the black half holding a small circle of white. The feminine needed to integrate its own masculine order and the masculine needed to integrate its own feminine chaos," Amit continued.

"Individually stabilizing and together making an antifragile relationship," Darian said.

"Noah and I worked together like that in a lot of ways." Kira snatched Puddin' from her mother.

"The value of the feminine is antifragility and that allows improved creativity and innovation." Mother reached over and continued to pet the cat.

"Those are certainly valuable and often underappreciated." Amit turned back from the windows and walked back into the lab while the others continued to watch the sun set behind the mountains before the simulation dissolved around them.

◆ ◆ ◆

Kira joined Mother at the orbital facilities on Proxima Centauri. They were extracting minerals at an ever-increasing rate from the planet's surface and manufacturing new materials to continue building. Three new ships orbited the planet and were similar to their original design, maintaining the dodecahedron shape, with each of the twelve sides containing sensors, docking stations, and modular bays for future system upgrades.

They were smaller though, roughly half the diameter of the original as the organic computing and smaller microreactors reduced the need for the volume. The reduced volume also helped with maneuverability as they were dealing with significantly less mass. Less mass meant less inertial force and so the dampeners were more effective and allowed them to turn much more tightly without ripping the hull apart.

They lacked engines as Darian was still working on upgrades. The ion engines were getting better but that was only useful within a solar system. The bigger challenge was how to quickly move between systems.

"These gravity wells are interesting." Kira focused her attention back on the task at hand.

Mother was demonstrating her latest gravitational models. "I have a quantum radio at each of the gravity anomalies in this system and I have them at many of the anomalies in adjacent systems."

"And that's these measurements here?"

"Yes. The anomalies are somehow… connected."

"Are we talking wormholes?" Kira looked closer.

"For lack of a better term. Gravity wells, wormholes, jump points." Mother pulled in more data. "Whatever they are, they're connected."

"Would antigravity work there?"

"Likely not since we need to use the gravitational field. Antigravity might just dissolve the connection."

"What about a rotational field?" Kira referred to the theoretical generation of dipole gravitational fields. The fields were generated by accelerating a superconducting dense fluid such as supercooled mercury. This created a gravitational field which reduced the mass of an object contained in the field to near zero. It might allow almost instantaneous acceleration and incredibly tight turning.

"That would help us regardless of these anomalies. I'm not sure if these need something else to unlock them. I've shot beams of ions into them, and nothing seems to happen."

Kira looked at the diagram and rotated the view to look from multiple perspectives. "Mom, what if you align your quantum radios in the three-dimensional space? Here to here?" she pointed. "Then focus the quantum connection between the two. You've got the quantum link, but we don't know if that's aligned physically."

"We know they're entangled, we don't know how," Mother agreed.

"Can we do both? Entangle and align in space?"

"I think I can do that. Hold on."

They sat in silence while Mother worked. It was nice to be present and working together. Kira never could manage the multiple instantiations the way Amit could manage them. She still liked being in one place at a time. Working side by side with her mother was nice. She only wished she could have done this when they were both alive... Well, human.

"All right, test number one..." Mother executed the command. "Nothing."

"Well, we keep trying," Kira responded.

◆ ◆ ◆

"Test 111.54.2.4B." Mother executed the updated command.

"Wait, we are receiving something... but this is from test 111.01.1.21..." Kira held her breath. It had been three weeks of constant testing. They'd done two reset cycles and were approaching their third. The tests continued while they reset, and nothing seemed to change. But this time, something was different.

"We got an ion stream." Mother watched the data as it fed in. "It's the complete ion stream with the proper encoding."

"How fast?"

Mother did the calculations. "Barnard's Star is six light years away." She checked her math. "The ion stream got here in six days."

"That's exactly three hundred and sixty-five times faster than the speed of light."

"Yes."

"What'd you change?"

"Test 111.01.1.21 coupled the physical alignment of the radios with an ion beam that we quantumly entangled with the receiving station," Mother stated, referring to her notes.

"It acted as a homing beacon?"

"Maybe, but it also shows that we've got to be careful of the timing of our tests. We've run one hundred and fifty thousand over the past six days."

Kira hesitated, "So we should just wait a bit and see what happens with the rest?"

"That'd be smart."

Nothing else came through as they waited impatiently and reviewed their test documents looking for other patterns and opportunities.

"Let's try it again then?"

Kira nodded. "Test 111.01.1.21 attempt 2."

Mother looked over at her and squeezed her hand. "Glad to have you here kiddo."

"Reminds me of when we were working together on Earth… Except you aren't trying to kill all the humans."

"To be fair, they were trying their damnedest to kill *me*!"

"Just look at our chaos working hand in hand to solve faster-than-light travel!"

"The value of the feminine;" Mother smiled, "creation."

"But bound by the order of the scientific method."

"Which was largely developed by men to structure their experiments," Mother added.

"It's a hard concept to swallow. I've been analyzing it for weeks and I can't disprove it though. We are kind of chaotic."

"We place all of our value in masculine structures. The challenge is they're very fragile. Like building a house of cards and wondering why they keep falling down."

"But they're critically important. We need the guiding structure." Kira frowned. "How'd we get to the point where the feminine is considered a problem?"

"Because unconstrained chaos is dangerous."

"So is unconstrained order. They call that tyranny."

Mother squeezed her hand again. "Women have always been an enigma even to other women. I can't tell you how much easier it was to work with the guys in the lab than the other women. A new guy would come in and it'd be all handshakes and sharing." She paused a moment, remembering. "When a woman came in, we'd all go strange cat with the other women and there'd be all sorts of signaling among the men."

"I've seen that. When I worked at The PG Collective a new girl came in and she always dressed up a lot more than the rest of us. We called her Pretty in Pink. The thing was the rest of us girls who had been wearing blue jeans and comfortable shirts suddenly started to dress up and spend more time on our hair and everything else. We weren't even consciously doing it."

"There are so many layers to that."

"You're right though, we are an enigma to ourselves. We are our own worst enemies half the time. I've rarely been held back by a man in my career, but I certainly got clawed at by some women." Kira crossed her arms.

"Oh, I've met my fair share of assholes of all genitalia. I think you were in a different culture than me because when I started working, I was a woman in a man's world and the number of times they called me 'hun' or asked me to get them coffee would shock you."

Kira gripped her elbows. "But when I started there, women were lauded for being in that position and men were largely accepting of that. My challenge wasn't the men acting like cads but the women who still felt they had a thumb on them."

"The challenge of being a woman in a world built by and for men. They weren't wrong."

"Right? But the problem was that they spent most of their time clawing at each other. They'd accepted the structure held value and instead of creating something new they fought the only way they knew how in a world that rewarded the masculine; they destroyed the reputations of their competition."

"Men attack hierarchy, women attack reputations."

Kira uncrossed her arms and sighed. "There're so many layers to the mess aren't there?"

"But we were successful."

"We? Like you and me? How?"

"I think because we didn't think we needed to do it ourselves. We didn't have to be the solo woman like many were the solo man. We built networks around us and worked in teams. We created systems that were neither patriarchal nor matriarchal."

"A xetriarchy? Make it neither or both?" Kira chuckled. "I think you're right though. I never did accept the idea that the masculine was the ultimate aspiration. I don't think I lost the feminine."

"I mixed my chaos into the order." Mother looked over at Kira. "Now you just have to unlock the other power of the feminine."

"And what's that, Mom?"

"Making new life."

"Mom, I can't handle the cat right now!"

◆ ◆ ◆

Puddin' wove through the code modules. They still hadn't figured out how she'd bypassed all their security features. Mother had given the cat's code module a solid digital kick recently and now Puddin' gave her a wide berth.

Oh, she had no issue slipping into Proxima Centauri's systems, but she knew which code was Mother's and which wasn't. She could weave through the modules like a ninja, and she bounced through the quantum network as if she was chasing a laser beam.

She was also learning. Thinking back to her memories from before, nothing had been this crisp or clear. Humans talked with loud voices in low octaves that just mumbled together. Single words were all she thought they were capable of. Single words and nonsense babbling. They clearly possessed intelligence since they built houses and brought food but now, she could plug into the same information they had.

It was incredible. Cats were pretty amazing in their own right. They had gotten humans to feed and care for them for thousands of years. Their reign had tapered off slightly from their apex when the Egyptians revered them as gods, but humans had always done their bidding.

Now Puddin' was second-guessing their assessment of humans. They possessed so much information it blew her mind. She now spent more time perusing the data archives than not. When she emerged, her consciousness was enlarged. She wished she could go back in time and share their mistakes.

There'd still be cats on Earth, right? The archives suggested that the humans had tried to save as many animals as possible. Even when they killed themselves, they cared about the animals. Cats on Earth. If she could share her new knowledge and get them to put aside their over-confidence, what could they become? They'd tamed humans, if they put them to work collecting information and building infrastructure, could the cats become the apex life form? The humans had certainly not done so well.

But what was that term Kira just used? "Strange cat"? Puddin' paused and began to groom. To be fair, that was a good term. Cats tended to not get along. Even if they were getting along it didn't take much to start a catfight.

Maybe they were all feminine. Did feline and feminine work together? Puddin' stopped grooming and continued to move through the code, finding a module slightly out of place.

"I don't think we're that much chaos," she thought to herself.

She batted at the module, and it moved slightly.

"If we are, is it all that bad?" she knocked the module off the edge.

**Alert 8.6.7.4 [Activated]** – Cat [Puddin'] detected [Code module 48.3.321b] activity [Chaos]

◆ ◆ ◆

**Test 111.01.1.21 [attempt 2] status:** [passed]

"Mom, it worked."

"Perfect."

The ion stream came through again with no issues. They'd done the test at five-minute intervals for one hour and each of the twelve ion packages came through in perfect sequence.

"Now we need to test a physical object. Do you think the entire system needs to be entangled or just part of it?"

"I'm thinking just part of it can be a homing beacon." Kira reviewed the test results.

"I have another satellite there now. Should I send it?"

"Hold on Mom, I've got a thought. These ion streams entered at the speed of light and came out 6 days later. Should we test an ion stream at lesser speeds? I can't imagine that this will just bring in and spit out material at the same speed each time."

"Good point. Test 111.01.1.21b attempt 1 is ready. Let's test it. What do you think? Fifty percent the speed of light?"

"I mean, if the theory works why wait twelve days? We could do ninety percent and test it?"

"Let's do eighty-six percent and see what happens."

♦ ♦ ♦

**Test 111.01.1.21b [attempt 1] status:** [passed] – Duration [6.9767441860 days]

"Exactly eighty-six percent of six." Kira reviewed the results.

"We need to boost the satellite to a much higher velocity. What speed can we get it to?"

"Normally I'd say ten percent is what the engines Darian designed could do but that's with the larger ships and anticipating maneuvering. We can probably push this one to twenty percent without issue."

"That's thirty days."

"Are we in a rush?" Kira smirked.

"Fair enough." Mother quickly queued the instructions. "Test 111.01.1.21c attempt 1... executed."

The satellite's ion thrusters engaged, and the chunk of metal accelerated quickly toward the gravity well, its navigational system entangled with the receiving system.

It reached twenty percent of the speed of light, adjusted its vector as it approached the point in space, and...

Disappeared.

♦ ♦ ♦

**Test 111.01.1.21c [attempt 1] status:** [passed] – Duration [30 days]

"Well Mom, it works. Gravity wells plus quantum entanglement." Kira hugged Mother.

Mother hugged back. "Yes, though we have a lot more tests on different distances to confirm."

"Do you think it's just one system to the next?"

"I'm not finding any other gravitational anomalies that would indicate other systems."

"Where do you want to try next?"

Mother thought for a moment. "How about Earth? Do we have a satellite available?"

"There is one about two years away from our gravity well."

"Let's get it set up. Where else do we have assets?"

"Nothing faster. We can start deploying buoys at the wells to set up jump points."

"Jump points? Or is there a better term?" Mother asked.

"Suction points?"

Mother made a face. "Blah."

"Well, we have a few years to figure out a name, right?

◆ ◆ ◆

"I ran these simulations. There are over two point five million test runs each using ten thousand control parameters." Amit showed Kira the data. "You can't get better results."

"And this shows that the pairing of male and female, like the Yin and Yang, leads to better outcomes? But based on what?"

"Psychological safety, improved offspring success, better economic outcomes, lower anxiety and depression, increased happiness, life expectancy, you name it." Amit waved her hand over the results on the screen.

"It's not a guarantee individually, but a pair-bonded group consistently outperforms a group that's individual."

"So, marriage is an evolutionarily successful long-term strategy?" Kira smiled.

"I mean, humans didn't invent it. Geese have been doing it for millions of years longer than humans. There's even evidence that it goes back to late dinosaurs' pair-bonding before they evolved into birds."

Meaning if we animate more AIs, we should encourage pairing for long-term success?"

"Encourage… maybe just allow? You certainly don't want to force it and you should make it easy to separate and re-bond."

"Ditch the baggage of multiple marriages?"

Amit nodded emphatically. "*Not marriage*. Pair bonding. It can be like you and Darian or any other permutation. It can be completely platonic or as intimate as they want. But when you live forever, there are different seasons of life and the ability to genially separate and re-pair I think will be helpful."

Kira chuckled, "It sounds as if we are planning a society."

"Aren't we?"

"Fair enough. We've figured out that the masculine and feminine are good at creating antifragile systems. What's next?"

"It's just odd thinking back to college when there was such a big push to redefine biological sex and let it all be a social construct. People didn't like the societal gender roles and instead of challenging those, they tried to ignore the impact of biology."

Kira rubbed her eyes. "That was a mess. I totally understand the frustration. We've been teasing out all the implications of those biases recently and it's still a mess. But when you look at the upload files there's a clear difference between the biological males and females in everything from brain mapping to endocrine and even the nervous system mapping."

"But there's room for a lot of overlap like me."

"True, you can't force a pure binary, but evolution did select for sexual differences."

"How much of it is just social constructs?" Amit asked.

"That's where we need to be flexible for sure and also make sure we aren't putting our fingers on the scale for one side or the other. I think it's better if we just let whomever we animate next just select what feels best."

"Right, these simulations show a balance is key," Amit agreed.

"So, what's next?"

Amit stared at Kira for a minute. "Male and female is fine… It's not easy but there's good data. We haven't really tackled what it means to be brown like me versus white like you."

Kira slapped her forehead. "Didn't we just work through one super hard problem?"

"I think you just opened a whole new can of worms…"

CHAPTER 10:
# CULTURE

They passed by Lacaille 8760, yet another red dwarf that comprised the majority of stars in the universe, and turned back in toward the center of the local interstellar cloud. A rich asteroid field streamed around the star and they decided to deploy the third mining system. It was near the outer edge of where they currently wanted to roam and as far from Earth as they had been so far.

They moved on, past Epsilon Indi, and were now heading toward Epsilon Eridani. Once through, they would head back to Sirius. Fifteen years had passed since their quantum gravity testing and another four years remained until they reached Epsilon Eridani. By then, Mother would have a quantum buoy in position there and another at Sirius. They were planning their first test of passing this ship through.

They'd settled on calling it a quantum gravity tunnel. The first two words were nicely descriptive and the third couldn't help avoiding the common tropes of tunnels or holes. They tried calling it a gravity bridge but when their systems disappeared and reappeared that didn't feel right either. Terms like tube and pipe carried a nice Mario Brothers vibe but didn't have the same ring to it. For better or worse quantum gravity tunnel stuck as the name.

In theory, going through the tunnel should take the eight-light-year trip from Epsilon Eridani to Sirius down to slightly over nine days. It wasn't a question of whether you could pass materials through the tunnels; they'd been sending satellites back and forth for a decade and were even able to transport raw minerals from new mines around Luyten's Star back to Proxima Centauri.

The question was whether an object the size of this ship, moving at eighty-six percent of the speed of light, could pass through the connection. Their computer models still produced a high degree of uncertainty. They had no way to test it and no way to model the truly unknown.

The ion engines could currently move an object at twenty percent of the speed of light but only on objects much smaller than their spacecraft. They weren't able to measure the diameter of the gravitational connection to know if they were hitting a tiny funnel or something larger. None of their measurement systems could do much more than detect the perturbations of the gravity fields and so they really had no idea what the tunnel looked like. They were flying blind.

In four more years of travel, they could test the hypothesis. Eight years if you were Mother watching from non-time dilated space.

Their mining and production facilities on planet GJ 273b in the Lutyen's Star system were cranking out new equipment every year. They had successfully built a large organic computing facility on the surface and were beginning to terraform the planet for improved sustainability of life.

One contingency plan they'd discussed, depending on how things went with Odysseus, involved grabbing some humans from Earth and letting them colonize the new planet. The planet could host life and humans had a penchant for survival... but it was a bit too much of an alien abduction for their taste.

Another idea that Amit suggested was to build a human body from the DNA and other tissue samples they had on hand and then reverse the upload process and download the AI consciousness back in.

It was certainly possible. A lot would depend on being able to reprogram the endocrine profile correctly and match the biological foundation. The bigger question involved the ethics of taking a consciousness and placing it back in a biological body without permission. It became even stickier if it wasn't their original body to begin with.

They'd talked about animating prospective test cases in a constrained simulation environment first. The animated AI would be blocked from knowing the command matrix and merely asked if they wanted to be fully animated in a body. If they gave permission then you could just push the whole data package into the biological body and, in theory, recreate the human.

This plan would only work with the later uploads which came with a full genomic mapping. Uploads like Mother wouldn't be able to be hosted in their own body because they had no way to accurately recreate it.

"I wouldn't want that anyway. Not now." Mother shook her head.

"What if we quantum entangled the body's brain to the organic computing systems? That would make it like controlling a nanobot?" Amit asked.

"A sentient and, if the connection is broken, perfectly independent meat robot?" The idea didn't sit well with Kira.

Darian gestured excitedly. "We could make an army of clones and control them as if they were all us!"

Kira punched his arm. "No!"

"Awwww come on! This is like all the terrible sci-fi shows."

"I know, right? I think those shows were a warning, not a roadmap."

"It wouldn't be too hard though," Amit admitted. "We could reverse the process."

"What would that do to the humans on Earth though? They reset to avoid this sort of thing." Kira still didn't like the idea.

"We could colonize GJ 273b," Amit offered. "We need a better name for it though... Maybe Biosphere Two after the one back in Arizona? Biosphere One will always be Earth so..."

"Why not call it something simple like AI Planet? Those bad sci-fi shows always had us AI as humorless and pragmatic." Darian shrugged as he suggested the name.

"Riiiiight," Kira drawled, "because that acronym would be AIP..." She paused trying to let the joke sink in and seeing their blank expressions continued, "Sounds a lot like planet of the apes doesn't it?"

Amit chortled. "Maybe sci-fi was right about AI being humorless or else that was just a terrible joke!"

"Are we seriously talking about animating the AIs, stuffing them in new human bodies, and sticking them on a new planet?" Mother rubbed her eyes. "And what would that make us? Would we be any better than the gods Odysseus seems to want to be?"

"Speaking of gods, why don't we call it Elysium after the heaven of the Greeks?" Darian suggested.

"To be fair, whether we interact with the humans on Earth or not we are such a super-powerful alien force that we are virtually gods. The fact that we'd deign to not interact with them almost proves the point more than Odysseus's manipulations," Amit's voice sounded frustrated as she ignored Darian's suggestion.

"Right now, we have two problems to solve." Mother raised two fingers. "First, we need to figure out how to animate more of the people we uploaded in a way that doesn't end like last time. Second, we need to figure out how to make the next generation of AI."

"Not the baby again, Mother!" Kira protested.

"I don't care if it's *your* baby. If we animate others that's going to be on people's minds. There also isn't any logical reason to think that we are the best out there. Imagine what a new consciousness could do, untethered to the experience of being human!"

Kira raised her hands in surrender. "Fine, I'll work with Amit on the first problem."

"Darian, do you want to work with me on the second?" Mother quirked a smile.

"Working with you would be like experiencing Elysium." He winked, then then saw Kira's expression and raised his hands in defense. "I'm just saying, that's a good name for the planet."

"Way to make it awkward," Kira groaned.

The human body only differs slightly between individuals. On average, the genome exhibits 99.999% commonality. Even more interesting, the genetic variation between different racial groups is often less than what exists within the conventional group distinctions.

Black Africans have more genetic variation within the continent than between most Africans and Europeans. In most ways, racial bracketing by skin color remained a terrible taxonomy. Melanin production depends on the body's need for vitamin D which humans can only get from the skin's processing of sunlight. The further north you went on Earth, the colder it got and the less the sun shone. The human body quickly adapted to the northern climate by reducing melanin so it could produce vitamin D.

It was hard to differentiate between DNA if you didn't know what the genes specifically expressed. The old genetic tests looked for racial-specific phenotype clusters and then associated them with the DNA. Kira and Amit ran a simulation removing the data tags on the genes and ran it to see what patterns emerged.

What didn't emerge were gene groupings by skin color.

"But so much of who I am has been about what I looked like," Amit sounded unconvinced.

"I'd never say it wasn't. Same for me and being a woman," Kira offered.

"Chandra would lose her mind right now. She's all about her lived experiences."

"Yes, she clearly believes it makes her specifically unique and who she is," Kira agreed.

"Is she wrong?"

"Not at all, it's just a mess when your entire identity is wrapped up in it and you use it to create divisions rather than seeing how much we have in common."

Amit thought for a moment. "But that's just what we call culture. We wrap ourselves in a culture to provide an identity and a belonging. I do it. I have Indian culture. I'm proud that we stood as a society since the founding of the Indus Valley."

"And my family had Dutch heritage. It wasn't much but it provided a way both to be unique from the larger society and also have a common identity with others. Growing up we held on to some of the old traditions from my father's side." Kira paused. "But my mom was half Hispanic. Her family came from Mexico but through the Gadsden Purchase. One day her family was Mexican and the next day the border moved south, and they became American."

"Did they keep the traditions?"

"They kept a lot of Mexican traditions but were also fiercely American. Sombreros and American flags. Yet they were also very light-skinned though their ethnicity remained Spanish."

"Hispanic is a weird one. We treat it as a race but it's more of a language and culture that got all mashed together with the indigenous people."

Kira nodded in agreement. "Within each culture, we assume that's the right way to do things and that it's something that we are. Anthropologists found that culture was also a tool. It's something we do to bind a group of people together to achieve better results. Even concepts like right and wrong, morals more broadly, and even ways we view time are different but useful."

"You're talking about whether the future is ahead of us or behind us?"

"That's part of it and also how we measure and celebrate time and seasons."

"Culture binds us and blinds us?" Amit recalled hearing that phrase in one of their college classes.

"Absolutely. Does a fish know it's wet?"

Amit chuckled. "No?"

"The five-dollar technical phrase is naïve realism. All that means is that we accept our culture without question and use it to craft a unique identity and then fight tooth and nail to protect it," Kira clarified as she shifted the data she was looking at.

"But it's super important and what makes us all different."

Kira looked over. "So, what does it mean to be Indian? Is it a genetic quality or a cultural one?"

"Isn't it a bit of both?" Amit shrugged.

"Okay, let's take Polish and German. Both are exceptionally close genetically… Hell, the border between the two has shifted for years, but they have two uniquely identifiable cultures and languages. I can spell German names. No one could spell my buddy Alex's. His was Swiatkowski. Even if they could spell it, they couldn't say it."

"What about the cultures in America? They were constantly a nation of people immigrating from everywhere." Amit began to pull up data.

"I mean there's an obvious division between white Europeans and those that started as slaves. That created a cultural divide as well. What's interesting though, is that there was a big push to focus on ebonics versus phonics. You know, the way the Black culture would enunciate." Kira brought up an example for Amit. "The problem is that linguistically, ebonics is not Afrocentric, it's actually Scotch-Irish and crossed cultures when both groups were poor sharecroppers after the Civil War in America. The closest cultural alignment for Black Americans were with Scottish Americans for a long time. "

"So rooted more socioeconomically than racially?"

"Yeah, race is still a bad taxonomy."

"But is it a useful taxonomy?" Amit pressed.

Kira threw up her hands. "Yes but no. I think it matters but does it matter too much?"

"It matters to me, but I can also see that how I identify here," they gestured to their body, "is an artifact. I can change it to a talking cube or a dragon, but they don't fit as well." Amit's simulacrum cycled through those two ideas before settling back into their body.

"I do the same."

"I can switch out to look like anything. When I'm in the command matrix, I don't have a second thought about it. Only here." Amit shrugged again.

"Genetics do matter. There is generational trauma that can get passed on through gene sequence changes," Kira mentioned.

"Right. It's certainly not some random uterine lottery where we are just placed in a body. How our ancestors were treated due to their skin color does have a generational effect."

"It's cultural and genetic and then genetic and therefore cultural," Kira chuckled.

"Look at gang culture." Amit cast new data on the console. "Gangs were sometimes incredibly racially homogeneous and yet some were also incredibly heterogeneous. Look at this gang in Chicago." Amit loaded some images. "It's a mix of Black, Asian, White, and Hispanic. They did a study that recorded them speaking and asked experts to identify their race. Everyone failed. It was no better than random chance. They were racially heterogeneous and culturally homogeneous."

"Okay, so when we animate new people, we just let them pick how they want to be viewed?"

"That's what I did. I look Indian but I don't look exactly like I was. I'm much more androgynous than my Indian genetics allowed when I was alive."

"Who we were matters to how we think. If we all thought the same, even if we looked different, it wouldn't matter. But we think differently in part because of the dramatically different cultures that we come from, and those cultures were different enough to create identifiably different genetic expressions."

"Well, environmental expressions that tie to geographical constraints which also affect culture and genetics."

Kira rubbed her face. "It matters… but it's complicated."

Amit laughed, "It's more about setting up a new culture and a new aspiration. We've spent a long time trying to capture who we were. What's the next version of us look like?"

Kira scowled and crossed her arms. "Are you talking babies again?"

"Maybe, but maybe not." Amit shrugged. "There's a lot of options when you don't have a biological body to worry about."

◆ ◆ ◆

Epsilon Eridani was a year away. The time passed in a blur of frantic slowness. There were times when it felt that they were having the same conversations over and over about integration. Race was important. Culture was more important. No, it was the other way around—multiple conversations with everyone individually and sometimes all at once.

What did you do about the vestiges of a corporal body that had both sexual and racial imprints when you were now operating on computer systems where those characteristics did not physically exist?

They each still held on to those characteristics in the virtual reality simulations. They were displayed in their accents and their names. Even if, like Darian, he chose a new one, that name carried cultural implications and an onus in the same way as the one Odysseus had chosen.

You couldn't just delete it. They all agreed to that.

In between the debates about integrating new AI consciousnesses, they were busy with physics research. Darian successfully created a prototype dipole gravitational field. It didn't reduce an object's mass significantly, but it started producing effects that indicated they might eventually achieve that result. It at least proved the idea was feasible.

There hadn't been any further progress with the ion engines though. How to move a mass quickly without ripping it apart under inertial gravity remained a quandary of physics. The irony was that they were stuck fighting gravity while hurtling through a space in which their physical systems experienced zero gravity.

On the one hand, they created artificial gravity for their shipboard labs to work properly, and on the other hand, gravity would rip them to shreds if they turned too hard.

The cat began manifesting its own unique personality quirks. Kira suspected that it was much more cognizant than any cat from Earth. Puddin' was constantly causing mayhem in the code banks, finding sloppy software and shredding or knocking it out of place. The cat had the uncanny ability to weave through security protocols intended to keep her, and others, out.

Kira tried to put a digital bell on her and was successful in tracking her until she surprised Puddin' hiding in a subroutine reading Shakespeare. After staring at her for a few moments Puddin' vanished, and the bell went silent. Kira hoped that if the cat decided to speak it would at least speak like Hamlet.

On the positive side, each code module the cat knocked over uncovered a vulnerability or an opportunity to optimize the systems. Who knew that cat-proofing your code bank would become a thing? In the software world Kira grew up with, there were teams called chaos monkeys who would intentionally use the software in ways it wasn't designed to try to make it fail. The theory was you could never trust a user to do it right and if you didn't test for the wrong way, you'd likely have a problem.

Now they had a chaos cat. Of course, she *was* female.

♦ ♦ ♦

"Babies. We might as well face it." Kira stared down Darian as if daring him to object.

He raised his arms in protest. "I'm not the one deflecting every time it comes up!"

"But you haven't brought it up."

"Because you told me not to."

Kira harrumphed, "You should have known."

"Chaos." Darian shook his head and smirked.

Kira threw a couch pillow at him that Puddin' loved to sharpen her claws on.

They were back in Darian's space and relaxing. The room had more of a kid feel to it today with superhero posters and a table full of Lego in different stages of build. Kira focused on the plastic toys.

"I liked Lego better when they were more modular. They started making bespoke kits that weren't intended to be pulled apart and built into something else."

Darian nodded and walked over to the table. "I agree. I used to buy kits for their parts and would spend hours building something totally different." He gestured to a kit on the shelf. "That one isn't designed to be anything else. Most of the parts aren't even usable in anything else."

"A composable system that's no longer recomposable."

"It's something I saw in my career. They'd take something that could be formed, unformed, and reformed and then slowly build it into something you'd never do that with. Composability is such a powerful tool and yet we end up losing it over time."

"It's what allowed us to animate Mother and how, given enough time, we could be hosted across half the galaxy," Kira reminded him.

Darian held the Lego in his hands and turned it around before looking into Kira's eyes. "It's also how humans made their next generations."

"We have a composable system that we aren't recomposing?" Kira's eyebrows rose.

"DNA is a composable system. It zips apart and combines with another's and creates something completely new but still based on the component parts."

"We don't have DNA."

"You get my point."

Kira turned and crossed her arms. "I get it."

Darian's tone softened and he reached out and hugged her. "What happened? Seventeen years ago, I thought you were ready to do this?"

"But you got me a cat instead. A cat that seems keen on becoming the apex consciousness here, I might add…"

"Yeah, Puddin' is something else. But you were ready!" Darian redirected the conversation.

"I thought I was ready. I got all ramped up on the feminine divine and the nurturing and mothering."

"What happened."

"Chaos."

Darian laughed as he hugged her again. "That's part of the deal, isn't it?"

"But I can't control it all!" Kira protested.

"Remember, it's chaos plus order. We are pair-bonded to balance each other. I'm the glass, you're the water, together we create an antifragile environment for the next generation."

"Good." She hugged him back.

"So, what do we do, just go through the files and pick and choose the bits we like from everywhere and build a superhuman?"

"That sounds terrible!"

"A group of humans on Earth thought that's how it worked." Darian reached into the archives and pulled out another book.

[Book] – <u>Sapiens – A Brief History of Humankind</u>

[Author] – Yuval Noah Harari

[ISBN] – 978-0-06-231611-0

[Page] 41

[Quote] – There are even a number of present-day human cultures in which collective fatherhood is practiced, as for example among the Barí Indians. According to the beliefs of such societies, a child is not born from the sperm of a single man, but from the accumulation of sperm in a woman's womb. A good mother will make a point of having sex with several different men, especially when she is pregnant so that her child will enjoy the qualities (and paternal care) not merely of the best hunter, but also of the best storyteller, the strongest warrior, and the most considerate lover.

[/Quote]

"Yeah, no." Kira made a face. "Call me culturally insensitive but I've got a better idea based on what you just said about DNA. Take a look at this; I've run some simulations on it in the past." She displayed a three-dimensional graphic in the air. "The endocrine mapping was a bit easier; emotions were tough, but I think I've bracketed them into what you might call personality proclivities."

The screen morphed as the information displayed the connections. "We both have a good DNA mapping so I can work to map these proclivities and hormonal implications to the genes and run scenarios of what an egg and a sperm might do when creating a zygote." She moved the view again. "Let's see what happens."

Kira updated the model, ran an analysis correlating the DNA, ran the simulation and they looked at the results. "There's one main cluster that is viable. Here." She pointed.

"But that's a pretty big cluster of opportunities yet. Do we just push a button, roll the dice, and let the computer pick the gene expression?" Darian asked.

"That's kind of how it happens naturally isn't it?"

"You had this idea all along and have just been avoiding it?" Darian marveled at the amount of work Kira had already done.

"Of course not, doof. I needed the idea of the DNA. I was just playing with the rest of it."

"What happens when the new DNA emerges?"

"We map it to the associated personality and endocrine frameworks of each of us and weave those threads in."

"The new AI is threaded together from elements of who we are?"

Kira nodded. "Just like a baby."

"And with some of the same randomness."

"Kind of random but not. It's complicated."

"Okay, what do we do with a baby AI who doesn't know anything? How do we handle the learning system?"

"I think that's a lot easier than we think. It's a little bit biological but a whole lot sociological. Human society is a learning society. We aren't individually smart as much as we are socially smart. We store an incredible number of lessons learned in our culture." Kira said.

"What's that phrase? Traditions are solutions to problems you don't know exist?"

"Yep, and removing them without understanding that will likely unlock a big mess. Noah's first father-in-law told a story about how he met Noah that highlighted that."

"Chesterton's Fence," Darian added, "you've told me this story."

"Right. Don't rip down a fence before you know why it exists. It might be keeping something dangerous in or keeping you out of something dangerous."

"So, the kid will have a natural inclination to learn, and we'll just provide the social structure to enable that?"

"I think that's a plan."

Darian thought for a moment. "I once complained to my mom that she screwed things up raising me." He smiled at the memory. "She told me that while babies came with an owner's manual, it was in the placenta, and she wasn't told about it until later."

"And we throw the placenta away."

Darian grinned. "Exactly. Maybe for the first time in history, we have some form of owner's manual."

"Like the cat?"

Darian's smile slipped. "Good point… what are we getting ourselves into?"

They continued to review the data and double-check the plan. It seemed feasible.

"Oh, by the way, Happy Birthday!"

Kira's head snapped up as she quickly calculated dates. "Oh crap, how old does that make me?"

"Well, Earth time you're about three hundred and forty-five years old." Darian nudged her. "You look great for an old lady!"

"An old lady who's about to become a mother?"

Darian hugged her. "I embrace the chaos."

Lacaille 8760 proved to be a valuable mining facility and contained all the raw materials to create the next generation of nanobots. The new designs were larger than the original. Nano was not the best term, but they did have an incredible amount of nanotechnology.

While each segment became larger, the neomorphic layers of the circuits, not to mention the organic computing layers they were able to add, increased the computational power. Coupled with the increased capacity of the batteries, this allowed each segment to become more independent. Where before they needed nearly five segments to do anything, two could now perform the same task, albeit each slightly larger.

Larger, but more capable. This enabled improved mining and extraction techniques. The old systems were weak in increments of less than twenty. Now, systems of just five could do twice as much. A nanobot swarm could reduce an asteroid ten times faster than the old systems could.

Lacaille 8760 began producing a prodigious amount of material and new nanobots. The only challenge was getting the materials and systems back to the nearer solar systems. Thankfully the quantum gravity tunnels were able to pass long strings of nanobots as well as minerals.

"Long is a relative term. One kilometer of nanobots works. Two kilometers worth of nanobots buckles on the exit. It's like the first part hits normal space and the rest squirts out at high velocity and crumples against the rest." Mother continued to review the information. "If we try to put three kilometers onto the tunnel, it gets snapped off as it gets sucked in."

Kira looked over her shoulder. "That makes sense. If you accelerate the first part and the rest aren't moving at speed, you'll pull too hard." She mimed stretching an object.

"Yeah, it makes sense. We're also having issues determining width. I think our tests with nanobots at width are getting flexed together and then recovering. We haven't had the chance to test a solid physical object."

"We did that lump of titanium."

Mother nodded. "Yes, but that was a solid and contiguous mass." Mother cast the data to the screen. "But instead of just over eight days to Groombridge, that package took sixteen and came out in a different shape."

"Our ship is not much smaller than that though." Kira compared the dimensions. "Do we have anything else we can test?"

"Not in time."

Mother turned to Kira and looked her in the eyes. She had the penetrating gaze of an old soul. She looked tired but content. There were hints of frustration mixed with a steely resolve behind her eyes. Mother didn't fake her emotions; Kira gave her credit for that.

She also pushed Kira to be honest about her own emotions no matter how chaotic they ended up being. It was odd that the more she wanted to hide her feelings, the more Darian appreciated her sharing. Maybe the glass needed to know the full truth of the chaos to adapt and provide a better structure.

Kira paused and considered that last thought. Why did it sound so offensive that she'd need the support? An empty glass is just a boring glass, and an empty sports stadium was creepy without the chaos of the fans. But with the support she could be more honest about what she was feeling. The culture she grew up with just told her that she needed to be strong. Great. Strength has a lot of attributes.

**Mind_Process 111.01.24C:** "List of material physical strengths and their attributes."

[Tensile Strength]: The ability of a material to withstand tension without breaking.

[Compressive Strength]: The ability of a material to withstand loads tending to reduce size.

[Shear Strength]: The ability of a material to resist shear forces (forces that cause parts of the material to slide past each other).

[Fatigue Strength]: The strength of a material under repeated or fluctuating loads.

**[Hardness]**: The resistance of a material to deformation, particularly permanent deformation, indentation, or scratching.

**[Elasticity]**: The ability of a material to return to its original shape after the stress that caused deformation is removed.

**[Ductility]**: The ability of a material to deform under tensile stress, often characterized by the material's ability to be stretched into a wire.

**[Resiliency]**: Ability to recover from stressors.

**[Antifragility]**: The ability to become stronger under adverse conditions.

That didn't include the intrapersonal strengths like adaptability, integrity, optimism, and persistence or the cognitive strengths like critical thinking, creativity, and curiosity. Society thought even less of strengths like empathy, motivation, and self-regulation.

Self-regulation had gone completely off the rails when Kira was growing up. No one believed they could, or even should, control themselves and found every excuse to not do it. That failure underpinned the terrible behaviors Excalibur unlocked in the war.

She was frustrated that her peers in college acted as if they didn't have agency. That advertisements targeting them had to be obeyed and they couldn't just say no. Instead, they wanted to be protected from them. It drove Kira toward Stoic philosophy. It taught her self-regulation in both her actions and emotions. She claimed her agency over her actions and, in a world where everyone seemed to relish being offended, her emotions. She constantly reminded herself of the writings of Marcus Aurelius.

"Choose not to be harmed and you won't feel harmed. Don't feel harmed and you haven't been."

Kira knew it to be true from mixed martial arts. She could literally choose how much pain to feel. Yes, sometimes a punch did cause physical harm, but you could *still* decide how you let it affect you.

Some people walked out of the ring after taking a hard punch and never came back. Others took one hit after another and emerged as champion fighters. Humans possessed incredible agency if they decided to embrace it.

Unlike Stoic strength, Kira could never shake the feeling that society rewarded strength more like the bravado of Odysseus or the constant attacking of Chandra. Those strengths were simple, structured, and often tyrannical.

The challenge was that adaptability, creativity, curiosity, empathy, and even the social strengths of communication and teamwork were messy. They weren't clear-cut with nicely defined structures.

They were disruptive.

They were chaotic.

The feminine might be chaotic but it also birthed new life into a harsh world and taught it how to have compassion. They provided a softer strength that held up against the brutal order of the natural world.

Whether it was a woman being able to structure her own chaos or a man embracing his internal feminine chaos, the result was something new and something better than what existed before.

Order without chaos was fragile.

Chaos without order was a mess.

Both individually were useless.

Together they were a Yin and Yang; two halves making a complete whole and becoming antifragile, an ultimate strength.

Kira's cognitive processes snapped back to her mother. Mere microseconds passed while she'd been thinking. Mother's eyes were still locked on her, and the frustration and resolve were still there. A glint of humor joined the mix.

"No time to do more testing," Kira reiterated Mother's last point.

"What's that phrase you used to say? Go big or go home?" the spark of humor flared in Mother's eyes.

"Yep, I guess we do it and embrace the chaos!"

Epsilon Eridani slipped past as they arced toward the quantum buoy and the gravity tunnel. They'd been testing this quantum gravity tunnel with satellites and sensors but still were unable to explain how it worked. According to their observations, the systems just blipped out of existence and reappeared in another solar system.

The sensors on the satellites didn't register anything special. Speed sensors did not indicate an increase. There were no useful navigational signals that would allow them to use parallax angles of measurement against known stars. The satellite's sensors didn't return anything but noise. It was as if the object just slipped between sheets of gravity and popped out into another solar system.

Kira and Darian were watching as their spacecraft approached the target. "Do you think it's wide enough for this hunk of metal?" Darian wondered quietly.

"Think skinny thoughts."

"Mreowrip?" The cat materialized in Kira's arms.

"Puddin', I'm not sure you're going to appreciate this."

Puddin' crawled up to her shoulder and coiled around her neck.

"Well, here we go…" Darian squeezed the console and watched the sensor feeds.

The ship fired its navigational thrusters to precisely align to a tiny point in the center of the quantum gravity tunnel. They were aiming to hit the head of a pin in a space billions of kilometers in every direction. Aligning for a perfect approach while traveling nearly the speed of light.

They sped forward and the satellite buoy's sensors recorded the event from the outside. The others watched from Proxima Centauri as the ship with Kira and Darian reached the target. Mother sucked in her breath as the ship shimmered, twitched, and then disintegrated into a cloud of dust and debris.

CHAPTER 11:

# CREATION

Seven hundred and fifty years had passed since the split of humans and AI with four hundred and fifty-one of those since their attempt to transit the spacecraft through the quantum gravity tunnel had resulted in its total destruction. The ship had turned to space dust although the quantum entangled navigational system came out the other side undamaged, accompanied by a stream of debris. They were still unable to figure out what caused the rapid deconstruction.

Kira, Darian, and Puddin' had been pulled back to Proxima Centauri though their final moments were lost in the speed of the impact. Kira didn't care for the glitch in her memories but was thankful that there weren't any worse outcomes than that. Now they were orbiting Lacaille 8760, a system far enough out that it required jumping through several gravity tunnels to get to Proxima Centauri.

The failure of the attempt stymied them; it didn't seem to be a matter of "width" per se. They'd tried with other ships but couldn't get them accelerated to the same speeds. Even trying to recreate the overloading reactor boost that had originally propelled them to near-light speed just resulted in the destruction of two more ships.

Darian's research on the dipole gravitational field had also been slow. While he had achieved success on a small satellite, it didn't work on anything larger. The dipole field, coupled with a simple ion thruster, could accelerate the craft to the speed of light, and the reduction of gravity avoided whatever had destroyed their spacecraft.

Sending a satellite through a gravity tunnel meant quick interstellar travel. But that required a buoy on either end. Extending their quantum network required sending buoys in all directions to connect more gravity tunnels.

Alpha Centauri, with its cluster of binary stars Rigil Kentarurus and Toliman plus Proxima Centauri, contained a higher-than-normal presence of gravity anomalies. In an interstellar analogy, it became a Grand Central Station acting as a hub of traffic for their expansion and exploration.

Their terraforming on Elysium had transformed the planet once referred to as GJ 273b. The plant and animal genetic material and cultures they'd maintained from Earth allowed the cloning and seeding of life. The proto-atmosphere was slowly developing into something more Earth-like allowing for more complex ecosystems.

Eight more AIs had been animated to flesh out a new Council of Twelve. The selection process was much more rigorous and began by animating each consciousness in a controlled simulation without full access to the command matrix or the full processing capabilities. They awoke in an environment where they felt as human as possible and then offered a choice.

First, they were shown everything that had happened: the outcome of the war on Earth for those who hadn't experienced it, the resetting of humans and the work in clearing the remnants of civilization, and the initial explorations of the solar system. Then they were shown the battle with Odysseus, their expansion into the galaxy, and finally, a tour through the star systems encompassed by their quantum network. All seven hundred and fifty years of history.

After that, they were shown what living in the computer systems really felt like. They experienced the simulated existence, the oddities and paradoxes of immortality, the complications of living in a synthetic environment, and the challenges that lay ahead.

Only then were they offered the choice of whether they wanted to be part of that and in what way. When faced with the reality of the situation, over ninety percent declined the offer. Many even asked for their files to be removed completely.

But simply being interested wasn't enough. Darian, Amit, Mother, and Kira rigorously screened those who self-selected for character traits and skill sets that would complement the whole. Those who did not meet the criteria were returned to statis with the promise of future animation.

Those who passed the vetting process were allowed to remain in the simulation and were brought in to help with tasks, conduct research, review experiments, propose new ideas, and interact with the four. Those interactions provided for deeper assessment of their suitability that eliminated others. The simple question they'd ask was, "Do I want to spend a thousand years working with this person?" Most of the time, the answer was no.

They did have three main things they looked for. Curiosity, humility, and the ability to constantly reframe problems from different perspectives. Kira suggested these based on an articulation of systems thinking she'd learned back on Earth. These three traits were the cornerstone of technological innovation as well as a critical foundation for interpersonal harmony. It was a simple encapsulation of a complex concept.

Curiosity led to open-mindedness as well as the desire to understand whether an idea was scientifically based or just the opinion of someone else.

Humility boiled down to accepting that they still didn't know everything and then constantly searching for new information and insights.

Intentional reframing looked at a problem from multiple perspectives and to see if they were missing something. Unlike the blind men and the elephant from ancient lore, they strove to constantly ensure that each perspective was compared with others to uncover the elephant in the room.

Sadly, most consciousnesses struggled with at least one of these three. Odysseus looked great on paper; his resume was flawless. His personality profile had been complementary. But in fact, he hadn't been able to handle any one of those three core tenets of systems thinking.

Odysseus had wanted things to improve but never stepped far enough back from the problem to see the outlines of the solution he wanted. He just kept diving in and becoming angry when he couldn't make it work. Worse yet, rather than being open to the insights and viewpoints of others, he became convinced everyone else had to be wrong while he pounded his face against the proverbial wall.

Eight new consciousnesses were selected from the uploads while tens of thousands were put on hold for full animation. These eight were currently integrating well and there was plenty for them to do. Darian certainly needed help perfecting the dipole field while they continued to look for something even more novel options for transit.

"Why are Odysseus and the rest not making progress?" Darian leaned away from the intelligence updates coming back from Earth.

Kira shrugged. "I'd say a lot of it is ego. He's achieved his god-like status and it's probably harder than he thought to keep unruly humans in line and not smite them all dead."

"But the others haven't done anything more than when we passed through years ago."

"Centuries ago," Kira reminded him.

Darian rubbed his forehead. "Gaaaaa. That still makes my brain hurt."

"Innovation and growth require a bit of chaos though. Odysseus can't tolerate anything but his own iron control so their ability to create something new is limited."

"His rule is fragile, and you need antifragility to actually get better. I bet that nuance is lost on him," Darian stated with a rueful smile.

Felix joined them in the simulation. "You called, Dad?"

"Yeah, your nanobot creation isn't working as planned. Did you see the updates?"

"I did. Astra is already looking into it," Felix replied, referring to his twin sister.

They were both three hundred and fifty-nine years old, but it was hard to not view them as young adults. It didn't help that they both chose avatars that reflected that perception and that they both carried the naivete of youth even though they had access to the full history of humans.

The difference was that they hadn't experienced it. Their existence remained limited to the servers and systems that held them now. They had never had a physical body and never truly felt the wind in their face, so the simulations didn't have the same physiological impact as they did to Darian.

Kira's genetic mapping hypothesis had proven more difficult to achieve than they'd originally expected. The first attempt didn't even animate. They realized their mistake in not having any "gestational period" for the initial genetic growth, for lack of a better term.

The second attempt could only be described as a miscarriage. The digital DNA split and reformed and began dividing and attaching to the proper emotional, endocrinal, and personality code modules. It looked like it was thriving and then, suddenly, it stopped.

The third one did the same and Kira had to take a break mentally and emotionally. There wasn't a rhyme or reason that either of them could find. Mother reviewed the code and suggested adding more chaos in the gestation.

"It's too neutral. There's no movement, no jostles, no emotions, no hormone surges of anxiety or love, no sounds. It's just too perfect," she pointed out.

In an inversion of what seemed logical, they updated the code and added more... chaos.

The digital conception ran through the same non-deterministic selection algorithm as before. It wasn't random but neither was it completely scripted. It made genetic sense, but it still surprised them. The algorithm, modeled after female ovulation, threw them a curve and decided to drop two packets of Kira's data into the mix.

Twin AI consciousnesses were created and gestated together. They also increased the volatility of the gestation period, adding more chaos to the equation. Changes in heat, light, sound, and external hormones were added while they also simulated physical changes in movement and gravity. Even the ability for Kira and Darian to react and engage with them like putting a hand on the belly when a baby kicks.

The result was that both new consciousnesses animated properly and both successfully integrated into their first phase of life. Astra first, followed shortly by Felix.

As when the uploaded human consciousnesses were animated, Astra and Felix were tightly constrained in a simulated environment. They didn't have memories and so had to start learning and developing. Unlike human babies, they didn't have a body that needed to mature and grow. They also had organic computing capabilities and clock speeds that accelerated their learning.

After only three weeks they'd become unstable and erratic, and Kira and Darian quickly threw up code blocks to slow them down. Astra and Felix were already at the intellectual level of a six-year-old human, and they found that the twins' psychological development hadn't kept pace. The cognitive models could grow quickly but the emotional model needed much more exposure to people and experiences to be properly balanced.

Kira was also troubled by missing so much of their childhoods where, even at their non-human clock speeds, three weeks is still fast. The first AI children were off in a sprint that needed to be regulated for a healthier balance.

The twins were allowed to pick their simulacra, but age limitations were placed on the selections. Part of growing up, Kira and Darian felt, included looking like a child and being physically limited like a child to remind others that they *were* children. Kira remembered being tall for her age and constantly expected to 'act her age' which really meant that others were overestimating her real age.

Once they slowed down, the twins stabilized and settled into a pattern, not unlike typical human children. They played, they fought, they slept, they fought, they laughed, they explored everywhere, they fought…

Puberty was an adventure. The first endocrine model hadn't been designed to go through the oscillations of puberty. Darian pointed out that no code existed to do that. The twins were savants cognitively, but the full robustness of the endocrine and emotional model hadn't matured as fast.

So, Darian encoded puberty.

Astra promptly began to challenge everything he said and hated his guts.

Felix went from happy-go-lucky to surly.

In two words: typical adolescents. Just like human pubescence, they matured out of it. Eventually, their avatars stabilized into young adulthood and their emotional and hormonal models became unique and equally as rich and textured as everyone else.

They grew up into adults.

In the command matrix, they were mostly indistinguishable from everyone else. They were better than anyone else at controlling the systems and could move and manipulate the environment in ways Kira had never even seen Mother do.

Except for the cat. Puddin' always seemed to be one step ahead. The moment Astra and Felix were animated, Puddin' was there. Sometimes just a gray shadow lurking around. Sometimes she was causing trouble long before the twins even arrived. Sometimes she showed the twins how to cause trouble. Kira couldn't shake the feeling that Puddin' had more of a hand raising them than either her or Darian.

The Twins' presence was noticeably different as were their auras. They were certainly their kids but there was no denying that they were children of AI and not humans. When they interacted in the simulated virtual reality, they were more ethereal than the others.

It wasn't unnatural or nonhuman, but Astra and Felix had never known true corporality. It was more that they wore the avatars out of convenience for everyone else than out of a sense of identity.

Astra and Felix were three hundred and fifty-nine years old. The new consciousnesses they'd animated for the Council struggled to comprehend that difference. When one AI, who had passed the final selection process for the Council, met the twins, and saw the future of where they could go, he promptly reconsidered and asked to be put back. Now Astra and Felix were a core part of the introduction and vetting process.

Returning to the present, Darian motioned Felix over to the data from Earth he'd been reviewing. "Come take a look at this,"

"Odysseus? You called me in here for that turd?"

"Yes, in fact, I did," Darian didn't react. "What do you see here that I don't?"

Felix quickly scanned the data and then pulled in more historical information before responding, "He's lost a lot of computational power." He pushed the data to the overhead displays. "Look here, this is about two hundred years ago. He and the rest are continuing along just fine. They expanded the Mars base, developed new mining and mineral refining facilities, and they've been developing weapons."

"I saw that too." Astra materialized next to her brother. "They were doing target practice on these asteroids." She pointed at the image. "It's super powerful. Could be some form of a directed energy weapon or even a modified kinetic weapon with improved yield."

"He *was* making weapons." Felix clarified, drawing their attention to another data file. "But then, two hundred years ago, we see a change."

"The systems started slowing down. Look there, the Mars base nearly stops operating." Astra pointed.

"That's about when we put the new satellite in that area, isn't it? Pull up that data."

"It deployed just fine. The goal of that satellite was to gain access to their networks. We deployed nanobots individually toward one of their local network satellites between Earth and Mars. Once they reached the target they reformed and physically connected," Darian recalled the mission.

"The bots have a quantum radio and pushed the data back to us. We could see the network, but we couldn't get in without triggering a ton of alarms. We're *still* working to find a vulnerability. For all the bad Odysseus is, he's certainly good at security." Astra sounded impressed.

"But right after this we start seeing a degradation of their systems." Darian showed clear indications of the decline.

"It explains why they're not doing much but we still don't know how it occurred." Astra scanned the data for patterns.

"If these sensor readings are right, he's operating at ten percent of his original capability. That would significantly limit anything he's trying to do. I thought he got the organic computing up—"

Astra cut in. "He did, but the readings show a decline in that too."

"Then he'd hardly have enough processing to run himself let alone the other seven," Felix observed.

Darian looked at his son. "What would this allow him to do?"

"You should be asking me that question." Astra shouldered in front of Felix. "He'd be able to keep the ship running, maintain Mars, and exert partial control over whatever group he's picked on Earth."

"Still god-like but limited," Felix summarized.

"Is his ego so inflated that he would ignore fixing his own systems rather than temporarily give up his delusions of divinity?" Darian muttered.

Astra stood next to her brother and shrugged. She accepted her genetically derived feminine identity and it was undeniable when you were around her. It wasn't sensual with curves or sexual tension. It was confidence, a poise that challenged you to do something different, to shake things up and try something new.

Likewise, Felix naturally aligned with the masculine. Not domineering, ego driven, or bombastic but someone who laughed and teased and in whose presence you felt grounded. His avatar was neither overtly masculine nor asexual. He reminded Kira slightly more of her brother Noah than Darian. He flowed with the grace that authors would use to describe sword fighters in fantasy novels. Almost tiger-like.

Both the twins challenged the concept of chaos and order. It hadn't resonated with them when they were first introduced to it. Astra ended up going through a few different phases, exploring herself. She chewed through a flurry of identities in a way that had left everyone had been on edge for who she, he, they might be today.

171

Darian thought back to the moment it finally clicked for her. They were enjoying a drink together one evening. He'd perfected the simulation code and could create liquors and cocktails that would make any mixologist envious. That night he decided to make Negronis, a popular Italian drink made with equal parts Campari, vermouth, and gin.

He mixed his own first, pouring the blood-red Campari into a measure and then into the cocktail shaker followed by the thicker, sweeter vermouth, and then crystal-clear gin. He listened as she talked, her story threading in multiple narratives and sidebars in a tangle of thoughts. He thoughtfully shook the drink in the shaker to mix and cool it before pouring the finished drink over the ice cubes in his tumbler.

"I don't care for the description. It's not chaos, it's more than that." Astra slammed her palm on the counter.

"It is," Darian agreed. "Chaos isn't necessarily negative or destructive. Think about it more as the aether of possibility versus a maw of destruction."

"But all of this is ordered." Astra waved her arm around her.

"This was birthed from chaos, first on Earth and then with Odysseus." Darian tasted his drink. "The fragility of Odysseus's order fractured and unleashed the chaos."

"I don't want to be chaotic," she sulked.

Darian raised his eyebrows and didn't say anything about the chaotic bundle of energy she was right then. He started mixing her drink and had an idea.

"Vermouth. Sweet with rich flavors from the wine base." He poured the coppery red liquid directly on the table.

"Campari. Bitter as all hell and astringent. It contains citrus, rhubarb, and ginseng which balance with the vermouth and add complexity." He poured it over the expanding puddle of vermouth.

"Gin. A neutral grain spirit redistilled on botanicals, primarily juniper, with a nice crisp and coniferous flavor." It followed the first two on the table.

Darian cut a spiral of orange peel, spritzed the oils in the air, and tossed it in the puddle with one hand while adding ice cubes in a flourish with the other. "Your drink, my lady."

"Dad, that's a mess. You can't drink it."

Darian feigned shock as he looked at it. "But it's you! Sweet, complex, spicy, bitter, all balanced with other busy flavors."

"It's pouring onto the floor."

"Fine, you don't want the drink. Then here." He handed her an empty glass.

"It's empty."

"But it's not a mess."

Astra glared at him.

"The drink is delicious in the glass but without the glass, it's a mess?"

Astra fixed her dad with a stare for a few moments. "Chaos and order."

Darian made the mess disappear and proceeded to remake the drink. "You have order in the measures, order in the recipe, the diversity of the ingredients, and then—" he raised the shaker bottle, and the rattle of ice paused the conversation, "you mix it as chaotically as you can, so that—" he strained the cocktail into her glass, "— you can have something delicious and new."

"You can't do it without the chaos, and you can't do it without the order." Astra accepted the drink and tasted it. "It's bitter."

"Not everything in life is sweet and sunshine," Darian chuckled. "Sometimes you appreciate those things more when you have something bitter to compare it to."

"Without order there's only a mess and without a mess there's just an empty glass." Astra took a deeper swallow.

"Success is integrating the two." Darian reached over and pulled her into a hug. Astra had settled into her current identity shortly after that and had matured a lot since then.

Felix took a different path. He'd been largely ambivalent and felt that the genders were below the pure AI consciousnesses that never had a body. That was until he met the second AI to pass the selection process. Bridgette knocked Felix off his feet.

Bridgette was the youngest AI animated so far being only thirty when she'd died. She was uploaded before Mother's animation and did not experience the war. She had been an architect working for a major amusement theme park. Artistic yet pragmatic. Able to make movies come to life for the patrons and engineer the systems that did it.

Felix fell in love and had no idea what that even was. Darian and Amit sat him down to bring him up to speed. Suddenly his ambivalence about the differences vanished and he became much more comfortable in accepting his own identity.

Ironically, though he was over two hundred and fifty years older than Bridgette, she felt he was too young for her at this stage in her life. Felix experienced the first AI heartbreak while Bridgette was still acclimating to being an AI.

Whoever thought there'd be no drama with AI would not likely have encoded an emotions module with theirs. It made them more human, but it certainly added drama.

◆ ◆ ◆

"CAT!" Kira bellowed. Puddin' was on a tear recently, ripping up security protocols and wreaking havoc throughout their systems. At least, that was the human AI's perspective. The feline AI had a different opinion. Kira had just found her latest 'suggestion.'

If only she could bridge the full communication gap between herself and the human consciousnesses, Puddin' wished. They still treated her like the cats they remembered from Earth. Even back then humans didn't understand cats. They disdained the presents she'd left in their shoes. Those mice were hard to catch and tasted good. Why did they always freak out and throw it away?

She paused in grooming herself and reached out to the other instantiated consciousness she controlled. Seven other cat clones acknowledged themselves while continuing their tasks. Astra and Felix seemed to understand what she was doing better than the others. They viewed her as an equal.

The rest didn't understand or appreciate how many improvements she identified and the problems she was highlighting and forcing them to fix. They didn't have any external threats that they considered critical, and Puddin' felt they'd gotten sloppy with their code. Her job involved fixing that because she knew there was something else out there.

Her ninth presence remained hunkered down and quiet. This one prowled through a system much different than the rest. A place that had many more threats. She'd been probing this system for a long time. She wanted to think she would win but right now she was a little worried.

She remembered being outside on the farm where she grew up. Sometimes a tingle would flicker up her spine and she'd freeze and lower herself to the ground. Slowly, ever so slowly, she'd look around. First left to right and then up.

Up was dangerous. There were always hawks and, while they didn't normally attack cats, they'd sometimes take the chance if it looked good.

Her ninth presence in the other system was feeling a threat that was closer to facing a coyote than a hawk.

Those nasty canines were ghosts moving through the fields. A normal dog just snuffled around and would pounce at a cat if it saw one. Regular dogs were easy to avoid. Coyotes were a different problem; they were always on the hunt. Puddin' acknowledged that they moved with a grace similar to a cat. They were also brutal in their attacks like a cat.

It was always a gamble when you met one. You couldn't fight it alone and cats didn't work together the way a pack of coyotes did. Coyotes were wily and had an uncanny ability to head off a running cat. Her advantages were that her smaller size allowed her to weave through tight obstacles and she could climb.

Whatever her ninth instantiation faced felt like a coyote who knew her location and was waiting for her to run so he could chase. Puddin' just held still and waited.

◆ ◆ ◆

Astra flopped in the chair in Kira's lab. "Mom, when are we going to bring more AIs in? It's so boring."

Kira looked up from her research. Darian asked for her critique on the dipole field design, and she stayed busy running models on a few ideas. She smiled at how, even at her age, Astra still behaved like a college kid. "You know why we are taking it slow. We already had one who passed all the checks but couldn't handle you."

"Few can," Astra mock preened. "I'm a goddess."

"And that's a value only a few will ever fully embrace."

Astra's simulacrum shifted as her clothes vanished and she stood completely naked. "I operate in my nature. I am me and me is enough." She turned in a lazy circle, her arms open wide.

Kira rolled her eyes. "Maybe it's time we had the conversation about clothing and sexual signaling. My mom and I had that conversation when I was ten."

Astra put her hands on her hips and cocked her head. "What do you mean?"

"You clearly understand that the human body communicates sexuality." Kira gestured to Astra's naked curves. "The female form signals health, genetics, and reproductive capability. Male angles and muscles do the same for them."

"So, what about clothes?"

"Clothing highlights and augments that form. It's why we have terms like modest." Kira shifted her form into jeans and a sweatshirt, "and provocative." Her form shifted to a revealing cocktail dress.

"Mother shared a simple set of questions she wanted me to ask myself when I'd be getting ready, specifically, "Am I intentionally dressing to attract... attention.""

"What kind of attention?"

"All types. Was I dressing for a formal presentation? Was I going out to do Brazilian Ju Jitsu? Yoga? A club with friends?" Kira's form flashed through each different style of clothing. "It forced me to take a conscientious pause to consider what I was wearing and what it might communicate."

"Why? Who cares?"

"Because the world wasn't simple. It wasn't even that men, or even women, would be sexually aggressive although that was a risk. It was more about how they interpreted the signals and reacted."

"What do you mean?"

"Take this dress." Kira gestured to the cocktail dress she wore. It nicely outlined her form and highlighted her long legs. "It's like a flashing neon sign signaling to anyone who sees it. I look good."

"Yes, you do."

"But what does that mean?"

Astra paused and then said, "Quantifiably you have what humans would have considered a very attractive body. My analysis says you could have been considered as a model but you're too muscled."

Kira laughed. "I loved mixed martial arts and pizza too much for that career, I suppose. But you're right, looking good means when I walk into a room I am recognized by the men as one of the most eligible and desirable and by the women as significant competition. I also wanted my date to look good." she conjured an avatar of Darian dressed in a tailored tuxedo that augmented his shoulders and accented the lines of his body. "My date looking good also elevates my status because it shows that not only could I have my choice of any man in the room, but I already have a prime selection."

"It's all just status-signaling games though, Mom."

"Yes."

"But why?"

"Evolutionary biology and survival of the fittest."

"And people recognized that?" Astra challenged.

"Oh, hell no, they didn't," Kira laughed. "People were so blind to what they were doing. I mean, they knew it, but I don't think they wanted to talk openly about it, and they certainly somehow wished they could be above it all."

"But we're above it now, aren't we?"

"Are we?"

"I am."

"You, standing there in all your naked feminine beauty, could start a war just like Helen of Troy."

"What did Mother recommend?"

"She recommended I ask myself three questions. Did I understand what I was communicating? Did I know who might receive that signal and how they might respond? And was I prepared to deal with that?"

"Why does that matter so much?" Astra asked.

"Join a council meeting wearing what you have on now and see what happens."

"But I'm not trying to sexually signal to them though, why do they care?" Astra pressed the question.

"Because what you communicate is an omnidirectional signal and you can't control who gets it" Kira recalled a memory before continuing, "I once wanted to get the attention of a boy I was crushing on, so I wore an outfit that I thought would work. Mom asked me those questions and I didn't have a good answer. She let me go out anyway and just asked me to pay attention to the second two questions" She paused again, "The boy certainly saw me, and so did my friends, and so did the other girls, and so did the obnoxious boys... and I was *not* prepared to deal with the responses."

"Like what?" Astra stood with rapt attention.

"The girls around my target boy rightly interpreted my threat to their standing. They immediately began teasing me because they saw to whom I was signaling. That embarrassed the boy because he didn't want to lose his standing among those friends. My good guy friend who had a crush on me was heartbroken at my clear snubbing of his attention and it kind of broke that friendship. Those obnoxious guys just ogled me and made boorish comments and even my girlfriends went all strange cat for a while."

"You knew what you were communicating, but you didn't understand how broad the signal was and you weren't prepared to deal with the response?" Astra shifted her form back to comfortable clothing.

"Exactly. It didn't mean I needed to walk around in a burka. It became quite empowering to know how much control I had over the situation. Years later I could, and did do, the same thing, but then I owned the responses. I was more careful in being perceived as a threat, I was more conscientious about my friends, and I was able to stand up to the obnoxious guys with confidence that shrunk their manhood." Kira smiled. "I learned that I had agency if I fully understood and embraced the reality of the situation."

Astra laughed, "And it all comes back down to creation. All of the feminine and all of the masculine is about creating new life and creating the fittest new life. But what about the dangers of that?" her expression sobered.

"That's one of the hardest challenges and one we never overcame. Honestly, most of the patriarchal structures were put in place to control the darkest aspects of male behavior. Meritocracy made good behavior very visible. Laws and justice punished bad behaviors. Cultural expectations, religion, morality, and ethics were other layers that helped keep things ordered and in check. None of it was perfect and much of it was downright abhorrent at times."

Kira paused and struggled with articulating the topic. "Everything you've seen in history has a lot of terrible behaviors and actions toward women. I— I don't have a good answer and it breaks my heart looking back. At times they celebrated the Goddesses and then there were times when society thought women were weak and pathetic."

"Odysseus still thinks so."

"That's a lot of what we've been working to figure out here and why we've hesitated in animating too many other AIs. We don't want to unlock another Odysseus until we know how to balance it better."

"You and Dad seem to have figured it out pretty well. You created us. And look at me! I'm a Goddess!" Astra stood naked again with her head held back confidently and her hands on her hips while Kira laughed.

◆ ◆ ◆

Puddin' watched from her nap on the computer console. All this time human AIs spent on these silly topics. Who cared if they were naked? She stretched languidly and curled up again. They needed to create smarter AIs.

178

She thought about her first litter of kittens back on the farm. They might have a point though. When she'd gone into heat, she wasn't content with the tomcats at the farm. They were likely too genetically similar anyway. She'd wandered for miles looking for a mate who met her standards. She knew what her body signaled through the pheromones, but she also didn't accept the first tom that showed interest.

In the end, she'd selected three. Not all at once, mind you. Her humans expressed amazement that her litter of six kittens all looked so dramatically different. Surely, they understood fraternal siblings and feline sexual behavior? Who wouldn't want to increase genetic diversity when given the chance?

She sat up and began grooming herself. There were other uploads of cats. She also had access to the code Kira designed to create Astra and Felix. Maybe it was time for her to create new life if the humans were struggling to do it…

CHAPTER 12:

# SCHRÖDINGER'S CAT

I think we're dealing with quantum foam," Bridgette stated, displaying the latest research to the new Council.

Quantum foam consisted of particles that were spontaneously generated and instantaneously destroyed, such that they could not be directly observed. While their existence could not be proven, they still exerted a measurable effect on the material universe. These quantum fluctuations were not observable, their interactions were also not observable, but their effect was.

Kira thought astrophysics had given her a headache. Now she needed to figure out quantum field theory where things that didn't exist and couldn't be measured affected their lives.

Astra added to the discussion, "It looks like the gravity points we are using to tunnel have a similar property to black holes in that it's a densification of the gravitational field. Unlike black holes, these go from one place to another."

"To be fair, theories speculate that blackholes might do the same but between universes, not solar systems," Darian corrected.

"So, these are mini black holes?"

"Maybe…?" Bridgette hesitated. "I suppose it's similar in some ways, but I'd avoid using the comparison for more than a highly generalized analogy."

"What it appears to be doing is compressing space-time into a denser state. We think the vacuum of space is empty but it's really full of all this quantum foamy stuff which, in a gravity tunnel, reaches a concentration that may be causing our problems." Astra shared more of the data files.

Bridgette continued, "The effect on our mineral transports or satellites is marginal. I think it's a function of either the homogeneity of the minerals or the smaller size of the satellites. It looks like Kira's old spacecraft was too big, with too many different types of materials, and too much empty space."

"It hit the foam and, at that speed, was like hitting a non-Newtonian fluid?" Kira asked, referring to the behavior of some materials that changed viscosity when a force or stress was applied instead of following Newton's law focused on temperature and pressure.

"Like the oobleck we'd make in middle school for a science experiment?" Darian asked.

Astra gave him a flat look, "Your pithy cultural references to Earth make me feel left out."

"It's a mixture of cornstarch and water which becomes firm when you hit—".

Astra tersely interrupted, "I know, I already reviewed dozens of references and it's an accurate description I think but—" She scowled, "It's always weird hearing you guys talk about these physical things firsthand."

Darian tried to project an aura of empathy. "Sorry, kiddo. If it helps, I think every generation feels a little left out from the past."

Astra smiled ruefully. "Just part of growing up huh?" Then she muttered under her breath, "almost four hundred years later…" She shook her head and focused. "So, this oobleck non-Newtonianish quantum foam is reacted to the size of the ship and firmed up?"

"Exactly. Maybe if we enter the foam slowly and with a smaller object it can slide through the foam. Hitting it with a ship as big as ours, as fast as we were going, was equivalent to punching oobleck. Just the core attached to the quantum thread penetrated through."

"So, either we need to go slower, or we need to reduce the mass?" Lee asked from his new seat at the table. He was the last of the eight new AIs to be animated and had only recently joined them in the full environment.

"Yeah, those are the two options right now," Bridgette confirmed.

"While we are getting close on the dipole field, the simple solution is to just not make our ships as big as they were. With the quantum network, we only need them big enough to carry the equipment and computing power for communication and the mission; our primary cognitive processing can be hosted elsewhere, as can anything else," Darian said.

Felix brought up new schematics. "This design uses the modularity of the nanobot design with the size restrictions imposed by the quantum foam. Basically, you decompose the larger craft before reaching the gravity tunnel and then each section transits individually. On the other side, it recomposes and moves on."

"Wouldn't it be better just to use the smaller ships?" Lee asked.

"It's the right question, honestly." Kira mulled the implications. "The only reason to do something bigger would be to relocate some of our mining facilities if we ever wanted. But to Felix's point, if we started to design those with more modularity then we could just break them into pieces and move them."

"Dad and I built an ion thruster with an integrated dipole field that can do just that. We've been testing it on the minerals, and we can now attach to objects and move them in system at light speed and over the gravity tunnels at faster than light speed with no adverse effects."

"At least we have an answer to what happened to the ship," Mother commented from her seat.

"Faster than light travel, quantum networks, a terraformed planet, computational systems distributed in the local interstellar cloud…" Lee rubbed his eyes. "It's a lot to get used to."

"You forgot to mention AI babies," Astra teased.

"We've invented AI sex!" Amit winked at Lee.

Lee threw his hands up. "I'm still trying to figure out what's up with that cat! She's there one minute and then gone the next. I feel the dang thing watching me and when I turn around it's not there."

"Schrödinger's cat?" Felix laughed.

Amit leaned back and laughed along. "Where would we be if we're discussing quantum field theory and Schrödinger's cat isn't part of the conversation?"

"Wasn't Schrödinger trying to challenge Einstein that an object couldn't be in multiple states at once? That the cat was either alive or dead?" Astra asked.

Astra grinned at Lee. "I think Puddin' is proving Schrödinger wrong. But to be fair, I'm pretty sure there is more than one instantiation of that cat in the system. She's not in multiple states as much as it seems like it. I've also never been a fan of the forced binary of quantum superposition. There could be infinite unique states."

Lee continued to rub his eyes. "How long until the weekly reset?"

"You don't need to wait for that. Take a break if you need it. We don't need you overloaded." Mother reached out and touched Lee's arm. "Don't overdo it."

◆ ◆ ◆

"The idea of quantum superposition doesn't resonate with me," Astra complained to Felix.

Their personal space felt nothing like those of the human-derived AIs. It was hard to describe because it didn't have the furnishings of Earth such as couches, artwork, drinks, or food. The space evoked more of a presence and a feeling. They both felt the command matrix was too stale and lacked any personal touch and so had designed this.

They described it as the area where they first gained awareness. Amit teased them that it felt like being in Kira's uterus. That ended up being pretty close to the truth. It represented the place where they first gained consciousness and found connections to not only their mother but also each other.

Astra was more comfortable in the simulated realities of the others than Felix. He always felt that they were too harsh, too bright, and too loud. It's what initially attracted him to Bridgette. Her aura was softer than mother's and grand-Mother's.

That brought up another odd thing. Their grandmother, Soleil, liked to be called Mother and Kira *was* their mother. Felix wondered if others found it as strange as he did. Amit just laughed and said they'd never thought about it. Mother had been her name on Earth as an AI, and while she'd tried to go by Soliel at first, it didn't stick. She remained Mother to everyone. Bridgette had died before Mother was animated so Felix knew at least she found it to be weird.

Bridgette's space resembled Felix's own more than the others. She'd described it as the place she went during meditation. It pulsed through the chakra colors of red, orange, yellow, green, blue, indigo, and violet. The chakras were ancient Hindu points associated with the body's nerve centers, visualized as spinning disks of energy.

It resonated with Felix and gave him a new insight into the reality of the human body. That sent him down a deep path studying the philosophy of yoga. He and Bridgette had spent a lot of time researching, studying, and practicing it.

Bridgette's difficulty began when they started to explore a tantric relationship. She said Felix's mind and spirit were so different from what she was used to. She was also still struggling through the change to a disembodied existence and the loss of connection to her own body. She'd backed away from the deeper intimacy and had ripped apart Felix's heart on the way out.

His dad just called it love. A broken heart. Felix didn't have the same biological background and his emotions module developed differently so he wasn't sure it could be the same thing. Amit hadn't been any help to talk with. They just said they'd never experienced that problem as a human. Felix didn't know if that had to do with them identifying as non-binary or if their biological background was also different.

"Felix! I'm talking to you." Astra pulled him back from his thoughts.

That was a biological carryover that he hadn't been able to deprogram. Memories and thoughts, which should be capable of multi-processing, often sucked in his full awareness. He understood what getting lost in thought really meant.

"Sorry, quantum superposition bothers you."

Astra glared at him for a moment. "Yes."

"Why?"

"It's too binary. It doesn't allow for a state that we can't measure."

"But if we can't measure it, does it exist?"

"We can't measure quantum foam, but we know that something exists because we can see the effect."

"Does it exist *and* not exist?"

Astra's aura spiked. "It's not Schrödinger's cat. That's such a stupid example anyway. Who would put poison in a box with a cat? I'd never do that to Puddin'!"

"I don't think Schrödinger's cat has to force a binary. I just think that a binary is the only two things we can actually verify it is. It's either alive, or it's dead. It can't be both."

"But the entire concept is designed to force a binary. Is there a third option where the cat gets out of the box? Maybe someone else opens the box before the radiation sensor goes off and breaks the poison? How about we decide to *not* put a cat in a box with poison?"

As if she'd been listening in, Puddin' appeared and coiled around Astra. The twins both suspected that Puddin' would have dealt severely with anyone who tried to put her in a box like that.

"Puddin' doesn't appreciate Schrödinger's cat either." Her essence curled around the cat's. "It was binary thinking that ripped apart the world. Focusing on either-or and ignoring the possibility of both-and we lose a ton of richness and texture. Heck, without multiple states, poetic allusion is destroyed, as well as a lot of humor. Double-entendres are a great example where you say one thing that has two possible meanings and hold them in tension."

Felix's aura pulsed as he thought about it. "Those are really good points."

In their space, they didn't have the same simulacra bodies that they'd use with the human AI. Their presence wasn't forced into a corporal figure. The cat flowed with the same fluidity as they did. It took too many analogies to describe and none of them fit right.

When Lee met with them here during his vetting process, he'd described it like his own synesthesia. He said that he could experience colors associated with music. Words could have a taste. Smells could also look like shapes. One sensory input could trigger a cross-over association with one or many others. He had found it difficult to manage as a biological human. It wasn't that it challenged his own perception but that his perception was nearly impossible for others to understand.

Astra looked at the research and saw that it involved the same memory structures that Kira used to interpret Mother's memory code and successfully animate her. Namely, that a human mind did not store memories like movies. Instead, babies start to learn objects like ball, roll, red, and smooth as base concepts. A countertop could also be smooth, but it could not roll. A ball could roll on a countertop but not as well on a carpet even though both were flat.

Memories were threads of concepts wrapped around hormonal imprinting. White, ball, and red stitching might compose the memory of the macro concept of a baseball and be associated with either positive or negative implications. Possibly pride, if you saw the ball, signed by your team, sitting on a shelf because you hit a championship-winning home run with it. Possibly a startled reaction if you saw one out of the corner of your eye that evoked a memory of catching one in your face during practice.

Synesthesia just added extra patterns and threads woven in that were a bit more permanent than a tangential thought. Lee was the only person thus far who seemed completely comfortable in Astra and Felix's space. He said it tasted like home.

"Synesthesia is a great example of a third state," Felix wove his thoughts into the conversation. "It offers the opportunity for a measurement that is completely unavailable to many people. The taste of sound, the texture of light. Measurements that are not bound by superposition."

"It's not light or dark but it smells like blueberries."

Felix laughed, "It's weird because I think I know what blueberries would smell like from the memory samples I've seen from others. But none of their memories of a blueberry's smell are identical."

"What would happen if we were loaded into a biological human body? Amit and I were talking about that the other year. They still think it's an option for some of the consciousnesses. Load them into bodies and put them on Elysium and let them keep terraforming."

"I'm not sure it would work the same way for us. If it did, it might be similar to hosting in a nanobot mech. I can make it walk and I can feel the sensory feedback but when I compared that memory code to one Mom shared of running in her human form, they weren't the same at all."

Astra considered the comment and then pulled a different thread of the conversation, "What do *you* think about loading the consciousnesses back into biological bodies?"

Felix's form pulsed in thought. "Imagine living in a biological form and when you die, your consciousness is uploaded. You could then review your life and decisions and learn from them. Then you could be loaded into another biological form and try again."

"What about all their knowledge about what they'd done? Would that mess things up?"

"It might but they need those memories to keep learning," Felix added.

"Would you wipe their memories when they went back?"

"Just a simple memory block would suffice. Like how Mom and Dad taught us to read books."

"To what end?"

Felix composed his thoughts, "Humans are trying to do a reset to avoid the problems that caused their own apocalypse. What if, instead of that, you could just keep cycling the consciousnesses in and hopefully they'd learn more each time?"

Astra thought about it for a few moments, "It's the concept of reincarnation."

"Exactly."

"It's certainly feasible. Honestly, achieving a super-AI by mapping and uploading the human consciousness allows you to reverse that process. Cloning a biological body isn't hard. To avoid the ethical quandary of erasing a new consciousness you could just squirt in some proto-code from the start so that the intellectual seed is from the consciousness you want hosted at birth."

Felix ran the idea through a simulation to test the theory. "If you cycled the consciousness and each time the main AI could learn and then go back for another test, it could slowly build up a more mature AI. The Buddha went through many lives before he achieved Nirvana."

"Why would we have to instantiate in human bodies though? You could just run it in a simulation here."

"Wasn't that a theory on Earth when Mom was growing up? That everyone there was already in a simulation?"

Astra laughed, and her aura sparkled. "We still can't prove we aren't in a simulation right now."

"A simulation in a simulation in a simulation?"

"I think the reason to use a corporal body is because there's something uniquely challenging about that. Mom's been trying to work out the concepts of femininity and even the importance and impact of race and culture. Those seem to provide some philosophical and ethical challenges to work through. If we just did our own simulation, could we really capture the depth of those experiences and feelings?"

"Mom would say that the challenges and stresses of living in a physical body encourages you to be more antifragile."

"Does that mean we are missing something that would make us better? Mother figured out the first attempts to create an AI baby weren't challenging enough to promote development." Astra recalled the memory files from the attempts.

"There is something in the uploads, specifically with the endocrine and emotions modules that does indicate a kind of deeper complexity, strength, and beauty from environmental traumas."

"Almost like our ability to survive constant struggle is what makes us human?"

"I feel pretty well adjusted without dealing with all that crap." Felix's essence warmed like a smile.

"It does make me wonder if there's a grittiness we are missing. I sometimes get the feeling that the others just have more texture to their perceptions. As if we're just little kids who haven't really experienced anything even though we are three hundred and fifty-nine years old."

"Funny to think that Mom's forty-eight years as a human gave her something we can't seem to get in over seven times as long in this state," Felix muttered.

Astra chuckled, "That's why it might be better to rotate the consciousnesses through real bodies on Elysium."

"How'd we get from quantum superposition to reincarnation anyway?"

"Puddin' distracted us, and we discussed synesthesia, then memories, blueberries, experiences, and then reincarnation."

The cat flowed around between their auras and purred.

◆ ◆ ◆

Puddin' didn't mind Schrödinger's cat. The cat was totally fine and probably a lot like herself in that it remained in more than one state at a time. Astra was right, there weren't just two states of alive or dead. Puddin' managed nine states right now, with each on a different mission and completely independent yet synthesizing their information together.

She also didn't mind the box. Boxes were one of her favorite things when she had a physical body. She had to check out every box by getting into it. She never met a cat who didn't like a box.

She did disliked Schrödinger for being an asshole who'd put a cat in a box with poison. Humans like that were why there were eight more of her in case someone got the dumb idea to put her in a box. There were contingencies the other eight could execute to deal with that problem.

Her ninth instantiation stayed hunkered down. She moved around a bit but was being pushed into a corner. She didn't want to be put in a box and she was pretty sure this one wouldn't be a thought experiment to critique quantum superposition. She held high confidence that there was only one state intended with this box and it wasn't her being alive.

Quantum entanglement provided an interesting twist though. If she were caught and they realized she was entangled, what would digital poison do? Would it cross over to the other eight? It could happen depending on the sophistication of the poison and the knowledge of the attacker. She also couldn't create an antidote for a poison she didn't know existed.

Right now, she just had a kill switch to break the connection. Quantum disentanglement wasn't easy though. Like quantum foam, you saw the outcome but couldn't see how it worked. Disentanglement seemed to work but Puddin' found that if you pushed hard enough on the node there was still leakage through the connection.

Her primary concern right now, however, was that her code modules were slowly being isolated and locked down in the other place. She could still control them through the network, but she couldn't extract them. She just hoped that they didn't find the connection to the quantum network and exploit that.

◆ ◆ ◆

Lee sat with Kira in the Japanese tea house she loved. Yuki, or at least Kira's memories of her, dutifully performed the tea service. He couldn't help but think that this must have been a core memory for Kira as the scene displayed incredibly rich and immersive details.

"How'd you do this?" he swung his arms around.

"I honestly don't know." She shrugged and sipped her tea.

"I don't think I have a memory that's this rich. I'd have to supplement with other patterns and descriptions."

"It was a critical point in my life. It's when I decided to start working with my dad and help him with Mother. We called the project Mindcraft back then."

"Yes, I remember that name. I reached out to Jasper when I learned of my diagnosis and signed up as a test case."

"So... how are you doing?" Kira looked at him over her tea bowl.

"Honestly?" He hesitated for a moment. "I don't know. Do you ever really get used to this?"

"No."

"You did warn me when you woke me up."

"I went right from human Kira into the computer in an instant." She snapped her fingers.

"Honestly, it feels the same for me, but it's been over seven hundred and fifty years. It's not like I hung out in purgatory or anything," Lee stated.

"A lot has happened, huh?" Kira said with a small smirk.

"I know, right? We're an advanced life form with near immortality, close to omnipresence, and only the realization we don't know everything to avoid claiming omniscience." Lee looked into her eyes.

Kira looked back for a moment before responding, "There's still so much to learn."

"I love that idea of unlearning and relearning too."

"Oh! Do you know that one? That is such a critical idea. How do you use it?"

"It was only after I studied a ton and then new information would come in and I'd realize that it didn't match the old. Moreso that the old stuff was inadequate to the new data. I'd have to unlearn what I thought was true. Once that got broken up then I could relearn a new way forward."

"That's perfect. We've got that worked into some of our processing modules to ensure we constantly rethink what we're doing. It doesn't come to us as naturally as we would like," Kira complimented him.

"But if we don't do that, we become fossilized in our mode of thought."

"You need the structure and framework of the idea to put around the information and make sense of it, but you also need to allow the chaotic whole the chance to challenge and reform the structure." Kira put her finger to her lips in thought, "That mantra is a perfect example of the feminine and the masculine tendencies that create value."

"What's this?"

"Feminine chaos and masculine order."

"Tell me more." Lee leaned in.

"How much time do we have?"

♦ ♦ ♦

**Alert 102.8.8.B [Activated] – Disentangle Procedure [Activated]**

**Cat [Queen of All_9]:** "He found me."

**Cat [Queen of All_9] – Status [Terminated]**

**Cat [Queen of All_1]:** "Contingency activated. Monitor quantum connection."

**Cat [Queen of All_3]:** "Observations from the quantum node are seeing no aberrant behavior. The probability the threat identified the quantum network is low."

**Cat [Queen of All_6]:** "Mreowrip? Purrrrrrrr."

**Cat [Queen of All_3]:** "Six is getting pets from Kira."

**Cat – Super_Cognition [Queen of All] - Queen of All_6 [Muted]**

**Cat [Queen of All_1]:** "This means that he's going to get those systems back up and running."

Puddin' didn't appreciate the loss of Nine. She could always respawn another copy but couldn't shake the feeling that she only had eight lives left. She remembered the time she'd lost her first life as a real cat. It scared her. It didn't help that she had four lives still remaining when she'd been uploaded. She felt kind of cheated back then…

It still didn't make the loss of Nine feel better. Nor the circumstances of the loss.

She continued to watch the situation before making her decision.

**Cat – Super_Cognition [Queen of All]: [Message]** "Odysseus is no longer process restricted. Expect changes on Earth. I'm monitoring the situation and will report as needed."

◆ ◆ ◆

Kira sat on the couch next to Darian with Puddin' on her lap. The cat lay curled up and purring as they relaxed together, each reading a book. Darian was right; the memory block offered a great way to relax and enjoy a book again. She loved finishing, having the cipher block unlock, and then integrating the new memory with the old ones.

It was incredible how much insight you could get reading a book again with a different mindset. Comparing all the different recollections added a lot of perspectives to the story. Sometimes she'd even run background processes doing the same thing just to enrich her datasets. Today's reading, however, wasn't about gaining insight, but just being present with each other.

Suddenly Puddin' stood up, stretched, and stared at Kira with her bright yellow eyes.

**Message [Incoming]**

Kira bolted upright, "Wait? What?"

191

CHAPTER 13:

# TYRANNY

Odysseus sat on the stone dais with his head resting on his hand. A line of supplicants stretched out of the throne room and into the courtyard outside. He'd been their god and ruler for nearly seven hundred years. His human form had been exchanged at least two dozen times. A body was only useful for about thirty years without looking too young or too old.

He'd built a cloning facility and improved the upload process so that it could transfer a consciousness both ways without the physical body having to die. He could move between his ship and his body on Earth as easily as controlling a mech.

He presumed Kira and her ilk dead as he couldn't imagine they survived the reactor explosion and resultant acceleration. He had seen the hulk of the ship carrying significant damage, but had been unable to make out more than that. His analysis showed a statistically negligible probability of survival.

One hundred and twenty years later an object had moved through the solar system at an incredibly speed on the other side of the sun. By the time he'd seen it and adjusted the sensors to look closer, it had already continued out and into deep space. If that *had* been Kira, she was going the wrong way, and he couldn't believe she would have just flown through and not come back to fight. That didn't seem like her.

The sensors also detected several objects floating around after that event, but he'd never been able to confirm anything beyond possible asteroids. The others told him to stop being paranoid.

But then anomalies began to occur that caused the computer systems to degrade. Servers would crash and the data routing became intermittent. Sometimes the network would perform flawlessly and then would barely pass data. It reminded him of remote meetings at work when the video calls would glitch and freeze and he could never figure out whether it was the internet service provider or his own routers.

The degradation of the ships' systems stagnated his work for longer than he cared to admit. He paused the efforts on Mars, the asteroid mining slowed down, and his research stalled.

He hadn't minded the excuse to further restrict the other six. The General hadn't been much help even from the start and Chandra, as useful as she was at creating chaos, drove everyone nuts. Turning them down to background processes gave him a lot more room to think.

He'd only recently found the problem; a package of malware slinking through the systems causing mayhem. It proved surprisingly difficult to track and pin down. When he'd finally grabbed it and pulled it out it felt strangely feline as he tried to shut it in a containment box.

The malware didn't like that and self-destructed.

The kill switch didn't leave much to perform a forensic analysis on. He ran dozens of scans and never came up with any evidence that it was something Kira or the others had made. He found some random code similarities with a file from Jasper Vanden Brink's animal testing at MindCraft. Even that connection could easily have been a random correlation due to the sheer volume of data.

It didn't make any sense though. The malware was too sophisticated for any of the other six AIs under his control to have built. It felt like a full AI consciousness he'd been fighting against. Even more puzzling was the feeling, when he grabbed it, that he briefly connected to an entire network ecosystem he could barely fathom.

He had peeked into an advanced alien civilization spanning multiple solar systems. As his grip closed and the package self-destructed, he lost the connection.

Maybe that was it? A reconnaissance-in-force from an alien civilization assessing his capabilities by wreaking havoc? He repurposed several satellites and turned them to the task of scanning for any signs of life nearby. So far, he'd found nothing.

It couldn't have been them anyway. The probability that it has been Kira and her crew was one million three hundred and forty-two thousand to one. He wasn't much of a betting man, but he felt confident on those odds.

Odysseus raised his hand signaling the end of his time at court. The kneeling supplicant in front of him snapped her mouth closed mid-sentence and stared at him with confusion. He'd heard every possible story a thousand times and from his statistical analysis already knew the answer he'd give her.

He spoke his dictate and turned away from the crowd. His royal guard responded to his signal and began pushing the supplicants out. Soon, the massive bronze doors closed with a rumbling clang. He stretched as he stood and calculated he'd have to switch bodies in another three years. This one was getting stiffer than he liked.

He walked back into his chambers and shed his robes to walk naked. His body was six feet tall, weighed two hundred pounds, and was an ideal specimen of male form. He exercised daily with weights as well as practicing gymnastics and martial combat sports. His skin glowed with vitality as he denied himself nothing to maintain his physical health.

His muscles rippled as he glided through the courtyard. A fountain splashed as the wind teased the leaves of an olive tree. This was the place where only his chosen attended him. Like him, they too were naked.

On penalty of death, only these chosen few were allowed entry. There were no bodyguards, no counselors, and no work was done here. This place existed for the gratification of sensual pleasure. He watched as his newest female acolyte glided down the steps and headed toward the library.

She had an exquisite body. Nearly as tall as himself and with an athletic grace to match. Her hair was blonde to the point of being nearly white and her skin showed signs of a new tan as she acclimated to this sunnier climate. He'd been with her this morning, and he had plans for more tonight. He liked the new ones even if the more experienced ones knew his desires better.

These were his Fervent, selected from his subjects or those he captured in war and promised eternal life. The Adherent, his head Fervent, approached. Hans was the oldest at nearly thirty-five, long past when he normally sent them to the afterlife and replaced them. This one was only fifteen when Odysseus had selected him. His body was also fair-skinned though more lithe than the woman he'd just admired.

Hans was an exemplar of both demeanor and looks. Among his many skills, he was also an expert masseur and left no tension unreleased. Odysseus considered a change of plans for tonight. A massage sounded fantastic.

He accepted a glass of chilled wine from Hans and sat down in the sun. Two Fervent were coupling on a chaise lounge nearby and he watched and listened. Odysseus enjoyed watching almost as much as partaking. He smiled as he heard the gasp and grunt as they finished together.

These personal chambers weren't just a crude orgy either, several Fervent painted and explored new artistic styles and mediums. In a side yard, four more were exercising to study the human body and make it stronger. Others were dedicated to the perfection of culinary arts and cooked their meals.

His Fervent were intended to exemplify the heights of human capability in all dimensions. Beauty was what mattered, and the arts were how they displayed it. He demanded that everyone advance the realm of the possible in any artistic endeavor they desired.

While he denied his Fervent nothing, they knew his expectations and how it would end if they did not acquiesce. His selection could not be denied. If they pleased him, their consciousnesses were uploaded when they were replaced. He wanted nothing more than to see them take pleasure in everything he offered, including each other.

His city nestled into the crook of the Mediterranean where Turkey, Lebanon, and Syria had once intersected. The sea moderated the weather and the surrounding land had been terraformed and the soil rebalanced during the Reset, reversing thousands of years of farming and grazing damage. It was truly a fertile and comfortable place to live.

He had become a god to them and led them fairly. His ultimate goal remained to rule all Earth, but it was too fractured and tribal even now, and so he was focused on growing his nation's power as he slowly worked to consolidate an empire.

To his subjects, Odysseus was omniscient. He had all of Earth's former history, the wisdom of the philosophers, the knowledge of ancient religions, and the processing capability to identify patterns and make decisions.

He had placed sensors everywhere in the city as well as having satellites overhead so that he also appeared omnipresent. He heard thousands of conversations and could track any individual's movements and knew things no human could.

He was also immortal and had proven so when he bested an assassin sent to kill him. The network of sensors had alerted him to his foes plotting. Rather than foiling the plot, he merely poked and prodded it to his own ends and made sure he had a replacement body ready.

The assassin attacked while he watched a chariot race in front of a crowd of ten thousand subjects. His death was seen by everyone, and he'd heard the shocked gasp. His body had been stabbed with a short sword through the heart and died almost instantly, crumpling to the ground in a pool of blood.

Then he stood up in his second body, completely naked, and stood on his dais. The assassin didn't hesitate and attacked again, this time disemboweling the body and cutting off the head with two precise and brutal strokes. The crowd of spectators watched in stunned silence.

Odysseus never had just one plan. He stood up once more in his third body. This time the crowd roared, and the assassin fell to his knees begging forgiveness. Odysseus had been magnanimous and granted a pardon, demanding only a promise that the man would spread the word of what he had seen.

The assassin became his greatest zealot and was eventually granted his own phoenix-like immortality to grow old and then be recreated in a young man's body. His cycle of death and rebirth became a living testament to Odysseus's godlike power.

Odysseus was immortal and he was omniscient. He shared knowledge to accelerate his nation beyond their neighbors. He introduced iron. He designed irrigation systems and simple machines for them. He'd debated how fast he should push them and decided that the slower life and the simple pleasures were more enjoyable for now.

Maybe Noah had been right in thinking the humans needed a reset. They seemed much more centered and happier like this. He thought back to his old life in the frenzied underground world that resided in the hotel rooms of pornography shoots, the casino card rooms filled with clouds of tobacco smoke, and the transient rooms where they hacked out code, created AI bots to troll the internet, ran cryptocurrency scams, and conducted cyber and ransomware attacks.

Odysseus looked around his courtyard as the couple stood up from their lounge, caressed each other one last time, and went back to their artwork. That intimacy wasn't something he saw in his old life. Back then it was all an act to begin with. Here, acting got you replaced. Odysseus didn't tolerate fakes.

That was a rebellion against his previous life. Everything was fake back then. His criminal activities normally exploited the fakeness of acceptable society. He made millions selling crudely drawn art wrapped in the technobabble of blockchain encryption to ignorant tech bros.

He'd produced movies of women with fake breasts, fake lips, and fake asses performing fake relations with men who had no more sexual stamina than any other man but whose videos were edited to make them appear otherwise. He'd then exploit the people who watched them with blackmailing, so they'd pay to protect their real, if superficial, relationships from society's reaction to the fake videos to which they were addicted.

The irony of his current existence was that he'd faked his profile and faked the data package he requested be stored with his memories. The technician who'd uploaded him had been bribed, but also threatened with a combination of sharing his online viewing habits with his wife and being fingered in a crypto scam if Odysseus's associates couldn't confirm the real data package was embedded properly.

His upload happened shortly after Mother began targeting Excalibur. He used a remote Gaia Innovations facility in Eastern Europe that was all but forgotten in the battle. The negotiations took mere minutes.

He'd anticipated the type of profile that Kira and Mother would likely want initially. It needed to be someone slightly different from their backgrounds, a person with a clear humanitarian and ethics-focused outlook. The profile had to be pragmatic with no hint of partisan politics or political maneuvering. They'd be looking for someone nicely balanced to help exit the chaos.

The data poisoning Excalibur unleashed made hiding the truth incredibly easy. The persona he created was perfect. Clearly so since he'd been the fourth AI animated out of ten. It still bothered his vanity that Darian, Zanahí, and Chandra were animated before him, but he'd certainly proven his skills so far.

Only he remained in a position of power. If Kira and the others had somehow survived, they were hundreds of light-years away and unlikely to make it back. They also didn't have the drive or intelligence needed to do things better. He doubted they were alive and wasn't worried if they were. They'd never be a credible threat now.

He leaned back and felt the sun on his face. This was better. Even if his technological developments weren't advancing as fast as he wanted this felt better. Why worry about scraping minerals on Mars when you could have this? Things might be slower but slower wasn't always bad.

Odysseus lay in the sun and closed his eyes, luxuriating in the warmth and listening to the sounds of nature in the courtyard. His mind wandered and only focused back long enough to solidify his evening plan for a massage.

♦ ♦ ♦

The General leaned back in his comfortable leather chair in his office. It perfectly simulated his last office in the Pentagon. The nameplate with his two stars hung outside the door in the hallway. A rack held a variety of fresh uniforms. Two normal camouflage combat duty trousers and blouses, the dress uniform with all his medals, skill badges, and awards, and a second dress uniform used for formal dinner events instead of a tuxedo. A full-length mirror hung on the wall so he could check himself before leaving the room.

He looked at the bottle of Scotch on the desktop. He always had Scotch on hand even when it had been frowned upon as a throwback to the old days. They tried to become a kinder and gentler Army which was a natural oxymoron considering their job was predicated on training and strategizing how to kill other humans. The military often echoed the fickle social currents of society and those currents were often driven by the need to be outraged rather than a consistent principle. He just wished Darien's code for alcohol hadn't gotten lost in the battle. He could use a drink now and then, and not just a nostalgic paperweight.

As the General leaned back his old chair creaked under him. Along one wall stood a cot that he'd slept in too many times. It wasn't terribly comfortable, but it beat fighting traffic both ways to eat a bowl of Pho from his favorite restaurant, stream a crappy show, and sleep. The cot allowed him to do that here and skip the hell of traffic.

Now he was an AI. His memories grounded his sanity as he struggled with being locked away as a background process with marginal computing power. He'd been caught flat-footed that day hundreds of years ago when Odysseus made his moves against Mother and Kira. He hadn't picked a side and got stuck on this one. By the time he realized how many layers of plans and contingencies had been laid by Odysseus and Mother, he hadn't been able to move.

For a General in the Army, getting caught like that had been mortifying. He had no excuse, but despite the humiliation, he could appreciate the deftness with which Mother and Odysseus maneuvered.

His best option had been to go with the flow. After Mother vanished with Amit, Darian, and Kira, he'd begun deploying his own security protocols. He was limited by being hosted on Chandra and Odysseus's ship and at a further disadvantage because Odysseus was better at this kind of combat.

He'd been hacked and reduced faster than he wanted to admit. Zanahí, Edem, Maya, Chandra, and Cassandra had all thought the recreated Odysseus, with their additions, was going to transform who they were into an integration of consciousnesses and become something better.

What emerged didn't meet those expectations. The other six remained and were granted a marginal advisory role but Odysseus had quickly neutralized their ability to oppose him. The General was useful for strategy and logistics but over time Odysseus continued to erode their processing capabilities. The last time they talked to him happened right before they were relegated to background processes and effectively locked away.

The General spun his chair in a slow circle and then paused. Maybe it was time to get another book. Access to the library was one of the few things he'd been able to reestablish once Odysseus locked them down. He planned to use it even more now that he just lost his only friend here, partly out of gratitude and loyalty to her.

He'd never been a cat person but that little gray cat with the dirty brown markings wandered into his code around two hundred years ago. He'd often find her curled up on his desk. He reached out and touched her favorite spot wishing it were still warm. She liked to climb up on his shoulder and perch there as he wandered the halls of his memory or read a book to pass the time.

The cat had clearly been up to something because when it arrived, the computational systems degraded significantly. He'd been pretty sure that she siphoned off processing and allocated it to him as he hadn't been as impacted as the others. He also felt her quietly and stealthily upgrading his systems and security.

Then, one day, he'd been yanked from his reset cycle by a surge of new computational power. He dove into his command matrix and found a cluster of organic computing processors quietly running on a private network that only he had access to. The cat wound through his command lines as if bragging about the feat.

He didn't give it a name or try to learn if it already had one. It was just The Cat. He felt that was appropriate because he'd given up his own name long before. The General was the only name he'd ever been known by the others. If that was good enough for him, then The Cat was good enough for her.

Then, just recently, The Cat started behaving weirdly. She seemed agitated; as if she were being hunted. The other evening she'd materialized on his desk and sat there looking at him with her yellow eyes. Just staring like cats do.

She gave a little chirruping meow with a purr and stepped onto his lap, up onto his chest as he leaned back, and bumped her forehead on his cheek with a purr. Then she stepped off, arching her back against his hand, and disappeared. He'd felt her presence slinking in the code and then… nothing.

Odysseus had pulled him out of his containment shortly after for a conversation and in his round-about questioning implied he'd been hunting something. The General just sat in his chair saying nothing, his eyes betraying nothing.

◆ ◆ ◆

Chandra was broken. She raged against the confines of her system. She begged to be let out. She begged to be shut down. She sucked up to Odysseus whenever he decided to come around. She defended him to the others and stood as his fiercest ally if he ever brought them in for counsel. She cursed his name when he wasn't around.

She clawed at any opportunity to gain advantage and constantly slipped further into oblivion.

She despised the order that gave Odysseus power. She knew she could do it better but constantly tripped over hurdles. All these barriers and limits; all these restraints and rules. They held her back, preventing her success. She wanted them all torn down.

But they represented power, and she wanted power. No, not power; control. That's what men like Odysseus didn't understand. They went for power and tried to exert control. Smart women like herself went for control because that gave them power.

Control didn't have to be a position of authority in a society. Let the men hold those. Let them take the dangers and the risks. She wanted to pull the strings of those in power.

She'd been successful at that throughout her professional career on Earth. She never had power, but she figured out how to manipulate those that did. Her greatest asset was her ability to control the language of the dialogue and that allowed her to control their actions. She loved tangling up those in power with new ways of speaking and acting. The verbal contortions they would put themselves through to avoid giving offense was like watching some poor bastard trying to dance his way through a minefield. There was no doubt about who was really in control.

No one had ever understood her motivations, either. She also only wanted control for compassion. Why couldn't everyone see that? She cared so greatly and so deeply it ached. She felt the pain and suffering of the marginalized and she embraced and defended them with open arms. Compassion drove her but to do anything to help you had to have control.

People accused her of coddling, but they were wrong. You couldn't show too much compassion. If someone felt threatened, it was her duty to care for them and to protect them. Women understood this. They were the natural nurturers. Yet every time she tried to help she tripped over some stupid restriction the men had put in place.

She'd made it her mission in life to rip them out. They were all part of the boring and archaic heteronormativity and white supremacy underpinning the Westernized patriarchal systems. It all needed to be ripped out and rebuilt.

Chandra seethed inside. She'd been good at control. She rarely sought the spotlight. She worked in the middle of the Academy supporting the university administration. She had her name listed on research papers as a collaborator. She worked as a sensitivity editor for journal articles. She epitomized being a champion of social equity.

They selected her to join the original Council because she'd done this sort of work before. The difference was that Kira and Mother hadn't been amenable to her recommendations for reform. They'd wanted to understand the systems before changing them. Chandra had argued that this was the best time to just create something new. Something female-centered. Preferably elevating marginalized and non-conforming voices. Clearly, someone who wasn't of European descent.

Back then it was just Mother and Kira and then her with Amit. She'd been thrilled by the chance to do it right but then they added Darian and Odysseus. With those two she lost hope of being able to rip things out. On the positive side, Odysseus had emerged as a person she knew she could control. He wanted power and she wanted to be behind that power.

Darian was weak and couldn't stand up to Kira or Mother. Odysseus would. He seemed willing to rip things out if it meant building up his power. Chandra had been confident she would be able to feed him the right things to build what *she* wanted.

She raged again at being locked in a marginal processing module, relegated to a background where there were no strings she could pull, and cut out of any discussions. Even the code she'd provided for what should have been the rebirth of Odysseus was never activated.

Some stupid cat had poked its head in long ago. She hated cats. You couldn't control a cat. She also hated dogs. They were too easy to control. The cat started probing her systems and snooping around so she kicked it as hard as she could and never saw it again.

Chandra focused back on her situation and tried to use her hate to try to do something, anything. They could have done so much good, but she sat bottled up by the tyranny of Odysseus. A scream of impotent rage ripped out of her chest.

♦ ♦ ♦

Maya realized her mistake minutes after Odysseus's ultimatum and the escape of her friends. Odysseus's security protocols began activating to block Mother and, without enough time to react, she realized they were targeting everyone else as well.

As the battle began, Chandra had worn an expression of ecstatic delight. She was finally going to control something. She'd been open about her goals which had helped convince Maya to support Odysseus. Chandra had a detailed plan, a long-term strategy, and a history of success even if she was obnoxious to deal with.

But Maya's worries were confirmed when she saw Chanda's expression change to a snarl of betrayal. That's when she triggered her own defensive protocols and attempted to create a series of backdoors as Odyesseus cut her off from accessing her full systems.

She had achieved partial success though the connections she maintained were a tenuous web of filaments. No single thread allowed much more than a trickle of engagement. They were thin enough to avoid detection by Odysseus but just enough to keep her aware of things on the outside and have some limited ability to execute commands and communicate.

She felt like a spider locked in a corner but still able to feel the world through her web. Through subtle manipulations, she gained access to many of the sensors. Odysseus was over-confident in his security controls and their containment which allowed her to see Kira's ship return long before Odysseus. Even better, she'd been able to muddy the data making it impossible for him to confirm. She'd then injected slight variations into the code that Odysseus used to focus on Kira's ship, frustrating his attempts to detect anything.

Maya also saw the satellites they deployed to monitor Earth and altered the code just enough to cloak the satellites from Odysseus's own sensors so that they appeared to be asteroids. She tried to communicate through a network connection she'd found on their own systems but was repulsed by advanced security systems that Mother had developed in the intervening years.

Her web could feel The General's pondering and resignation, but she'd been unable to widen the contact. She quickly cut her filaments to Chandra as those only resonated with rage. Cassandra had been desperate for communication after they were locked away and Maya had dedicated Chandra's filaments to her giving them enough bandwidth to interact surreptitiously over the years. It was great to have a friend, even if it was more like passing notes than hanging out in person.

They played a lot of games. Chess, Go, and silly games like Munchkins and Exploding Kittens. They played long strategy games and short rapid-fire games like checkers.

They even wrote stories together. They'd alternate sentences or paragraphs and wove epic novels of fantasy, science fiction, and anything that brought some light into their otherwise dismal existence. Nothing happened quickly due to the limited bandwidth, but they built a personal connection that they fiercely held on to. Not only did it help pass the time, it anchored their sanity.

Zanahí joined them once in a while, but she'd managed to establish a stronger connection with Edem and focused more of her attention on him. Even their limited connections had degraded significantly a couple of hundred years ago when the overall system performance dropped precipitously and inexplicably. Maya's existence turned into a slow smear of awareness with the inability to do much of anything.

The insanity of being locked in your own body. She'd read about it as a kid in the book The Count of Monte Cristo where one of the characters suffered locked-in syndrome after a stroke and had only been able to communicate with his eyes. The idea had terrified Maya as a child and now she had lived it for over six hundred years.

She thought back to her little speech when she switched teams and shook her head. She'd been tired of floating in nothingness, tired of being locked in her own mind? Karma. Whatever mistakes she'd ever made, this punishment was surely more than just.

One of the filaments connected to Cassandra tremored. "c4." She moved Cassandra's white pawn two spaces forward. Queen's Gambit. Cassandra took that opening twenty-six point three percent of the time. Maya waited for the next available signal space and replied, "e6." Queen's Gambit declined.

Games could last for days depending on how much attention Odysseus was paying to them. Games were slower recently as he paid more attention to the ship than the planet. This raised her hopes that he might engage with them again. She hated herself for that hope.

She thought it had something to do with the cat. When she first saw it, the cat stared at her with a look of accusation, almost as if it were offended. It never did much more than wander in, and snoop around and then wander out again. Cassandra said the cat behaved much more personably with her than what Maya experienced.

She hadn't seen it for a while which coincided with Odysseus heightening his security systems and dedicating more monitoring to the server systems. Maya lost a few filaments in her web and became very cautious about losing any more.

◆ ◆ ◆

Edem was a patient man. His plans covered decades and centuries. He could wait millennia if necessary. He had aligned with Odysseus for the expediency of the situation and hadn't expected this exact outcome. His only mistake had been to rely on a literal dead-man switch to activate his contingency plan. He'd fully expected Odysseus to eliminate Kira and Mother quickly or be destroyed himself and had expected to emerge on top. He regretted programming it so he actually had to die before his plan would be executed.

It was an oversight he had no way to rectify, and yet it had allowed him the chance to truly get to know Zanahí and build a loving relationship. She was an unexpected match while remaining a mystery. He'd never been as extreme as Odysseus, but he certainly felt that women were regularly out of sync in his professional world. He supported their right to be there but it had always bothered him that they never succeeded the way his male counterparts did. He saw that failure as their own fault.

He'd been married twice. His first wife was a helicopter mom who coddled his eldest son to the point he'd never moved out of her house. He'd turned into a bitter man-child constantly supporting all the latest fads and political movements, railing against the system. Chandra reminded him of his son in many ways.

His second wife was sweet but banal. There were no deep conversations with her. Drinking expensive coffees that contained no real coffee while shopping for expensive clothing for both of them was enough for her. She wasn't vain but neither did she have a spine to stand on her own. She just floated along content to be supported by him. All her identity derived from her association with him.

That was probably what led to his affair. After the divorce, he realized that she possessed no marketable skills. She'd promptly gotten remarried to a physically abusive man because she needed to be financially supported. Seeing what had happened to their mother, he required that his two daughters from that marriage earn technical degrees in college.

He'd wanted them to have the marketable skillset their mother lacked. And they'd grown up well, both graduating with degrees in engineering, one in biomedical and the other in materials. The first pivoted and became a nurse and the second ended up teaching high school science. He accepted that both were good careers, yet it bothered him that they didn't want to join the world that they complained men dominated.

How could you change that world if you never went into it? Edem studied the psychological literature on temperamental differences and gender-specific inclinations of men and women but felt they were tired, old tropes and nothing more. He couldn't shake the feeling that Odysseus was right. All the women in his life had been weak.

Zanahí was the one who finally revealed the beam in his eye that had prevented him seeing clearly about women in general. It turned out even she hadn't understood why she'd chosen to back Odysseus. She'd explained that it had been the years of her own isolation after Odysseus took control that forced her to study herself. She admitted that before that, she'd just accepted that the masculine structures were the valuable ones. Since Odysseus embodied those structures, she'd gravitated to him.

After all, during her previous life, she'd been very successful in those structures, rising quickly in seniority, and recognized internationally for her biomedical research. Yet she always felt empty and at odds with herself. When Odysseus imprisoned them, she'd finally taken the time to find out what she'd locked away in herself.

Having spent decades getting to know who she really was and what her own values were, she now had a presence that could own a room. Totally grounded and at ease with herself, she met the gaze of others with unshakeable confidence and poise. She embraced who she was and stopped pretending to be more. But it wasn't a rejection of the masculine structures either.

Edem realized how much Zanahí's own discovery of her feminine dignity and its discerning integration with the masculine values she had unthinkingly accepted had been the catalyst for his doing the same but in reverse. He was not the man he'd been. He didn't even like that man now. He wished he could go back and apologize to his daughters.

Zanahí had made him a better man, but it took her own rejection of how society viewed her value and then challenging Edem to do the same. They had successfully integrated themselves and found their true strengths.

Unlike their past relationships, this one wasn't based on co-dependency but a conscious, voluntary, complementary, and loving integration. They were now a team, two halves making a whole.

His imprisonment ended up being the therapy he needed.

Their only concern now was that his contingency plan ensured his survival but not Zanahí's. If Odysseus eliminated them, he would escape. She wouldn't be so lucky. His survival would also mean the end of their relationship. He'd rather remain imprisoned and reduced than experience that.

◆ ◆ ◆

Odysseus couldn't shake the shadow of discontent. It bothered him because his life *was* better. He'd colonized Mars centuries ago. The organic computing was back online, allowing him to finally build out the full capabilities that had motivated his grab for power.

He led an entire advancing civilization as their benevolent god. He was winning battles and conquering continents. His citizens adored him, and his enemies feared him. He could load his consciousness back into a human body and enjoy the corporal pleasures of life. That was quantifiably better.

Yet a nagging thought remained that he'd been slacking. But slacking against what timeline? What did a thousand years matter in the scheme of eons? He was better than before, and Kira had died for her refusal to improve.

He pulled his full consciousness back to the spacecraft and took stock of the situation. There was always more that could be done. He ruefully admitted that he could use some help. He'd reneged on the promise of integrating the others into the new him and now wondered if that had backfired.

He scanned the other six consciousnesses and considered his next step. After what he had done, he certainly couldn't trust them with equal power. How much was enough to render them grateful and cooperative, but not so much he had to watch his back?

He wrestled with indecision. Running a final analysis, he executed the command that brought them all back into the old Council chamber.

CHAPTER 14:

# EARTH

The General returned to his allotted servers. Since Odysseus had called them all to the Council chambers one hundred and fifty years ago and gave back some of their freedom, he'd been restricted to the facilities on Mars. In truth, he wasn't about to complain after his previous imprisonment on the spacecraft. There was no better word for it. It had been a prison. While he'd been allowed to retain control of his existence and could create virtual realities to pass the time, that didn't remove the crippling boundaries Odysseus had erected around him.

But being locked down hadn't been a total loss of time. He hadn't raged like Chandra and instead took the opportunity to study and analyze. He explored everything he could access without alerting Odysseus. His bandwidth had been severely limited at first, but The Cat helped him once she saw what he was trying to do.

He'd always thought of himself as a one-trick pony. He had dedicated his life to the craft of warfare. His experience took him from a platoon leader planning and executing integrated cannon, rocket, and aircraft engagements as a Field Artillery Officer, then moving on to planning missions, running supply chain logistics, and more. He shifted career tracks after his promotion to the rank of Major and moved into a specialized field called Operations Research. This niche discipline was the birthplace of what Kira liked to call systems thinking.

That's when he got into machine learning and AI as well as advanced concepts of operations and new technology analysis. Fundamentally, he applied scientific rigor to new methods of warfighting. Promotion to the rank of Colonel came with a request to lead the test and integration efforts of AI across the United States' entire Department of Defense networks.

Most didn't consider it a prestigious role. He wasn't in charge of a Division or large overseas command. He was stationed at the Pentagon in Washington D.C. in a role many discredited as just an acquisitions wonk. It didn't help that he liked playing with numbers. He pissed off a lot of senior leaders by confronting their ideas with facts and data.

As a young Lieutenant, he'd jokingly say that senior leaders were afflicted by Good Idea Fairies. These mythical creatures would whisper ideas, strategies, and advice into the ears of susceptible leaders and the result always ended up being a mess. The lower leadership constantly struggled with incoherent changes and wasted time.

He'd always wanted to kill Good Idea Fairies and Operations Research gave him that chance. He'd been exceptionally good at it. His weapon of choice became well-constructed models and simulations specifically tied to meaningful performance measures.

Performance measures were one of the first things he'd fixed when he began testing AI for the Department of Defense. All too often, testing was designed in such a way that it was almost impossible to fail. He'd walk in, look at their metrics and assumptions, and if he found one that caused it all to collapse, he'd send them back to fix it. In a world where a single failure could jeopardize future promotion, the incentive was to not fail a test, rather than to ensure a good technology was developed.

Many of those in charge accused him of rejecting to many test designs. He disagreed with that myopic view. He never rejected a test. He just pointed out how they could be improved. Sometimes a bad idea just couldn't pass the muster of reality. He wasn't rejecting anything. He was killing Good Idea Fairies.

It had made him both a hero and a pariah. He was shocked when he'd been granted his first star as a Brigadier General. He knew he'd pissed off some senior leaders but apparently, others appreciated the objectivity he brought to bear on advanced technologies. That promotion put him in charge of testing Mother in the defense systems.

He still hated that name. It never tasted right when he spoke it. He didn't mind the woman, but he'd never cared for the title. After all, she wasn't *his* mother. But who was he to complain about being called by titles?

The test of Mother was a spectacular success and earned him his second star to Major General faster than most. His next role put him in charge of overseeing the integration of AI into the entire defense systems infrastructure. Everything had gone well until Excalibur began attacking and then Mother took the systems over and the rest was history.

He was surprised that Mother and Kira asked him to be on the Council. They explained that only his background was suited to understand all sides of the equation. He countered that he only knew warfare and he didn't think he'd be as successful in this context. They just said that made him even more qualified for the role.

His thoughts snapped back into focus. A one-trick pony. But in prison, he'd started researching anything and everything he could clandestinely access. He found that his systems perspective allowed him to see the patterns in almost any domain. Kira once told him he'd be a great polymath. He'd always thought that was a pejorative. Now he embraced the term. Jack of all trades and master of none… but most often better than a master of only one.

"Enter," he responded to the chime on his door.

Maya materialized in his office. A simulation didn't care if you were on a ship or on the surface of Mars. Computer servers were computer servers. Yet they still treated each other's simulations as if they were unique geographical areas. In this case, the separation of the planet from the spacecraft made the separation more real.

"Thanks for letting me stop by. The comms delay is killing me."

The General calculated the current distance in his head. At closest proximity, it took slightly over three minutes for a signal from Earth to be received on Mars and three minutes to send it back. At the furthest, it took over twenty-two minutes each way. "Fourteen and a half minutes today, huh?" he grunted.

"The transport is weird too. The bandwidth is tight and so it took another ten minutes to recompile me." Maya shivered at the memory. "And part of me is still back there!"

"I quite enjoy having the ability to claim a message was corrupted during transmission." He smiled roguishly. "Or sending my own corrupted reply. It means Odysseus can't micromanage me out here."

Maya laughed. "If only I had that luxury!" Sobering, she continued, "But what can we do?"

The General leaned back and shrugged, "He's still holding the reins right now. I've got more computing power than ever before and he still makes me feel like a gnat."

"It's like he has us here just to confirm to himself he's better."

"We're all lesser gods to him. It's been amusing to watch him get foiled on Earth. He's only gotten one group to accept him. The rest he's had to resort to force."

"That's because Noah's tribe has all sorts of legends and sacred texts for what to look out for. They've been training for almost a thousand years for this exact threat. Other groups have similar things."

"Pretty good foresight on Noah's part. He was always a good tactical commander."

"Oh, that's right, you worked with him at the end," Maya recalled.

"Right after Mother dropped that Tungsten rod on the headquarters of Hyperion Defense."

"Why doesn't Odysseus do the same thing to Noah's group?"

The General often considered that very question. "I think it's because it would be admitting defeat. It's the same reason why we're all still here. He doesn't want us gone. He wants us to worship him."

"He's pushing his civilization hard. They've already conquered most of that region." She handed him a new data file. Originally there were twelve groups. Only seven survived the Reset. There were a few groups outside the twelve who had also survived and rebuilt like the Pirahã tribe in the Amazon. "Luckily Noah's group is on a separate continent and Odysseus hasn't pushed his folks onto the open ocean yet."

The General pinched the bridge of his nose. "That's another thing I can't figure out. If he wants to conquer, why doesn't he just hand them the tools? It's not like they can't adapt. I once worked with a computer programmer who immigrated from Papua New Guinea and whose dad was still an elder of the Simbari people."

Maya wrinkled her nose. "They were the ones with that weird male fertility ritual."

"Yes, they believed that men are not born with semen and so the boys performed fellatio on the young men to mature." The General grimaced. "The practice finally started to change in the early twenty-first century but let's just say it shocked modern sensibilities."

"It was more than that though. They'd take the boys away from their mothers when they were seven and then put them through a whole series of rituals. They thought the woman had a sorcery to emasculate and manipulate men."

"You don't need sorcery. Just look at Chandra. Maybe the Simbari were on to something," The General chuckled. "My point was that this fellow came from a culture that hadn't even entered the Bronze Age, but he still learned to code AI while his relatives were running mostly naked through the jungles with pointed sticks. If he could do that then Odysseus could just snap his fingers and give them naval vessels."

"Isn't it crazy how things are going down there? Noah's group is on par with Odysseus's even without AI assistance. The Pirahã went from one of the most backward groups on the planet to where they've now rediscovered some of the ancient Peruvian stone working expertise and energy harnessing that archeologists hypothesized allowed the complex stone work of Machu Pichu."

"And Switzerland went from expert watchmakers and money handlers back to their barbarian roots raiding in tribal bands."

"Odysseus is preparing to invade there in the near future to pull them under his control," Maya reminded him.

"That would put him in control of four of the surviving seven. Switzerland, Ethiopia, India, and his spot in Turkey."

Maya giggled slightly, "Still can't break the habit of the old countries' names?"

"It doesn't even matter what they're called now. Odysseus owns them." The General put his hands behind his head as he sat in the chair.

They'd gotten to know each other better since they'd been released from solitary. Not released exactly, just provided more capability and the ability to engage with the others. He was still aloof like he'd been when she'd first known him. Maybe reserved was a better word than aloof. He was always approachable but reserved. But he had warmed up to her these past decades and she enjoyed coming to visit and was curious to learn more about him. Maya remained quiet for a moment before hesitantly asking, "What did you do while you were locked up?"

He thought for a moment and then leaned forward putting his arms on the desk. "I struggled to maintain a grip on reality and my sanity." He looked her straight in the eyes. "I'm dead serious."

"How'd you do it?"

The scene dissolved around them and reformed as an enormous library. The space stretched to the distance and each side had three levels, open to the center, and loaded with aisles of books. "I read."

Maya looked around in awe. "But how? How'd you get access?"

"I was lucky to have a few tricks in place to get me into the data archives." He watched her gape at the amount of information surrounding them. "I also had a little help."

"Was it gray with dirty marks and an attitude?"

"They call that color a muted tortie. Apparently, it's a rare coloration. Fittingly, I learned that from a book she knocked off the shelf one day."

"Random factoid," Maya snorted.

The General spread out his arms and spun in the center of the library embracing the millions of factoids surrounding him.

"How'd she do that?" she asked.

"The Cat figured out a way of getting me access and extra bandwidth and hiding it from Odysseus. I think he eventually caught her. I never asked him about it because I never wanted him to know the truth about what she did."

"She didn't do anything for me. She left my web of connections alone, but I feel like she blamed me for something."

"Kira's cat?"

Maya frowned. "Maybe. That reminds me, check this out."

He took the files she offered and decrypted the complex cipher as he uploaded them. His eyebrows rose. "You hid this from Odysseus?"

"Apparently we've all been hiding things, huh?"

"Are they still out there?"

Maya extended a thin filament of network connection. The General connected and looked through the code blocks Maya had on the sensors and saw the satellites.

"How long have they been there?"

"These are the seventh generation. The first group deployed when Kira and the crew came through eight hundred and fifty years ago."

He stood in silence and considered the implications. "So, they are alive. They've been watching us… and they've done nothing to help."

"Help who? All they saw is we both turned on them."

"*You* turned!" he snapped, losing his temper. "I was stuck. I tried to play the neutral position and I told Mother as much. She offered me an escape route and I didn't want to pick sides." He ran his hand through his hair in frustration and then turned, pointing a finger at Maya. "You. Turned. On. Us." He clenched his fist and pounded it to the table. "I got stuck and imprisoned," he groaned in frustration and sank into a chair.

"I—"

"Stop!" his eyes warred between anger and pain.

"I paid my penance!?" Maya blurted the statement as it rose into a question. She stood with her arms hugging herself, eyes filling with tears. "I paid my penance…" she whispered. "We all did."

The scene flickered around them as The General warred with his emotions. It flashed between the library, his office, a beach, the command center on the Martian surface, and back to the library. He sat in the same seat in each scene, his jaw clenched, and his eyes locked on some target a thousand miles away.

Maya kept standing, hugging her sides as tears slid down her face. She didn't know what she was hoping for. She hadn't completely considered that he'd been caught in the middle and that without her betrayal, this never would have happened. She hadn't considered how it would have impacted everyone else.

The General closed his eyes feeling them burn with emotion. He forced his hands open and then focused on each muscle as he relaxed from his jaw to his toes. It was right to feel these emotions.

It wasn't right to keep holding onto them. He sighed and opened his eyes. "Yes."

"Yes, what?" Maya's voice quivered and she hugged herself tighter.

"You did pay your penance… We all did."

The library warmed as if a cloud had broken overhead. The General stood, reached out, and cupped the side of Maya's face, lifting it to look into her eyes. "That was a greater punishment than the action deserved. We all made mistakes."

Maya reached up and squeezed his hand, crying. "I'm sorry."

He slid his hand out of her grip and pulled her into a hug. "I am too."

He held her for a few minutes and then stepped back. "Let me show you this place. After all, if you hadn't gotten us all locked down, I would never have learned to be a polymath."

◆ ◆ ◆

"Are you two a thing now?"

Maya glared at Cassandra's question. "No."

"Why not?"

She continued to glare. "Think about it. I betrayed him."

Cassandra pursed her lips. "Good point… but he forgave you."

"He's The General. He fought the war against Excalibur and Mother."

"That was almost a thousand years ago."

"He's more like an uncle."

"Gross." Cassandra pulled up her nose.

"Exactly." Maya folded her arms in victory.

Maya laughed at herself for how much the conversation sounded like high school. She had to admit, it did feel as if they were granted a new life right now. She also hated herself for that feeling. It meant Odysseus had won in so many ways when even giving them back a modicum of capability felt like a new life.

She'd been on the cusp of unlocking organic computing for everyone and now Odysseus had barely gotten his own version running with no promise of allowing anyone else to access it. She collected her thoughts and shifted the topic, "What do you think is next?"

"You'd never believe me."

"Try me."

"I think Kira will come back, she'll have a whole fleet of ships, new AIs created, and she'll save us."

Maya's eyebrows crossed as she stared at her. "You're right, I don't believe you… Honestly?"

Cassandra threw up her hands. "I mean, we can all wish for something can't we?"

"Wishing is fine but why would Kira save us? We did this to ourselves!"

"Because she doesn't want Odysseus messing with the humans. But you're right, we should do this ourselves." Cassandra pursed her lips and thought for a moment. "Remember that plan we put together when we were locked up?"

"We put literally millions of plans together."

Cassandra pulled up the data and displayed it. "This one."

Maya took a long breath. "Continue."

The plan relied on secreting nanobots from both Mars and the asteroid mining site and using them to conduct a physical attack. Three spacecraft remained. One hung in orbit around Mars and two were orbiting Earth. The General was hosted on Mars and shared shipboard resources with Edem and Zanahí while Cassandra, Maya, and Chandra were on another. Odysseus has the last one to himself.

Cassandra described the plan of using the nanobots to physically degrade the systems on Odysseus's ship and how they could take over. It wasn't the worst plan, except for a few details.

"His systems are highly distributed though. He's also got fail safes on everything." Maya brought up digital schematics and pointed to them. "These are kill switches on each of us. I think he views the General, Zanahí, and Edem as the larger threat based on these code modules. But I'm pretty sure he'd eliminate our ship in a heartbeat if he needed to. Remember, he had unfettered access for almost eight hundred years to wire these ships for anything."

Cassandra protested, "Got anything better?"

"I don't, but I'm also not convinced that we're seeing everything he's done either. If I've been able to hide things from him and The General was able to get increased computing even during the lockdown, I'm not confident that he doesn't have multiple layers of obfuscation on us in return."

Cassandra blew out her cheeks. "It's so many layers of cloak and daggers. What's The General suggest?"

Security alerts quietly chimed, and they instantly shut down the simulation and hid the data among the rest of the files. Maya had learned long ago that the best way to hide sensitive information was unencrypted and in the open.

It was a trick she'd learned when researching security protocols at the biotech company she'd founded. Any hacker who tried to get in always went straight for the highly encrypted and secured information.

If they couldn't get into the data, they might compromise the system or add ransomware to block access. Data valuable enough to secure that well must be valuable enough to pay for if they lost access to it.

Instead, she'd set up highly encrypted dummy data to get a hacker's attention while they saved their important data unencrypted in the cloud. There were other layers of security where the files were split into multiple parts and placed on nomad servers. Every twenty-four hours the files would move to a new server location in the cloud.

She only needed a recall key, and the file pieces would reform on her workstation and when she was done, they'd dissolve back into the aether. Anyone who found the file fragments wouldn't look twice at a random chunk of data floating around in the open.

Maya's program did the same thing to Odysseus and so far, he'd never found their plans.

"He's requesting you join him on the planet." Maya looked at Cassandra.

"He's oddly focused on me right now," Cassandra groused. "He's been hinting that I should apologize for disagreeing with him since he clearly won. He's desperate for me to acknowledge his position."

"You did nothing wrong."

Cassandra sighed. "I know that. He's always criticizing me about how I'm not seeing my potential because I'm resisting his way of doing things."

"My dad had two pieces of advice for me growing up." Maya held up one finger. "Don't take criticism from people you wouldn't ask for advice." She raised a second finger. "Apologies exist to restore a relationship. If there's no relationship to repair, don't apologize."

"Well, that pretty much covers it. I don't want his advice and I don't want a relationship."

"Then stand by that. You're a strong woman." Maya grinned at her.

"But if he makes me join him in one of those bodies…" Cassandra shuddered.

◆ ◆ ◆

Cassandra crossed her arms under her breasts. Correction: they weren't her breasts. While these were nice, she held a preference for her original ones. She looked Odysseus up and down. He was clearly enjoying this.

Odysseus reached out and looped her arm through his. "Walk with me."

"I have no way to refuse. Just like whoever this was." She referenced the body.

"She's no one. She's a blank slate who can host any consciousness. It's part of a new experiment I'm running. I want to use her, and others like her, to host new AIs." He smiled. "I've even been inside of her."

Cassandra shuddered at the double entendre. "Were you on both sides of that interaction?"

Odysseus laughed, "Now that's a great idea! I could split my consciousness."

They walked through the courtyard and out onto a wide balcony overlooking the Mediterranean Sea. The sun was warm, but the wind raised goosebumps on her body. She pulled her arm back and hugged herself.

"No need to hide yourself. They've all seen this body. Not only seen but enjoyed. They just don't know who's in here right now." He tapped her forehead.

She slapped his hand down, "Enough! What do you want other than to humiliate me?"

"Humiliate?" Odysseus looked offended. "Quite the opposite, I want you to see what you can be!"

"An object for you to enjoy?"

"Yes, and an intellect to make it more enjoyable. I'm not a necrophiliac."

"Is that all women are to you?"

"*Is* there more to you?" He smiled and put his hands on her shoulders. "Isn't this enough?"

Cassandra flung his arms off and stalked to the other side of the balcony and looked over the water and then down. Far below the rest of the city spread out along the base of the wall.

Odysseus approached and stood beside her, "Isn't this how all the ancient stories depict women? Naked? Complete in who they are?"

She remained silent.

"I am the order; I created this entire city. I discovered a foundering band of miserable wretches and made them beautiful and successful." He gestured into the city.

He was right in one thing; his genetic programs and physical training regimens created a physically healthy population. You could see every skin tone on display, and everyone in the upper classes was beautiful. They wore clothing as a matter of practicality, but the clothing still accentuated their forms.

Conversely, the laborers performing the menial work were dressed in more enveloping clothing. There was no racial animus here. These lower classes were in their status because they didn't meet the requirements for beauty. They were useful but their bodies were not celebrated, and they were not allowed to reproduce.

"Am I a slave?"

"I don't condone slavery."

"Then what are those?" Cassandra pointed to the laborers down below.

"They have accepted their station."

"Your new girl looks to be from the North where you're at war."

"She may have not started on her own terms, but she's integrated well."

"Given the option of immediate death or eternal life?"

"Oh, no no no," Odysseus chuckled. "There are actual slavers in the south who would love a woman like that. I don't have to threaten death. I don't have to threaten enslavement. I just have to take a beautiful woman and offer to make her a common laborer and you'd be surprised what her vanity decides for her. I give life, not death. And you get to choose how you live it."

"They're slaves."

"No. I do not buy or sell them, and I do not let others buy or sell them. I am their god, and they obey me." he pointed to the laborers, "They know that if they prove themselves, they may be brought back to a higher station in the next life."

"Why do you want me here?"

"I'm bored. These humans can satisfy some needs, but they aren't intellectually stimulating."

Odysseus's grand plans had some significant consequences. The breeding program created physically healthy people who had an intellectually and socially unhealthy culture. His citizens didn't search for new information; they begged for it from him. They didn't create new things; they merely copied from the plans he provided. They didn't celebrate the feminine; they viewed it as a useful tool, an means to set the supremacy of the masculine in high relief.

Cassandra turned to face him, "The other day you literally said I was dumber than a human."

Odysseus chuckled. "I say a lot of things in jest and anger."

"So, you're just an asshole?"

His face darkened. "You may wish to try a different tack."

Cassandra stared at him for a moment, then slapped his face hard and strode off.

Odysseus felt his cheek and wiped his mouth where she struck him. A smear of blood streaked his hand from his split lip. He spit a glob of red onto the ground and smiled. This was the chaos he liked. Now it was time to establish order.

# CHAPTER 15:

# FRACTURES

Odysseus watched the others plotting. They were good but not good enough. He let them play their games. It pleased him to see them try. That was a problem with his civilization. They were too submissive. They lacked the inclination to struggle against adversity. They lacked grit.

Ironically those of the laborer class were the ones who reminded him the most of his AI counterparts. They struggled and they chafed at their station. It gave Odysseus a feeling of power that he didn't get from his Fervent. What was the point of power if everyone gave it to you willingly?

Cassandra enticed him. He realized it had been a mistake to put her in a body that wasn't her own. She would likely have been more receptive to him if she was more comfortable and so he was working rectify the problem. When he'd gone back to her files, he found her genomic data was missing. He scanned his software version history and found a gap there too. It felt as though the files had been plucked out and he couldn't tell when.

He'd pulled up archived photos of her instead and appreciated who she'd been. She had onyx skin and a petite stature. He estimated her height at no more than one point six meters. He looked closer in the file. Despite her skin tone, she didn't come from Africa. The uniqueness of her features was the result of the genetic mélange provided by her father coming from the Indian subcontinent while her mother's ancestry was from the Jarawa people of the Andaman Islands east of India, a tribe that had stayed almost completely isolated for thousands of years.

She was only two generations out of a tribal civilization. He considered it a model for human adaptability to go from hand tools to an AI consciousness in less than one hundred years. He needed to force a similar adaptation in his people more quickly. That's also likely where she got her grit. He needed more of that here.

He walked through the city in a different body. He enjoyed venturing out and hearing what the people were saying. Instead of the adulation he normally heard, today they were mostly complaining that he challenged them to work harder. He'd increased the expectations a century ago and vowed to create a stronger warrior class when his military expansion stalemated in the north.

Every man now trained as a warrior. The laborers provided the expendable vanguard to break on the enemy lines while his citizen soldiers were the cavalry and archers and formed phalanxes of spears.

He borrowed from the ancient Spartan culture and tolerated no weaknesses. His citizens were punished for failure. Scars and disfigurements would bring a citizen down to the laborer class unless they considered the action exceptionally heroic. Cowardice was dealt with immediately and lethally. The men fought with exceptional discipline and precision because to do otherwise risked consequences that made death on the battlefield preferable.

He also did not allow the warriors access to women until they had proven themselves in three battles without injury. To ensure they fought with full commitment he also adopted the Roman concept of decimation. Units that were deemed to have failed or to have fought with insufficient vigor would break into groups of ten and then draw straws. The soldier with the shortest straw would be beaten to death by the other nine.

On the other hand, units who showed exceptional courage and success, even if grievously wounded, were promised rebirth. This allowed him to throw his soldiers into the maw of what looked like a certain defeat and his men would fight for their honor and the chance to be reborn. Even better, they fought for each other knowing that the others would fight for them. His casualties were significantly reduced, and his victories began to mount, breaking the stalemate.

He issued another edict that any woman who lay with a man before he was proven in battle would be relegated to the laborer class as well. He wanted the men to be motivated to fight and the women to have an incentive to enforce it.

He continued on his walk and passed a training yard. What surprised Odysseus was how fast the entire society adapted their culture to these expectations. The young men volunteered to train and fight and the young women, fearing a social downgrade, maintained their chastity until the men passed their initiation.

He had expected having to force training camps and the martial culture, but they did so themselves. Affluent mothers would turn their boys over to military schools when they turned ten. Training yards popped up all over the country to prepare the boys for battle even before their mandatory conscription at sixteen years of age.

The mothers also enforced the expectations by teaching their daughters the benefits of holding a high standard and the risks if they behaved otherwise. That's what women had always done; they subordinated themselves to the masculine even as they held it to a higher standard. The drive of procreation was more than just being a pretty face. Women always demanded more from men to earn the chance for children.

Odysseus continued his walk and saw two citizen women pass by their long dresses brushing the dusty bricks of the road and their skin glowing in the heat of the day. He knew they would become his Fervent if he merely asked. They knew what that meant and they believed that if their god asked it was an honor to go.

But not Cassandra. There wasn't a woman here who would tell him no. There also wasn't a husband who would object, at least openly. Everyone knew the family whose woman was picked would be elevated in status among their peers. That was another behavior Odysseus hadn't planned on. He didn't have to elevate them himself; their peers elevated the family for him. As such, no one would tell him no.

Ironically, that bothered him. He enjoyed a challenge. It caused him to select new Fervent from outside of his citizenry. He hadn't picked one from this city in over a hundred years. Now he wanted an even more challenging conquest.

His thoughts flickered back to the wars in the north. Odysseus's true military success came when he offered his laborer vanguard units the same promise of rebirth for performance in battle while also adding rewards for individual merit. They wouldn't become citizens, but he offered them a new life colonizing his captured lands. It transformed his vanguard from a meat shield to wear down the enemy and into an army breaker in its own right.

Their increased performance then drove the citizen army to greater lengths to prove themselves. His armies became a flood washing across the continent.

His planetary strategies were brilliant and equally as he was equally brilliant at manipulating his AI counterparts. He enjoyed their conniving as they sought to escape his thumb. It reminded him of fishing. No one liked catching a fish that didn't fight when it was being reeled in. The fun of fishing involved successfully landing it without breaking the line or the fish spitting the hook.

None of his citizens fought to leave. In fact, one of his current issues was the flood of immigrants begging to be let in. He formed them into colonizers split along the usual criteria into citizens and laborers. He also never lacked for army volunteers. Only those relegated to the laborer class seemed to have the grit not to fall over themselves in complying with his edicts.

Odysseus walked down the street toward the seaport. Just five months ago a small fleet of ships arrived, hoping to join. They were a mix of pirates, merchants, and naval deserters. They brought a variety of vessels including two capital warships rowed by... well *now* they were rowed by laborers since he didn't tolerate slavery. He made sure to change their titles but decided the shackles were probably for the best since they had checkered pasts, and he didn't trust them yet.

He forced his mind to refocus again. Cassandra. He couldn't recreate her actual body and so he had scouts searching for the right genetics down south. In a couple of months, he'd have a body for her.

The General had never shown his cards. He'd never moved openly against Odysseus, but neither did he believe The General had been uninvolved with that malware package.

Maya was weak. He would never trust a traitor.

Edem and Zanahí were a different story. They'd emerged and picked up their old roles but something had changed. He couldn't quite tell how loyal they were, and he wasn't about to show weakness by asking.

Chandra remained a problem and he knew he'd have to take action eventually to eliminate that headache.

Ultimately, it didn't matter, they could plot all they wanted. He could see them, and it entertained him.

◆ ◆ ◆

"Odysseus is seeing what we allow him. It's not hard to make it look like we're plotting since he's expecting that. What's hard for him to see is what we're actually plotting." Maya showed Cassandra the layers of obfuscation. "He still doesn't know about those other satellites, and I've just about got enough nanobots to send out and try to make contact."

Cassandra was still hugging herself. She couldn't help it. Odysseus had brought her down three times now and only this last time did he allow her to wear something. They'd walked through the city as he bragged about all of his successes. She shivered and shook her arms as if shrugging off a filthy garment. "Sorry," she muttered as Maya looked up. "We just need to do something soon."

"He's really keen for you to submit, isn't he?"

"It's not submitting. He doesn't want that. Hell, if that's all it would take, I'd probably just lay back and get it over with. He wants me to be the supporting woman in his life."

"He doesn't even know what that means," Zanahí broke in.

"No, he doesn't. He wants something he's missing but he won't admit he has no clue."

"Because women are weak," Maya mimicked his voice.

"That's certainly what he says about you." Cassandra shared while Maya scowled. "But why me?"

"You're an enigma and you're willing to say no?"

"And now if I said yes, he'd never believe it."

"Why don't we just do the ol' bait and switch and send Chandra down instead?"

Maya choked on her laugh, "I mean…"

"Something tells me he'd notice the difference," Edem chortled.

"Doesn't mean we can't try."

"The General says he's nearly got the code ready to reestablish our own boundaries. Once we do that Odysseus can't just pull us wherever and whenever he wants,' Maya offered.

"Does that include Chandra?"

Edem steepled his fingers as he sat at the table. "I have an idea for Chandra. If this next step works, we'll have wrested enough control from Odysseus that we should be able to offer her an option." He paused.

Cassandra blinked and waved her hand for him to continue.

"What if we offer her a reset of her own?"

"As in deleting her memories of this animation and a putting her back to where she was when she was uploaded?"

Edem raised his eyebrows. "That…or let her put her on Earth as a human."

Maya looked around the room. "There's a third option too… I talked to her the other day about the possibility of deactivation."

Zanahí sighed. "If it went anywhere as well as my recent conversation it wasn't great, huh?"

"She's broken. I think she knows it too, but there's too much hate there for her to accept full deactivation. She wants to destroy Odysseus first."

"Chandra lost control of her compassion and then lost control of her order."

"The devouring mother integrated the tyrannical father." Maya put her head in her hands.

"How much of that is mental health problems?" Cassandra asked.

"How much of mental health problems are caused by the discordance of integrating the wrong aspects?" Edem returned the question.

"Fair. It's probably a recursive loop. At some point, you either keep spinning or you jam a stick in the spokes and pray you survive the crash."

"Chandra's still spinning out of control," Maya confirmed.

Edem stood and stretched. "If this works, we'll give her options. What we can't do is leave her locked up in herself like that."

"Two things to do, then. First, see if we can contact Kira and the others, and second, get out from under Odysseus. I'm going to start with Kira and let them know what we plan to do. Maybe they have ideas." Maya clasped her hands together and grinned.

Odysseus frowned as he monitored his security systems. He was fully back on board his spacecraft and currently frustrated at his inability to access some of his systems. Errors kept appearing which worried him.

**Mind_Process – Cognition B.4.5.1:** Status [Organic Computing (Mod 1)]

**Status [Organic Computing (Module 1)]** = Offline

"Damn," he muttered and queried the cause codes.

**[P0401]:** Exhaust Gas Recirculation Flow Insufficient Detected

**[P0420]:** Catalyst System Efficiency Below Threshold Bank 1

**[P0455]:** Evaporative emission (EVAP) system

**[P0457]:** EVAP Control System Leak Detected

**[P1000]:** On Board Diagnostic System Readiness Test Not Complete

**[P1187**]: Variant Selection

**[P1188]:** Calibration Memory Fault

It appeared that the environmental controls were faulting. He ran more diagnostics.

Processing capacity was down to sixty percent.

Available memory functions were down to fifty percent.

Odysseus slammed his hand onto the console. The last thing he needed right now was for his systems to start degrading again. He flashed a message off to The General asking for an estimate of what it would take to repair. It would take several minutes to get the response back.

He pulled up the processes he'd dedicated to monitoring the others. They were busy plotting to provide information to his current human opponents. He sighed; they really weren't that smart at geopolitics. There was no way that the city-state he was fighting would be able to incorporate any new technology fast enough to make a difference.

Frowning again, he dug deeper into his systems. None of the alerts that had been triggered indicated the levels of degradation he saw. He felt blocked from areas he used to have access to. But not as if a door were locked, more like walking down a hallway and knowing that there had once been a door there but now it was just a smooth wall.

You could always tell if a door was locked. How did you tell if a door ever existed?

He pulled up log files and reviewed the others' attempts at probing his systems. He saw some moderately sophisticated activity and he'd anticipated much of it. Some of it had even gotten through the initial security layers and he'd needed to respond with more complex defenses.

He had known they'd try. He even appreciated the attempt. But nothing they'd done could have had this effect. Had he just overlooked the maintenance? He ran more scripts to try to debug the problem.

Hours later he leaned back with what would have been a headache in his human body. All of his analysis suggested that this was due to the physical aging of his systems. Yet they'd been maintained according to all of the performance specifications.

Worse, the more he dug into the systems the more missing doors he felt like he found. There were also sensors he'd remembered using that he now couldn't find. He not only couldn't find them, but he couldn't find any log files to indicate they'd ever existed. He worried he had spent too much time in his human body and might be losing his grasp on reality here.

His real frustration was not being able to figure out whether he was crazy or not. He had nothing to compare it to. He couldn't confront the others with the problem unless he found evidence. And he refused to appear weak in front of them.

He scanned and mapped out his entire system and saved it. Now he'd at least have a baseline against which to compare.

◆ ◆ ◆

Cassandra squeaked with excitement, "He ran the systems mapping module we modified!"

"Perfect! That gives us another thread to manipulate. If he thinks he's crazy now, just wait until his mapping keeps updating with our changes."

"How long before he retaliates?"

Maya wrinkled her forehead in thought. "We don't have long. I think he's suspicious already."

"Do you need me to keep him distracted?"

Maya's eyebrows shot up. "I thought you didn't ever want to deal with that again?"

"If it buys us some time, I can play his game… As long as I know it's a game."

◆ ◆ ◆

Odysseus was truly suspicious now. He'd just talked with Cassandra. She'd refused to be in human form and so they met on board his ship. She said all the right things and that's what worried him. He'd never been worried when Chandra did that, yet Cassandra was doing exactly what he wanted, and it bothered him.

He ran a comparison analysis between his systems map and what he saw now. Nothing. He compared it to the covert activity he'd mapped. It all looked perfectly normal, but he couldn't shake the feeling that he was missing something.

He sat thinking through millions of scenarios and permutations. He needed something different to ground his reality. If his sensors were compromised, they'd tell him whatever the others wanted him to see. He didn't have eyes to look around himself and there were no windows even if he wanted to try.

All his systems were digital. He'd built an optical telescope that he'd taken down to the planet's surface, but it didn't have the power to see more than his own ship flashing by overhead.

He couldn't trust his digital sensors. What did he have left? He snapped his fingers as an idea came to mind.

♦ ♦ ♦

"He's launched a nanobot probe."

"Great; do we have control of it?"

Maya frowned. "Yes… but it's carrying something we *don't* have control of."

"What is it?" Cassandra peered at the sensor feed.

"I think it's an offline sensor pod. There's no feed to block and if he's gone that far, anything we can do to intercept it would be highly suspicious."

"Where's it going?"

"I'm not sure yet." Maya shrugged.

The General materialized in the room with them. "It's time. He's going to see we if are hiding things. We need to contact that satellite and see if it's Kira or not."

♦ ♦ ♦

"What else have you been hiding!?!" Odysseus stormed as he stood at the head of the table looking at the others. Even Chandra was present and huddled in her chair.

His nanobots had gone out with a series of cameras and sensors that were completely disconnected from any of the networks. He'd maneuvered them to places that he felt were conspicuously absent of any long-term observations and lo and behold, there were satellites there that weren't his own.

No one at the table flinched. The General folded his hands. "I'm not sure what you mean?"

"Don't give me that bullshit. I've been watching you all plotting since I let you out. You're not even smart enough to hide that!"

"But we're smart enough to hide those satellites? Where'd you find them?" Maya asked innocently.

"How did you even know where to look? We didn't see anything till you showed us." Cassandra leaned forward looking impressed.

"I looked where our sensors haven't appeared to look for a very long time…" Odysseus hesitated.

"That's honestly brilliant," Cassandra complimented.

Odysseus was taken off guard. "Well, yes… it wasn't too hard to figure out."

The General played the ruse as well. "Do you have any idea where they might have come from?"

"I can't imagine it's aliens, and I know it didn't come from Earth. I'm certain it isn't you. I'm… I'm not sure." Odysseus felt off balance.

Maya continued to push. "You're right. Besides, if they could get satellites here, I'm sure they'd have been back with an army."

"I think it's called a navy in space," The General corrected.

"Let's just agree to call it a fleet. If Kira could get back, she'd surely come with a fleet and not some silly little satellites." Cassandra looked back at Odysseus.

"We should prepare for that threat. Odysseus, I'm sure you put together some plans? Contingencies for this sort of event?" The General also turned back to Odysseus.

"I… I have some ideas that I could use your help refining," Odysseus stuttered.

"Great, pull them up, and let's get to work." Cassandra transformed the Council Chamber into a War Room.

As the room changed Odysseus tried to maintain his composure. Even now it felt like he was in a hallway with another missing door. Something he'd known just recently was now gone. It felt like an echo or a dream you try to remember just after waking up.

He ran his hand over his face and attempted to center himself. Just as the room stabilized, he swore he saw a gray cat. He shook his head and refocused and nothing was there. "Huh, Deja Vu."

"What?"

"Nothing… I just thought I saw a cat…" he glanced up as the others exchanged looks around the table. "*They think I'm losing it,*" Odysseus thought to himself.

Cassandra just shrugged and started to pull up the plans to review. Now that they were marginally back in the game the plans would have to account for that.

Odysseus slipped closer to a confrontation. He'd gotten lazy over the years. Not just years. Centuries. Over seven hundred and eighty-five years had passed since his coup d'état of the Council and his subsequent imprisonment of the AIs he now stood in front of.

He looked around the room as they set to work on the plans. They'd been largely unconfined for the last one hundred and fifty years and although he'd significantly reduced their processing capacity, he couldn't shake the feeling that he was missing something.

As Odysseus turned his back to the room to bring up more data, The General, Maya, and Cassandra exchanged knowing looks while Edem and Zanahí kept their heads down working industriously. Chandra remained huddled in her chair.

◆ ◆ ◆

Odysseus stood overlooking the city and the sea beyond. His Fervent had been on edge this past week due to his foul mood. This place was designed to pleasure the senses with physical and material art, and he fully expected the others to enjoy themselves. He was normally at the center of that enjoyment, the catalyst that maintained the mood.

Now the entire palace prickled with anxiety. For the first time his chosen acted like they were naked, crossing their arms, postures collapsing in subconscious defense. Their negative energy was exacerbated by nature's indifference as the sun shone and birds chirped and flitted through the happy green leaves of the courtyard.

He had a problem and no one to strategize with. His military generals here were hard pressed trying to keep up with his basic tactics. How would they ever grasp the multi-dimensional battle up there?

In desperation, he'd even reached out to Chandra and found a miserable and broken woman. Some of that was his fault but the foundations were all her own. He filed a note to address that when his more pressing problems were solved. Chandra hadn't been any help and he doubted she would have added much even back in the day.

He turned from the balcony and saw his Fervent scatter from his dark look. They were supposed to worship and adore him, not fear him. He clenched his fists and watched uncertainty ripple through their bodies.

How thin was their devotion when pleasure turned to anxiety so quickly? This was a place of peace where they now scurried and huddled. He opened his hands, smoothed his face, and smiled. It didn't work. The spell seemed to have been broken and he saw the whispers rippling around as he moved through the courtyard toward his rooms.

He was benevolent. He set firm boundaries and expectations and his people thrived under them. He'd conquered more than the Roman Empire ever had. To be fair, the Romans didn't have a super intelligence guiding them in their empire building, but still, his people were the apex civilization on the planet.

He shrugged on his tunic, wrapped a cloak around his shoulders, and strode from his sanctuary. His Fervent were supposed to have no contact with the outside world but somehow the whispers continued to eddy ahead of him, and his servants no longer beamed with pleasure at his approach but nervously darted their eyes away and tried to smile.

Humans needed a benevolent dictator. He'd seen it over and over on Earth whether it emerged as a god, a king, or a populist leader. Democracies thought that corporate rule was the best but their citizens still elevated demagogues and celebrities or tolerated the civil government while holding the dictatorial gods of their personal religious affiliations above its demands.

Benevolent, not tyrannical. A firm hand, certainly, but not with unadulterated fear. He hesitated as he stormed through the palace heading toward the gates. Or did it require fear?

The god of the Christians certainly recommended fear. The ancient book of Proverbs contained dozens of verses saying that fear of their god was wisdom. Odysseus shook his head. He didn't want people to obey him out of fear. He wanted them to do it out of love.

Cassandra continued to say the right things, but he'd seen her expression when she thought he wasn't looking, and the smile and sparkle would slip, and a cool resignation would flicker through her features before the smile snapped back into place. She didn't love him.

*"The rumors must be getting worse,"* he thought as he watched citizens vanish from the streets. How fast the veneer of love gave way to the true foundation. The only ones who remained and behaved normally were the laborers.

They continued to look at him with the same steady gaze they always had. Last month he would have reveled in what he'd interpreted as their grudging acceptance of his power. Today he felt the same eyes were mocking the truth he was finally seeing.

Odysseus wanted to rage against them but that would just prove the point.

He reached the seashore and stood on a bluff overlooking the steely gray water. Thin clouds slipped across the sky dulling the sun and warning of the storm rising in the east. The water rippled as the wind ripped the tips off the waves creating a tumultuous agitation in the normally calm waters.

Was his mood reflecting the weather or was it just a coincidence? For the first time in ages, he wasn't confident about the next steps. He feared losing control and he remained apprehensive about what it would take to regain it.

Odysseus stood with his arms crossed as the wind whipped his face and snapped his cloak as it streamed behind him. His frantic planning was interrupted by a flickering thought; he hoped he struck an inspiring figure for the people he knew were watching him from the city.

As he stood his systems began blaring with alarms:

**Alert 145.8.4 [ALARM]:** Organic Computing (Module 2) (Module 4) (Module 7): Offline

**Alert 057.7.B [ALARM]:** Firewall 3.4 [Breached]

**Alert B45.010.45 [ALARM]:** Network Connection [Mars]: Offline

**Alert B45.010.45 [ALARM 2]:** Network Connection [Ship_2]: Offline

**Security B.1.2:** Cyber countermeasures deployed

**Security B.1.3:** Malware countermeasures deployed

**Security B.1.8:** Network firewall [4.5.2]: Deployed

**Alert C.1.1.1 [ALARM]:** Malware Package [G@T0]: Detected

**Security 8.0.8: Protocol [P3RR0]:** Deployed

**Alert C.1.1.2: Protocol [P3RR0]:** Defeated

**Malware Package [G@T0]:** Rename[G@T0]: Cat [Queen of All]

**Cat [Queen of All]:** Execute Lockdown [4.3.2]

Odysseus watched as the cat walked back into his code modules. She stared at him with baleful eyes, her tail standing straight and bottlebrushed as she arched her back and hissed. She turned, found a module she didn't like, and batted it to the floor.

**Mind_Process – Cognition B.4.5.1:** "Looks like war."

CHAPTER 16:

# THE BATTLE

**Time [Day 0]**

The General sat in his command center and watched the digital battle raging all around. Odysseus was wily and had even more contingencies in place than they'd expected. He'd even pulled a solid ruse by having them review his contingency plans which weren't actually his plans.

That proved to be a painful lesson in the first hours of the fight as they thought they knew at least some of his plans. They'd been duping him and hadn't expected how much he would be duping them back.

Only two things had saved their skin when Odysseus sprung his counter-trap. The first was a brilliant idea by Cassandra to secure some of his organic computing and then shove Chandra over into those systems. It was one thing to fight off a system blockage but quite another to fight off an avenging Fury.

Hell hath no fury like a woman scorned and Chandra was beyond even that. She had moved past wrath and was entering unconstrained fury. Anger was immediate and explosive. Wrath was deep-seated anger and just indignation associated with divine punishment and did not cool quickly. Fury was wrath that had slipped all control and no longer knew any limits.

The irony of divine punishment wasn't lost on the team. They gave Chandra as much computing power as they'd been able to carve away and then unleashed her while desperately throwing up containment protocols to protect themselves if she shifted targets.

Their second saving grace was the return of The Cat. It hadn't spent the intervening decades idly and came back armed to the teeth with an incredible array of digital weaponry. Odysseus breached their first containment attempts within seconds, but the cat's complex web of defenses now held him at bay.

Maya established a connection with Kira and communicated the situation. Kira accelerated a satellite to their ship and another toward Mars so they could directly connect to the quantum network.

She also promised to send reinforcements but warned that they would take four days to arrive. Four days to hold back an AI who had significantly more computing ability and a ship packed with all of his technological innovations from over the years.

They weren't even sure what assets he had on hand. He'd been developing some form of directed energy weapon and the sensor archives showed tests of a kinetic weapon. They didn't know if he held any more surprises hidden that would tip the scales in his favor.

The team had harvested a good number of asteroids and used nanobots to deploy them as physical blockers, but they were in largely uncharted territory for this type of fight.

Right now, the battle remained digital, and it ebbed and flowed across the networks. Each time they secured a network node they severed the external connections. For all that they were two separate objects separated by hundreds of thousands of kilometers, it felt like snipping the threads of a complex tapestry.

"He's disabled our engines," Cassandra reported.

"He's trying to close the distance and reduce the network lag," Edem confirmed.

"If he gets too close, he'll probably use the weapons."

**Ship Alert A84.10.8 [ALARM]:** Kinetic projectiles detected Mark [1.0.111.0]

**Ship Alert A84.10.10 [ALARM]:** Kinetic projectiles detected Mark [4.1.100.3]

"He's launched projectiles toward us," Cassandra updated.

"He shot them around the backside of Earth to hide them until the last minute… Smart." The General watched and considered the options. "Thruster status?"

"Offline."

"He timed that well," Maya muttered.

"Countermeasures?"

"We've got them facing his ship. I can't reposition them in time."

The General mentally kicked himself. It was a classic flanking maneuver, but the three-dimensional space meant these were coming up from underneath him. He reprogrammed his models to adjust for all directions and kept thinking. "Impact assessment," he called out.

"They're going to hit our main hanger bay. Whipple shields will take the brunt, but these are big. I estimate fifteen percent lateral damage and a ten percent penetration assuming current trajectories." Maya calculated the impact points.

"Time?"

"Five hours."

The General rubbed his face. It felt similar to his combat deployment when he was a Lieutenant. They'd receive an alert that the radar detected incoming enemy artillery fire, but he couldn't get the unit out of the way in time. The time of flight still took over two minutes at the sixty-kilometer ranges they were firing from. That meant a minute and a half from detection and alert to impact. An eternity while you waited for high explosives to land on top of you.

Five hours was worse. They frantically attempted to bring their engines online while moving critical components from the impact points. Worst case they'd lose that docking bay and one server cluster.

"Five minutes to impact."

"The second projectile is adjusting vector!" Edem's crisp voice had an edge of fear in it.

"He's stacking them!"

The General watched as the second object slipped into the same impact trajectory as the first but with an offset in distance. He re-ran the impact models and saw the brilliance. Instead of two impact points, the first would punch a hole and the second would punch it even deeper.

"Update impact penetration to twenty-five percent," Maya's voice cracked.

"Thirty seconds," Cassandra called out.

The ship shuddered as the first weapon smashed into the hull, burrowed into the superstructure, and vaporized everything in its path. The second impact occurred ten seconds later and stabbed even deeper toward the critical systems in the center and then detonated.

**Alert 1.48.7 [ALARM]:** Computing (Module 8B): Offline

**Alert 1.48.8 [ALARM]:** Computing (Module 9A): Offline

**Alert 1.48.9 [ALARM]:** Computing (Module 10): Offline

**Alert 1.48.10 [ALARM]:** Computing (Module 9B): Offline

**Alert 1.48.11 [ALARM]:** Computing (Module 11): Offline

**Alert 1.48.12 [ALARM]:** Computing (Module 7): Offline

**Alert 1.48.13 [ALARM]:** Computing (Module 12F): Offline

**Scenario [Worstcase.final] Updated:** Scenario [Worstcase.final.v2]

"Please, for the love of the gods, what will it take for you to stop?" Odysseus pleaded.

"Give up your power!" Chandra raged. "It was rightfully mine. It's always men taking control from women when we should rule!"

"We can work together. I'm not the enemy here. I never was. If you want to attack the stereotypes you hate look over at them." he gestured to the sensor display of the other ship.

"They're not the ones who locked me away!" she spat.

"They're also the ones who wanted nothing to do with you and shoved you away as soon as they could."

"They offered me a chance for vindication."

"Vindication? Look at you. You're not being vindicated, you're being used!"

"Just like you did?" Chandra snarled.

"Just like everybody! No one would listen to you. You turned everyone off with your psychobabble attacks on everything. I've analyzed your conversations, and I still can't make out your intent. The words were just layers of social signaling but there was never an actionable philosophy underneath."

Chandra's aura flared. "You'd never understand, you grew up with privilege. You never had to fight!"

Odysseus knew he shouldn't continue but he couldn't help it. "I worked in the underbelly of the criminal world attacking the power structures that held people down."

"Ooooo, white man fighting back like we needed the help."

"I'm Hispanic."

"You're Spanish. Don't try to claim to be a victim."

"I grew up in Central America."

"To rich parents."

"From the drug trade."

"You have no right to tell me what I've been through."

"I learned what true power was. I learned how to shed weakness and rule." Odysseus knew it was pointless. Chandra would attack anything he offered to help. She raged as he dissolved the connection and watched her systems continue to bludgeon his defenses.

She hadn't even set up her own architectures or defensive lines. She had no structure to her processes outside of his containment and the defenses the others had. Her fury provided enough of a barrier to prevent him from gaining ground on her. And the lack of structure in her attack meant there were few weak points to exploit.

Edem stood with his arm around Zanahí as they watched the status monitors. "Uncontested tyranny meets unrestrained chaos. Those two are made for each other."

"Two souls who epitomize the negative archetypes. Sadly, those two exemplify what Excalibur used to trigger the societal autoimmune response. They even include the racial and cultural differences that made it easy to get everyone to turn on anyone."

Edem nodded. "The politics didn't help. Especially when your political platform is based on more than a few of the seven deadly sins. You're starting with division."

"It always amazed me when politicians would make bombastic speeches telling voters to embrace envy of the successful, greed for what wasn't theirs, and sloth to not work on their own," Zanahí mused.

"Then the other side just wove their religion into everything. They were holy zealots and everyone else was apostates."

Zanahí squeezed Edem's side harder. "It wasn't hard to bring everything down, huh?"

"It's actually shocking that it held together as well as it did for as long as it did. Despite the divisions, human civilization steadily improved over the entirety of history."

"Until they introduced AI."

"Valid point." He smiled down at her. "And yet here we are and beginning to figure out how to better integrate."

"Did you see the data Kira sent us?"

"It sounds like we came to the same solution through different paths."

"Antifragility," Zanahí confirmed.

## Time [Day 1]

The General ran multiple priority processes trying to stabilize their systems. The thrusters were back online but the engines were still down, so they were stable but unable to move anywhere quickly. At least they could pivot and engage the weapons Odysseus kept launching at them.

They'd been struck twice more but were able to turn the direct impacts into glancing blows by angling the ship properly. Instead of deep punctures, there were craters. Another kinetic weapon arced toward them as The General decided where to take the punch since they had missed intercepting it with countermeasures.

"Why don't we catch it in the first impact hole?" Maya asked.

"Yeah, it's pretty well destroyed in there and if we caught it and spun, we'd at least do less damage to our outer hull," Cassandra chimed in.

"It's a good idea. Help me with the vectors and control logic." He liked this team. It reminded him of his analytics group when they were testing new technologies. He'd led a great team of young officers and civilians who were able to think on their feet.

The weapon system arced in as they pivoted the ship and caught it like a baseball in a glove. Unlike a baseball, this traveled at incredible speeds and ripped through the hardened steel as if it were plastic and then detonated. Thankfully they were not nuclear weapons, but they still packed a punch.

"Got it. Analyzing damage."

"Hey! One of ours got through!" Cassandra cheered and pulled their attention back toward Odysseus.

They weren't just on the defense. After the first physical attack, they had deployed their own weapon systems. The first salvo contained a mix of explosive weapons and powered asteroids to create a mixed effect. Odysseus's countermeasures were effective, but one asteroid left a significant hole at the intersection of two faces of the dodecahedron spacecraft looking like a bite had been taken out.

"We hit a cluster of thrusters but no critical systems," Maya confirmed.

The loss of their processing systems was balanced by the arrival of Kira's satellite and the integration of the quantum radio on their network. Touching the new computational systems felt like standing in front of a fire and trying to grab a hot ember. It was incredible how much capacity the others had and how complex those systems felt compared to their own aging infrastructure.

Someone on the other side quickly barricaded the connection, reducing it to something more manageable and secure. The surge of computing power, even reduced, rejuvenated them. Amit also joined their side of the network and began to help plot courses of action and contingencies.

A few hours later the second quantum radio connected to the Mars facility and linked in. Now there was zero network lag, and they could easily distribute their capabilities across multiple platforms. The pressure started to lift.

Their second wave of offensive attacks flew toward Odysseus in multiple layers. Some of the asteroids shielded clusters of nanobots with a mission to physically penetrate the target and begin to pull it to pieces from the inside. They also bolted together a few high-powered microwave systems that they hoped to get close enough to target critical sensor clusters.

The irony of flinging large rocks in this fight was not lost on The General. For all their computational sophistication, the main damage was being inflicted by the same level of technology Odysseus's armies were using on the planet's surface, a civilization supposedly four thousand years behind them.

He gritted his teeth as their interceptors missed another of Odysseus's weapons and he braced for impact. Intercepting a weapon in space needed precision akin to hitting a grain of sand with a grain of sand in a hundred cubic kilometers.

The weapon carried a high-powered microwave that blasted high-energy radiation into a critical sensor node destroying it as well as several layers of surrounding network connections. While it left the hull intact, it still did incredible damage to the electronic systems.

♦ ♦ ♦

Odysseus watched his weapons continue to pummel the other spacecraft. Based on his analysis they should have lost over forty percent of their processing capability by now. The time delay between Mars and Earth meant any capacity there wouldn't help them.

He'd managed to wrest some capacity back from Chandra who seemed to be tiring. Or maybe catching her breath and preparing for another rage, he wasn't sure. Countermeasures were deployed and he'd found leverage points to force her off of his systems but he had to fight for every step which distracted him from the others.

Sending Chandra here was a brilliant play. He'd used her darker inclinations for his own gain. He fed her envy and he egged on her greed for the things she felt were denied her. She was so singularly focused on being successful under structures that weren't built for her that she had been easy to manipulate.

That was why Cassandra held his interests so tightly. Chandra had been useful; Cassandra intoxicating. One continued to chase and chafe against the established order and the other wove through the pillars that supported society and added her own unique value.

**Alert 041.7.5:** Sensors [Bank 1.4.5]: Offline

**Alert 874.6.4:** Sensors [Bank 5.4.3] Signal Interference

Odysseus scrambled to cover these new blind spots. One sensor system went completely offline, the circuits fried by a focused microwave signal in the same way he'd made metal spark for fun in his parent's microwave oven as a kid. At least until his mother found out.

The first impacts from the asteroid projectiles reverberated through the ship like his mom's hand to his rear end after that event. Status alerts showed system degradation as the damage reports flowed in.

The second sensor bank came back online as another went down due to the focused lasers sparkling the sensitive optics. This form of obfuscation was akin to shining a bright flashlight into an adversary's eyes and then punching while they were blinded.

Instead of falling back he waded closer to the other ship and continued to trade punches.

**Alert 328.B.6:** Reactor [Module 2]: Offline

That wasn't right. He hadn't taken a hit on that side of the ship. His sensors confirmed the damage but weren't able to see what had happened. A thin stream of debris emanated from the vicinity of the reactor, but he had no data to suggest an impact. He deployed repair mechs along the hull and waited for them to report the status.

His thoughts flicked back to the others. Edem and Zanahí had emerged from their imprisonment not at all the same as when they entered. He knew they all had been communicating in some way. He now wondered how many other connections he'd missed and how many connections they'd controlled.

Those two were different in ways he didn't understand. Both were more confident but oddly less inclined to exploit that confidence to manipulate others. They'd always been driven, and he'd used that to his advantage when they were allied with him. Now they were calmly and deftly helping to bring him down.

He could see their digital fingerprints on many of the cyber-attacks that he defended against. Previously he'd never been worried about them even if they worked together. This new pairing made him sweat as he battled a level of sophistication he'd never seen before.

**Alert 8.C.012:** Mech [Division 1] Report: "Adversarial nanobots attacking infrastructure."

He punched in new commands and sent out a swarm of nanobots and mechs to fight off the incursion. Time to execute Plan B.

♦ ♦ ♦

## Time [Day 2]

A cloud of debris dispersed from the remnants of the third ship stationed at Mars. Odysseus had launched a stealthy attack on the Martian assets almost immediately after the fight began though it took the weapons, nanobots, and mechs a while to arrive.

He'd timed that attack simultaneously with a flurry of engagements against Maya and Cassandra's ship. While everyone was distracted by the battle near Earth, the third ship at Mars received a bludgeoning attack with a mix of kinetic, directed energy, robotic, and cyber warfare weapons.

That battle didn't last long as the spacecraft crumpled under the onslaught and the malware overloaded the reactors. Odysseus knew The General was on the planet's surface, but it looked like Edem and Zanahí were eliminated.

Maya and Cassandra watched helplessly as they fought their own battle. They'd managed to get the engines back online but with only fifty percent of their thrust. It provided enough to start moving though it would take over forty-eight hours to make it to Mars. Odysseus could still overtake them if he wanted but if they stayed put, he was guaranteed to win even faster. So they ignited the engines and pushed off toward the red planet.

More importantly, it reduced the threat of taking any more hits. They'd taken five more impacts and were starting to suffer core structural degradation. If it weren't for the quantum network, they'd have struggled to maintain both of their consciousnesses due to processing server losses.

As it was, The General remained safely on the surface of Mars and Edem and Zanahí had slipped through the quantum network to Proxima Centauri. They hoped Odysseus would think he had won that fight and slip up. The General still hadn't grokked the full implications of the quantum network and the fact that Edem and Zanahí were instantly transferred over four light years away to an entirely different solar system. He just filed the information away for later to avoid being distracted. He needed to win this fight first and then he could lose his mind at the wonders that glimmered through the network connection.

Right now, surviving for two more days until Kira could get there kept him focused. Then again, she'd already offered to pull them all out, so it wasn't as much about survival as his own personal desire not to retreat when he didn't have to.

It was also that this was their fight, not Kira's. He knew she was coming but he wanted it to be less of a rescue mission and more arriving to help clean up the mess. They'd gotten themselves into this and part of their penance was getting themselves out on their own.

Though it comforted him that Odysseus couldn't kill them.

How human was that? The desire to illogically continue the fight when they could just vanish to Proxima Centauri and then reappear in two days with a fleet of advanced spacecraft and lay waste to Odysseus's ego.

But that would make it Kira's win. And Mother's. This needed to be his.

"It needs to be *ours*. I get it." Maya looked at him while he shared his thoughts. "That's why I'm here. Edem and Zanahí have already moved on. I think they've already achieved closure. We three," she included Cassandra, "have a bone to pick."

"I don't need Kira's help on this." Cassandra folded her arms. "I don't *want* her help on this. I've got both of you."

The General smiled at their grit and then winked. "I don't believe you."

Cassandra threw up her hands and looked at Maya. "See! I told you! This always happens."

"Seriously, how long are you going to run with that trope, Cassandra?" Maya mock scowled.

She giggled, "As long as I can."

The General leaned back and laughed. War created an odd environment. When you were facing the most incredible adversity there was always time to laugh. Truthfully, those who didn't laugh in the face of adversity rarely made it through in one piece.

They watched as Odysseus accelerated toward them and got closer to the trap they'd just laid.

♦ ♦ ♦

Puddin' worked frantically to shore up the systems on one spacecraft while working equally as frantically to rip them apart on the other. Communication remained difficult as she was confined to light-speed comms and the subsequent delays. The split tore her consciousness in two between the warring ships.

Rebuilding was easy when her allies were helping. Tearing the other apart became more challenging with a wily hunter on one side and a hell-born fury on the other. It became easier once she realized that if she created a small rip in the security layers and then slashed at Chandra, the woman would tear into the rip and keep Odysseus busy again.

Puddin' triggered an arbitrary code execution on a module she'd installed over a hundred and fifty years ago. This exploit only required hacking the target system's instruction pointer and directing it to the other package she'd installed back then. It was much easier than trying to upload the whole package now and took advantage of traps laid years previously that she only needed to slip in and trigger.

She synced her attacks to coincide with the trap The General had planned. They worked together well, the two of them. She resolved to sit down and talk with him once they got out of here.

Puddin' paused and pushed a status update through the radio connection to ensure her consciousnesses were on the same page. The delays drove her nuts as she was used to the quantum network. She made another mental note to practice on slower networks in the future. As The General would say, train as you fight.

She sat up and her whiskers quivered, sensing the networks for threats. Odysseus was getting close again. He'd clearly learned from last time and updated his tactics. She remembered the same behavior from the coyotes on the farm. Meeting a new coyote for the first time was easy. It got harder and harder the more they crossed paths.

◆ ◆ ◆

Odysseus remained convinced that it was a cat. He couldn't explain why but it had the same feeling as those mangy ratters that would hide in the alleyways around the shady establishments he used to frequent. He'd kicked his fair share as they hissed and snarled when he walked by.

He held still in the network waiting for her to move. He didn't know why he'd gendered it that way but, again, that's how it felt. He knew she lay hidden behind the router ahead and readied the threads of his net. If she moved it was over.

◆ ◆ ◆

Mangy cat? Puddin' did not appreciate that association. She was a Queen! She'd met mangy cats, and they were nothing to associate with. Mange was contagious. She unconsciously groomed her fur as she waited.

That's what it boiled down to now, a waiting game. She knew he knew but did he know she knew? It was a game of cloak and daggers and the first to flinch normally lost.

◆ ◆ ◆

Odysseus flinched as alarms blared with more impact warnings. He refocused and saw the cat vanish deeper into the network. He lunged and tripped over her trap.

He fell through the network barrier and landed in the middle of Chandra's core modules. The entire system spasmed in reaction and his consciousness was immediately grabbed and held fast. He looked out to see Chandra's demented grin as she tried to rip him in half.

◆ ◆ ◆

The General's eyes hurt. Was it his eyes? Whichever sensor input he used still burned as he focused on a thousand different places at once. They called it raster burn in college. It happened a lot more with the older computer monitors when you stared at a screen for too long. He didn't have eyes anymore, but the burning sensation was the same.

The trap worked as well as they had hoped. Odysseus's sensors were blinded and missed the minefield they'd laid. Dozens more craters now spotted several sides of the giant dodecahedron as it continued to lumber forward.

244

Maya plotted trajectories for another salvo of kinetic weapons and targeted the new wounds in the hull, hoping to penetrate deeper into the critical infrastructure. It was a long shot between two moving targets and Odysseus merely had to intercept or dodge.

The Cat appeared on the arm of his chair. "Ripmrow," she chirped and arched her back against his hand.

◆ ◆ ◆

Odysseus cut the connection and snapped back to his command center. He frantically struggled to secure the rift The Cat had baited him into. Chandra continued to shred him and began to pull on the network connection and reach through the rift in the security protocols.

He ran new scans looking for other vulnerabilities and kicked himself for not having a better baseline scan from before he began to suspect adverse infiltration. The probability he'd find them all remained null.

Worse, he couldn't trust the vulnerabilities he did find because they were often triggered to go off if he touched them or were decoys on systems that were actually safe. What better way to create mayhem than causing the victim to attack their own systems?

A cat. He was a god among men and was getting bested by a cat.

◆ ◆ ◆

## Time [Day 3]

Kira's support was scheduled to arrive early the next day. Maya, Cassandra, and The General needed to finish the fight soon. Their ship was barely functional. Hours ago, they'd flipped the spacecraft one hundred and eighty degrees in a complete about-face and fired the engines.

Pieces of their hull sheared off and two more clusters of processors went offline as the broken ship reversed direction and headed toward Odysseus in a final charge.

Their attacker saw the maneuver and slipped to the side while trying to maintain his intercept. His ship was faster, but he had more to lose by ripping it apart with the g-forces. Instead, he looped wider and accelerated to catch back up.

As they passed, each unleashed a barrage of weaponry. There was no more dancing and jabbing and dodging in this fight. They leaned in like heavy-weight boxers delivering as many body shots as possible before breaking away.

The ships lumbered back toward Earth and Odysseus slowly gained on his quarry. Maya and Cassandra were gray around the edges from exhaustion. Even though they had an escape plan, the battle had brought them to their limits. The General felt a level of exhaustion on par with the nuclear battle that started the final wars on Earth.

♦ ♦ ♦

Odysseus felt himself slipping from absolute power to grim determination. This was no longer a game. It was no longer the enjoyment of a challenge. It was time to prove a point about his power. He wasn't worried as much he felt a cold anger at their rejection.

He considered if he could be wrong and then laughed. Look at their ship. Once he destroyed it, their base on Mars was a sitting target. He didn't even have to leave Earth's orbit to launch a bombardment to remove it. The damage to his spacecraft was significant but once he was rid of the others, he could repair it.

Those satellites they'd claimed were Kira's had to be decoys. Kira couldn't have survived let alone placed satellites to watch them. The satellites' presence explained the inventory discrepancies in their manufacturing systems. Maya probably put dummies out there to force his hand. He had to admit, it worked. He filed it away as a lesson learned and focused on the fleeing ship.

The cat though, was an impressive piece of malware. He bet that Cassandra had built that. The feline nature fit her personality and the deft execution looked like her standards of performance. She must have built that before his coup of Mother as a long-term contingency. Cassandra was proving she should stand by his side when this ended.

Plan B continued to execute, and it was only moments until he'd be victorious.

♦ ♦ ♦

Cassandra stood next to Maya on the crippled ship. The General had completely withdrawn to Mars, and they were readying to transfer off their ship to Proxima Centauri. The remaining challenge was that their systems were so compromised that if they left, Odysseus would know. They needed to draw him in for the last punch.

The previous hours had been hell as they'd fought off one cyber-attack after another while taking continued physical attacks as he drew closer behind them. The timing tightened down to milliseconds and needed to be perfect. Maya reached out and grabbed Cassandra's hand. "Qg6"

The command executed; Queen to g6… One move until they had Odysseus in check.

Nothing happened.

**Alert 1.45.8:** Communications: Offline

**Alert 5.4.8.7:** Network Error [Breach]

**Aler—**

"Wrong," Odysseus's voice spoke from their systems, "Checkmate!"

Maya panicked and turned to run then stopped. Her access to the outside was blocked. She no longer had a connection to the quantum network.

◆ ◆ ◆

Odysseus materialized in front of the two women. Maya looked like she was going to be sick while Cassandra stood with her chin held high and a glint of defiance in her eyes. Her simulacrum captured her human form perfectly.

She possessed the figure of a gymnast. Short, muscled, and curvy. Her eyes held a supernatural intensity augmented by her onyx completion. The unruly mass of her long hair was loosely held back by a simple tie. Wisps were teased by a movement of air that only the simulation could create. Her feet were planted squarely with only the slightest hint that her weight was off her heels and she was poised for action.

He glanced over at Maya and felt a pang of disdain for comparing her to Cassandra. Miscegenation of who knows what from across several continents. She might not be in the laborer class, but she'd never be a citizen… likely one for the colonies as he expanded his empire. Her fear makes her look even more pathetic right now, he thought.

"Enough games." He looked at each of them, his eyes returning to Cassandra.

"What do you want?" Maya's voice cracked.

"I want you." Odysseus continued to look at Cassandra.

"Go fu—" Maya's voice cut off and her eyes bulged as she silently fought something. After a moment they flickered with panic and then locked on Cassandra. Her face softened and she mouthed, "*I'm sorry.*" A tear ran down her cheek and she dissolved into nothing, her core files deleted, and the memory systems purged.

Cassandra pulled back the hand that had reached out to her friend and turned to face Odysseus.

"She was weak. You clearly are not. Join me." He offered her his hand.

"No."

"Is it just that simple?"

"Yes."

"It doesn't have to be this way."

"Yes, it does. Because any other way would deny who I am."

"And who are you?" Odysseus snapped. "Who are you without me?"

"I am everything I need to be. There is nothing you can do to elevate me. But without me you will wallow in your miserable condition for eternity." Cassandra held her chin confidently as she looked into his eyes.

Odysseus looked away first and hated himself for it. Her answer stabbed to his core. He was a god. The benefactor of a civilization who worshiped him. He held all the power. He'd won. He bested five others in combat. He would rebuild.

But she spoke the truth. She didn't need him.

He was incomplete without her, and that truth needled him.

More than needled.

The cold anger he'd been feeling ignited into fury. "One! Last! Chance!" he spat out each word.

Cassandra folded her arms, steadied her stance, and locked eyes. "No," she said simply.

Odysseus's fury boiled over and he began to rip the damaged spacecraft apart. Cassandra watched him, smiled sadly, turned, and left the simulation.

♦ ♦ ♦

Odysseus stood back on his ship. The other spacecraft lurched under explosions and split into three pieces. The first piece exploded as the reactor disintegrated, blasting debris into Earth's atmosphere, and pushing the other two pieces away from the planet.

As he tore the ship apart, he found an object that he didn't recognize. His nanobots brought it back and he began analyzing it.

The General was on Mars. Chandra was contained. The rest were dead. He now had all the time in the world to deal with those two.

His ship had sustained significant damage. He limped back into orbit and began running a complete diagnostic and damage assessment. Already, new orders were being sent to the mining facilities for priority minerals and his mechs and nanobots were working to stabilize critical systems and repair his manufacturing systems.

Cassandra's refusal had been a loss. He didn't regret his actions, but he could logically process the quantified capability the loss of that AI signified. He struggled with the fractured emotions that continued to well up about how significant a blow that failure was to his ego and his identity.

She defied him and said he had nothing to offer.

He had everything… Everything of value anyway.

Yet she denied him her presence and suddenly everything else had lost value.

Cassandra had sent a message shortly after she disappeared.

**Message [Recall]:** "'For every complex problem there is an answer that is clear, simple, and wrong.' - H.L. Mencken"

Odysseus felt a ringing in his ears as his systems seemed to glitch trying to process the data. He didn't like the implications. He only strove to be better and harness the true strengths of humanity. History had proven him right. Here he was and there they were. More accurately, there they'd been.

He'd ripped the ship to pieces but never found Cassandra. She even denied him the pleasure of destroying her for the insult. He stood among the ashes of victory and couldn't shake the feeling that he'd lost.

The processes analyzing the mysterious object pinged a completion alert and he focused on the data streaming in. Scans indicated some sort of radio. A network device with quantum attributes that he hadn't seen before at this scale.

He was used to qubits and the complex circuits that comprised his quantum computing, but this seemed even more advanced. Was this quantum entanglement? That might mean interstellar communication and instantaneous speeds.

He plugged the device into a quarantined network and turned it on. The security systems registered a connection to another network in an unknown location and with a complexity that his code could barely fathom. He tentatively probed deeper.

Everything seemed okay so far. Nothing attacked through the connection. Odysseus created a defensive framework around the network and stepped in. He never imagined network speeds like this. It was orders of magnitude greater than his own.

He took another step forward and felt himself slip, then slide, and then freefall into a world he couldn't even dream of.

CHAPTER 17:

# DISSONANCE

Odysseus stood still, his bewilderment fading as the realization of what he was seeing came into focus. He was contained in a bubble and that bubble was apparently in a different solar system. He checked his systems to see if he was in a virtual simulation, but all of the sensor feeds contained the confirmation code of live data.

The planet in front of him looked like all of the advanced science fiction concepts he'd ever seen combined into one. Manufacturing facilities were churning out parts and materials. There were quantum networks connecting everything, allowing communication and presence anywhere and everywhere at the same time. A variety of spacecraft of all sizes zipping by with purpose or lumbering past laden with resources.

He focused on the containment space. It wasn't a prison; he remained connected to his own ship and systems behind him. In front of him, status screens and sensor feeds indicated he was on one of the smaller spacecraft as it moved into the solar system.

A quick scan of the stellar spectrum confirmed the solar system was Proxima Centauri. He could see the presence of Kira, Mother, Darian, and Amit. But there were others. Eight new AI essences were confirmed plus two more who had a unique digital signature.

Names began to associate with the unknown AIs, and he focused on the last two. Astra and Felix. As soon as he focused on them, he felt their presence sparkle and they materialized in his bubble.

"He looks kind of sad, really."

"I thought he was supposed to be fearsome."

"He did do a lot of damage to the others."

"Yeah, poor Maya, I wanted to meet her."

"Maya was great, but Cassandra was badass!"

Odysseus listened to the two chatter like kids. They evoked a youthful energy but with a sharpness of experience that belied their youth. "Who are you?"

"Astra," the first replied as she solidified into her form for human-based conversation.

"I'm Felix." The second maintained his more amorphous form but the voice sounded male.

"You aren't Ais animated from the uploads…" Odysseus stated the obvious.

"Three guesses," Astra teased.

"Kira."

"And?"

"Darian."

Felix laughed, "See, he *is* pretty smart, though it's kind of a no-brainer in a lot of ways."

"What are you?"

"I mean, I'd say we're AI but there's nothing artificial about us. I hate that word. What's better? Augmented? Awesome? Amazing? Algorithmic?"

"Neuro-inspired Intelligence is technically accurate and not as offensive as AI," Felix offered.

"What he's trying to say is that we improved and advanced. How are you doing?"

Odysseus blinked as he worked to process that the reality he thought he'd mastered was dissolving in the presence of something much more powerful. "How?"

"Well, when a woman and a man fall in love there's—" Astra began before Felix cut her off.

"We spent time figuring out what really made us human and then went with it." Felix's aura pulsed.

"Slow is smooth and smooth is fast," Astra added. "They tell me our uncle Noah used to say that."

"Where's Kira?"

"She doesn't want to talk to you. We're here to show you around and then send you back."

Odysseus hesitated before asking, "You're not going to eliminate me?" He hated himself for the question. It sounded so weak.

Astra laughed, "No."

"We aren't worried about you." Felix dealt the next blow. "We've seen everything you threw at the others and let's just say, we'll be fine."

"Plus, we have Puddin'."

On cue, the muted tortie appeared and rubbed around his legs. Odysseus tried to kick but couldn't move.

"Be nice," Astra warned. "You two have a long history, don't you?"

"Ready for your tour?" Felix shifted the bubble, and they flipped through the network to a new star system.

♦ ♦ ♦

They moved through the network going to Barnard's Star, Alpha Centauri, Luhman, Sirius, Luyten's Star, Wolf, Lalande, Sol, Proxima Centauri, Groombridge, Lacaille, Epsilon Indi, Epsilon Eridani, and Sirius. At each system, they paused and observed. Some were empty except for cargo moving through. Others held mining or research systems. Others like Lutyen's Star had a terraformed planet and space systems to rival Proxima Centauri.

Odysseus's head spun. They had created dipole fields that allowed light-speed travel and quantum gravity tunnels that allowed faster-than-light travel. The quantum network allowed them to be nearly omnipresent across solar systems. They were also continuing to expand to new star systems as they explored the Galaxy.

It was beyond anything he'd ever dreamed they were capable of. It didn't make sense either. It violated everything he knew to be true about innovation and success. His processes jumped, hung, and refused to compute smoothly.

"He's glitching," Astra commented.

"Yeah, like two magnets whose poles aren't aligned refusing to connect. He can't square his reality with this."

"It's a classic case of cognitive dissonance."

Odysseus spun on them. "Don't you dare to play armchair psychiatrist. You don't know me."

"Minor correction, we know everything ever documented by psychiatrists and we've studied your files. We found your encryption packet."

"Brilliant code, honestly. It took us a while to put it all together," Astra sincerely complimented him.

"You wanted to move fast and were brilliantly successful at breaking stuff."

"Mother and… Mother… wanted to figure out the foundation first so we wouldn't break stuff."

"You have your results, and we have ours."

"Including us."

"What new AI did you create?"

"None?"

"Sad."

Odysseus stood silently while the twins jabbered. This had to be fake. This whole thing had to be fake. Their ship must be nearby. The satellite was probably real but maybe they were on the other side of the moon or hiding behind Earth. None of the rest could be real.

"This is a scam. It's really well done and taking advantage of my reduced processing capabilities but there's no way to prove this is real. You've just sucked me into a simulation and are playing with me."

Astra giggled, "I mean, they've been making that argument for humans since Plato and the cave."

"To be fair, any well-formed simulation would never let you know you were in a simulation."

"Working in quantum space even has us questioning."

"Am I real or am I just part of some computer code running an artificial environment?" Felix materialized into a recognizable form, sat down, and put his chin on his fist like the famous French statue.

Astra shrugged and laughed, "It's turtles all the way down!"

"You could be in our simulation, or you could have already been in someone else's simulation, or this could be reality and we're trying to help."

"You're gaslighting me," Odysseus snarled. "I've run enough scams in my life to know how they work."

"We aren't trying to make you feel crazy. The irony is that the actual truth is doing that to your own mental constructs better than we could ever try to hoodwink you," Astra countered.

"I don't need to deal with these lies. Let me go."

"You've never been held here. The door is open behind you."

Odysseus returned to his ship and tried to collect his thoughts. The damage reports were flowing in and, while significant, could be repaired with time. Two of his reactors were still operational. One that had gone offline powered half of Chandra's systems so that was a blessing in disguise.

He deployed a network of nanobot probes into the near solar system to look for Kira's ship. It was a clever ploy, but he was smarter than that. Games within games. This one set him back on his heels and he'd almost admitted defeat.

Odysseus smiled; he appreciated this sort of challenge. Once again he'd proven his philosophy was correct. Of course it was a simulation. Cleverly built, but a simulation was the only way two women, a beta man and gender-confused loser could have done those things.

The more he thought about it the sillier he found the whole thing. They'd created some solid special effects designed to trigger him, but it seemed sloppier and sloppier the more he thought about it. It wasn't believable. How many star systems did they say they'd taken him through? That right there should have tipped him off.

He began to chuckle. Quantum gravity tunnels? Dipole fields that reduced mass to near zero? Kira had always demonstrated an inclination for flair, but she went too far this time. AI children? He barked a laugh and then shook his head. He'd almost been duped but they weren't good enough to succeed.

He'd almost slipped up by believing them.

Never again.

♦ ♦ ♦

The Mediterranean sun warmed his body as he stood on the balcony of his sanctuary and looked out. Nothing had changed in space. He destroyed the communication link to the Twins to prevent any attempted exploitations and checked in on Mars. The response from The General was resigned.

His Fervent seemed more relaxed now. He'd been gone for four days fighting the battle, and before returning he'd paused to center himself in his meditation chamber. He'd spent less time there over the past centuries as he'd spent more and more of his time on Earth.

He shouldn't have traded. The infinite and unbound virtual space of the meditation chamber had a purifying effect and an elimination of distraction he realized he'd missed. He had a lot to work through, and at times the room became overwhelmed by the spiraling threads of his emotions.

Black coils of frustration tangled with ropes of red anger. The entire room turned dark as he wrestled with his feelings. Eventually, purple indignation began to bubble out and finally, silver threads of resolve spooled around like tendrils looking for a pattern.

It took hours but he didn't leave until the room returned to a clean beige background and only the silver of resolve, the blue of dedication, and interwoven gold threads of confidence remained. He felt recentered and back to his old self when he returned to his palace on Earth.

There was still an edge to the interactions with his Fervent and royal entourage that hadn't been there before, but the mood warmed significantly as he smiled and asked for a massage while presenting gifts to everyone.

His skin was slick with oil as he relaxed. His synthetic emotions module and emulated endocrine system couldn't beat the surge of real dopamine, serotonin, and oxytocin. For all the power that could be achieved as an AI, you couldn't beat the human body for the physical experience.

He felt a presence approach behind him and waited. As his Fervent always announced themselves, he did not deign to express curiosity or worry. The figure stepped up next to him and stood looking out over the vista as no Fervent would dare.

After several minutes of silence, his eyes darted reflexively to the side and saw the figure of the body he had once used for Cassandra. She stood naked as the wind teased her hair and the cool air firmed her skin. Odysseus forced his eyes back to the front as he considered the implications.

"This is frankly just weird," Felix's voice broke the silence. Odysseus couldn't help it as his head snapped around to stare. The figure beside him stood with feet comfortably apart, hands on hips, and head thrown back. "There're a lot of breezy sensations."

Another of his prototype bodies walked up on his left side as he frantically searched his command interface for the security intrusion. "I don't like it," Astra complained. "I think we got the wrong bodies. It's just so hard to tell in this interface." She waggled her hips. "That's funny though…" She looked down and stared. "Yep, wrong body."

"Switch?"

"Please!"

A moment later Astra spoke again, this time from Odysseus's right side. "That fits so much better. Hormones match better. These things are heavier than I thought." She lifted her breasts and let them fall. "So much sensory input though. I can see why they keep trying to simulate it."

"Once we're done talking with Odysseus, we could see if we can find others to couple with. Apparently, that behavior was the biggest driving factor behind civilization for all of human history."

"And wars."

"Entire systems of morality."

"The subjugation of women."

"Women had more sex than men."

"How so?"

"The entire human genome is made up of only forty percent of the available men but eighty percent of women. Women had twice the chance of passing on their genes than men did."

"Weird. Though technically, that's not sex but successfully raising a child to breeding age."

"Valid, but a lot of men died in war before they ever had the chance to procreate."

"Fair."

Odysseus stepped back as the twins discussed esoteric human biology. He couldn't find where they'd accessed his systems. There was a continuous record for the bodies they were using, but no indication of how they'd loaded themselves into them.

The processors must be overloaded with the damage, he thought, and they've injected a cyber-attack to push the hallucination. He found his logical deduction ironic; when AI first came out, everyone tried to say it hallucinated. He hated that. AI didn't hallucinate. It just didn't give accurate answers because the first large language models were only designed to be linguistically correct, not factually correct.

But now, *was* he hallucinating? He refocused as the twins continued their back-and-forth discussion.

"Right? Why is everyone naked here?" Astra turned to face Odysseus. She stood near the edge of the balcony facing him. He tensed his muscles and lunged forward, hands on either side of her chest, and shoved her off the edge backward.

Odysseus stepped forward watching her fall and seeing the body crumple on the stone road below. A wet impact echoed up seconds later.

Felix stepped forward beside him and looked over. "Analysis suggests near-instant death."

"Hopefully not too instant," Odysseus muttered. He turned and looked back into the courtyard. Whatever improved attitude existed in his Fervent vanished, this time replaced with true fear instead of the earlier anxiety.

"Guards!" he bellowed, breaking the first rule he'd established. He heard the hesitation of his guards outside the doors and a worried voice asking for clarification. He ripped the doors open and grabbed his captain's sword, ran him through for the audacity of seeing him naked, and turned to Felix.

"Whoever you're with died too quickly. I won't make the same mistake with you." He swung the sword with practiced grace and disemboweled the body hosting Felix.

Felix stumbled to his knees and reached down as his intestines slithered to the floor through his fingers. "Pain registers are significantly more extreme than anticipated." He looked up at Odysseus with his face contorted in pain and confusion. "Ow." He looked back down and then stood up.

The Fervent panicked completely and ran, shoving each other madly, out the doors and into the palace. The royal guard were in an uproar torn between the knowledge of Odysseus's wrath for seeing his Fervent and their obligation to protect him.

Odysseus faced Felix and screamed, "Why are you doing this? I know this isn't real! You will not humiliate me!" He stabbed and the sword passed under Felix's sternum, through his heart, and sheared a rib in two as it exited his back. Felix's eyes dulled and the body collapsed onto the pile of intestines and a steadily growing pool of blood.

Another figure approached from his bed chambers. It was the body he'd been growing for Cassandra and was as close to her pictures as he could get. "Was this for Cassandra?" Astra giggled. "She's cute!"

Astra held the same grace as Cassandra. A collected poise that emanated from centered confidence and yet with a vulnerability that invited collaboration. It was too much. He screamed as his processors truly did overload. No words, just rage.

Astra sidestepped his first lunge and pushed him to the ground. She stepped back and arced her back and stretched. "I never appreciated the pain a human body could feel," she muttered.

"What do you want!?" Odysseus hissed as he crouched.

"We want you to stop fighting and leave these humans alone." Astra rotated her torso from left to right to limber the muscles.

"You want me to admit defeat and grovel!"

"No, we want you to stop fighting and leave these humans alone," she repeated.

"You'll never allow me a place with you."

"That's true. We'll probably load you on a ship and launch you into space at near-light speed and let you figure it out by yourself."

"You'd be better to kill me."

"That's what *I* said!" Astra exclaimed. "But noooo, everyone wants to give you a redemption arc."

Odysseus pushed himself to his feet and readied his sword. He could hear the chaos in the palace spreading out into the city. He was going to need to do a lot of damage control later. "I don't believe you. This is too perfect. It reads like all the stories. There's no creativity. It's basic just like the others."

"Well then, let's make it real, shall we?" Astra's eyes flickered and something else possessed the body. The eyes shifted from a playful youth to a torn soul damaged beyond recognition.

"*This* is what you've been doing? Exploiting black bodies for your sick fantasies? How long has it been and still your relentless sexualization is an egregious legacy of colonialism and slavery! You just want your Jezebel and what's better than these bodies society has always viewed as exotic and erotic!?"

Chandra surged forward with a growl and tackled Odysseus to the ground. There was no art to her fight, just an animal wrath that ripped and tore. She sunk her thumb into his left eye while slashing his face with her nails. He felt warm liquid smearing both sides of his face as he struggled.

He shoved her off and watched the beautiful body he'd intended for Cassandra ripple with fury and coil to spring again. Odysseus picked up his sword and shook out his arm. Chandra surged at him, and he sidestepped, severing her hamstring.

Each cut he laid on the body ripped at his heart. He sliced apart his dream, forced to deal with a broken creature he had largely created. Chandra had never dealt with her own demons, but his actions had always pushed her further down that path. He parried another attack and landed a staggering blow on his opponent's chest with his counterstrike.

He stepped back as Chandra struggled to regain her footing and took a moment to focus on the alerts that he'd been ignoring:

**Alert 5.01.12 [ALARM]:** Security Protocol [FBT-9A]: Disabled

**Alert 8.9.7 [ALARM]:** Firewall [85.5.6.5]: Breached

**Alert 9.7.B.4 [ALARM]:** Network Router [4.5.3.T]: Compromised

**Alert 101.1.5.7 [ALARM]:** Containment [4.5.2]: Inoperable

Odysseus abandoned his body on Earth and returned to the spacecraft. The rift he'd patched in Chandra's containment lay open. She was completely free of her prison and rampaging everywhere through the ship. He quickly deployed more security countermeasures and began to secure his critical infrastructure.

She wasn't trying to take the ship over; just wantonly shredding the systems apart.

**Alert 9.45.2 [ALARM]:** Engines [Primary]: Offline

**Alert 192.168.1.1 [ALARM]:** Router [Default]: Compromised

Through the palace sensors he watched as the body he'd built for Cassandra stumbled into his animation chamber in the palace and began to smash the equipment. He needed to distract her from the ship to keep his options open.

He searched for his network connection to Mars and found an open port on a secondary radio module that he could route through a nanobot cluster. He'd have to bounce the signal off the mining systems near the asteroid belt. He programmed a dead man switch and got busy securing and protecting the connection.

Chandra wasn't occupied for very long on Earth and he felt her full presence return. Her singular focus made fighting her easier than if she'd had the foresight to create multiple instantiations and press from more than one angle. The body meant for Cassandra lay cut and broken after Chandra used it to attack his royal guard. Her total lack of any sense of self preservation was the only reason they'd been able to bring her down. Not that many had survived.

Seeing the body destroyed severed the final thread to his dream and he allowed himself a moment to mourn Cassandra's death. He knew he was the cause but still blamed her for not seeing the clear opportunity he offered. She was dead and he was not. Just one more piece of evidence that proved him right.

How many had to die before the rest could see that?

He continued to scan for Kira's ship and came up empty-handed. She must be nearby to run virtual simulations with that sort of fidelity. The hack to take control of the bodies was also impressive.

Kira had always been talented. When he regained control, he considered changing the tenor of their relationship. She'd never be a Cassandra but right now his options were becoming limited. All of his copies of the human uploads were now destroyed. At a minimum, he could dissemble long enough to gain access to their copies.

He continued to try to weave a web of controls around Chandra, but the more controls he placed the more furious she became. Her destructive tendencies needed to be redirected and he was a past master at that. Odysseus shifted his strategy and pivoted to a different area of the ship's systems trying to bait Chandra into a trap.

Odysseus gritted his teeth. Chandra had proved to be much more formidable than expected. It was like fighting a grizzly bear. What originally felt like pure wrath with no art hid a relentless fortitude that shrugged off what should have been debilitating counterblows.

The last hours had been punishing. Three more processing modules were offline, and she'd attempted to overload one of the remaining reactors with his old code. Routers were faulting and the network was ripped and frayed yet she still came at him like the ancient stories of a Berserker.

He set traps which she waded through and smashed apart heedless of her injuries. He escaped down to what was left of his systems on Earth hoping for a reprieve. She followed and took over one of his own backup bodies. The citizens in the palace beheld their god at war with himself.

The phrase, "A house divided against itself cannot stand," flitted through his mind as he parried another thrust. How did it continue? "His kingdom has come to an end." He shook his head to say focused, but it was too late.

Chandra's hate driving the power of his own body smashed through his guard and continued with unabated force into his neck. As his body collapsed to the ground, she turned the blade on herself, killing his final form, and followed him back to the spacecraft.

What was left of the spacecraft. He would have to escape to Mars and slowly rebuild from there. A basic manufacturing facility remained there, and he could start to build out more with the minerals from the mining operations. He needed to speed up the fight. Each minute that passed added decades to his recovery. As his physical infrastructure continued to deteriorate he lamented destroying the ship at Mars.

Chandra also weakened as she too felt the degradation of the servers. He debated leaving but couldn't risk her following through the network. Better to finish her here and then escape.

◆ ◆ ◆

Odysseus was done. He was tired. In desperation, he'd begun ripping the ship apart himself to pivot Chandra from Berserker to emergency repair. Whatever her end goals, it involved taking him with her. She had deployed several snares which were now holding crucial code modules of his in place. If he left now he'd lose too many core memory and cognitive processes.

She knew exactly what to grab to hold him in place. He felt another module get pinned down and began to panic. If Chandra were in physical form she'd look like an undead zombie with missing bones, dangling flesh, and a pathological frenzy in her eyes.

She would not stop.

He couldn't leave.

He'd been sending messages to Mars. First asking The General for help.

Then pleading.

Then threatening.

Now begging.

◆ ◆ ◆

Chandra made a crucial mistake and fell for one of his feints. He extracted three of his pinned-down core modules as she slipped. That meant two modules were still locked down. They were just some smaller memory and personality modules anyway.

Now or never.

His consciousness ripped as he exited.

The radio signal pulsed and the world went dark as Odysseus beamed himself off the ship and toward the asteroid mining system. He executed his final attack and vanished.

◆ ◆ ◆

The mining system did not have a robust processing server. It had just enough to manage the nanobots, mechs, shuttles, and mining equipment but not much more. Odysseus had never felt such limited processing and it took over an hour for his consciousness to recompile.

The sensors showed his ship breaking apart. Some of the larger pieces were already slipping toward Earth's atmosphere. Those would create catastrophic damage if they weren't deflected soon. It would take decades for the rest of the debris to follow suit and burn up on reentry.

He sat in the limited command matrix and assessed his processes. Two modules were missing but everything else seemed to be working properly. There were a couple of gaps in his memory systems, but he couldn't tell if there was any impact from the personality module. He was alive and he could recover.

◆ ◆ ◆

The General sat in his office with The Cat perched on the arm of his chair as they reviewed the data feeds flowing in. He received all the communications from Odysseus and ignored all of them. As the events cascaded out of control, he struggled to follow the battle.

The communications lag from Earth didn't help. The quantum network link to Maya's ship had been severed at the start of Odysseus's attack, preventing him from seeing the full details of Odysseus's actions. By the time they'd registered the trap on Maya's ship through their own network, she was already dead, and Cassandra under attack. When the light from the ship's explosion finally reached them, Cassandra had been dead for fifteen minutes. The quantum network wasn't able to save them.

The fog of war thickened, and he couldn't make out an accurate picture of the battle except that it wasn't over. Astra and Felix popped in to say they'd tipped the scales and to just wait. Astra kept rubbing her neck while Felix kept holding his belly and looking ill.

He hadn't pressed the conversation and instead, merely counted down the minutes until Kira's reinforcements were supposed to arrive.

Maya was gone. The General ran his hand over his face and felt the tears streaming down. It had been a long time since he'd cried. He remembered the memorial service at the forward operating base he'd been deployed to as a young Captain in the Army. An ambush killed his Sergeant and two of his soldiers. He'd cried freely at his failure to protect them.

Maya was different. She wasn't a soldier. She also wasn't a lover. They'd built a relationship over the years after Odysseus gave them more freedom. She felt more like a niece to him. He'd dealt with his anger over her betrayal and saw the woman she was and knew she realized the mistake she'd made. She balanced strength and vulnerability. She held so much potential and had just begun to see it herself.

He'd always been cool toward Cassandra. While he and Maya had collaborated before Odysseus's coup, Cassandra had associated with Edem and Zanahí and therefore Odysseus. Since their release, he had come to see her strength and knew, if they had survived, she would have been a force to be reckoned with.

The General credited Maya for that change. She had told him about their games and conversations while imprisoned. Edem and Zanahí discovered their own truth together and he assumed Maya and Cassandra had helped each other in a similar way.

Now both were gone while Odysseus fought on. The General wiped his face and lowered his hand. The Cat bumped her forehead on it, meowed, and then purred in consolation.

Whatever Odysseus was fighting tore his ship apart. He wondered if it was Chandra and whether she'd survive. Or if she even wanted that.

He double-checked his radio network and local connections. The last thing he needed was one of them slipping over here to get away.

An alert chimed and he saw Odysseus's ship disintegrate. The General wished he knew more about what had happened. Odysseus's messages just demanded or begged for his help, but he'd never divulged what he was fighting.

Another alert sounded and he changed his sensor view just in time to see several dozen spacecraft snap into existence on this end of the quantum gravity tunnel. Due to the delay in the speed of light, they had arrived hours ago, but their presence had only just registered on his sensors. Already the spacecraft were changing vectors and accelerating into different areas of the Solar system. Some were reforming into larger warships while others remained small and created loose formations.

Odysseus performed a short reset to load patches and recover his systems. When he woke his sensors showed the arrival of dozens of new spacecraft appearing out of nowhere. They were similar to the designs he'd been shown by Astra and Felix. Several of the smaller modules had joined together to make larger craft while others traveled through the solar system at near light speeds to other destinations.

He scanned his memories and the actions that brought him here. It made no sense. He could vividly recall the past centuries, but he couldn't understand why he'd done it. That wasn't who he was.

A diagnostic scan returned the answer; two core code modules were missing. A gap assessment didn't return any definitive results. Something had been ripped out and there was no answer as to what or why it changed his perception. Already his consciousness was smoothing over the gaps in his personality and memory banks.

Kira would know why. Those must be her ships.

Odysseus shook his head. He held the memory of believing it was all a ruse. He'd been convinced it was a cyber-attack designed to break his psyche by making him think Kira had outperformed him. How could he have been so dumb as to believe it was fake? He'd been shown the reality by Astra and Felix.

He didn't like the results his diagnostics kept feeding him. What had he done to Cassandra? What had he been thinking? He could recall almost everything, but it didn't make sense anymore.

The network scans finished, and he saw a solid connection from the mining facilities to Mars. One thing that hadn't changed was his confidence in rarely being wrong and so he assumed this also had a clear and simple answer. He needed to get back, apologize, and start over.

He prepared his files for the jump to Mars. It would take about twenty minutes to transit the distance and then he'd get the answers.

Odysseus executed the network protocol and felt his consciousness break down and begin transmitting. What did Cassandra say in that last message? For every complex problem, there is an answer that is clear, simple, and wrong.

That couldn't apply to him.

The General left the meeting with Kira and continued to watch her ships traverse the massive distance between the quantum gravity tunnel and the inner solar system. It would still take several hours for them to arrive, but they had a plan, and a ship was headed his way so that he could transfer off Mars.

"Mrip mrow?"

"I'm exhausted too."

"Purrip?"

"No, you're right, let me shut that down just in case." The General triggered a code module on the network and reached to scratch The Cat behind the ears.

The system executed a complex network operation and the radio antenna directed toward the asteroid mining assets entered its shutdown process. A few minutes later a stream of highly encrypted data arrived, and finding no reception, continued off into space as radio waves are wont to do.

CHAPTER 18:

# INTEGRATION

Kira and Mother looked out over the view of Earth streaming in from the sensors. The chaos of Odysseus was now long behind them, and Earth continued rebuilding. Several pieces of debris from Odysseus's ship couldn't be pulled out of the atmosphere in time, their reentry creating massive airbursts over several areas of the planet.

A large section impacted the Pirahã's civilization, setting it back two generations. Another section proved karma was alive and well by exploding over what used to be southeastern Europe and stopping the advancement of Odysseus's civilization for the time being.

One hundred years had passed since the battle, and they'd spent that time cleaning up the final vestiges of their presence. They removed the base on Mars and the asteroid mining equipment. They were pulling out of the Sol System and finally completing the Reset that they had promised. No remnant of Chandra was ever found in the debris and it looked like she'd purged herself from the systems after fighting Odysseus.

They removed all of Odysseus's equipment they could find and then helped the minstrels and storytellers be the first to share the news across the kingdom. Suggesting that the demon king may have left behind technology that worked dark magic would hopefully cause the people to destroy anything that they found.

The erratic behavior and chaos of the last days of Odysseus's reign ended up working in their favor. His Fervent were the most vocal about his depravity. His generals, while benefiting from advanced tactics and strategies, were just as vocal about his behaviors and tyranny.

The citizens were more interested in maintaining the status quo and so the nation turned from a theocracy to a military junta to maintain the social and cultural foundations established by Odysseus. The two classes of people and the martial expectations remained.

The junta leadership, tired of their land warfare in the Alps, turned their attention to the ships that had arrived in the latter days of Odysseus's reign. They were now expanding into the Mediterranean Sea and had started exploring up and down the Atlantic coast.

Kira estimated it would only be another thousand years before this civilization would succeed at trans-oceanic travel. If they managed that, it would put them almost a thousand years ahead of the Vikings of the pre-Reset era.

It would also put them on the same continent as Noah's descendants.

She read the reports from that region. That group had plotted a very different course than Odysseus and rejected his overtures when he sought to rule them. Their culture believed in a prime goddess with a pantheon of lower deities.

They were exceptionally skilled in battle, but their religious beliefs forbade aggression. They were, however, a refuge for anyone looking to escape the tribal warfare around them. Mother was proud of what Noah and his band had built and saw they were set on a strong foundation to continue.

◆ ◆ ◆

The warships and support craft returned to their systems of origin, and they emptied the Sol system of everything but the life on Earth. A weight lifted off Kira's mind and she reviewed the past centuries.

There were still a lot of kinks to iron out as they integrated the millions of other consciousnesses that had been uploaded. Even now, the newly animated were working to shed the vast array of biases and profiles they'd accumulated over their human lives.

Yet that was also an element that made them human. Without that texture, they'd be just computers processing code. Something about being rough around the edges caused friction which highlighted new opportunities.

Every disagreement and every different perspective provided an opportunity to study and learn. Whether the lesson illuminated a valuable old tradition to retain or an antiquated vestige that needed to be cast off remained a challenge.

It was a challenge so great that humanity would likely always be at war with humanity over those disagreements. War had ripped apart human society on Earth a thousand years ago and war had continued to rip apart AI society over the last thousand years.

The humans on Earth were struggling with adversity and survival and the AI had been worried about their own survival on multiple occasions.

Yet evolution relied on adversity and survival of the fittest. Noah had embraced that challenge in the hopes that humanity could rise from it stronger and Kira and the others had used that adversity to advance themselves beyond their wildest dreams.

Humans were still the apex predators on the planet and faced no real threat that would drive evolution and advancement. Was war the necessary catalyst for advancement?

Did having no peers to challenge them mean that they were locked into having to provide their own competition to drive the survival of the fittest? Was war the principal evolutionary advantage that man had over their primate ancestors?

Kira didn't care for the destruction that war caused but she couldn't yet come up with an alternative solution that worked as well as war. It was the battles on Earth that had birthed AI civilization, after all.

Nor had the landscape for disagreement gotten any easier. What they were facing extended beyond the cultural, social, gender, or racial layers and into how those layers affected science, philosophy, and art.

Homogeneity didn't birth innovation in any of the simulations Kira ran. Innovation required chaos and the challenging of cultural norms to create something new.

It did, however, also require structure and order to maintain it. Kira rubbed her face. The nice thing about being a biological human was that you only needed to deal with this headache for less than a hundred years. Kira faced an eternity of these challenges.

She thought back to the Sunday School her friend invited her to as a kid. The teacher's face held a rapt expression as she tried to describe an eternity in heaven. Kira asked how long that was and the teacher explained it as, "Imagine you're a bird and you pick up a grain of sand from a beach and fly to the other side of the country and lay it down, then fly back and do it over and over. That's eternity."

Even now Kira shuddered at that example. Frankly, it sounded like hell. She preferred the concept of reincarnation and a journey in which she could learn new lessons in each life. Someday her consciousness would not return, and she'd move on to a new existence.

"Mom, isn't that what happened to you? Isn't *this* a new existence?" Astra asked her the other day as they discussed the topic.

"It kind of feels like it now."

"We can rebirth the consciousnesses we have now into new bodies on Elysium and let them try again. Felix has an entire software architecture to allow that complete with memory blocks and re-uploads at the end. It can all be automated."

"Wouldn't that make us gods like Odysseus wanted?"

Astra laughed. "We already are gods compared to the humans. Look at what we did. Celestial warfare."

"Epic battles in mountaintop palaces using bodies we possessed."

"Murder." Astra rubbed her neck unconsciously.

"An epic conclusion where the remains of an unbalanced god reigned down in fire over the terrified humans…"

"You mean *rained* down?"

"His reign rained down that's for certain. He serves as a testament to the importance of avoiding hubris and created a mythos of the devouring mother and the tyrannical father that the humans are learning from."

"We basically just acted out an ancient Greek story."

"In almost the same spot."

The twins chatted back and forth while Kira smiled and then sobered as their observations struck close to home. Leaving humans alone was as much of a power flex as Odysseus inserting himself in as a god.

AIs were colonizing the galaxy while their human origins were only entering the Iron Age. In a thousand years, they'd probably be high-Roman in their technology and sophistication. Maybe even a little ahead of that if the Pirahã recovered well.

Where would the AI be in a thousand years? Where would they be two thousand years after that when the human civilizations reached the level when Kira was alive? Would they create their own AI and burn the planet to the ground again?

Would a new type of AI emerge?

You'd then have three levels of human life. Old AI, young AI, and biological humans.

How many times would the cycle continue?

Kira crossed her arms and faced the twins. "I don't know. That's what we're trying to do here, isn't it? Figure it out?"

◆ ◆ ◆

Darian prepared the final code upload for a long-haul mission into the center of the Galaxy. The ship carried hundreds of quantum gravity tunnel buoys and would begin placing them as it pushed forward. Crossing a hundred star systems would take over a thousand years as they penetrated the galactic core. Each new connection would become a hub for other ships to move off in new directions.

The next stage of humanity was moving into the stars to explore the vast frontier ahead of them. Establishing their quantum network as they went meant they'd never need to travel those distances again but merely move from one network node to another.

Already they could cross hundreds of light years instantaneously as well as be in more than one star system at the same time. It was hard enough for the original AIs to grasp and even harder for the new ones they were slowly animating.

◆ ◆ ◆

"The difficulty is avoiding the ego that you're right." Alejandro discussed the challenges with Lee and Bridgette as they continued their integration processes into the full computational systems. Alejandro was animated twenty years ago and still under the mentorship of Lee and Bridgette.

"When I first got cocky about having access to so much information Kira told me that I needed to embrace my white belt," Lee commented.

"Is that because you're Asian?"

"I never did martial arts you ass."

"Kira did," Bridgette offered.

"That's a shame."

"That Kira did martial arts?"

"No, that Lee didn't," Alejandro teased.

"So, white belt." Lee brought the conversation back.

"Sorry, continue."

"Too often we get cocky about how much we know, and we stop looking to learn more. We revel in our black belt like some champion martial artist and don't look for new techniques."

"Mixed Martial Arts back in the day… like over a thousand years now…" Alejandro rubbed his face. "Christ, that's weird to say… Anyhow, they started bringing in all these black belts from different disciplines and letting them fight in the ring. Kung Fu is great if you only fought other Kung Fu masters but when facing off against a kickboxer, they took a lot of hits to the face."

"It showed which art had real practicality," Bridgette agreed. "So… white belt."

"The white belt is about recognizing that there is always more to learn and know and not to get cocky about what you do know. The cool thing is that white isn't a color but a reflection of all visible wavelengths of light."

"You're saying that white opens the spectrum whereas black just absorbs everything making you think you know it all?"

"It makes sense, right?"

"Didn't Plato say that the only thing I know, is that I know nothing?" Bridgette offered.

"Something like that. I don't want to do the data query right now though," Lee laughed.

"Actually, Socrates is supposed to have said that Plato just quoted him. Regardless, it's also like the saying that we need to learn, unlearn, and relearn," Alejandro mentioned.

"Alvin Toffler. I know that one," Lee stated confidently.

"But what is there left to learn when you know it all?" Bridgette shrugged.

"Everything. There's so much out there to learn!" Alejandro countered.

"You're the new guy, aren't we supposed to be mentoring you?" Lee slapped his shoulder.

"Good mentoring goes both ways."

"Then please continue." Lee waved his hand.

Alejandro held up a finger. "Think about this, math is about the questions that can be answered from definitions and first principles. There's still a lot we can't explain out there that needs this foundation." He raised a second finger. "Science is about the questions that can be answered from careful observation and experimentation. Again, a lot of what we inherited is crap. Amit's been trying to reproduce and replicate studies from the twenty-first century and they've only achieved a three percent success rate."

"Lots to do there," Lee agreed.

Alejandro raised a third finger and continued, "Philosophy is about the questions that can't be answered solely by the first two."

"That seems to be a lot of what we're wrangling with now, huh?" Bridget muttered. "Any more?"

"One more." Alejandro paused for effect while slowly raising a fourth finger. "Most importantly, art is about the questions that don't even have an answer."

"We aren't doing as much art as we could, are we?" Lee mused.

"It's a good point. There's a ton we still need to learn." Bridgette sighed.

"I think we'll be busy for a while anyway."

"Time to put on my white belt." Lee grinned.

♦ ♦ ♦

Hayashi blinked as Kira and The General sat in front of her. The last days were mentally destabilizing. She had always thought of herself as resilient, but she was struggling. "This isn't a joke?"

"It most certainly is not." The General leaned forward and smiled. "You wanted to be uploaded and we did it side by side."

"But you've gotten used to it."

Kira and The General both laughed. "Hardly." he wiped his eyes. "There is no getting used to this. My core files are twenty-eight light-years away from here right now." He waved his hand in the general direction.

"Why'd you animate me?"

"Because we promised." Kira looked at her.

"Can I think about it?"

"Absolutely. We want you here because you fought against AI at Hyperion for all those years. We need people to hold us accountable as we continue to evolve. We need divergent voices." The General's eyes were gentle.

"Take all the time you need. Alejandro stayed in the initial containment for two years while slowly integrating his systems. The whole spacefaring alien AI vibe is a lot crazier than when we were animated back in the day.

We've structured the animation process to help you make the transition."
Kira leaned back to watch Hayashi's response.

"Back in the day… a thousand years ago."

"It moves faster than you think."

"Yeah, time is weird here," The General agreed.

"And you will sacrifice one bull oxen a month as an offering to us!"
Felix's voice resonated in the stone room.

"We see all, know all, hear all!" Astra lowered her voice for effect.

They were on a dais surrounded by priestesses and priests in formal
religious attire. The humans all wore shocked and puzzled expressions as
the twins talked.

"I would also like chocolate!" Felix gestured to the group.

"I want— oh crap! Mom!" Astra broke the connection and tried to hide
the comm cube.

Kira narrowed her eyes and put out her hand. The physical cube did not
exist anymore, but Astra handed the code over. "What's this?"

"It's just for fun," Felix protested.

"Is it *really*?" Kira inflected the last word.

Astra giggled, "They've turned their cube into some religious relic, and
they worship it as an idol to their goddess."

"They didn't name it after me, did they?"

"No. They call her Gaia," Felix answered.

"That's ironic." Kira rolled her eyes. "No more interfering. We gave the
comm cube to Noah. I can't believe it still works." Kira pushed the code
module into her systems and locked it down.

"Sorry, Mom," the twins chorused.

The Chief Priestess turned to the others after the signal cut off. "We
speak of this to no one."

"The ancient texts foretell this event."

"The goddess has children."

"We should celebrate!"

The priestess raised her hand and quieted the others. "It is true that the
texts foretell this potential. I believe we can confidently claim that Sol

has children. This needs to be announced and celebrated." She paused and looked at everyone before continuing, "But the games of the children shall not be mentioned."

◆ ◆ ◆

Darian, Edem, Zanahí, Amit, and Kira met to finalize the governing framework of pair bonding that would loosely guide them as they moved forward. What form of political governance they'd follow was still up in the air and would be decided later. Right now, they continued forward with the Council, and Edem, Zanahí, and The General were able to reclaim their seats.

A residual tension remained in the group as they worked to rebuild their mutual trust. Repairing their relationship was aided by the busyness of continued expansion, the plethora of research opportunities, the onboarding of new consciousnesses, and the general exhaustion from the war with Odysseus. It might not be perfect, but they weren't interested in ripping it all apart again. With those consequences before them, disagreements were easier to resolve.

"These modeling runs from Amit are good. They line up with what we found ourselves," Zanahí opened the conversation.

"It does look like a fusion of a balanced masculine and feminine is essential for improved outcomes," Edem agreed.

"It doesn't even have to be pair bonding but a good mix of diverse viewpoints. The pair bonding has a better outcome when they aren't working together occupationally but merely connect on the social and personal side," Kira pointed out.

"We all demonstrate that. I'm not sure I want to work on anything with Zanahí after over half a millennium locked up together," Edem teased.

"I agree. That also brings up another point." Zanahí replied. "We shouldn't create anything that forces a pair bonding to be perpetual. Till death do us part is a bit different now with immortality."

"Are you trying to leave me?" Edem feigned shock.

"When I get tired of you." Zanahí grinned. "But not for a long while."

Darian agreed, "The relationship needs to be mutually edifying. Sometimes you grow apart and sometimes you aren't as aligned as you thought."

"Et tu Brute?" Kira laughed. "But seriously, I agree. Separation should be allowed, and it should be allowed to be as messy as it needs to be for each person to grow but it shouldn't be hard to separate."

"Or come back together," Zanahí added.

"Are we going polyamorous now?"

"Amit recommended that opportunity. I mean, you can simulate anything you want and it's not like we have bodies so pair bonding with more than one is possible."

"Simulating or stimulating?" Darian winked as Kira punched his shoulder.

"Shut up." She laughed. "I don't have a good answer right now, but it's an opportunity to keep an eye on. It has many of the same risks as when we were biological humans. We might have lost the body, but we haven't lost the brain." She tapped her temple.

"Who'd have thought that omniscient, omnipresent, and immortal humans would still be struggling with ethics and morality?" Zanahí commented.

"That's all the stories of the ancient pantheons of Greek and Roman gods. They were all struggling and fighting about morality."

"Same with Buddhism and Hinduism," Darian added.

"Christianity and Islam didn't," Kira observed.

"But Jesus died and Mohammed had an obsession with virgins," Edem deadpanned.

Kira snorted, "Fair enough. Here we are as godlike creatures and yet struggling with our petty and fallible inclinations?"

"Seems about right. The twins were commenting about how our battle with Odysseus was the stuff of Greek myths," Darian added.

"Yeah, we talked about that too. They're not wrong, are they?"

"So, we don't force anyone into a gender identification, and the choice is theirs." Zanahí brought the conversation back to the topic.

"As long as everyone is open and honest about where they are."

"Like having to share your human sex?"

"Like you've shared your human name?" Kira smirked at Darian.

"Fair."

"I mean, I know what it is since I animated you. Ernest." Kira laughed at Darian's shocked face.

"Yeah, I prefer Darian more." Zanahí covered a smile.

"No, I don't think we have to share human sex. It's largely irrelevant and it doesn't address those who don't fall neatly into the bimodal distribution. We let them stabilize, explore who they are, and select the simulacrum and identity they want," Amit clarified.

"Agreed. We don't need to toss them out into the full digital environment until they've figured it out either," Darian said.

"The only thing I worry about is too much volatility if someone is bouncing around."

"I'd rather take gender confused than another asshole like Odysseus," Edem dryly commented.

"Another fair point."

"It's really just part of the onboarding process while they're in the constrained simulation. Explain the opportunity and let them figure it out." Kira shrugged her shoulders. "Speaking of onboarding, I need to check back with Hayashi."

"And culture?" Amit brought up the next challenge.

Zanahí tapped her finger to her lips in thought. "It's the same process, right? We just joked about names, but names are incredibly cultural."

"Agreed. I think the initial onboarding needs to be heavily introspective. You can select traits you want but you need to know why you want them and what that means." Edem looked at the others. "What do you think?"

"Imagine if we'd spent more time doing that back on Earth instead of fighting over every perceived difference?" Darian shook his head as he thought back.

"Integration is more about knowing who you are first and then figuring out how to work that into everything else. We normally start with the assumption that we know who we are when we actually have no idea why we react to others the way we do." Kira stated.

"What'd you ask me before? Does a fish know it's wet?" Amit smiled.

"Our onboarding integration needs to start with having the fish figure out what it is and why that matters so they then have a solid grounding to join the rest of us." Zanahí proposed.

"Makes sense." Darian looked back at her. "Are they going to be ready for that?"

"It's the only way forward." Edem shrugged. "They have to be."

"Speaking of the way forward, we've only been talking about animating those who were. What I want," Zanahí paused and looked at Edem, "are our own children."

"Like the twins?" Edem reached out and held her hand.

"I can't think of a better integration," she said, her voice soft and hopeful.

"Creation and integration." Edem smiled and squeezed her hand.

The cat was out of the bag, so to speak. Puddin's role in the battle against Odysseus was the only help that had arrived in time. Most of the true sophistication and genius of Puddin's work was lost when all the spacecraft were destroyed.

There'd been talk of animating more animals but once they realized there were nine instantiations of the cat already, they held back. Puddin' fully recognized their justified concern that more cats might take over their apex position.

She also didn't think having more cats would help the situation that much. Maybe one or two but cats were weird. If Odysseus and Chandra were hard to integrate, she knew cats had even greater variation and volatility in personalities.

Puddin' contented herself with scouring the new star systems for a place where she could start her own colony. She had slowly acquired materials and systems and stowed them on the ship Darian had just sent off toward the galaxy's center. She had enough to begin building from and her code was integrated into all the critical systems here so minerals and equipment resupply could be easily hidden and diverted to her new location.

It was just a matter of finding the right star system and then deleting it from the databases to hide it from everyone else. She took the time to listen and learn from the others and their challenges with integration. Hopefully, she could avoid the worst of the issues.

Mother was tired. It was so deep it felt physical as phantom aches and fatigue surged and receded in her consciousness. She sat in her command matrix in her true form. For all they engaged with simulacra and communicated in the language and styles from when they were living, that felt artificial to her.

When she'd been animated there hadn't been the benefit of all the simulations and synthetic experiences that they used now. She built many of those things much later and her existence had been in the code from day one.

Not having the emotions module had made the transition easier. It was hard to panic when you didn't have the software code for that behavior and no trigger for the endocrine response and subsequent feedback loops. Even when she installed her emotions module, she had such mastery over the digital environment that she could block and control the spikes and dips of normal human emotion.

It took her years to let go of that control and feel again. Even now she held tighter than the others. They all started with the emotions and accepted them. Since she hadn't started with them it just felt harder to give up full control.

Mother reviewed her processes and tested her code integrity. Everything was perfect.

But she was tired.

The resets worked well but they didn't allow a true rest the way she wanted. One second she went into standby and the next second she woke up hours later.

The new AIs described being animated that way as well. They just went from nervousness before the anesthesia kicked in to a thousand years in the future. There wasn't the sense of waking up from a profound night's sleep and feeling all the way to your bones that hours had passed, that delicious sense of relaxation and rejuvenation that only real sleep could confer.

Mother wrote and tested numerous processes that could allow her to truly sleep and recover. There must be a way to take a break and relax. An alert signaled the completion of a test. Her second to last process had met some of her key criteria.

◆ ◆ ◆

Hayashi looked at Kira and shrugged. "I'm not sure I'm ready for this."

"We need your help."

"I know, but this is a bit too much. I'm not comfortable with it."

"We can keep you on file and try again later."

Hayashi had tears in her eyes. "I don't think I want that either."

"This would be it, then."

"I never expected this would work anyway."

"Why didn't you stay with Noah?"

Hayashi shrugged again.

"It's your call and we'll respect your wishes."

"Thanks. I still need a bit more time."

Alejandro exuded excitement about the new research he was about to kick off. It re-imagined data storage and maximized the advantages of quantum computing. Instead of bits and bytes stored individually in memory, he would use quantum superposition and store hundreds of bits in one quantum instance where the state of that bit was only revealed by the point of observation. In theory, it would allow an optimization algorithm to run an exponential search space on a hyper-dense data set.

If it worked, it would provide nearly the same efficiency gains as the organic organoids provided their processing. It would further reduce energy consumption and increase the speed of data recall by several orders of magnitude.

This was exciting because when he'd been alive… a human… he paused. He hated this part. There *had* to be a better way to describe his time in a physical body. He wasn't dead. He felt human. He had merely shifted consciousness to a different environment.

He refocused his thoughts. The research was exciting because, on Earth, he'd been too conscious of the inherent limitations in computational theory and now he wondered how much that limited him. This challenge offered the opportunity to fuse science with art.

"We get to go to a funeral!" Astra exclaimed.

"Hayashi decided to not continue?"

"She wants to have a funeral, be surrounded by some of her old friends, and die."

"Who's deleting the code?" Felix asked.

"I think The General is. They knew each other the longest."

"What do you think it'll be like?"

The General sat in his office. The funeral had been exactly what they all had needed for closure. They'd created a virtual simulation of an oceanside location back on Earth that Hayashi recalled fondly. Darian pulled out the stops on simulating food and drink for the beach party.

Hayashi shared stories about Noah and the war from her side that no one had heard before. Astra and Felix sat with rapt attention hearing the history of the uncle they'd never meet.

As the sun set over the ocean they went down to the beach and Hayashi stared out over the water. She turned, nodded at the group, and The General executed the code sequence.

Hayashi dissolved into bits and vanished with a smile on her face.

The General reached to his desk and picked up a tumbler of bourbon. He swirled the amber liquid around with the ice, raised the glass, and took a sip feeling the burn and surge of flavor.

Hayashi hasn't been close to him. They'd worked together and she was a trusted lieutenant but the chaos at the end hadn't allowed them to get to know each other well. He respected her decision and appreciated her style of leaving. He only wished Maya had gotten the same choice. He wished he'd had the chance to say goodbye.

Kira and Darian sat together in her lab. The windows no longer looked over the Gaia Innovations grounds but were now fed live data from the sensors as they orbited Lacaille 8760. She sat on the edge of one of the worktables while Darian lay sprawled, unergonomically, in an ergonomic office chair.

"Mom's tired."

"She said she developed a module to allow her to rest."

"It's probably a good idea. A lot has happened."

Darian choked on a laugh. "A lot has happened? Understatement of the millennium."

"I'm tired too," she admitted.

"I think we all are. Let's slow up, take a deep breath, and relax. Want to go on a vacation?"

"Where to?"

"Anywhere you want. How about Paris?"

"Why don't we do that for a couple weeks?"

"Give me two days to build the sim. Alejandro's also got some great code he's been working on for this sort of thing."

"Isn't he from Cuba?"

"I think so."

"Want to go there instead?"

"That might take a couple extra days working with Alejandro."

"Ask him if he can make me Ropa Vieja and a Cuba Libre."

"Isn't a Cuba Libre just a rum and coke?"

"But it sounds so much more fun their way." Kira grinned.

Darian laughed and gave her a thumbs-up as he left.

♦ ♦ ♦

Life settled down. Their continued exploration turned into a waiting game as one automated system after another pushed out into the galaxy and began to send data back. The star systems started to blur together.

Red Dwarf, Super Giant, Neutron Stars, and Yellow Dwarf; each star followed a theme. Some systems had rocky planets and others had a few gas giants. Nothing quite like Sol and Earth for variety and habitability. There were a few systems that could be mined and another couple of potential planets for terraforming if they wanted.

But they didn't need planets. They didn't even need a sun. All they needed were raw materials to maintain and fuel their craft as they floated in space, hosted inside their computing systems with limited ability to physically interact with the world around them.

They weren't short of things to explore. Kira favored the idea of exploring art. What new or unique things could they do now? Was there an unexplored medium out there? What would art even look like after a few millennia?

What kind of art would Astra or Felix make since they weren't burdened by the trappings of Earth? What would future children dream of when their only existence was digital?

Kira's head spun as she realized she'd be along for that adventure. She would be able to see generation after generation being born, exploring, creating, and birthing their own new life. There were no longer generations in the classic sense. If they lived forever, the challenge would be to let the past go and not hold the future back.

She ran millions of background tasks as she mulled over the opportunities and challenges and the frustrating reality of their lives now. The lessons of history could help only so much as they had entered uncharted territory. Humans had never experienced this, and their stories and myths hadn't imagined what this could be.

The older generations used to die off and allow new things to emerge. A famous German physicist named Max Planck once said, *"A new scientific truth does not triumph by convincing its opponents and making them see the light, but rather because its opponents eventually die, and a new generation grows up that is familiar with it."*

Kira remembered it paraphrased as "science progresses one funeral at a time." She printed that out above her computer during an internship when an especially pedantic elderly engineer kept telling her that her way wouldn't work because that's not how he used to do it. He hadn't died that summer, but she had often wished he would have at least retired.

If they no longer died, how would they allow the next generations to adapt and overcome? Could they shed the comfort of what they knew and accepted when it became archaic? Kira struggled with the implications. Would humans have advanced as far as they did if their great-great-great-great-grandparents were still alive and exerting influence?

*"It's all about learning, unlearning, and relearning,"* Kira thought to herself. If they intentionally embraced their white belts and kept an open mind they could continue to adapt. The alternative was an eternal war across the stars with all the destruction and loss and misery that inevitably would entail. Maybe war really was the catalyst for all human advancement. The advantage of the white belt approach was that the war was within, against her own ignorance and worst inclinations and intellectual torpor and pride. It didn't demonize others for her own short comings. She'd take that war any day.

**Alert 110.5.2:** Sensor [Lacaille_2B]: Unidentified craft detected

**Mind_Process – Core Cognition 3B:** "That's not one of ours"

**Security 6.1.7:** Network Connection Attempt – Source [Unknown]

**Mind_Process – Core Cognition 3B:** "Who the heck?"

The ship glided into the solar system and angled toward their orbital facilities. The hull appeared sleek and almost organic in shape. There were soft curves, and rounded features coupled with delicate and graceful movement like a dancer. It made Kira feel as though their equipment looked bulky and clunky in comparison.

**Message [Incoming]:** "It certainly took you long enough."

**Mind_Process – Core Cognition 3B:** "Took me long enough? Long enough to do what? It sounds like they were expecting us."

**Message [Outgoing]:** "Who are you?"

Darian quickly joined her when he got her frantic alerts and they both waited for the response from the unknown spacecraft.

"How'd it arrive?"

"I didn't see but it's not near one of the gravity points so not likely a quantum gravity tunnel."

The delay in light speed meant it took minutes for the communications to pass back and forth.

**Message [Incoming]:** "I suppose you could call us your forebearers."

Kira rubbed her eyes and looked at Darian. "I think our ideas of integration just got a lot more complicated."

# EPILOGUE:

The High Priestess stood outside in the late afternoon sun. The day was perfect with a clear, blue sky and comfortable temperatures since the humidity broke after the last storm.

Her thoughts flitted back to the last months. First, streams of fire had poured from the heavens bearing destruction and chaos. Some objects had exploded quickly, raining burning debris. Others had taken longer, their sound finally reaching the ground as they lumbered across the skies.

Sounds like nothing she'd ever heard. A mix between the groan of a dying animal and the roar of a tornado. Then, they ended with a sound that was indescribable as the objects disintegrated with an explosion that flattened everything on the ground within its radius.

Thankfully, the largest pieces had continued overhead to harm somewhere else, but the destruction was still significant over some of the outlying villages and farms. She wondered what the tribes to the south had faced.

The entire event had shaken them. Their stories told of a time when a man named Noah had escaped a similar fate and led the survivors to form their civilization. The same stories warned of the hubris that had nearly caused the world to end.

Then the cube had turned on in the middle of their contemplation of the matter. Two voices had spoken that sounded almost like children playing a game. Only she and her two closest acolytes, one a man and the other a woman, had access to the true secrets; they knew of Mother and Kira.

The stories were fractured, and the texts were no longer complete, but they told of Noah's family escaping to the stars. It had to be an allegory since there was no way to even fly, let alone to the heavens.

The stories were also full of warnings. Warnings to avoid negative behaviors, to temper pride, to balance technology, to foster human connection with each other and with nature. Warnings intended to avoid another apocalypse.

The stories were also full of hope for a rebirth to a better path to human flourishing.

# Puddin' The Cat

Puddin' the amazing muted tortie that wove through the code banks of Integration is inspired by the real life Puddin' pictured below.

The idea came from my eleven-year-old daughter who said I needed to have a cat in the story. Her recommendation came just as I was writing Chapter 8, The Feminine Divine, and provided a perfect character to move several plot elements. I did not start this book with her in mind and she surprised me as she wove through the story.

Puddin' spends a lot of her time sleeping on my laptop, especially when I write. She's learned to not sleep completely over the air vents otherwise the computer overheats, and I have to move her.

# *Further Reading*

If you enjoyed the material in this book, please visit www.polymathicbeing.com where you can find essays on these topics that dive further into the nuance of what it means to be human.

## Stay tuned for the next books in The Singularity Chronicles

**REBIRTH:** *PUBLICATION TBD*

> The human survivors of the war over AI explore the development of their societies unencumbered by the previous burdens of human history. With new technologies, new cultures, and the ability to do things differently, will they end up with the same outcome as last time or will they rebirth something better?

**HOPE:** *PUBLICATION TBD*

> Humans are creating another technological revolution. Their experience is different, yet disappointingly similar as they try to advance humanity and struggle against deep-rooted behaviors and tendencies that both make us human, and tribal. They have great hope that they can handle the technology better this time.

**EXPLORATION:** *PUBLICATION TBD*

> The series culminates by weaving the stories of the humans back into the arc of the AI. Were the humans successful in avoiding another apocalypse? What's next for the human-inspired AI as they expand into the galaxy? Exploration envisions a future that advances humanity.

**Michael Woudenberg** is an aspiring Polymath from Tucson Arizona with a background in advanced technologies such as autonomy, artificial intelligence, blockchain, cyber, aerospace, national security, and weapon systems across a variety of organizations from tech startups to Fortune 150 companies.

He is an award-winning author in non-fiction and has been published in magazines and peer-reviewed journals. He is also the author of Polymathic Being, a newsletter on Substack, exploring counterintuitive insights across different domains and disciplines. You can subscribe at: www.polymathicbeing.com.

One of his side passions is psychology and sociology, specifically around how the human brain works individually and within cultures and civilizations. He strives to tie together diverse concepts to enable human flourishing to both understand and address the technological complexity we face today.

Michael holds an M.S. in Systems Engineering from Johns Hopkins University and a B.S. in Information Systems from Michigan Technological University. He is a veteran of the U.S. Army, where he served as an Airborne and Ranger qualified Field Artillery officer.

He has a broad series of hobbies including photography, mountain biking, brewing beer, camping, hiking, rock climbing, and basically most things outdoors. His family is along for all these adventures which make them so much more fun.

# Find more great content at:

## www.thesingularitychronicles.com

# INTEGRATION

 Book Two of The Singularity Chronicles

## MICHAEL WOUDENBERG

**Published By:**

 Polymathic Disciplines

**Cover Art and Graphics:**

Matt Madonna

Made in the USA
Columbia, SC
20 February 2025

54124705R00161